LONE WOLF

Published by Kensington Publishing Corp.

LONE WOLF

DIANA PALMER
KATE PEARCE
REBECCA ZANETTI

ZEBRA BOOKS
KENSINGTON PUBLISHING CORP.
www.kensingtonbooks.com

ZEBRA BOOKS are published by

Kensington Publishing Corp.
119 West 40th Street
New York, NY 10018

All Kensington titles, imprints, and distributed lines are available at special quantity discounts for bulk purchases for sales promotion, premiums, fund-raising, educational, or institutional use.

Special book excerpts or customized printings can also be created to fit specific needs. For details, write or phone the office of the Kensington Sales Manager: Attn.: Sales Department. Kensington Publishing Corp., 119 West 40th Street, New York, NY 10018. Phone: 1-800-221-2647.

Zebra and the Z logo Reg. U.S. Pat. & TM Off.

First Printing: May 2021
ISBN-13: 978-1-4201-5149-7
ISBN-10: 1-4201-5149-5

ISBN-10: 978-1-4201-5150-3 (eBook)
ISBN-10: 1-4201-5150-9 (eBook)

10 9 8 7 6 5 4 3 2 1

Printed in the United States of America

CONTENTS

COLORADO COWBOY

DIANA PALMER

In Memoriam:
Patricia Gail Dorroh Nash
My Friend
1950–2020

CHAPTER ONE

It was snowing. Esther Marist was cold and frightened walking along the highway. She pulled her blue fox jacket closer around her and nervously pushed back a long strand of platinum blond, curly hair. She was still wearing the gray wool slacks and the purple silk blouse she'd put on that morning. There was a dark stain on the hem of one pants leg. It was blood. Her mother's blood.

Her pale blue eyes stared into the darkness without really seeing it. Her mother, Terry Marist, had just been killed in front of her eyes, from being picked up and literally thrown down the staircase by her latest gigolo boyfriend.

Terry had several homes. This one was in Aspen, Colorado. It was the prettiest of the lot. They'd come here against Terry's wishes, several weeks ago, because her gigolo boyfriend was meeting somebody. Esther hadn't been able to hear all of it, but there had been something said about Terry financing a scheme of his that two partners were involved in. They were going to meet the men here. Darrin had forced the two women into Terry's Mercedes and driven them here from Las Vegas, where Terry had reluctantly financed several days of reckless gambling by her vicious boyfriend.

Terry had finally realized what Esther had known from the beginning, that Darrin was dangerous and money-crazy. But it was too late. Esther's mother had paid the price, and if Esther couldn't get out of Aspen before Darrin Ross found her, she'd be paying it as well.

Her mother had tears in her blue eyes as she shivered and clawed at her daughter's cold fingers. Her leg under her short dress was twisted horribly from the fall. Her blond hair was covered in blood from where her head had collided with one of the banisters. She was gasping for breath and then Terry realized that there was a cut on her mother's throat. Blood was pulsing out of it like a water fountain. Esther knelt beside her mother and frantically tried to stop the flow with her hands, but she couldn't.

"I'll call an ambulance!" she told Terry quickly, glancing up the stairs in fear that Darrin would come. She started to pull her cell phone out of the pocket in her slacks and remembered that she'd left it upstairs in the drawer of her bedside table, charging.

"No," her mother choked. "Too late. I'm . . . dying."

Terry put the huge seven-carat pink diamond ring she always wore into Esther's palm and closed her daughter's fingers around it. "Keep the will I gave you last night. Keep the ring, too. He thinks . . . I put it on the dresser, like he . . . told me to. Run," she whispered frantically. "I'm so sorry . . . ! You can go to . . . your . . . grandfather . . ."

But before she could say anything more, she made an odd little sound and the light left her eyes. Her pretty face was white from the blood loss. Upstairs, the boyfriend was cursing. "Where is it?" he was raging. "Where's that damned ring? I saw her put it . . . right here . . . on the dresser!"

Esther felt for a pulse, but her mother's eyes were open, her pupils were fixed and dilated; darkness was settling in them, just like when one of Esther's pets had died and she'd watched the same thing happen to their eyes. Terry was dead. Darrin had killed her! Tears ran down her cheeks as she took one last look at her only refuge in the world. Her mother was gone and she would be at the mercy of Terry's murderous boyfriend.

Esther knew better than to stay. Darrin Ross was drunk and he was very dangerous when he drank. He'd taken up with her mother weeks ago, despite Esther's pleas. *But he loves me*, her mother had said with a laugh, *and you'll get used to him*. Esther hadn't. And once he started knocking her mother around when she wouldn't give him as much money as he wanted, Terry Marist had realized the mistake she'd made. Darrin was abusive and frightening. Terry was sorry, but she was too afraid to try and leave him.

He'd become obsessed with the enormous diamond ring that Esther's mother had been given on her eighteenth birthday by her father. Even though they were estranged, Terry Marist spoke of her father sometimes and told her how kind he'd been to her when she was a little girl, before Terry married a man he didn't approve of. The ring had sentimental value. But past that, it was worth a king's ransom. Darrin had tried to take it off her finger once, when she was asleep, but Terry's poor hands were arthritic and swelled badly. He'd been sure at the time that all Terry had would be his one day, so he'd found an excuse to give her about what he was doing. He was just massaging her poor fingers because she'd been crying out in her sleep. Esther knew better. Terry hadn't.

Now, Terry had truly left him and Esther was going to be next unless she could get away before he came downstairs. He was still upstairs, searching for the ring. He yelled that he'd seen her take it off and put it on the dresser, because he'd threatened her if she didn't. So where was it?

That explained why Terry had it hidden in her hand. Esther had given her mother one last, anguished look, grabbed her coat and purse off the coat tree, and ran out into the snowy night.

She had only the money in her purse, her unspent allowance. She didn't even have a credit card, having always used her mother's. The money was all in her mother's name as well, and Darrin would have access to it; but not at once. He wouldn't know that Terry had cut up her credit cards so that Darrin wouldn't have access to them, soon after they'd arrived in Aspen. She'd had the premonition then and shared it with her daughter. Terry was truly frightened after the terrifying trip up from Vegas, with Darrin driving the Mercedes, laughing about how much money—Terry's money—he was going to spend on this new venture of his.

Most of Terry's estate was tied up in stocks and bonds and property, not easily liquidated. The ring Esther wore was free and clear and could be hocked or sold for a fortune. Where could she go? She was twenty-three years old and she'd never worked a day in her life. She'd been pampered, taken care of, her every desire fulfilled. Her mother's great wealth had cushioned her, spoiled her. If her mother had only loved her . . .

Well, over the years she'd managed to accept the neglect, while the housekeeper, Agnes, had shared holidays with her and been a wonderful substitute mother. Esther's mother was perpetually in search of the right man, so there was a succession of them in the villas she kept both in the United States and other countries. Esther had learned quickly to stay out of the way. Her mother didn't like having a grown daughter; it interfered with her vision of herself as a young and beautiful woman. Despite the face-lifts and spas and couture garments, her age was getting hard to hide. When she was at her lowest ebb, cast off by a younger lover, she'd met Darrin Ross. And it had all started to come apart. Even the slight affection Terry had felt for her daughter was suddenly gone, in the passion she shared with Darrin. But so soon, the passion turned to fear. Darrin drank heavily and used drugs, and he had very expensive tastes. Terry became a hostage to his desires. Along with her, Esther, too, became a victim. And now her mother was dead and she was cast adrift in a cold and frightening world, with no family.

Her mother had mentioned a grandfather. But who was he? Her mother spoke once of a falling-out she'd had with her remaining parent over her choice of husbands when she'd married Esther's easygoing, gambling father. Her father was long dead, but the feud apparently remained. Esther knew her grandfather's last name but not where he lived, because she hadn't been told. She couldn't go through family albums or correspondence, because those were in the main house back in Los Angeles, where Terry and Esther had lived. Esther didn't even have her cell phone. It was in the drawer beside her bed, still charging. She'd forgotten to bring it downstairs this evening, having come running when she heard her mother scream.

She could have cried, but it would do no good. She was

running for her life. She could call the police, of course, but Darrin would tell them it was a terrible accident. He wouldn't tell them that he'd thrown Terry down the staircase, and when the police left . . . It was too terrible to think about.

There had at least been three 911 calls from the address previously, though, when Darrin had attacked Terry over money. Agnes had called the police despite Terry's pleas. Try as he might, Darrin couldn't intimidate Agnes, who had powerful relatives. He wasn't drunk enough to do that, but he had pushed Terry into firing her. A temporary housekeeper had been engaged to work in her place, and Esther's heart had been broken at the treatment her surrogate mother had suffered. Terry had taken Darrin's side against her daughter for protesting. Darrin had threatened her with a black eye if she interfered with him again or if she dared to call the police. Those 911 calls would be on record. Even though Darrin was sure to swear that Terry's was an accidental death, there would be an investigation, because of Darrin's prior abuses. Surely he'd be found out!

Esther was far too afraid to do anything. She would call the police, she decided, so that at least Darrin wouldn't have the opportunity to hide the body. She'd do it anonymously, however, and from a pay phone. If she could find one. She'd never used a public phone. She wasn't sure where to go. But they recorded those calls, didn't they? And what if Darrin's friend at the police station recognized her voice and traced the call before she could get out of town? What then?

Buses ran. But Darrin would be after that diamond, and even worse, after her mother's will. Esther hadn't understood why her mother had stuffed the legal document into her purse the night before. *You must keep it close*, she'd said, *and never take it out of your purse*. Esther had asked why. Her mother had looked horrified and murmured something about a terrible threat. Darrin was jealous. He thought she was seeing someone else. He wasn't about to give up his luxury bed and board and he'd already started drinking. Her mother had seen an attorney, unknown to Darrin, and changed her will so that Darrin inherited nothing. In one of his rages, Darrin had gone with Terry to an attorney and had her revise her will to leave everything to him. Intimidated, Terry had agreed. But two days before her death, she got up enough courage to go back to the attorney and change the will so that her daughter would inherit everything. She told the lawyer she'd had a premonition. So now Esther stood to inherit the incredible amount of wealth, and she had the new, revised will, naming her beneficiary. She had the diamond, too. But the will and the ring were only useful if she lived.

She had to get out of town and somewhere she could hide, where Darrin couldn't find her. When she was safe, she could decide what to do. Tears stung her eyes. Her poor, sweet mother, who had no sense of self preservation, who trusted everyone. Esther knew what Darrin was the minute she saw him. Her mother was certain that he was only misunderstood, and he was so manly!

The first time Darrin had struck her mother in the face, Terry had realized with horror what sort of person he really was. But it was too late. He intimidated her to the point of separating her from every friend she had. He watched her, and Esther, like a hawk. The abuse had grown so much worse when he insisted on coming here to Aspen, to the grandest of Terry's many homes. They didn't dare tell anyone. He had a friend on the local police force, he told them, and he'd know if they tried to sell him out. They didn't have the nerve. Agnes, the only one in the household who wasn't afraid of him, had called 911, and been fired. Poor Agnes, who'd sacrificed so much to take care of the little girl Terry ignored. It broke Esther's heart.

And now her mother was dead, and Esther was running for her own life. She didn't have the price of a plane ticket. But she knew that Darrin had that friend on the police force. He might have someone who knew how to hack credit card companies to find out if a card in Terry's name had been used. So it was just as well that Esther didn't have the card. She couldn't fly, because she didn't have enough for a ticket. She couldn't take a bus because she could be traced that way. Even a train would keep records of its passengers.

But what about a truck? A big rig? She was walking beside a major highway and a huge semi was barreling through the snow that covered the road. Impulsively, she stepped out into the road. If the truck hit her, she wouldn't be any worse off, she thought miserably. At least she'd be with her mother.

The truck driver had good brakes. He stopped, pulled to the side of the road, and got out, leaving the engine idling.

He opened the passenger door and looked down at the pretty little blonde. Her long hair was tangled and she was wearing a fur jacket—probably fake, he thought gently, like that gaudy paste ring she was wearing that sparkled in the headlights. She didn't look like a prostitute. She looked frightened. "Miss, you okay?" he asked in a drawl.

She smiled wanly. "I'm sorry," she said, almost choking on anguish. "I've just lost my mother and I wasn't . . . wasn't thinking. I have to get to my cousin."

He smiled gently. He was an older man. She didn't

know why, but she felt that she could trust him. "Where's your cousin live?" he asked.

"Up near the Wyoming border," she blurted out. Her mother had mentioned a friend who'd lived there once, but she couldn't remember a name. "Benton, Colorado," she added.

He chuckled. "Now that's a hell of a coincidence. Come on." He led her back to the truck and knocked on the sleeper cab. A sleepy, heavyset blond woman opened her eyes. "Jack?" she asked the man. "What's wrong?"

"We've got a passenger. She's headed to Benton, hitch-hiking."

Esther started to deny it, but this was working out better than she'd dreamed. "I have to get to my cousin," she explained in her soft voice. "My mother . . . just died." She choked up.

"Oh, honey." The blond woman, dressed in jeans and flannel, tumbled out of the sleeper and caught Esther up in her arms, hugging her. "There, there, it's okay. We'll get you to your cousin."

Esther bawled. She'd lucked up. At least she had some hope of getting away before Darrin could catch her. And he'd never think that she'd be hitching rides in big rigs.

"You get right in front with Jack. I've been driving for twelve straight hours and I'm burned out." She chuckled. "We're a team. Well, we're married, but we're both truckers, so I'm his relief driver."

"It must be interesting," Esther said.

"Interesting and never dull," the woman said, smiling.

"Thanks so much," Esther began.

"We all have dark times," the driver, Jack, told her. "They pass. Buckle up and let's get going. You had anything to eat?"

"Oh, yes, I'm fine, thanks," she lied.

He saw through that. Her pale blue eyes were full of anguish. "There's a great truck stop a few hours down the road. We'll pull in and have some of the best barbecue in the country. You like barbecue?"

"I do," Esther said, and smiled.

"Okay, then. Let's be off!"

The trucker's wife was Glenda, and they were the nicest couple Esther had ever met. Down-to-earth, simple people, with no wealth or position, but they seemed outrageously happy. They made her feel like family.

She paid for her own supper out of her allowance that she hadn't had time to spend, and theirs, despite their protests. "You're giving me a ride and you won't let me pay for gas, so I'm buying food," she said stubbornly, and smiled.

They both laughed. "Okay, then," Glenda agreed. "Thank you."

"No. Thanks to both of you," she returned.

After supper it was back in the truck again. Four hours down the road, the truck stopped and Glenda got behind the wheel.

Esther was amazed at how the small woman could handle the big truck. "You're amazing," she exclaimed. "How in the world can you manage such a huge vehicle?"

"My daddy taught me to drive when I was only eleven," Glenda said as she pulled out onto the highway and the big truck started to slowly accelerate. "I can drive anything, even those big earthmovers. I love heavy equipment," she added with a flush of embarrassment. "It's why I married Jack. He drove these big rigs, and I loved them. Well, I loved him, too," she confessed. "The big lug. I couldn't do without him."

Esther, who'd never really been in love, just nodded as if she understood. She really didn't. She'd lived like a hothouse orchid all her life, kept at home because her mother didn't like it if she had friends; they interfered with her boyfriends coming and going from whichever house they were living in. They rarely stayed in one place. Esther had been sent off to school, to a boarding school, and she'd hated every minute of it. When she came home, her mother was curt and unkind to her. Esther got in her way. She was younger and prettier than Terry, and when Terry's boyfriends came to the house, many of them flirted with Esther instead. Terry spent most of her time avoiding her mother and her mother's lovers. She wanted to leave, but she had nothing of her own. Everything belonged to Terry, and she wasn't shy about sharing that tidbit with her daughter if she ever rebelled. Terry could be icy and she was distant most of the time. Sweet Agnes had been Esther's anchor. She still missed the housekeeper.

Now here she was, alone and terrified, out on her own for the first time in her twenty-three years, with her mother lying dead back home. And Darrin no doubt hunting her for that diamond ring that was worth millions of dollars, not to mention that he needed her to be executrix of her mother's estate so he could get to the money. He had the false will, which would give him access to part of the property. He would want it all. But he and her mother weren't legally married, so he had no clear title to her estate. In the will that he thought was the true will, Terry had only made him beneficiary to her bank accounts. He hadn't read it thoroughly enough to realize that, and he certainly didn't know about the revised will in Esther's purse. When he found out, he'd be quite capable of getting one of his underworld friends to go after her.

The thought arose that if Darrin could find her, he could probably force her to sign something giving him access to Terry's entire estate, no matter what violence it required, and do that without a pang of conscience. But he had to find her first, and she was going to make that very difficult.

They got to the outskirts of Benton before dawn. Esther couldn't afford to go to a motel and have people see her and wonder who she might be, because it was a very small town. Impulsively, she asked the couple to let her out at the end of a long driveway. She saw a small cabin in the distance with lights blazing inside it, through a drift of snow.

It looked like a wonderful refuge, if she could convince whoever lived there to let her stay, just for a day or two, until she could make other arrangements. Surely it was a couple, maybe with kids, and she could work something out.

It was an impulsive move, but she had these rare flashes of insight. Usually they were good ones.

"That's where my cousin lives," she lied brightly. "Thank you so very much for the ride!"

"You're very welcome." Glenda hugged her. So did Jack.

Glenda handed her a piece of paper. "That's my cell phone number. If you need help, you use it," she said firmly. "We'll come, wherever we are."

Tears stung Esther's eyes. "Thanks," she choked.

Glenda hugged her again. "You take care of yourself."

"You do, too."

They climbed back into the truck and waved. They looked very reluctant to leave her. It made her feel warm inside. She forced a smile, turned, and walked down the long trail to the little cabin. She'd memorized the name on the side of the truck. One day, she promised herself, when she had her fortune back, she was going to make sure that the pair had a trucking business of their very own.

As she struggled through the deep snow, her ankle boots already wet, her hands freezing because she didn't have her gloves, she felt as if she were slogging through wet sand. The night had been an anguish of terror. Her mother, dying, apologizing, Darrin raging upstairs, Esther terrified and not knowing what to do or where to go. She shivered. She had no money, no friends because they never stayed in one place long enough for her to make any since she'd left boarding school, she didn't even have a change of clothing. And the fox fur, while warm, wasn't enough in this freezing blizzard. She must have been out of her mind to get out of a safe truck with only the hope of a warm place to stay in the distance. A couple must live there, she told herself. Surely they wouldn't turn away anyone on a night like this!

It was almost daylight by now. She was just a few steps away from the front porch of the cabin when her body finally gave out. She fell into the snowdrift with a faint little cry, lost in the howling wind.

Inside the cabin, Butch Matthews was just turning off the television. It was late. He didn't sleep much. Memories of the war in Iraq, where he'd lost an arm to a mortar attack, still haunted him. He had nightmares. He was all alone here in this cabin on the outskirts of Benton. He'd been engaged once, but she'd gone back to an old boyfriend because, as she put it, she couldn't bear the thought of sleeping with a one-armed man.

He sure could pick them, he thought bitterly. Well, he had a good job with the state wildlife division, and he was a licensed rehabilitator. He looked down at his companion, a three-legged wolf named Two-Toes, who was old and almost blind.

"At least I've got you for company, old man," he sighed, tugging at the neck of his blue-checked flannel shirt. "Damn, it's getting cold in here. I guess I'd better get in a little more wood before it all freezes."

He patted the wolf, ran a hand through his own thick, short black hair. His dark eyes went to the sheepskin coat hanging by the front door. He wasn't a handsome man, but he had regular features at least. He was tall and fit, despite losing part of his arm up until just below the elbow. He had jet-black hair and dark brown eyes, and big hands and feet. He also had an inner strength and an oversized dose of compassion. Everyone liked him, but he didn't mix well, though, and he kept to himself. The loneliness got to him once in a while. It got to him tonight. He was more alone than he'd felt in his life. Both his parents were long dead. His fiancée had bailed on him. There wasn't anybody else. Not even a cousin . . .

He opened the door and his eyes widened. There, in the snow, was a body. It had blond hair and a fur jacket.

"Good God!" he exclaimed. He ran to her, turned her over gently. She was beautiful. Perfect complexion, long blond hair, pretty mouth. And unconscious.

"At least you're a lightweight," he murmured as he shifted her so that he could get her over one shoulder in a fireman's lift.

He carried her quickly into the house and eased her down on the leather sofa. "Don't eat her," he told Two-Toes firmly.

The old wolf sat on its haunches and panted.

Butch closed the front door and found an afghan that he'd bought at a summer festival in Benton. He eased the woman out of the fur jacket and winced. She was wearing a very thin silk blouse. No wonder she was almost frozen. And what was she doing out in the middle of nowhere, without a suitcase? He noted the hem of her slacks as he wrapped her up. Something dark had stained them. Blood?

He wrapped her in the afghan and went into the kitchen to make coffee. While it perked, he got down an extra mug. Something hot might help. He wondered if he should call an ambulance. Hopefully, she'd only fainted. He'd have to check her pulse and breathing. He'd had basic first aid courses as part of his army training, and later, forest service training, so he knew how to handle emergencies.

He poured coffee, turned off the pot, and carried the mugs to the coffee table.

He sat down beside the woman and shook her gently by the shoulder.

She opened her eyes. They were blue. Pale blue. She looked up at him, disoriented. "I passed out," she said in a soft, sweet voice.

He smiled. "Yes, you did."

She blinked and looked around her. "This is the cabin. I saw it from the road . . ." She'd have to make up some excuse for being here, and she wasn't good at lying. If he tossed her out, she didn't know what she'd do. On the other hand, what if he was like Darrin? Faint fear narrowed her eyes.

There was an odd growling sound nearby. A dog, maybe? She loved dogs. If this man had pets, he must be nice. But her heart was pounding with mingled fear and worry and grief.

"It's okay," he said, watching the expressions cross her face. She looked very young. "You're safe."

"Safe." She sat up, just in time for Two-Toes to amble over and sit down beside her.

Esther's eyes widened and she held her breath.

"That's just Two-Toes," the man said in a pleasant deep voice. "He's blind. He growls when he doesn't know people, but he's never bitten anyone. Who are you, and what are you doing out here in the middle of the night?"

She recovered her senses and looked at him. The man was tall and well built. One shirtsleeve was empty at the bottom. He wore boots and jeans and a flannel shirt. He had dark hair and eyes. He was smiling.

"Well?" he prompted, but not in a mean way.

"I thought my cousin lived here," she lied. "Barry Crump and his wife, Lettie . . ."

"No Crumps here." He frowned. "In fact, I don't think I've ever known anybody with that name."

"Oh, dear," she said, biting her lower lip.

"I didn't see a car when I found you."

It was a question. She flushed. It made her face brighter, vulnerable. "I don't own one," she said. And she didn't. Not anymore. "I hitched a ride."

"That's dangerous," he pointed out.

She was drawing blood with that tooth in her lower lip. She sat up, displacing the afghan, and ran a hand through her tangled hair. "Oh, coffee," she exclaimed, and almost fell on it. "I'm so thirsty!"

"Feeling better now?" he asked.

"Oh, yes. I was just so tired. It's been a long night," she added without elaborating. "I've never fainted before. I guess it was the cold." She smiled shyly. "Thanks for saving me."

"No problem. I'm a licensed rescuer for damsels in distress," he teased.

"What's a damsel?" she wondered.

"Damned if I know, really." He chuckled. "But you were in need of rescue. I slay dragons, too, in case you ever need one taken care of."

She grinned. Her whole face lit up and she was extraordinarily beautiful.

"Who are you?" he asked.

"Esther," she said quietly. "Esther Marist." She cocked her head and studied him. "Who are you?"

He smiled. "Butch Matthews."

"Thanks for bringing me inside," she said softly. "I guess I'd have frozen to death out there." She shivered. "I'm not really dressed for this much snow."

Butch Matthews was no dunce. Something traumatic had happened to her. He could sense it. She was wearing high-ticket items. He knew real fur when he saw it, and that fox jacket was real fox. Her shoulder bag was real leather, like her high-heeled shoes. She didn't have a suitcase, so she'd left somewhere in a hurry. She was wearing a huge pink gaudy ring on one finger. It sure didn't go with the fox jacket. Nobody had a ring that size that was real, he was sure of it. Damned thing covered almost a whole joint of her finger.

He recalled hearing a semi stop out on the highway, a

few minutes before this little fragile blond turned up on his doorstep.

He sat down in the armchair across from the sofa with the coffee table between them and sipped his own coffee.

"Now," he said, smiling. "Suppose you tell me what's wrong?"

Wrong . . . ?"

"Come on. Two-Toes and I are mostly harmless."

She laughed. "*The Hitchhiker's Guide to the Galaxy*," she blurted out, because those two words were what were written about Earth in the guide.

He roared. "Truly."

Two-Toes inched toward her, sniffing.

"Friend, Two-Toes," he told the wolf, ruffling his fur. "Friend. Don't eat her."

Esther looked, and felt, horrified.

"I'm kidding," Butch teased.

She looked from him to the big wolf. She'd never seen one in person, and this one was twice the size of any dog she'd seen. He moved closer to her and began to sniff her. Impulsively, because he didn't seem aggressive, she put out a small hand. He took a deep smell, and suddenly laid his head in her lap.

"Oh, goodness," she said softly. She stroked his head, a smile breaking out on her worried face. "My goodness, he's so sweet!"

Butch was speechless. Mostly Two-Toes avoided contact with anyone who came in the door, except Parker, his Crow friend who'd just married.

"Well," Butch said heavily. "That's amazing."

She looked up. "Why?"

"He's not usually that friendly."

She laughed.

"Not to most people," he amended. "Can I get you something to eat?"

"Thank you, but no. The truck drivers were kind enough to find a truck stop. I got coffee and supper. They were so sweet to me."

"Most truckers are good people," he said.

She drew in a breath. "It hasn't exactly been a night for that." She caught herself and gave him a worried glance.

"Can you talk about what happened?" he asked.

She hugged the wolf and lowered her eyes. "My mother . . . died tonight."

"Good God! Where?"

"Back in"—she hesitated—"where we were staying. Her boyfriend wants all her things. He was drunk. She was all broken up and there was blood everywhere. She told me to run. I didn't think, I just ran!"

He saw a panorama that was disturbing, and this fragile little thing right in the middle of it. "You're afraid of him. The boyfriend."

"Terrified." She drew in a short, sharp breath. "If they find me, they'll make me testify. If I testify, he'll kill me. He has friends in organized crime. He made threats to my poor mother." She closed her eyes and shivered.

"You should go to the police," he said.

"He has a friend in the local department," she replied. "The mob pays him."

"I see." He frowned. "How did your mother die?"

"He threw her down the staircase." She looked at her lap. "I think it broke her spine. Her throat was cut from hitting something on the way down. She only lived a few seconds . . . after . . ."

"Dear God!"

He got up and went to the sofa beside her, pulling her

against him with one strong arm. He smelled of soap and aftershave. He was very strong, and warm, and she was aching for comfort. She curled close to him and cried her heart out.

He'd never felt needed in his whole life, not by anybody. And here this beautiful stranger came walking in out of the snow and made him feel ten feet tall with her fragility, her vulnerability.

She drew back after a minute. "I'm sorry, it's just that there's so much . . . !"

He smoothed her hair. "Don't worry about it." He got up. "Come on. This isn't a five-star hotel, but it's got two bedrooms and you're welcome to one of them. The door even locks," he added with a grin.

She smiled. She trusted him implicitly, without even knowing him. "Tomorrow, I'll find someplace to go and see about getting a job."

"What sort of job?" he asked.

She flushed. She'd never worked a day in her young life. But she was strong and she could learn. "Whatever there is," she said finally, and smiled at him.

He admired her spirit. "I'll see if I can help," he said. "But you can stay here for the time being. I'm out a lot. I work for the wildlife service. In my spare time, I'm a re-habilitator."

"Oh, I see! Two-Toes," she began.

"Yes. Two-Toes and other assorted mammals, including a fox. The others live in the outbuilding. It's heated, sort of, and at least sheltered. Two-Toes, though, he's company." He stopped suddenly, close to admitting how lonely he was. He'd been engaged, but when she found out he'd lost his arm, she'd broken the engagement. His parents were long dead. He had nobody, unless you counted his friend, Parker.

"I like animals," she said.

"We noticed," he chuckled, indicating Two-Toes, who was following her.

"He's sweet," she said softly, rubbing her hand over his thick fur.

"Yes, he is. Now if you'd had a big bologna sandwich for lunch . . ." His voice trailed off with amusement.

She just laughed. "You wouldn't eat me, even then, would you, sweet boy?"

The wolf sat down and his tongue lolled out while she petted him.

Butch just shook his head.

The bedroom had a bed, a chest of drawers, and assorted guns.

He made a face. "I guess you hate guns . . ."

"I don't mind them," she said, smiling.

Both eyebrows went up

"My dad used to take me to the gun range with him, when he was alive. He was a Class A skeet shooter."

He was fascinated. "Can you shoot a shotgun?"

"Just the lightest gauge, the 28," she replied.

"Just," he said, shaking his head. He'd never met a woman who'd even pick up a shotgun, much less risk the noise and recoil of shooting one.

She was looking around the room.

"It's just a spare room," he said. "I had the bed put in because once in a while, somebody comes from one of the agencies and needs a place to stay. But it's not often. It's messy in here," he added.

"I don't mind clutter," she said softly.

"You don't even have a change of clothes," he mused.

"I left in a hurry." Tears stung her eyes.

"Do you want to call anybody?"

"There's nobody to call," she said miserably. "It was just Mama and me. I've got a grandfather, but I don't know where he is. I don't even know who he is. Mama hardly ever talked about him. I can't even call the police. Darrin would find out where I am and come after me."

"Why?" he asked. "Because you saw what he did?"

She opened her purse and took out the will. "Because Mama changed her will and I've got it," she said. "She stuffed it into my purse a day ago and told me to keep it there. She always had premo . . . premonitions." She swallowed tears and grief.

He was noticing the gaudy ring she wore. Costume jewelry, of course. He wondered why she hadn't chosen something less ostentatious, that looked less like a fake. Women were incomprehensible to him most of the time, though. He'd never been able to keep one for long, especially his fiancée. She was hung up on cowboys when they met, and thought that he had a ranch in Wyoming. He'd never lied to her about that. He owned a hundred acres and a few horses, but he was no land baron. Perhaps she'd been wrapped up in daydreams. She hadn't been that crazy about him after a few dates, and to be honest, she'd been pretty drunk when he proposed. He'd thought she was innocent until he took her to bed, where she taught him things he'd never known. Probably it was just as well that she'd left him. Hearing her talk about past lovers made him uncomfortable. It was something he'd never have done.

"Well, I'll leave you to it," he said gently. "Bathroom's down the hall and it has a lock. I hate having people walk in on me when I'm having a shower, even if it's other men." His face hardened for a minute and she wondered if it was because part of his arm was missing, but she didn't say so.

"Thanks for giving me a place to sleep," she said gently. "I'll find something as fast as I can and get out of your hair."

He just smiled and closed the door on her.

She was too tired to take a shower. She took off her slacks and blouse and slid under the covers, nervous and sick and worried. It would be a miracle if she got a wink of sleep after what she'd been through.

But she felt safe. That kind man in the other room had been generous. He didn't know her from a snowball, but he was willing to trust her in his home. It made her feel humble. She had to make sure that she found something soon, so that she didn't have to presume on his hospitality. He wasn't a man who had a lot of material possessions, she could tell, but it didn't matter to her. He had a good heart. She closed her eyes and, amazingly, went right to sleep

He tapped on the door around eight. "Breakfast. Hot coffee. Great company!" he called through the door.

She burst out laughing, still half asleep. "I'll be right out."

She got up and put on the clothes she'd been wearing the day before, her eyes wincing at the blood stain still on the hem of her slacks. Maybe she could wash it out later.

They ate in a companionable silence. He'd made scrambled eggs and toast and bacon to go with the coffee. They were great.

"You're a wonderful cook," she said.

"You only think so because you're half starved," he pointed out good-naturedly. He leaned toward her. "The toast has been scraped. I burned it!"

She giggled.

He grinned and went back to eating.

"Is there a local paper, and does it have want ads?" she asked.

"Yes." He got up and retrieved it from the sofa, handing it to her.

"Thanks." She sipped coffee while she searched through the Help Wanted column. She sighed. "Well, I can't drive an eighteen-wheeler or handle cattle, and I'm pretty sure I'm not cut out to be a shepherd. But there's a waitress job going in town at the Gray Dove." She looked up. "I hate to ask . . ."

"But can I drive you to town," he finished for her, laughing. "Sure. Let me feed Two-Toes and the other critters and I'll drive you in."

"Thanks!"

He shrugged, not even looking back.

His truck wasn't new, but it was well kept and it ran smoothly. She grinned. She'd never been in a pickup in her life. "This is great!" she exclaimed as they went down the road.

"What, the scenery?" he asked, curious.

"This truck!" she said. "It's just awesome!"

He was stunned. She was wearing expensive clothes, he could tell, but she went goo-goo over a truck. He laughed softly.

"What is it?" she asked.

"It's just a truck," he pointed out.

"Yes, I know, but I've never ridden in one. It's just super!"

His eyes widened. "You've never been in a truck?"

"Well, no," she said, hesitating. Her face colored. She shouldn't have admitted that.

He felt guilty when he saw the joy drain out of her. "Listen, don't mind me," he said. "There must be dozens of city people who think cars are the only way to travel. But I'm glad you like the truck." He grinned. "There was this song, about a man who loved his truck."

She laughed, the joy returning.

She was pretty when she laughed. He had to drag his eyes away.

She didn't notice. She was on fire with life, with a new beginning, with a sudden feeling of safety and refuge. She took a deep breath and forced her mother's tragic face to the back of her mind. She had to look ahead. And that meant a job, for the moment.

CHAPTER TWO

The owner of the Gray Dove, Mary Dodd, tried not to gape at the sight of Butch Matthews with a pretty young blond woman. He hadn't dated anyone since he came home from the war and his fiancée threw him over, so it was something of an occasion. But she was quick to hide her surprise.

"I've never done any waitressing," Esther confessed. "But I'll work hard, and never complain, and I'll learn, if you'll teach me. I won't even care about salary . . ."

"You don't have to sell me," the woman said gently. "I read people pretty well. It's not as if we have hordes of people rushing in here trying to get work," she added with a smile. "If you want the job, it's yours."

Esther relaxed. "Thank you!"

The owner went on to tell her about uniforms, which would be provided, and working hours. She'd start the following Monday.

Esther thanked her again, with such enthusiasm that Butch had to hide a smile.

They went out together, onto the sidewalk.

"Are there cabs?" she asked suddenly, worried.

"It's five minutes from the cabin," he pointed out. "I don't mind driving you."

"Are you sure?" she asked, concerned. "I'm causing you a lot of trouble."

"And if I minded, I'd say so," he replied softly. "Okay?"

She let out the breath she'd been holding. "Okay."

"How about riding around with me for a bit?" he asked. "So you get to know the area."

"I'd like that!" she enthused.

"Yeah, right, you're not fooling me. All that enthusiasm, it's just so you can be near the truck," he drawled.

She burst out laughing. So did he.

"Busted," she confessed.

He drove her around town, pointing out the various businesses. There weren't a lot. Benton had a little over fifteen hundred souls. It was like a big family, he explained. People didn't mind each others' business, but they cared about each other.

"That sounds very nice," she commented softly

"Isn't it like this, where you come from?"

She hesitated. Then she shook her head. She sighed and looked out the window. "We lived a lot of places, but none of them was ever home," she explained. "Mama was, well, adventurous. She was always in love with somebody, and she never chose anybody who was good for her. Darrin was the latest in a long line of horrible men she . . . lived with."

"What about your dad?" he wondered.

"He died years ago. He was a sweet man. I loved him very much. I loved Mama, too, but . . ." She hesitated. She glanced at him. "She did love me, in her way."

"I'm guessing that you had to find ways to avoid some of the men, Esther," he said without meeting her eyes.

She drew in a long breath. She looked out the window again. "Yes."

What a hell of a life, he was thinking. "Was your mother as pretty as you are?"

"Much prettier," she replied, smiling sadly. "She never looked her age. I brought a boy home from school one day and he spent the evening with Mama." She shook her head. "I wasn't much on boys, anyway. Watching Mama with an endless parade of men sort of soured me, I guess."

He felt sorry for her. She had a little material wealth, from the look of her, but without love, it wasn't much.

"How are you going to like waitressing?" he asked quietly. "I'll bet you've never had a job in your young life."

"You'd be right," she said on a long sigh. "But I'm young, like you said, and strong, and I can learn how to do anything I set my mind to."

"I'd bet money on that," he said with a gentle smile.

"I have to find somewhere to live . . ."

"Why can't you stay with me?" he asked simply.

She was shocked. "But, people might talk," she began.

"Sure they might. I don't care. Do you?"

She was thinking about being on her own. She could probably find someplace that she could afford, but she'd be all alone. She grimaced.

"Or does the idea of living with a one-armed man turn you off?" he asked, and there was such bitterness in the remark that she turned her head and gaped at him.

"Is that what happened?" she asked softly. "Your girlfriend turned her back on you when you came home from overseas? What an idiot she must have been!"

Now he was the one gaping, so much so that he had to right the truck back on the highway.

"You took me in and I could have been anybody," she continued. "You live with an injured wolf that you could have had put down instead." She smiled. "You're not a missing arm with a man attached, you know. You're a man who lost his arm."

"Damn!"

Her eyebrows arched. "Excuse me?"

He pulled over onto the grass beside the road and threw the truck out of gear. He looked at her, long and hard, and his lean face was taut with bad memories. "I was engaged to be married," he said quietly. "My reserve unit, army, was called up, so I went to Iraq with a friend of mine, Parker, who lives locally. He carried me through a hail of bullets, after I took a hit from mortar, in Iraq. He saved my life." He stared out the windshield at the distant mountains. "I came home wounded and was mustered out. My girl was waiting for me. I got off the bus and she saw the empty sleeve." He hesitated.

She put out a soft hand and touched his shoulder. "And?"

He grimaced. "She said she was sorry. She couldn't bear the thought of going to bed with a one-armed man. She put the ring in my shirt pocket, smiled, and just walked away. I stayed drunk for two weeks. Parker snapped me out of it and helped me get a job. This job, working as a wildlife rehabilitator for the state of Colorado in this district, and that helps put money in the bank. But I've sort of been off women ever since."

"No wonder," she said quietly. "What a burden she might have been. You had a lucky escape."

He glanced at her, frowning.

"Sorry," she said, grimacing. "I open my mouth and stick my foot in."

The frown went away. "I've never thought of myself as being lucky."

"What sort of wife would she have been, if she didn't love you enough to just be grateful that you came home at all?"

There was a faintly stunned expression in his eyes. It hadn't ever occurred to him that Sadie might not have loved him in the first place. They were good in bed together, but she'd never been emotionally attached to him. He'd almost died with pneumonia the winter they were engaged, and she'd never even come to see about him. Parker had nursed him until he got well.

"Talk about being blind," he murmured. "No. I don't think she loved me at all. We were good in bed together. It was only that. She was on the rebound from another man when I started going with her."

"Does she still live here?" she asked, without knowing why she asked the question.

"No. The old boyfriend turned up and she married him. They moved away."

"When did he turn up?"

"Oh, just before I came home . . ." He stopped in midsentence. "Why didn't I remember that?"

"You stayed drunk for two weeks," she pointed out.

He glanced at her again and this time he was smiling. "You're a tonic."

"You mean I taste bad?" she teased.

He pursed his chiseled lips. "I can't comment until I've decided that for myself."

She blushed scarlet. "Oh, gosh!"

He burst out laughing. "Sorry. Couldn't resist it." He put the truck in gear and pulled back out onto the highway. "Are you a witch?" he teased. "You know things you shouldn't."

"We had an ancestor who died in Salem who was accused of witchcraft, so who knows?" she teased.

She was bright and beautiful, and Butch felt as if the sun had just come out in his dreary, cloudy life.

"What about you?" she asked. "Do you have family?"

"Just Parker, and we're not related," he said on a sigh. "My parents were older when they had me, and I was their only child. They've both been dead for years."

"So, you're alone, too," she said in her soft, quiet voice.

She looked out the window, fighting tears again. It was so painful, remembering her mother lying at the foot of the staircase.

"You miss your mother," he said, noting the faint glitter of tears in her averted face.

"She was so trusting," she said, her voice catching, because the loss was very new. "She never saw the evil in people. Especially in men. It was one after the other, most of my life."

"Addiction."

She turned toward him. "What?"

"Addiction," he repeated. "It's not much different than being addicted to alcohol or drugs, or even gambling. It wasn't something she could help."

She was silent for a minute, thinking about what he'd said. "I didn't think of it that way."

"We're all at the mercy of our urges from time to time," he said quietly. "But I'm sorry you had to lose her in such a way."

"Me, too." She wiped her eyes with the backs of her hands. "She was all I had left in the world."

"You need to talk to a lawyer," he said. "You can't let your mother's boyfriend get away with murder."

"He's very slick," she muttered. "He could talk people into believing anything."

"You were an eyewitness to what he did," he pointed out.

"Yes, and he has friends who are big-time criminals," she replied. "The minute he knows where I am, he'll come after me. I have Mama's will." She also had Mama's multi-million-dollar ring on her finger, but she wasn't mentioning that. It was gaudy enough to pass for paste, which suited Esther just fine.

Butch was thinking. "There has to be some way you could point a finger at him."

"You think?" she asked on a heavy sigh. She glanced at him. "It would put you in danger as well, and I'm not doing that. Not after you've been so kind to me. They have a good police force in Aspen," she added quietly. "I know, because Mama had to call them, when Darrin hit her . . ."

"So there's a record of it?"

"There is. In fact, there were three incidents while we lived there."

"And that will put him on the suspect list, at least." He glanced at her. "If you want to go back, I'll go with you," he said unexpectedly.

"But you don't know me from a bean," she pointed out. "I could be lying."

He chuckled. "Nope."

"Are you always so trusting?" she wanted to know.

"Not with most people. But you're an open book, sunshine," he teased. "You couldn't hide anything. Your face would give you away." He paused to grin at her. "I'd love to play poker with you."

She burst out laughing. "I guess I'd be pretty lousy at that, anyway. The only gambling I've ever done was at the slot machines in Vegas, and I lost every penny I put into it."

"I used to play poker. I never won, so I gave it up. Now it's checkers or chess, when I have the time."

"I'll bet you . . ."

His phone rang. He pulled off on the side of the road and looked at the screen, then pushed a button and put it to his ear. "Where? When? Sure. I'm on my way. Don't let it out of your sight, okay? Fine."

He hung up. "I have a call to make," he told her. "Do you mind going along?"

"Not at all. What do you have to do?"

"Rescue another wolf, but this one isn't blind or missing a leg," he said. "You'll stay in the truck while I deal with it. Got that?"

"Okay," she said.

He put his foot down on the accelerator. "Two boys with rifles were shooting for sport," he said angrily. "They are not sure they hit it, but they're in custody anyway."

"It's an endangered species?"

"No. They got arrested for animal cruelty. They had a rope around its neck and they were dragging it behind a pickup truck." His face was taut with anger.

"I hope they lock them up for a year," she muttered.

"Me, too."

It wasn't a long drive. Butch pulled off the main road across from a convenience store and cut off the engine.

"Stay put, okay?" he emphasized.

"I will."

She watched him go over to a pickup truck, which was flanked by a county sheriff's deputy and a state police officer. Butch bent over something, ran a hand over it and stood back up. He glanced at the truck.

One of the deputies picked up the wolf and carried it to the bed of the pickup, where Butch kept a cage.

"Go easy," she heard Butch say as the man slid the injured animal into the cage.

"How will you get him out when you get home?" the deputy asked.

"With a lot of swearing and a little bit of luck," Butch replied with a laugh.

"I'll follow you home and get him out for you," the deputy said.

"Okay. Thanks, Roy."

The other man waved and went back to his vehicle.

"Is he badly injured?" Esther asked.

"A couple of broken ribs, feels like, and a lot of scrapes. I know what to do for them, and there's a wildlife vet I can call to check him over. I'll do that when we get home."

"Those stupid boys," she muttered.

"They're going to be very sorry for what they did, believe me. They won't get away with it."

"I'm glad."

The deputy was waiting at the cabin when they got there. Butch went around to open the passenger door and Esther got out.

It didn't help that the deputy, young and single, stared

at Esther as if he was looking at a delicious ice cream sundae.

"Uh, the wolf?" Butch prompted.

Roy cleared his throat, flushed a little, and laughed. "Sure thing. Coming."

He lifted the wolf out and carried him to one of the out-buildings where Butch kept his injured wildlife. The wolf, fortunately, was in too much pain to fight. Several minutes later, the men came out of the building.

"Thanks for the help, Roy," Butch said, and shook his hand.

"That's one beautiful girlfriend you've got there," Roy said. "Is she local?"

"No. And she's not my girlfriend." He hesitated. "She's my fiancée."

"Well! Congratulations, you sly dog, you." Roy chuckled. "No wonder you were giving me the evil eye."

"Can't help it. She's gorgeous and I'm ugly," Butch said.

"Baloney. If you need help anytime, though, you can call me."

"Thanks."

He went into the house to find Esther in the kitchen, looking for a cookbook.

"Hey," Butch said. "What are you up to?"

She turned. "Have you got a cookbook?" she asked.

"Uh, no, not really," he said slowly.

"Well, if I'm going to stay here, I have to earn my keep," she said softly. "So I'm going to learn how to cook."

Anticipating a few weeks of burned meals, he just smiled and said that was a great idea.

"I may have done something bad just now," he added slowly.

"How bad?"

"Well . . ."

She propped her hands on her hips and gave him a mock glare. "How bad?"

"You really are a dish," he murmured, starstruck.

"Butch," she prompted.

"Oh. The bad thing." He snapped out of the daze. "Well, it's like this. Roy, the guy who helped me with the wolf, he's single and woman-crazy and persistent."

Her eyebrows arched. "And?"

"And a real rounder. He was giving you the eye. So I told him something. It may make you angry . . ."

She cocked her head.

He cleared his throat. "I sort of told him we were engaged."

Her eyes glimmered with pleasure. She smiled. "You did? Really?"

"You're not angry?"

"Oh, no," she said softly. "I was already worrying about your reputation. You work for the state government and . . ."

He chuckled. "I don't really think they concern themselves with our private lives," he pointed out. "I was thinking of your reputation. You're sort of green, honey. I don't mean that in a bad way, just that you're not very, well, brassy. And Roy . . ."

"And Roy's a rounder," she finished for him.

"Exactly."

She smiled slowly. "Okay."

His eyebrows went up. "You don't mind?"

She laughed. "No. I don't mind at all."

He studied her quietly. "It's just while you're staying

here," he said. "I mean, you don't have to think of it as binding or anything."

"Oh."

He couldn't quite decipher the look on her face. "Anyway, I've got to go out and see about my new charge."

"I don't guess I could come with you?" she asked.

"He may be dangerous . . ."

"But I'll be with you," she said.

He felt a foot taller. "Okay, then,"

She grinned and followed him out the door.

The wolf had lacerations all down one side, probably the one on which he'd been dragged. Butch had an antibiotic ointment that he smoothed over the cuts after he'd cleaned them, having muzzled the animal first.

"I can't really afford to lose the other arm as well," he teased as he glanced at a spellbound Esther, standing next to him.

"I understand. Any animal can be dangerous, though, even a house cat."

"So true."

He smoothed his hand over the wolf's head. "Poor old man," he said gently. "I'm sorry to belong to a species that could do something so terrible to an animal."

The wolf opened one eye and looked at him, almost as if it understood him.

"I'll get you well and you can go home," he added. "Just rest now. The vet's coming over soon to see about you," he added, having called the vet as they walked into the shed room.

"He's so beautiful," Esther said as Butch closed the cage. "They're losing habitat so fast. Animals have no place to go. Civilization is making them extinct."

"Pretty much," Butch had to agree.

"What else do you have in here?" she wondered.

"Come and see."

She paused by the injured fox and winced. She was wearing a fox coat, although it was blue and this beautiful animal was red and white.

Butch bent down to her ear. "It's a dead fox. What you're wearing," he pointed out.

"Oh." She smiled shyly. "How did you know I was thinking that?"

"I'm taking a mail-order course in how to read minds," he teased.

She chuckled. "Okay." She moved with him to the other cages. One of them held a strange animal. She'd never seen one like it. "What is this one?" she asked.

"A badger," he replied. "Don't get too close. They can be aggressive."

"So can wolves," she returned.

"Yes."

She turned to Butch. "What you do, it's awesome," she said. "All these poor creatures would be dead if it wasn't for you."

He felt warm all over. She made him feel different. Useful. Better than he thought he was. "If I hadn't done it, somebody else would have," he began.

"Yes. But nobody else did. You did." She smiled.

He drew in a breath. "You really are a boost for my ego," he mused. "I won't be able to get my head through the door."

She laughed.

"We should go," he added. He adjusted the thermostat in the building, which controlled the gas heat, and shepherded her out the door and back into the cabin.

* * *

They had mashed potatoes and a small piece of cube steak for supper, with fruit for dessert. Butch had cooked. Esther peeled the potatoes.

"I peeled them too much," she said sadly.

"You did fine," he replied. "Especially for somebody who's never set foot in a kitchen before," he added with a grin.

"Thanks. I'll get better. I just need a cookbook and some practice."

"The cook at the Gray Dove is awesome," he pointed out. "I'll bet she'd be happy to give you some pointers if you just ask her."

"What a great idea! I'll do that."

"You might also mention that we're engaged," he added, because he knew the cook, and she was very conservative.

He was very protective already. She liked that. She smiled to herself.

He saw the smile. "What?" he asked.

She looked up, eyebrows arching.

"You smiled when I said that," he told her.

"Oh." She flushed. "It sounded, well, protective." She shifted. "I've never had anybody who tried to protect me. Mama was always looking for the right man. I know she loved me, but I was sort of an afterthought. And she didn't like having a grown daughter. She went to spas, had face-lifts, all those things really beautiful women do to try and look younger than they are." Her face was bland. She looked up at him. "What use is it?" she asked solemnly. "I mean, you may look younger, but it won't change how old you are, will it? And if you have to do so much work on yourself to deny how old you are, who's going to know or want the person you really are?" She made a face. "I'm making it all muddled . . ."

"You aren't," he replied, and he was serious as well. "I know exactly what you mean. My former fiancée was like that," he added bitterly. "She was always using creams and lotions and dyeing her hair, wearing clothes that were too young for her. She couldn't stand the thought of a new gray hair or a wrinkle in her face."

"That's just sad."

"It is." He studied her. He smiled. "You really are a knockout."

She flushed. "That's all on the outside," she said.

"I like what's on the inside even better," he returned softly.

The flush deepened.

His eyes were probing. "Haven't you ever had a boyfriend?"

She laughed softly. "They couldn't get past Mama," she said. "She was so beautiful . . ." She bit her lip. Tears stung her eyes. "Sorry. It's still so new."

"And so painful," he agreed. He slid his big hand over her small one and held it just for a minute. He let go then. "Don't let that steak go to waste," he said, forcing laughter. "It's one I bought from a local rancher. Filled up half my freezer. Grade A beef, no antibiotics, no hormones, just good beefsteak!"

She grinned. "I like steak," she said. "But just once in a while. I mostly eat fish and vegetables."

"Desserts?"

She paused and then shook her head. "I don't like sweets."

"Neither do I. Well, I like a chocolate pie once in a blue

moon. The cook at the Gray Dove makes them. I eat there about once a week."

She beamed. "So I'll see you at work one day a week?"

He chuckled. "Yes, you will."

She finished her meal and her coffee. "Want more coffee?" she asked, getting up.

"One more cup. It keeps me awake at night if I have more than that," he said.

She sighed. "I don't sleep, whether I drink coffee or not," she said. "Mama was always wanting to go somewhere. California, Nevada, Idaho, New York City, overseas. I don't think we ever spent more than a month at home. I don't like traveling."

"That makes two of us," he said. "I got moved around a lot in the military. Up until then, I'd never been out of Benton in my whole life."

"Honest?" she asked, surprised. She put his coffee mug down in front of him.

"Honest. My folks were ranchers." He chuckled. "Hard to go off and leave the cattle while you party in some other country. One guy I know went to Tahiti for a month. When he came back, his cattle were gone. He went to ask his foreman what happened to them, and his foreman was gone as well. The guy forged his boss's name on a bill of sale and sold the lot. Took the rancher two weeks to track him down. He hadn't had time to spend much of the money, so he got it back and recovered his cattle. Foreman went to prison."

"Good enough for him," she said.

"It also taught the rancher a valuable lesson," he added with twinkling eyes. "Not to be too trusting."

She chuckled. "I can see the point."

* * *

After they finished supper, Butch got Esther's fox fur and helped her into it.

"Where are we going?" she asked.

"Walmart," he replied. "You can't wear the same clothes to work every day."

She flushed. "I didn't think about that."

"We'll get you some slacks and shirts and a coat that won't attract attention," he said.

She sighed. "I guess it does look a bit out of place. But maybe people will think it's fake fur," she added.

"Not in this part of the country, they won't." He laughed.

"At least I still have some money," she said, and gave him a long, hard look that indicated he wasn't paying for anything for her.

"What an expression," he mused. "Have you ever knocked anybody out with those dagger-eyes?"

She relaxed and laughed softly. "Just making the point that I pay my own way," she replied. "And you'll get rent as soon as I get my first paycheck. I won't argue," she added softly. "You've been kinder to me than anybody ever was, except my parents."

Now he was flushing, high on his cheekbones. "Okay, then," he said, remembering that his former fiancée had begged for pretty things and never offered to do a thing for him. "Let's go."

CHAPTER THREE

The store was crowded, and the first people Butch met were his friend Parker and Parker's new wife, Katy, and his stepdaughter, Teddie. They were an interesting combination, because Parker was Crow—and had the jet-black hair and dark eyes and olive skin to prove it—and Katy was blond and blue eyed.

"Hey, buddy, how's it going?" Butch asked.

Parker grinned at him, his arm around his wife. "Things are great. How're you doing, Sarge?" he asked, and his eyes went curiously to the pretty blonde in the fox jacket standing so close to his friend.

Butch slid his one good arm around her and pulled her gently close. "She's my fiancée. Esther, this is my friend Parker, and his wife and daughter."

"Nice to meet you," Parker said. "Fiancée, huh? And you didn't say a word to me about it?" he teased.

"We haven't known each other long," Butch said, smiling down at a worried Esther, "but we both . . . just knew," he said, shrugging.

"I know how that feels." Parker chuckled. He looked down at Katy. "I knew, too."

Katy laughed up at him. "Me, too."

"How's Two-Toes?" Teddie asked excitedly.

"He's doing great. He likes to watch game shows." Butch chuckled.

"How does Esther like living with a wolf?" Parker teased.

"He follows her around like a puppy," Butch said, amused.

"He's so sweet," Esther said gently. "We've got a new wolf, too." Her face clouded. "He had a vicious introduction to people."

"Indeed he did," Butch muttered. "There were arrests. And there will be prosecutions. Poor old wolf. He'll live, but he may not be able to go back out into the wild either." He shook his head. "We live in strange times."

"How's Bartholomew?" Butch asked the little girl.

She grinned. "I can make him trot without falling off now!"

"Good for you!"

Esther looked puzzled. "Bartholomew?" she asked.

"He's my horse," Teddie said, smiling at her. "He was a rescue. Dad's teaching me how to ride him!"

"Mom's also teaching you," Katy said with pretended annoyance.

Teddie hugged her. "Sure you are. But Dad's at home when you're teaching. Well, when he's not breaking horses for Mr. Denton, anyway."

"It must be nice," Butch said to Parker, indicating Katy. "Your very own daughter. I'm so jealous!"

"You need a couple of your own," Parker told him with a grin at Esther's high color.

"We just got engaged, give us time." Butch laughed out loud.

"We have to get going," Parker said. "It's *Warriors and Warlocks* tonight, and this is a special one. The bad guy's going to get his. At least, the previews almost promised that he was."

"Don't you believe it," Butch drawled. "I have it on good authority that J. L.'s wife, Cassie, likes that bad guy a lot, and she's resisting any attempt to kill him off."

"Spoilsport," Parker teased.

Butch grinned. "I like him, too."

Parker glanced at Esther. "Do you watch the show, too?"

She shook her head. "My mother didn't even own a television," she said, and her face went taut again.

"She just lost her mother," Butch said, pulling her closer. "It's fresh."

"I'm truly sorry," Katy said gently. "I've lost both my parents. I know how it hurts."

"Thanks," Esther said in her soft voice, and her blue eyes were warm as they met Katy's.

"It gets easier," she added.

"It does," Parker agreed. "Okay, female troops, let's head out."

Katy made a face, but Teddie laughed.

"It's sort of like being in the military." Katy laughed.

"Oh, I can certainly identify with that," Butch said, and smiled as he waved them goodbye.

"Your friends are nice," Esther said as they walked down the aisle that contained women's clothing.

"They are," he agreed. "Parker's a special case. He saved my life overseas. Damned interesting guy, too," he added. "He has a degree in theoretical physics."

"What?" she exclaimed, her eyes wide.

"No kidding. He goes off to the nation's capital from time to time to work with one of the letter agencies, deciphering code. He's got a mind like a steel trap."

"He's Native American, isn't he?" she asked.

"Crow," he replied. "He has cousins on the reservation up in Montana."

"He seems to really love the little girl."

"He does. I expect he and Katy will have some of their own. Parker's been on his own for a long time. A family is just what he needed." He hesitated. "It's what I need as well. Being alone is for the birds."

She grinned.

He grinned back. "Do you like kids?"

"I love them," she replied. "I haven't been around them much. We had a housekeeper who had two little granddaughters who would come to see her in the summer. She had to bring them to work a couple of times. Mama was mad about it, but I loved it. Children are special, Agnes was the best grandmother." She sighed. "I really missed her after Darrin made Mama fire her. See, Darrin didn't like her." She made a face. "Children make the world a magical place," she said with dreamy eyes.

"I've always thought so myself. Parker brought Katy and Teddie over to see Two-Toes when I first brought him home. He loved Teddie at once."

"She seems like a sweet child."

"Her dad was in the military, a doctor. He died while he was completing a tour of duty in Iraq." His face closed up.

"That's where you were, isn't it?" she asked.

He drew in a breath. "There sure are a lot of pretty sweaters over here," he said instead of answering her.

She didn't push. She knew he'd had a hard time in the

military. "Yes, these are lovely," she agreed, not mentioning that it was the first time in her life that she'd been in a store that didn't sell couture garments. She was actually enjoying herself.

Finally, she ended up with two pairs of slacks and four colorful pullover sweaters, two gowns, a sweatpants set and some serviceable underwear. It amused her that Butch went to look over the electronics when she went into the lingerie section of the store. He was a conundrum, she thought. But she liked him very much.

Her first day on the job was grueling. She wasn't used to standing for long periods of time, and she was amazed at how hard it was. At the same time, she was fascinated with the fact of earning a living for herself. She'd never had to worry about money. In fact, she'd always been able to buy anything she liked. This was different. It was exciting. Everything about it was new, and her enthusiasm was visible.

The owner of the café, Mrs. Dodd, chuckled when Esther was taught how to take toast out of the toaster and butter one side, then put both pieces of bread together so that the heat melted the butter on the slices.

"Imagine, getting excited about toast!" she chuckled.

Esther just laughed. "It's all new and exciting," she said. "I've never had to work a day in my life."

The owner's eyebrows arched.

Esther flushed. "I lost my mother . . . recently," she said gently, not going into details. "She took care of me. Now I'm learning to take care of myself."

"And doing nicely," the older woman said, smiling kindly. "The standing will get easier. But you need tennis shoes to work in, honey, not hard-soled ones," she added gently, indicating the high heels Esther was wearing with her slacks. "Standing is hard enough in comfortable shoes."

"I'll get Butch to take me back to Walmart after work and I'll buy a pair," Esther assured her. "Thanks for the advice, too."

"So few people ever take any. You're a breath of spring," came the reply. "Okay, ready to move on to taking orders?"

"I wish my memory was better." Esther groaned.

"That's why we have pads and pencils." The other woman chuckled. "You can practice on me before the lunch rush. Ready . . . ?"

By the end of the first month, Esther was dashing back and forth between the tables and the kitchen with a light step in her new tennis shoes and making a small fortune in tips. She put her long hair in a ponytail at work. Her waitress uniform fit in all the right places, which was causing her some problems. She was pretty, and men noticed.

She'd never had to work at discouraging men, because her mother had been around to absorb any interest she was likely to get. But one of the deputy sheriffs, and a couple of cowboys, were growing more insistent about wanting to take her out, either to dinner or a movie. And Esther didn't want to go. She had more reason than many women to distrust men, especially after Darrin. Besides, she wasn't interested in other men. Just in Butch, who became more important to her by the day. She was careful to remind other men that she was engaged. She only wished she had a ring, to prove it. Butch hadn't mentioned the ring at all.

* * *

She dumped her tips out on the kitchen table before they started supper. They shared cooking, which Butch was teaching her. She'd already produced several very edible meals under his tutelage. She and Butch sat down to roll her loose change into coin envelopes. This was one of their nightly rituals. It was something they could do together, and Esther loved the companionship. They had their respective jobs, and Butch was out of the house a lot. Sometimes, he had to go out of town overnight, but he left her with Two-Toes and she felt safe. Besides, there was that 28-gauge shotgun he'd loaded for her. It was locked in the gun safe, but she knew where the key was. If she could bring herself to shoot somebody. Hopefully, Two-Toes would be a deterrent if she was ever really threatened.

There had been no news of Darrin, although Esther had secretly looked online, on Butch's laptop, and found an account of her mother's death. It was brief, just mentioning that it was an accident, citing her monied background, and mentioning that there had been only a memorial service. Nothing about homicide. So Darrin was still out, obviously, and probably looking for Esther. It made her nervous, but she was careful to conceal her worries from Butch.

"Quite a haul," he teased as they separated the various denominations of coins.

She laughed. "Yes, it is. We should buy you a new coat."

His high cheekbones flushed. "You need a raincoat," he protested. "I can't wear nice coats doing the work I do. It gets messy when you work with animals."

She smiled at him, liking the way his eyes crinkled at

the corners when he smiled back. "I have a raincoat," she protested.

"One you bought at that thrift shop," he muttered.

"Hey, don't knock thrift shops," she returned. "Most of the stuff they have is barely worn at all. It's got a hood and it's warm." She searched his dark eyes. "Butch, I don't need fancy things anymore. I like it here, just being a normal woman."

"Truly?" he asked. "I haven't said much about it, but that fur jacket you wear is real, and the clothes you were wearing that first night didn't come off a rack." He didn't add that he'd been suspicious of her. She could have been a thief, for all he knew. In fact, that was still a possibility. She didn't act like a rich woman might. And, too, there was that gaudy fake diamond ring she wore. Maybe she thought it would give her the appearance of wealth, even more than her clothes.

"No, they didn't," she confessed. She thought about what she wanted to tell him. He wasn't wealthy. She didn't want him to be intimidated by the life she'd left. "I had a small savings account that my father left me," she prevaricated. "It was my birthday, so I splurged."

"Your mother had money, though." He was probing. Curious.

She sighed. "Well, not really," she lied. "She had a nice little nest egg that my father left, some stocks and bonds and certificates of deposit. Too, there was the house in Aspen." She didn't mention the others her mother owned. "It was free and clear. Plus she owned a good amount of land that she inherited. But it was all tied up, you know, and it wasn't easy to get to any of it. Darrin wanted it all. He'd have sold it to buy drugs. I'm sure he still does want it, but I have her will. He can't get to it unless he finds me." She shivered delicately. "I'd honestly rather be locked up than have to face him." Her eyes were troubled. "He's very dangerous. In fact, he served time for assault. But Mama didn't find that out until it was too late to do her any good."

"We should get a daily paper, one from Aspen, just to see if there's any news about her death," he added.

She almost panicked. She didn't want him to know how wealthy her mother had been, what her estate was worth. It would change things, between her and Butch. He was a proud man. He wouldn't even let her buy him a cup of coffee. It would be a disaster if he learned anything about her real background.

She'd tell him someday, she thought, but not right away. She was having fun, learning about him, being with him, having a real relationship with another human being. Her mother had been distant, barely affectionate. There hadn't been anyone else in her young life who was affectionate, except her father, and Agnes, who had truly been a surrogate mother. But that was long ago. She'd become standoffish like her mother, she'd become used to never touching or being touched. Well, except for unwanted touches from various men her mother brought home.

"I'm sorry," he said after a minute. "I know you're missing your mother."

"It's okay," she said. "It's getting easier, as time goes by. But I don't know what I'd have done if you hadn't taken me in, Butch," she added with a warm, affectionate smile.

He shrugged. "I didn't mind. It gets lonely here. Not so much, now," he added, and he returned the smile. "I have somebody to share the chores," he teased.

She laughed. "True."

"You weren't really looking for a cousin, were you, that night?" he asked abruptly.

She shook her head. "I was afraid to go into town. I looked on a map. Benton is really small. I didn't want to just show up there, a stranger that people might ask questions about. I was traumatized to boot." She sighed. "I saw the cabin from the road and it looked, well, welcoming. I guess that sounds odd. But I knew it would be safe here." She met his dark eyes, curious about the look in them. "I don't know how."

"I'm just glad you showed up," he said quietly. "I don't mix well with people, and I had a rough experience with my ex-fiancée. I guess I'd turned into a hermit."

"A very nice hermit," she said softly. "You're easy to get along with."

"So are you, honey," he replied. "You make a house a home, however trite that sounds."

She smiled from ear to ear. "What a nice thing to say!"

He drew in a long breath, watching her pretty hands working on the coins. He picked up some and started separating them. "They have a machine that does this. I need to get you one."

"It wouldn't be nearly as much fun," she replied. "This is something we do together." She flushed. "I mean . . ."

His big, lean hand slid over hers. "I like doing this with you, too. There's no need to feel embarrassed."

She laughed self-consciously. "Thanks. I don't think I've learned discretion yet. I just blurt things out."

"That's not bad at all. I speak my mind, too."

"I guess people at least know where they stand with us, don't they?"

"What did you do, when you lived at home?" he asked.

She hesitated while she tried to think up something.

"Well, not much, really. Mama didn't want me to get a job, and I'd already gone away to school for several years."

"A boarding school?" he asked, thinking of someplace with uniforms and firm rules. "I'll bet you were picked on a lot."

"Yes, I was," she exclaimed. "How did you know?"

"Because you're beautiful and shy, a combination that provokes people who aren't," he said. His face hardened. "Hell would freeze over before I'd send a child of mine away to any sort of boarding school."

"That's how I feel," she replied. "It was miserable. Mama sent me presents for Christmas and my birthday, but she never came to see me." Her voice was bitter. "It was worse when I came back home, at eighteen." Her face tautened. "It was a constant parade of men, and sometimes she didn't bother to close the bedroom door . . ." Her face flamed and her expression was horrified as she met his eyes.

"You can tell me anything," he said in a gentle tone. "I don't gossip, and you won't shock me. Okay?"

She bit her lip and went on sorting change. "I've never, well, done stuff like that. She screamed a lot . . ."

"Women do, when they're enjoying a man," he said very softly. "It's natural. It doesn't mean they're being hurt."

"Oh." She took a deep breath. "I tried to ask her, but she changed the subject. I never had any close friends. I was too ashamed of my home life to take anybody home with me. Mama would walk around in see-through negligees when she had men living with us."

He was getting a sad, painful look at her life. No wonder she was so naïve. He liked it. He had little experience with innocent women. She was a new experience.

He smiled.

She looked at him, her blue eyes wide and curious.

"I like it, that you don't know much about men," he explained. He grimaced. "I guess that sounds Neanderthal."

"Oh, no," she said at once, and her cheeks flushed. "It sounds, well, protective."

He cocked his head. "That's how I feel when I'm with you. Protective." He scowled. "You need some assertiveness training. I'll teach you."

"You will?" She smiled at him. "What's assertiveness training?"

"Telling people to go to hell when they start annoying you," he replied tongue in cheek. "I was a natural, but you'll need some educating."

She burst out laughing. "I do like you," she said huskily. "You're so much fun."

Something no other woman had ever said about him. He felt ten feet tall. When he was with her, he forgot about his injuries and limitations. She made him . . . whole.

"So you never had a job?" he persisted.

"Not really. Mostly I stayed in my room and listened to music. Or I painted." She sighed. "I had a sketch pad and canvases and acrylic paint. I really loved doing still life portraits of flowers." She frowned. "I suppose Darrin trashed them all."

"You never know." He was smiling. There was an art supply store in town. He'd have to take her over there one day and get her some paints. She had spare time when she wasn't working. It would give her something to do when he was out of the house.

"Cook taught me how to make that chocolate pie you like so much!" she said abruptly. "If we can afford the ingredients, I'll make one for the weekend!"

He laughed. "She did, huh? I think we can afford to

splurge a little on food." He searched her eyes. "You are one of a kind," he said softly.

"So are you, Butch," she replied, flushing a little.

He just looked at her, aware of feelings that were slowly getting the better of him. He would have liked nothing better than to take her to the nearest minister and marry her out of hand. But it was early days yet. He had to take his time. And meanwhile, the man who'd killed her mother needed to be found out and brought to justice. He was working on that, without telling Esther.

He felt it was necessary, but he wasn't comfortable with the idea. Once she was over her grief and out of danger, she'd probably go back to Aspen, where she'd inherit the house her mother owned and those stocks and bonds. Once she had her life back, this time with him might be just a forgotten episode in it. He'd be relegated to a memory that she might take out from time to time. She liked him, but it was unrealistic to think that a woman so pretty and sophisticated would want to settle down in the wilds of Colorado with a crippled man who had nothing except his paycheck to offer.

"Goodness, you look morose!" she exclaimed, studying him. "Was it something I said?"

"Not at all," he said smoothly. "I've got a visiting dignitary to take around tomorrow. I was thinking about where to take him." It was the truth, but he stretched it a little.

She hesitated. "You're sure you don't mind letting me stay here with you? I mean, I could probably afford an apartment . . ."

"Do you want to go?" he asked abruptly.

"No!" She took a deep breath, oblivious to the joy that washed over his features before he contained it. "I mean, it's nice here, with you and Two-Toes. But I'm a strain on your budget."

"Some strain," he muttered. "You keep the house as neat as a pin, you do half the cooking, you cheer me up when life sits on me too hard. I'd . . . miss you, if you left."

She brightened. "Okay, then."

He felt his own heart lift.

"Something I've been meaning to ask," she began slowly. She flushed. "Maybe I shouldn't, though."

"Spill it, chicken."

"Well, are we really engaged?" she asked without lifting her eyes.

His eyebrows arched. "Why the question?"

She shifted restlessly. "There are these guys who eat at the restaurant every day," she said worriedly. "They're nice, I mean. But they keep asking me to go places with them and I don't want to. It's, well, it's bothering me."

"Why don't you want to go out with them?" he wondered aloud.

She drew in a breath. "I just don't. I'm nervous around most men. It's hard to trust when you've been through what I have, with Mama's lovers."

His heart jumped. "You're not nervous with me."

"No, I'm not." She smiled at him warmly. "I love being with you."

The flush on his cheekbones grew more ruddy.

"Gosh, I'm sorry," she bit off, wincing. "I just open my mouth and words fall out. I shouldn't have said . . ."

"I love being with you, too," he said curtly.

Her expression lightened. "Really?" she asked.

He laughed. "Really."

She sighed. "Okay, then."

"So you don't like being bothered by other men. I could offer a suggestion."

"A suit of armor?" she asked.

He pursed his chiseled lips. "An engagement ring?"

Her lips fell apart. "A ring! You mean it? Honest?"

It wasn't the reception he'd expected. She was excited. Happy. Enthusiastic. He felt warm all over. "Honest."

She grinned. "That would be lovely." She hesitated, and her happy expression turned morose. "Oh. You mean, like a prop, so they'd leave me alone?"

He smoothed his big hand over her small one. "I mean, like a real engagement ring that would lead to a real marriage. Well, someday," he amended, so she wouldn't feel threatened or obliged to him. It would certainly keep gossip down. He didn't want her reputation to suffer, here in this conservative small community.

She stared at him, her eyes bright with feeling. "Wow."

He chuckled.

She grinned. "But you don't know me very well," she began.

"Same here. We could get to know each other. For a few weeks, I mean." He grimaced. "I'm not putting it well."

She sighed. "I would love to be engaged to you, Butch."

"You . . . you would?" he stammered.

"Oh, yes. You've been kinder to me than anybody in my whole life, except my dad and Agnes. I could . . . take care of you, you know? I mean if you got sick or hurt, I'd be there."

A confusion of emotions turned him inside out. She wanted to take care of him. Damn! He'd never had anybody of his own. Not really. And this beautiful little blonde looked at him and didn't see a haunted man with a missing arm. She saw someone she cared for.

"I'd do the same for you," he replied.

"You already have," she teased. "You rescued me from freezing to death in the snow."

"I'd forgotten."

"I didn't. I never will."

He drew in a long breath. "What happens when you end up with your mother's house and those stocks? You've still got the will, and her lover won't be able to get away with it forever. What then? When you have your old life back?"

"I don't want my old life back," she said simply.

He was still hesitant. His eyebrows drew together. "Esther, how old are you?"

"Twenty-three."

His face hardened. He averted his eyes.

"What's wrong?" she wanted to know.

"Honey, I'm thirty-six . . ."

"Oh, yes, you're definitely over the hill, I can tell."

His eyes widened as he looked at her. She was grinning. He burst out laughing.

"Thirteen years isn't so much," she said gently. "I think you're gorgeous."

He cleared his throat, embarrassed. "Well!"

"So, are you going to buy me a ring?" she asked. "Something inexpensive." Her eyes twinkled. "I like turquoise."

"It should be a diamond."

"I don't like diamonds," she returned, and didn't mention that she was wearing a real seven-carat one on her hand, and that she had a safety deposit box back in LA full of expensive jewelry. "I'd rather have something elemental, something natural. Something down-to-earth."

"Okay, then. Suppose we go into town tomorrow while you're on your lunch break and look in the jewelry store?"

She smiled from ear to ear. "That would be great!"

And it was. They avoided the diamond counter because she insisted, and they went to the gemstone section. But she fell in love with a blue topaz ring instead of the turquoise she'd originally wanted.

"Oh, that one," she said, indicating it. "It's Caribbean blue. I love it!"

"Could we see that one?" Butch asked Mr. Granger, who'd owned the jewelry store for thirty years.

The older man chuckled. "Yes, you may. Is it for a birthday?"

"No," Esther said softly. "It's going to be an engagement ring. I don't really like diamonds," she added.

Mr. Granger glanced at the huge seven-carat diamond on her right hand and saw at once that it was a real stone, with a clarity and brilliance that he'd rarely ever seen. But he didn't remark on it. He pulled out the tray of rings and let Esther try on the blue topaz one.

"It fits!" she exclaimed, her eyes on Butch's amused face.

"It looks good on that pretty little hand," he replied with a warm smile.

She laughed. "I love it. Can I have it?" she asked, looking up at him with soft, shimmering blue eyes.

She could have had the store if she'd asked for it when she looked at him like that. He'd rob a bank, he thought amusedly. "Sure you can," he said.

He gave Mr. Granger his credit card and waited while the owner ran it. He signed the ticket, they thanked the older man and walked out of the store.

"We are now officially engaged," Butch told her.

"Not yet," she said. She pulled off the ring, there on the sidewalk, and handed it to him.

"We're not engaged?" he asked, and felt his heart sink.

"We're not, until you put it on for me," she said softly, searching his eyes. "Then it's official." She held up her left hand.

Heart hammering at his ribs, he slid the ring onto her finger. It was poignant, he thought. A moment that would live in his heart forever, no matter how old he got, no matter what happened down the road.

"Thanks," she said in a soft whisper.

His fingers brushed her flushed cheek. He didn't smile. The dark eyes piercing hers were full of some deep emotion.

She reached up and touched her fingers to his chin. "I'll try not to embarrass you," she said quietly. "I'll never do anything to make you ashamed, and I'll take care of you if you need me to."

His lips compressed hard. He averted his eyes, because the emotions she was kindling in him were new and vaguely frightening.

Now she was embarrassed. She'd said too much. "Oh, look, isn't that Parker?" she asked abruptly, indicating a truck that stopped just a few parking spots down from theirs.

He got himself together, with an effort. He felt ashamed of himself for the way he'd reacted, but it was getting harder and harder not to reach for her and kiss her half to death. He had to fight his impulses in a way he'd never had to before. She was very young, and very green, and he didn't want to scare her off. If he made a dead set at her, he might ruin everything. Time enough to lead up to that. He had to go slow. Slow! The engagement, he reminded himself, was just the first step. It would take time.

"Yes," he said after a minute, following her gaze. "I think it is."

"Oh, gosh, I've got to get back to work," she exclaimed,

looking at the cheap watch she'd bought along with her new clothes. "I'll see you about six, yes?"

He nodded. "I'll pick you up at the restaurant. Have a good day."

"You, too." She forced a smile that she didn't feel and went across the street and back to work. She couldn't understand why Butch had suddenly become so distant. Was he regretting the engagement? Had she pushed him into something he really didn't want? Tonight, she told herself, they'd sit down and she'd find out. She was so fond of him. He'd been kind to her. She didn't want to make him unhappy.

CHAPTER FOUR

Esther was doing well at her job. She enjoyed the local patrons, whom she was getting to know, and the infrequent out-of-town people who showed up at the restaurant. There were occasionally people from New York who came to Benton to see Mrs. Denton about the television show she wrote for. In fact, she learned that Cassie Denton had worked as a waitress at the Gray Dove before she married J. L.

Not that Esther asked the New York people questions, but she listened raptly when they talked about changes that would show up in the series later on.

"It's so exciting!" she told Butch that night. "They say the bad guy is going to turn over a new leaf!"

He knew who the bad guy was. He had a wide-screen television, and he and Esther and Two-Toes never missed an episode of *Warriors and Warlocks*. "I like him, even if he is the bad guy," he confessed while they were sipping second cups of coffee in the living room after a nice supper.

"So do I. It's a great series. Well, it would be, if I could stop blushing," she added, because there was bad language and nudity, a lot of nudity, in it.

"Think of it as free sex education," he teased.

She averted her eyes. "It's not, really, you know. Most of the women get used. The ones who don't aren't interested in having a home and a family, they just sort of sleep around." Her blue eyes met his. "Is that really what it's like, in modern society? I never mixed in it. I had a girlfriend once, my last year in boarding school. She'd slept with a lot of men and had an abortion. She thought having children was stupid. It would get in the way of her happiness." She sighed wistfully. "I love children. I could never think of them as a liability. And if I got pregnant, I just couldn't . . ." She stopped, shocked at what she was saying to him.

He just smiled. "I told you. I'm unshockable."

"Oh." She smiled shyly. "Okay."

"All too often, an accident causes real issues between a man and a woman, especially if he wants a child and she doesn't. It would be hard to shame a woman into giving up eighteen years of her life to raise a child she didn't even want," he added, but his eyes were suddenly sad.

She just looked at him. She knew there was something he wasn't telling her. She could feel it.

He glanced at her and sighed. "My ex-fiancée and I had a few spontaneous episodes," he said delicately. "She got pregnant."

"She didn't want it?" she asked delicately.

"No. She went to a clinic the minute she knew and told me afterwards." His face was harder than stone.

She got up out of her chair and crawled into his lap, laying her blond head on his chest with one soft arm wrapped around him.

He was stiff at first, it was so unexpected. Then he realized that she was comforting him. It shocked him, how much he liked it. His good arm curled around her shoulders, lightly, so that he didn't make her uncomfortable.

"I'm so sorry," she said. She knew that he was a man who'd love a child.

His chest rose and fell against her. His heartbeat was oddly fast and strong. "I couldn't have forced her to have it," he said. "And under the circumstances, I suppose it was the right thing to do." He idly smoothed her long blond hair in its ponytail. "I didn't even know I wanted a child until she told me that. I grieved for it. She said it wasn't the first time she had it done, and it was like having an abscessed tooth pulled."

She made a gruff sound in her throat.

He didn't have to be told that she'd never have made that choice if it had been his child in her body. She'd have fought to keep it, even fought him to keep it. He was surprised at how well he knew her already. It had only been a few weeks since she'd shown up at his door, and it felt as if he'd known her forever.

They were both so lost in thought that they didn't hear the truck drive up. They didn't hear the perfunctory knock at the door, which suddenly opened to admit Parker. He stood in the doorway, grinning at the picture they made— the delicate little blond, still in her waitress's uniform, and the taciturn wildlife officer, curled up together in a big easy chair.

"Oh!" Esther exclaimed, embarrassed, and started to get up.

"Stay put," Butch told her, his arm tightening as he chuckled. "Parker's family. And we're engaged," he reminded her.

She was still. She smiled shyly at Parker. "So we are," she said, and tried to sound sophisticated. Which she wasn't, despite her wealthy upbringing.

"What's up?" Butch asked the other man.

"Are you guys doing anything special on Sunday?" Parker asked.

Butch and Esther looked at each other. "Nothing much," Butch said.

"I don't work Sundays," Esther added.

"Why?" Butch wanted to know.

"Teddie wants to go ice skating. There's a rink nearby and it's open all year. You guys want to come along?"

Butch made a face. "Not sure I can get on skates." He looked at Esther, who grimaced.

"I never learned how," she confessed. "I'd fall and break something and what would my boss say?" she asked plaintively.

Parker just chuckled. "Okay. When we find something a little less reckless, we'll invite you again. Rodeo maybe, later in the year."

"I love rodeo!" Esther exclaimed.

"Me, too," Butch seconded.

They were both beaming.

Parker just shook his head. "Hey, there, Two-Toes," he said, greeting the wolf, who'd been out in the kitchen drinking water. He knelt down and ruffled the animal's fur affectionately.

"He's so sweet," Esther remarked.

"He took to her right off," Butch added with a warm smile at the pretty woman in his lap. "I always knew he was a great judge of character," he added with a chuckle.

"I'll say. He loves my girls, too," Parker said, referring

to his wife and stepdaughter. He stood up. "Well, I'll be off."

"Thanks for the invitation," Esther said. "I'm sorry I'm such a stick-in-the-mud."

"Not at all." Parker returned at once. "Variety really is the spice of life. How boring if we all liked the same things all the time!"

"True," Butch said. "See you."

"Night, Sarge. Esther." He went out, closing the door behind him.

Butch gave Esther a long, penetrating stare. "You lied."

She went red as a beet. "You don't know," she retorted.

He laughed and hugged her close. "Yes, I do. You can skate like a fairy, can't you? I'll bet you float on the ice."

"I took lessons from the time I was three," she confessed. "Mama wanted me to be a contender, but I wasn't crazy about being on the ice all the time. I quit when I was in my mid-teens. I don't think she ever forgave me." She pulled back. "See, that was what she wanted to be, a star on the ice in women's single competition. She didn't have the gift, but I did, and she pushed and kept pushing. Dad didn't like the way she nagged me, but he died and I was left with her." She sighed. "It was the only time she really cared about me, I think, when she was trying to use me to fulfill her own dreams."

He smoothed over her back. "My dad was the same," he confessed. "He wanted me to be a pro football player." He made a face. "I hated football. I was a soccer freak. I still am. I never miss a game."

"I like soccer, too," she said.

"Who's your team?" he asked.

She grinned. "Real Madrid."

His eyebrows arched. "Not the US team?"

She flushed. "Well, I used to know a guy who played for Madrid. He was a friend of my dad's."

His eyebrows arched.

"He was much older than me," she said. "I liked him because Dad did. He was married and had two kids, anyway," she added with a pert smile.

He laughed. "I guess you don't like older men." He sighed.

"I like you," she replied. "But you're only older in your mind," she said solemnly. "You don't look as old as you feel. I'm muddling that . . ."

He drew in a breath and coaxed her back down against his chest. "War makes men old," he said. "I'm still older than you, though, by a good bit."

She smiled against his shirt. He smelled of soap and cologne, good smells. "Why do you think that matters?"

He stiffened for a minute. "Well . . . people talk, you know."

"Butch," she murmured, "like you care what people say."

"I don't. But it might get back to you."

"Oh, I don't care what people say, either. Friends won't mind, and nobody else matters."

He chuckled. "You're a breath of spring."

"Awww. You're just saying that because I finally can make a biscuit that wouldn't kill a man if it fell on him."

He grinned. "You're a natural born cook. I'm amazed that you don't strike envy in the heart of the cook at the Gray Dove."

"She likes me."

"Everybody likes you," he replied. "So do I. A lot."

She sighed. "I like you, too."

They sat like that for several minutes, during which Butch became a little uncomfortable. It had been a few years since his erstwhile fiancée had thrown him over, and Esther was beautiful. He didn't want to make her feel unwelcome, but he did want to get up before she noticed anything she shouldn't about the way his body was reacting to her.

"Men's room," he murmured. "Sorry."

She laughed and got up. "No problem. We all function, at some time or the other," she said with a pert glance.

He just stared at her and sighed and shook his head. "You gorgeous blonde. You'd shame a flower," he mused prosaically.

Both eyebrows went up. "What have you been drinking?" she asked sharply.

He threw up his hands and turned toward the bathroom. "That's what you get for trying to share poetic thoughts with peasants," he called over his shoulder.

"I am not a peasant, and just for that, I'll burn the coffee!"

He laughed as he closed the door behind him.

Esther had worried that Darrin might have tracked her to Benton. But as the days passed without any contact, she began to relax. Well, she began to relax a little. The memory of her mother's death still haunted her. It wasn't right, to let Darrin get away with it, but she'd burned her bridges. She hadn't said anything about the murder. Wouldn't that make her an accessory after the fact? Because she had knowledge of a crime after it was committed, and she didn't report it to the authorities?

It was one more thing to worry her. She'd have talked about it to Butch, but she was still hiding her real background from him. He thought she came from just well-to-do parents; but her mother had been a multimillionaire, and all that wealth would one day come to Esther, whether she wanted it to or not. She couldn't hide for the rest of her life.

She supposed that she needed to get a good attorney and start trying to make up for having been so cowardly. She'd run away, but in all honesty, it hadn't been much of a choice. If she'd stayed, Darrin might have killed her as well, to get rid of the only eyewitness to his crime.

Butch had a computer, and she'd asked to use it to check her email. Instead, she'd pulled up a search engine and looked for any further indication of her mother's death. There had been a big updated notice about it in the Aspen paper, only a fraction of which was available online without paying a fee to subscribe to the newspaper. It said that a well-known socialite had been found dead in her home by her boyfriend. It was thought that her daughter, now missing, might have pushed her to her death. There had been a violent argument, Darrin had told authorities, so the police were asking for anybody with information of the whereabouts of Esther Marist to come forward.

Esther's hands had jumped off the computer keys as if they'd been burned. Now she didn't dare go back! She had no money and no way to get any, other than her salary and tips at the restaurant. She couldn't even afford an attorney. What if they believed Darrin and she went to prison? It had happened to innocent people before this. Oh, why had she run? she wailed mentally. Why hadn't she gone straight to the police and told them exactly what had happened!

She'd only complicated her life by running away. Now she was as much a fugitive as Darrin would be if she'd told on him. And had he managed to get access to her mother's fortune by now? If he had, he could afford the best attorneys in the world to represent him. And the best private detectives to find Esther.

She worried for days about what she'd read. She hadn't known how to erase her search history on Butch's computer, but she noticed that he almost never used it except to send emails back and forth and log on to the web page he kept to discuss wildlife rehabilitation. Hopefully he wouldn't bother to check what Esther had done. And she had sent an email to an old friend whose email had been changed, so that it would come back as not forwarded. So she wasn't totally lying, anyway.

Two weeks went by, during which Esther went to work, came home, counted her tips, made supper with Butch, and generally worried herself sick.

She had a little money now, so she'd had Butch take her back to the local Walmart to get a few more items of clothing. It wasn't what she'd been used to, but there was great satisfaction in earning her living, paying for her own clothes. No more pampered little rich girl getting anything she asked for. Terry had been generous. Of course, Terry had also substituted money for love and hugs and understanding. It had been the housekeeper, Agnes, who had kissed away the little girl's tears and bandaged the cuts and made Christmas special for her. It had never been Terry, who was constantly on the road with some new boyfriend to exotic and luxurious places.

If she ever had a child, Esther told herself, the baby

would never be left with a housekeeper, not even for a day. Her child would go where she went, and she'd love the little one so much! She thought about children a lot. She and Butch spent time with Parker and his wife, Katy, and Katy's daughter, Teddie. Esther loved Teddie. The little girl was sweet and smart and loved horses. So did Esther. When they'd lived in California, when her father was still alive, her father had owned a ranch and they rode horses together. Her mother had no use for animals of any sort. Sometimes, even through the sadness of loss, Esther thought about her mother's reaction to her daughter living with a wildlife specialist and rehabilitator, who had a wolf in the house. It amused her no end.

"What are you cackling about?" Butch teased, joining her in front of the television with a refilled cup of fresh-brewed coffee. It was well after supper and they were watching an episode of *Warriors and Warlocks*.

"I was thinking about my mother," she said, smiling as he sat down beside her. "She wouldn't let me have pets. She thought all animals were filthy. I was imagining her reaction to us living with a wolf in the house." She chuckled. "It was funny."

He leaned forward, the cup held in his one hand. "It's getting easier for you to talk about her, isn't it?" he asked.

She nodded. "Still stings a little," she confessed, smiling at him. "But I can remember some of the fun times now."

"Was she a good mother?"

She rolled her eyes. "She was in love with love. There was a new boyfriend every other month and she loved to travel. She was mostly gone after Daddy died. I lived with our housekeeper. I never saw much of Mama until I was in my last year of high school. Even then, she made sure I was out of the way when she brought people home." She laughed softly. "It bothered her to have a grown daughter. She didn't want her friends to see me and conjecture about her age."

He sighed. "Pity."

"Yes. You can't change how old you are. You can only disguise it."

"I could always color my hair . . . ?"

She laughed and punched him playfully, almost upending his coffee mug. "Oh, you! Anyway, you're in your prime of life right now. Why would you want to be younger?" She leaned toward him. "I don't like men my own age," she said in a conspiratorial tone. "So if you start looking younger, I'll have to move out!"

He chuckled. "Never. I'd send out search parties and bribe you to come home."

"Bribe me with what?" she asked, and arched her eyebrows several times.

"Chocolate," he said with twinkling dark eyes. "It's your greatest weakness."

She drew in a long breath. "I guess it is. I never met anything chocolate that I didn't like."

He sipped coffee and put the mug down. "We need to talk about what happened to your mother," he said abruptly.

She bit her lower lip. She hadn't told him about Darrin's accusations. She probably should . . .

"There was a investigator in town this morning, at the police department. I'd stopped in to check with them about Darrin."

Her face went white. She wasn't even breathing.

He saw the terror in her eyes. "He was looking for you. Honey, I don't know how to tell you this. They think you pushed your mother down the staircase."

Tears stung her eyes. She had to react as if it were a

surprise; she didn't want Butch to know that she'd read that in the Aspen newspaper. She hadn't even planned to tell him about it, because she didn't want to worry him.

"Oh, don't do that," he said tenderly, and pulled her close. He wrapped her up against him, kissing her soft blond hair. "Don't! I won't let them hurt you!"

She clung to him, shivering a little. "Darrin's good at telling lies, when he's sober," she said. "I thought he'd say it was an accident," she added miserably.

"Apparently, the coroner lodged some doubts about her injuries not aligning exactly with an accidental fall."

"I'll bet that put a stick in Darrin's spokes," she muttered.

"I don't doubt it. But it puts you in a dangerous position," he added. "I know you're not capable of murder, certainly not of killing your own mother. But he could claim to have seen you push her down the stairs."

She nodded. "I worried about that." She closed her eyes. "I can't even afford a lawyer. And if Darrin has access to Mama's bank account, he can afford the best. Even if he can't, he can sell stuff she had, for money to help keep him out of prison. It's not right."

His lean hand smoothed up and down her spine. "We'll come up with something."

"Is the investigator still in town?"

"I don't know."

"I guess Darrin could afford to hire him, too."

"He wasn't hired by your mother's boyfriend. He was an investigator with the district attorney in Aspen."

"Oh, dear," she moaned.

"Honey, you've got your mother's will in your pocketbook," he pointed out. "That being the case, do you think Darrin's anxious to find you?"

She grimaced and drew back. "That would give me a motive for murder."

"Yes, but it would be bad for him, wouldn't it, because it would prove that you inherited your mother's estate. He'd be left with nothing."

"Oh." That hadn't occurred to her. She stared at Butch. "It would put you in danger, if that investigator finds me." She sat up. "I need to find a place to go . . . !"

"No, you don't," he said shortly. "I lived through hell in the Middle East. I'm not afraid of some two-a-penny bad guy who has to get drunk to beat up a woman to make himself feel big!"

Her expression softened as she looked at him. She smiled gently. "Do you know, your ex-fiancée was a total idiot?" she mused.

He chuckled. "What brought that on?"

"You're very protective of people you like," she said simply. "I'm glad I'm one of them."

He smiled at her. "I can't lose you," he said. "I can't make a biscuit," he added, tongue in cheek.

"You beast!" she accused.

He leaned forward and kissed her pert nose. "I thought I might talk to that investigator, if I can find him."

She felt her whole body shake with nerves. "I don't know, Butch."

"You can't live your life in fear," he pointed out. "At some point, you have to stand up to him. I'll be right there with you."

"You could be right there in jail alongside me, too," she said abruptly. "Accessory after the fact? I saw a man commit a murder and I didn't report it."

His chiseled lips fell apart. He hadn't considered that.

"Now do you see why I didn't go after Darrin to begin

with? If I'd had the sense God gave a billy goat, I'd have gone to the police that same night and they'd have protected me. But I was afraid that Darrin had a contact in the Department. Instead I made myself a fugitive, and the only person who's going to benefit by that is Darrin. It was a colossal mistake." She sighed. "I was so scared of him, so traumatized by what I'd seen." Her hands clenched on her jeans. She looked up at Butch. "I don't know what to do. I don't want to go to jail. I don't want you to go to jail, for protecting me."

He caught her hand in his and held it tight. "We're a matched set. I'm not turning my back on you."

"I know," she said, and a glimmer of humor escaped her. "You can't make a biscuit."

"Damned straight," he replied. But his dark eyes were saying a lot more than that. "Now, suppose we watch the series and forget about Darrin and the investigator and the rest of the world for a few minutes?"

She snuggled up closer to him with a contented sound. "Okay."

He slid his arm around her and rested his cheek on her hair as the commercials ended and the program came back on.

Esther went back to work the next morning, still perturbed about the changes in her life. One of her first customers was a casually dressed man in slacks and a sports shirt with a leather jacket over it. He sat down at a table where he could put his back to the wall and started looking around.

She went with her pad and pen, her uniform spotless, and smiled at him as she put down utensils wrapped in a napkin and handed him a menu. "What would you like to drink?" she asked. "And do you need a few minutes to look at the menu before you order?"

"Not really." He had a nice voice, friendly and calm. "Black coffee, scrambled eggs, biscuits and sausage."

She nodded, writing it on the pad. "How would you like your eggs?"

"Over easy."

"Okay. Be right back."

She was aware of his eyes watching her as she went to the counter to give the order to the cook. It wasn't unusual. She drew attention because she was pretty. She didn't think much about it.

He was served and she went to wait on other customers. She noticed that the man had finished his meal and she went back to hand him the check, smiling.

"Esther Marist?" he asked quietly.

The smile faded, to be replaced by a look of sheer horror.

"Don't panic," he said quietly. "And don't run. I know you didn't push your mother down a staircase. Please, sit down for a minute."

She sat, too frightened to think that it might cost her her job to be familiar with a customer.

"I've already spoken to the owner," he said. "She knows why I'm here." He indicated Sadie, another waitress, who was suddenly waiting tables, filling in for Esther.

"I didn't even think about that," Esther said. She met his pale eyes. "I ran. I'm so sorry. I was terrified. He was drunk and making threats . . . !"

"It's all right," he said gently. "I've interviewed a dozen people who know you. Not one considered you a suspect. Neither do I. Darrin, on the other hand, has a rap sheet as long as my arm, and priors for assault. He was arrested on suspicion of murder a few years ago, but the charges couldn't be proven beyond the shadow of a doubt. There's not much guesswork involved in how your mother died."

She let out the breath she'd been holding. "She was so trusting," she said. "I knew what Darrin was, the day I met him."

"Your mother had a history of choosing the wrong sort of partners, I'm afraid," he replied. "This time, it ended badly."

"Darrin was furious because she wouldn't buy him a sports car," Esther said quietly, staring at the table. "She argued, and he just . . . hit her. She staggered and he hit her again, then he picked her up and hurled her down the staircase." Her eyes clouded. "She'd given me her will the night before, shoved it into my purse and told me to hold on to it, in case something bad should happen. I didn't realize why, not until she was gasping for breath. She told me to run. I did. I was so afraid . . . !"

"It's all right," he said gently, calming her. "Nobody will blame you for that. Certainly not the authorities back in Aspen. But you will need to come back and testify."

"Darrin has friends in organized crime. He also has somebody in the police department," she added solemnly.

His eyebrows arched. "He does?"

"Yes. So the minute I go back, I'll have an accident, and Darrin will go free. I'm the only eyewitness. Isn't that how it works? If I don't testify, he can't be convicted."

The man looked thoughtful. "I suppose so."

"Then what can I do?" she asked. She noticed that he was giving her diamond ring a long, careful scrutiny, and that there was the faintest smile on his face.

"Where's the will?" he wanted to know.

She thought it an odd question. She was about to tell

him, however, when the bell on the front door rang and Butch walked in, tall and handsome in jeans and chambray shirt, boots, wide-brimmed Stetson and a shepherd's coat. He looked around, spotted Esther, and made a beeline for her.

"Butch," she exclaimed, with some relief, and smiled at him. "This is Mr. . . ." She paused. "I'm sorry, I don't know your name," she said.

"Cameron," the other man replied, and shook hands with Butch, who pulled up a chair.

"Butch Matthews," came the answering greeting. "You're the investigator."

Cameron nodded. "I've just been going over the case with Miss Marist here."

"I wonder if you could put it off until the morning?" Butch asked with a smile. "I'm sorry, but I've got an emergency and I need her to help me with it. It's Two-Toes," he told Esther.

"Oh, no!" she exclaimed. "What happened?"

"He got out into the road," he said heavily. "A truck hit him . . ."

"He's not dead!" she exclaimed, almost in tears.

"No!" he replied at once. "But he's bruised and I'm pretty sure his hind leg is broken. I need you to help me get him inside." He looked at the investigator and indicated his empty sleeve. "She's handy. I can't manage a lot of things on my own."

"Well . . ." The investigator hesitated. "I could go with you, I guess . . ."

"Two-Toes would eat you. He's a wolf," he added, his dark eyes meeting the other man's. "I'm a wildlife rehabilitator, and he lives with Esther and me. She's the only other person he'll allow to touch him," he informed the other man, with a quick warning glance at Esther, who read it at once and didn't blurt out that Parker was familiar to Two-Toes and would certainly help if asked.

"I'll come with you right now." She turned after she got to her feet. "I'll be working in the morning, if you could come back then?" she asked. "If it's not too much trouble?"

"No trouble at all," Cameron said with a forced smile.

"Okay, then. Butch, let's go. I'll stop by and tell them why I'm leaving . . ."

She headed to the counter, with Butch right behind her.

CHAPTER FIVE

"Okay, what's going on?" Esther asked Butch when they were in the truck and headed home. "Parker would have been glad to help you get Two-Toes inside."

"Sure he would, if I needed help. Two-Toes is watching television. Sorry I had to scare you, but I had to get you away from Cameron in a hurry and that was the best way. You looked upset when I walked in. Why?"

"He asked me where the will was. Mama's will." She frowned. "Isn't that an odd question for an investigator to ask?"

"It would be, if he was one," Butch said curtly. "One of the sheriff's deputies called Aspen to ask if an investigator had been sent out here. They said no."

Her lips parted on a breath. "Oh, my gosh, Darrin's found me, hasn't he? You're in danger!" she exclaimed, looking at Butch with sheer horror in her eyes.

His heart jumped. Her life was in danger and she was worried about his safety. It was enlightening. Flattering. He felt like dancing. Except that the situation was dire and getting more dire by the minute.

"Yes, I'm afraid the man knows your mother's boyfriend.

Aspen authorities told the deputy that the coroner actually did find your mother's death suspicious, but they aren't looking at you. They're looking at Darrin. The way she was tossed down the staircase isn't something a woman your size would be capable of. They're fairly certain they can prove Darrin did it, so he's after ready cash for a quick getaway."

"Oh, dear." She wasn't remembering just Cameron's question about the will, she was remembering the way he was studying the diamond ring on her finger. Quick cash. Yes, that ring could be pawned for a small fortune, certainly enough to get Darrin out of Aspen, even out of the country in a hurry, before murder charges could be filed against him.

"Even if he got the will, it would have to go through probate," Butch was saying, although she was only half listening.

"Well, yes, but Mama had things he could pawn," she replied. She didn't mention the ring.

"You don't have any of her stuff with you, except that fox fur," he said. "So you're safe if we can get that will in a secure place."

She hadn't told him about the ring. Why hadn't she taken it off and left it at home? It was going to put a target on her back!

"Esther, did you hear me?" he asked.

She looked up. "Yes. Sorry. I was thinking about Mama." She fought tears. Even though her mother had been a trial to her, she was the last parent Esther had, and now she was alone in the world.

"Don't cry," Butch said gently. "I'll take care of you," he added. "Nobody is going to hurt you here. Benton is a very small town. Everybody knows everybody else's business. If any strangers come looking for you, nobody's going to tell them anything," he told her.

She grimaced. "Butch, somebody told Cameron where I was."

He frowned. "I guess so. He must have been very convincing."

"Darrin knows people everywhere, people who do bad things," she told him. "I was always afraid of him, even from the first. Mama had no judgment about men, ever."

"There are women who look for dangerous men," he said. "I always thought of it as like an addiction. You know, people go nuts over gambling and have to go into rehab? Stuff like that."

She nodded. "That was Mama. She had a different man in tow every few months."

"What a hell of a home life that would have been for you," he said, imagining it. "You're shy and pretty." His lips flattened as he considered that, and added her sad expression to his collection of facts about her past. "How many times did you have to find ways to get out of the house?"

"A lot," she said. "I had places I could go, even schoolmates who would hide me out for a few days. It made Mama furious, but sometimes it was the only way out. Some of her men liked threesomes," she added with evident distaste.

"Good Lord," he said reverently. "You've had some hard times."

"Well, they do say that steel has to be tempered." She smiled at him. "I guess I'm really tempered."

"Tempered," he agreed. His eyes dropped to her soft mouth. "And sweeter than honey," he added in a husky tone.

She sighed and smiled up at him. "We don't know each other very well," she said out of the blue.

"Don't you think we should?" he asked seriously. "After all, we are engaged. We could, you know, get married. If you wanted to, that is."

Her heart flew up over the world. "You want to marry me?" she asked, and the pleasure she felt was as clear as a sunny day.

Butch saw that and it amazed him. "Yes," he replied. He hesitated. "I mean, it wouldn't be a bad idea, since you're living with me." He grimaced. "I'm sort of old-fashioned. My former fiancée was a wild girl and I was younger. But now, I guess I'm getting more conventional. It doesn't look good, you living here without us being married."

She smiled with her whole face. "I love it that you're sort of old-fashioned," she said gently.

He smiled back. He'd done more smiling with her than he had since his fiancée departed. She made him feel strong, courageous, all the things he hoped he really was.

They got out of the truck and walked into the house.

"I'd love to marry you, Butch," she said huskily, as they walked through the door and into the living room

His high cheekbones flushed. "You would?"

She nodded, moving closer. One soft little hand smoothed up the front of his shirt. "You want a real marriage, don't you? I mean, we wouldn't have separate bedrooms and live like friends, or . . . anything like that?" she faltered.

"Yes, we'd sleep together," he said, his body already tautening just at the thought of this beautiful little blonde in his arms all night. But he gritted his teeth. "It won't bother you?" he added roughly. "I mean, I only have one arm . . ."

"That's okay," she said softly, lifting her face. "I have two. I'd give you one of mine, if I could . . . !"

She stopped because his mouth covered hers, fierce and hungry and tender, all at once.

"I think I dreamed you," he said gruffly, and he kissed her again.

She loved being in his arms. She loved the feel of his hard, hungry mouth on her lips. She loved it that he wanted her. She wasn't so naïve that she couldn't feel that. But he might think she was experienced, and she had to tell him.

She pulled back just a little, her mouth swollen, her body singing as she looked up into turbulent dark eyes. "Butch," she began shyly, "you know that I've never . . . I mean, I don't know how . . ." She groaned.

"You've never had sex?" he asked, and despite his earlier suspicions that she was innocent, he was shocked. She was so beautiful!

She shook her head. "Seeing Mama with all those men," she replied. "It soured things for me. I mean, it was like just animals, she went from one man to the next, constantly. Some of them wanted me." She shook her head. "I was afraid of most of them, especially Darrin." She looked up. "But I'm not at all afraid of you," she confessed, studying his hard face. "I love being with you, talking to you, going places with you. I love kissing you . . ."

She stopped as he bent and kissed her again, but this time with exquisite tenderness, holding her against him from head to toe, letting her feel his own hunger.

She started to jerk away, but he held her, without pressure, and smiled down at her. "This is something you'll have to get used to," he explained gently. "Men get aroused when they kiss women. Doesn't mean I'm going to jump on you all at once. Okay?"

She laughed away the embarrassment. "Okay."

He drew in a long, slow breath. "Well, our first time is going to be an experience," he commented.

"Because I don't know anything?" she asked.

He shrugged. "Because I haven't been with a woman since I lost my arm. I guess I'll wobble all over the place and make a mess of the whole business."

"No, you won't," she said gently and nuzzled her face into his throat. "We'll manage. People come home from wars in all sorts of conditions," she added quietly. "I don't think most women care what condition that is, when they love their husbands."

His hand smoothed over her soft, fine hair, almost to her waist in back when she let it loose, as she had earlier. "I was so busy thinking about my men that it never occurred to me that I'd end up half dead. If it hadn't been for Parker, I wouldn't be here. He's got several wounds that he sustained because he carried me off the battlefield. He's a hell of a guy. My best friend."

"He likes you, too. It shows."

"Men form bonds in war," he said solemnly, nuzzling the top of her head with his cheek. "You go through so much horror. It makes for lasting friendships, especially when you get out and have to deal with the aftermath. I was in the hospital for a while, and then they started trying to talk me into a prosthesis. I tried one or two, but the things just don't have what they need to have, to replace an arm. I mean, you can't lift with them. You can't feel through them. They're only good to pick up stuff, and I can even do that with my teeth if I have to."

She smiled. "I knew a man in college who had an artificial arm. He was one of the adjunct instructors. He'd been in the Middle East, too. His prosthesis was high-tech. He actually had sensation in it, and it was linked to his muscles and even his brain so that he could control it."

"Must be nice," he sighed. "On my paycheck, I might afford one if I could save up for about thirty years." He laughed. "By then, I'd be so old, I wouldn't care, you know?"

She grinned. But inside she was thinking that she'd have all the wealth she needed to do that for him, when her mother's estate was settled. She didn't dare tell Butch that. He thought she was an ordinary girl with a well-to-do mother, down on her luck. Even with their brief relationship she knew that he wouldn't react well to being married to a millionaire. It would kill his pride, even in the modern world, to have a rich wife who had more money than he'd ever make.

But she pushed that thought to the back of her mind. It was a problem for another day. On this day, Butch had proposed, and something much better than a pretend engagement to save her reputation and keep people from asking too many questions.

She smiled as she drank in the clean, manly scent of him. "I never want to leave here," she murmured absently. "I want to take care of you. I've never really had anybody, not since my father died. Now I'll have you."

His arm tightened. "And I'll have you, honey girl," he whispered. "I'll take care of you all my life."

She snuggled closer. "When?"

"When what?" he murmured.

"When are we getting married?"

He drew in a breath. "Spring weddings are nice . . ."

She lifted her head and looked up at him with something like horror. "You want to wait?"

That blatant disappointment could have made him strut. "No. I don't. But I thought you might . . . you know, so that we could save up for a fancy wedding gown and a reception," he began.

She reached up and kissed him softly. "I don't want a fancy wedding gown and a reception," she said. "I just want you."

"Oh, baby, that's not something you should say to me right now," he ground out.

"Don't you want me, too?"

He was almost shivering with need, and trying to deny it. "We have to drink some coffee," he told her, moving her aside. "Right now. I'll make it."

She sat on the sofa where he'd all but dumped her, staring after him with wide, stunned eyes. It took her a minute to get her breath and realize that he was at it again. Protecting her. From himself. She grinned from ear to ear and walked into the kitchen.

"You're a sweet man," she said gently, and went to get the sugar dish and some cream from the refrigerator.

"Just looking out for my own," he said, and winked at her.

They sat together on the sofa, but a little apart, going over plans for the wedding.

"I just want the two of us and maybe Parker and his wife and stepdaughter," she said. "Unless you have somebody you want to invite, too. Do you?"

"Yes. J. L. Denton and his wife," he replied. "I used to work for J. L. until I lost my arm. He's been good to me over the years."

"I'd love to have them there. And I'd really love to have her there, so I could pump her for information about that bad guy in her TV series and see if he's really going to turn out to be a decent person!"

He just laughed. "She never talks about scripts, so give it up. But she'll be happy to meet you. She doesn't look like a famous person, you know. She's thin and red-headed and shy."

"Really?!" she exclaimed.

"You lived in Aspen, didn't you? Don't all those movie stars come up there, and millionaires and such?" he teased.

She had to fight to control her reaction. "I guess so, but we were mostly on the ski slopes," she improvised. "Mama loved to ski."

"Can you?" he asked.

"Oh, yes. I love it. Mama was dating a ski instructor before Darrin," she said. "We stayed with him until Darrin came along."

She was clouding the explanation. Butch realized it but he didn't understand why. "Your mother had money, didn't she?" he asked.

"Yes, in investments," she returned. "Not much except that, though," she lied with a smile. "You know, you can't just pull money out of an investment brokerage. And Darrin will never get his hands on that, because I'm the beneficiary on all her investments." She gave him a sly glance. "So we'll have stocks and bonds and our kids will end up with them, because they're long-term investments."

He let out a whistle. "Thank God!"

"Excuse me?"

"I really don't want to be Mr. Esther Marist," he said dryly.

She burst out laughing, a little too enthusiastically, because his reply was close to the bone and he didn't even know it. "So we'll have rich kids and they can worry about the stock market. Right?"

"Kids." He was looking at her with an odd expression.

"Kids," she replied, and the look she gave him was both shy and excited. "Do you like kids?"

"I love them," he said huskily.

She recalled that his fiancée had gotten rid of his. She reached over and slid her hand into his big one. "I'm an only child. I'd love to have several children, if we could afford them."

"Nobody can afford children," he teased, "but they have them anyway. So will we." His dark eyes held her blue ones. "Our daughters will be beautiful if they take after you."

She flushed and laughed. "You're very good-looking, too, Butch," she said, sighing. "Our boys will have to look like you."

"We'll put in an order for one, right after we're married," he said with a big grin. "You do know that the stork brings them, right? There's bound to be some sort of store where you can order the kid you truly want."

She grinned. "You nut," she accused, and hit him playfully. "We'll take what we get and be grateful."

"Works for me," he said, and grinned back.

They were married at the local Methodist church on a Sunday after church in the chapel, with most of Benton in the pews. J. L. Denton and his wife, and Parker and his wife, stood up with them as best men and matrons of honor, and Teddie, Parker and Katy's daughter, was the flower girl.

The church was full of roses. They were a present from the Dentons. The smell was awesome. Standing up with Butch in a pretty white dress off the rack at a department store, with a veil that she found at a thrift shop, with Butch in his only good suit, they were married by the church's minister.

When Esther came to the vows, she looked up at Butch and spoke them with her heart in her eyes. She hadn't planned on getting involved with anybody when she ran away, but it seemed as if fate had pushed her into Butch's cabin and given them both a second chance at happiness. Esther had come to adore him in the weeks they'd been together. Butch was happier than he'd ever been. It was a marriage that would succeed. They were both sure of it.

They exchanged the simple yellow gold rings they'd purchased, and when they were pronounced man and wife, Butch lifted her veil and looked at her for a few seconds with an expression she couldn't puzzle out before he bent his head and kissed her with breathless tenderness. Seconds later, before she even had time to enjoy it, they were running down the aisle and out the front of the church.

The girls in the Gray Dove with whom she worked had produced a beautiful wedding cake and they'd organized the reception, which drew most everybody in town.

Esther in her lacy white dress felt like Cinderella, and Butch was definitely her idea of Prince Charming. He'd certainly charmed her. The only shadow on her happiness was the threat of Darrin, somewhere out there, waiting for a chance to pounce. He'd get what money was available, most likely, because Esther couldn't be found. But that investigator, Cameron, had found her and Darrin knew where she was. Cameron had seen the diamond ring on her finger, the one that Butch thought was paste. It sent cold chills down her spine. She was worried for Butch, who had been so kind to her.

"Hey, this is a wedding, not a wake," Butch teased at her ear. "Why so sad? Are you having second thoughts?" he added, and looked suddenly worried.

She bumped her hip against him. "I am not having second thoughts," she murmured. She peered up at him with mischievous eyes. "And you'd better eat lots of cake. You're going to need all the energy you can get, later."

It took him a few seconds to puzzle that out and he actually flushed.

She laughed softly, flushing a little, too, at her own boldness. "Sorry," she said.

"Don't be. I love it." He grinned down at her. "You'd better eat a lot, too, honey girl."

She sighed. Let Darrin do his worst. This was her wedding day, and she was married to a man she could love and respect. In fact, she thought, as she looked up at him while he accepted congratulations from the Dentons, she already loved him. It was like a jolt of lightning. She loved him! And what a time to find it out. He was marrying her to protect her. Maybe he wanted her, too, but men could want without loving, hadn't she learned that from watching her mother flit from man to man?

She wiped the consternation from her face and clung to Butch's hand while she teased Mrs. Denton about the series and the bad guy who might turn out to be a hero.

"Give it up," Cassie Denton told Esther with a sly laugh. "You'll never find out until they actually air the last episode of the season. But," she added, "you're going to love it. Honest."

"Okay!" Esther said, and grinned from ear to ear.

She'd been full of joy and laughter until they got back to the cabin and went inside together. Everything was different, now. She wasn't a house guest, or even a fiancée. She was a wife.

She looked up at Butch with all her worries in her blue eyes.

He smiled. "Nothing's changed except we're married," he said softly. "So suppose you change into some comfortable clothes and we'll go out to eat? Then we can go riding, if you like. J. L. said we could go around the bridle path at his place, and he's got plenty of horses."

"Oh, that's so nice of him! We haven't been riding together," she added. She hesitated, worried again that she'd put her foot in her mouth.

"I can ride, tenderfoot," he teased, reading her expression. "I'm not graceful getting on or off, but I know my way around horses. You sweet little woman. Were you worried?"

She nodded. "I wouldn't do anything to hurt you, even with words."

His chest felt twice its size. He smiled at her. "Lord, Esther, every time I look at you, I feel like I've won the lottery. You're beautiful and sweet and kind." He shook his head. "I don't know what I've done in my life to deserve a wife like you."

"Awww," she said. She went close and hugged him. "I feel like that, too. You're such a sweet man, Butch. I'll be the best wife in the world, honest. I just need to, well, I need . . ." She searched for the words and flushed.

He chuckled, deep in his throat. "You need a dark room."

She let out the breath she'd been holding. "Well, yes," she faltered, and looked up at him. "How did you know?"

He leaned down. "I wasn't always experienced," he told her. "My first time, I got my zipper caught in my underwear and fell over a chair."

She gaped at him. "What did you do?" she exclaimed.

He laughed. "I ran for my life, of course. She told everybody she knew, so it was really bad for a while. I was in the service before I had my first real experience. Fortunately, the zipper didn't get stuck that time."

She was laughing. "I can't believe it."

"She was a very sophisticated girl," he recalled. "The one where I had the zipper issue." He made a face. He studied her. "You'd have laughed, but not at me. You'd have laughed with me, and I wouldn't have been embarrassed."

She smiled. He knew her very well already. Her eyes were bright with joy as they met his. "I'd never laugh at you," she said softly.

He bent and kissed her lightly. "You look very pretty in that dress," he said.

"It's off the rack," she replied, "but I thought it looked bridal."

"It does. Very. Okay, go get changed and let's find something nice to eat on our wedding day."

"We could go to the little Scottish place," she called over her shoulder.

He scowled. "What little Scottish place?"

She poked her head out of her bedroom door. "McDonald's," she teased, and closed the door. She could hear him laughing, even through the wood.

They had hamburger and fries and then drove over to J. L.'s place, where one of the cowboys was waiting to saddle horses for them.

"This one is nice and tame," the cowboy said as he led it out.

Butch's face hardened. Did the man think he needed a rocking horse because he was disabled?

"This horse is for Miss . . . Mrs. Matthews," the cowboy said quickly, wincing at Butch's offended expression. He tipped his hat to her and returned her smile. "I thought you might like an easy horse at first, ma'am."

She laughed. "I would. I haven't been riding for a while. Thank you."

"This one's for you, Mr. Matthews," the cowboy said as he went to retrieve a gelding. "Rudolph. He's not quite as tame as the other," he added dryly.

Butch chuckled. "I can ride anything that has a mane and a tail," he said.

"That's what the boss told me."

"Why Rudolph?" he asked as he sprung into the saddle, unhampered by the lack of his left arm.

"If you aren't careful, he'll toss you into a tree and you'll have a red nose," the cowboy replied, tongue in cheek.

Butch burst out laughing. "Enough said." He looked back at Esther, sitting comfortably in the Western saddle. "Ready?" he asked.

She grinned. "Ready!"

They went off on the bridle path that led around the ranch. And if the cowboy thought it was an odd way to celebrate a wedding, he didn't voice his thoughts.

"It's so peaceful here," Esther said on a sigh as they rode, with only the creak of saddle leather and birdsong around them to break the silence of the woods.

"I like peaceful," he teased.

"Me, too. We had a house in Los Angeles when my dad was alive." They still had it, she just wasn't ready to share that with her new husband. Not yet. "It was noisy and polluted. I hated every minute we spent there, although I loved my dad."

"Did he look like you?" he asked, curious.

She shook her head. "He had dark hair and gray eyes. I look like my mother."

"She must have been beautiful," he remarked, his eyes warm on Esther's face.

She smiled. "She was. But it was all she thought about." She frowned, staring down at the pommel of the saddle. "She was terrified of wrinkles and even one gray hair." She looked up at him. "It's not a bad thing, getting older."

"We, the aged population of Benton, applaud your consideration."

She chuckled. "Stop that. You're not old."

"Older than you, cupcake," he said softly. "Maybe too old."

"You are not, and stop talking like that or I'll get off this sweet rocking horse and throw something at you."

He felt lighter than air. "Okay."

"Age has nothing to do with how people feel about each other," she continued.

"You're very young, even for your age," he mused.

She met his eyes. "I'll grow three gray hairs and soak my face in water so it wrinkles, just for you," she said with a twinkle in her blue eyes.

He made a face. She made one back.

"As long as you're happy, honey girl," he said gently. "That's all that matters."

"I've never been so happy in my life, Butch," she replied, and it was the truth. "I love being with you."

"I love being with you, too."

They came to a crossroads. "Right is back to the ranch, left is off to J. L.'s lake, where he likes to fish," Butch told her.

"I'd love to see the lake," she said.

"Okay, then." He hesitated, frowning. "It's starting to snow."

She knew already how quickly snow could turn to ice. "You want to go back, don't you?"

"I think we'd better," he said reluctantly. "Neither of us needs to take a toss on our wedding day, and it gets icy here when the temperature drops and snow hits the ground."

She smiled. "Okay."

He shook his head as they turned back. "And that's what I like most about you."

"What?"

"You never complain. You never fuss. Life with you is . . . easy," he said after a minute. "But that's not the word I want, either. You make everything seem simple, even when it's not. You're the best companion I've ever had."

She smiled. "I'm glad. Because you're my best friend, Butch."

"Best friend." He said the words as if they bothered him.

She realized belatedly that they did, and why. She reined in her horse gently, and Butch paused beside her.

"I don't mean that the way you're probably thinking," she said, flushing a little. "I mean, you don't get excited just being with a friend, do you?"

His eyebrows arched and his eyes, so sad a moment before, were now twinkling. "You get excited with me?" he asked softly.

She cleared her throat. "We, um, we should move along, don't you think? Snow's coming down faster."

CHAPTER SIX

The snow was deep by the time they got back to Butch's cabin. Esther's ankle-high boots were going to get full of snow on the way to the front door.

Butch solved that problem very easily by hefting her over his broad shoulder, catching her behind the knees with his good arm.

He chuckled at her surprise as he bumped the truck's door shut with his hip. "We learn coping skills when we lose limbs," he teased.

She laughed, too. "Yes, we do. Thanks! My feet would have frozen. The snow's halfway to my knees already."

"We're most likely going to get snowed in for a day or two," he remarked as he put her gently down on the porch. "That being the case, I'd better get out back and make sure my furry house guests have enough to eat and that their water bowls are plugged in so the water doesn't freeze." He sighed. "Then we hope we don't lose power, or I have to go out and water them two or three times a day."

"How do you get water when there's no power?" she asked, and was honestly curious.

"Melt snow, if it's the only way. But we have an emergency generator. I can connect it to the well head if I have to."

"Wow. Science!" she teased.

He grinned. "All the comforts of home, regardless of the weather. And it's the weekend, so I don't have to work— except for feeding our furry guests. I won't be long."

"I'll start supper."

"Damn," he muttered. "I should have stopped some- where and gotten us takeout, so you wouldn't have to be in the kitchen cooking on our wedding day!"

"I love to cook, since you taught me," she protested. "Really. It's not even like work."

"You sure?"

She smiled. "I'm sure."

"Okay, then. I'll go see to the animals."

She went into the kitchen and started looking through the meat in the freezer.

She cooked a beef casserole and made biscuits to go with it. Dessert was vanilla pudding from a mix, with some Cool Whip and peaches mixed in.

Butch just shook his head as he savored the dessert. "Honey, you have a way with food," he said. "You can take the simplest things and make them uptown."

She grinned. "Thanks. It's better if you have yellow cake or shortcake and put peaches and ice cream over it and then add the Cool Whip, but I didn't have ice cream or cake."

"We had cake at the fellowship hall." He groaned. "They told me to bring the rest of the cake home with us. I forgot!"

"They'll save it for us," she said with certainty. "I'll phone the Gray Dove later, to make sure. It's not a problem, you know. We're eating dessert!"

He sighed. "You're the easiest person to live with," he said.

"So are you."

He looked up. "I'm really not," he told her. "I'm impatient, bad-tempered from time to time, unreasonable . . ."

"You're just you," she interrupted. "We all have times when we're irritable. I get that way, too."

"I've never seen you irritable."

"Well, I don't get that way often. Never with you," she added, her eyes soft with affection.

He finished his dessert and sat back to enjoy his second cup of coffee. His eyes slid over her with pure appreciation. She was wearing jeans and a long-sleeved yellow sweater that brought out the highlights in her blond hair.

"Why do you wear your hair up like that?" he asked curiously.

She laughed, touching the high topknot held up with a yellow scrunchy. "It gets in my way when I'm cooking," she explained.

He pursed his lips. "But you're not cooking right now."

She rolled her eyes, but not with irritation. "Men," she laughed. She took the scrunchy out and shook her head, so that her long blond hair settled around her shoulders.

"You take my breath away," he said, and he wasn't smiling.

She met that intent stare and couldn't look away. The tension in the room was suddenly so thick it could be felt. Even old Two-Toes, asleep on his rug in the corner, lifted his blind eyes momentarily before he curled up again and went back to sleep by the fireplace.

"What we need right now," Butch said in a husky tone, "is a nice, warm, dark place."

Her heart raced. "I think I know the very one," she replied breathlessly.

He stood up and curled her fingers into his. "I'll be slow, and careful," he said softly. "I promise, I won't hurt you."

"I know you won't."

She followed him into his bedroom. The light was already off. He closed the door, leaving them in total darkness. Esther could hear her own heart beating. She felt the heat of him as he moved closer, felt his breath on her forehead, her nose, and then on her mouth as he bent and kissed her with exquisite tenderness.

He sighed. It was like drowning in velvet. He murmured that and she smiled under his mouth, because it felt like that to her, too. She slid her arms around his neck and waited for whatever came next.

She was unprepared for the sudden flash of desire that sparked between them when his hand slid under her sweater and up to the catch behind her back. He loosened it, feeling her stiffen, just a little.

"Nothing to be nervous about," he whispered against her lips as his fingers moved around, just under her soft, firm little breast and teased it.

She'd never felt such sensations. She jerked a little, surprised that such a light tracing could produce such an explosion of pleasure.

"Am I going too fast?" he asked at her lips.

"No. Oh, no. It feels . . ." She swallowed. "It's like falling into fire," she choked.

He let out the breath he'd been holding. "It feels just like that," he agreed.

His fingers moved up, up, teasing the nipple into sudden hardness, causing sensations in her untried body that she'd never felt in her life. She moaned softly.

"I can use something," he managed. "If you want me to."

Her arm tightened around his neck. "You said . . . you liked children," she whispered.

"You said you did, too," he ground out.

"Then why are you talking about using things . . . ! Oh, do that again! Please . . . !"

She was arching backwards, moaning even more harshly as he fumbled the sweater up under her chin and put his mouth squarely over her hard nipple. He suckled it, feeling the shudder that went through her, hearing the soft cry of anguished desire.

"Yes," he said, as if she'd spoken.

He propelled her to the bed and eased her down onto the coverlet, his own body shuddering with need. It had been so damned long . . . !

She was a little embarrassed when he coaxed her out of her clothing and stood up to get rid of his own, but she was on fire for him, so that the embarrassment was quickly gone.

When she felt his nude body over her own, she hesitated, uncertain.

"It's part of being together," he whispered, bridling his own desire to kindle hers. "Trust me, honey girl. I'll make it good for you, however long it takes."

That relaxed her. He wasn't in a hurry, and he wasn't

rough. Her fingers slid up and down the muscles of his back as he balanced on what was left of his arm and moved his mouth tenderly all over her body.

She moved involuntarily, so caught up in pleasure that it felt as if her body was on fire. Everything he did was new and exciting and wonderful.

"Still okay?" he whispered.

"Better . . . than . . . okay," she choked, arching and shivering as he touched her in a new place, an embarrassing place, but it felt so good that she didn't even protest. "Oh, my goodness . . . !" she cried out as pleasure shot through her like an arrow.

His mouth pressed down hard on her soft belly. He thought of her having his babies with real hunger. She was writhing under him now, so lost to passion that she wouldn't have protested anything he did.

He took her from one level of pleasure to the next as he slowly eased over her, parting her legs with his own. He moved down into stark intimacy, but she was blind with need, arching up toward him, not protesting as he slowly, surely, invaded her.

"Oh!" she whispered with wonder. "Oh, is that what it feels like? It's . . . !" She lifted off the bed as his hand moved between them, arousing her so that the tiny barrier he could feel now wouldn't interrupt her pleasure. At least, thank God, he knew what he was doing. He wouldn't have hurt her for the world.

He moved down against her, each thrust going deeper, slower, as his mouth finally found hers in the darkness.

She was whimpering. But her body was arching rhythmically, shivering with pleasure, her nails biting into his back. Whatever she was feeling, it was definitely not pain.

He felt a sense of pride he couldn't remember ever experiencing with any other woman, not even the fiancée with whom he'd thought himself in love.

Her long legs wrapped suddenly around his and she pleaded with him. He could taste her tears in his mouth as he gave her what she wanted, driving into her with such passion and strength that he very quickly brought her to ecstasy.

She hung there, in thrall to a pleasure she hadn't known existed, shivering, sobbing. Then she felt him driving for his own satisfaction, felt his muscles coil as he pushed down one last time, with all his strength, and cried out with the force of the pleasure her body gave him.

"It's good, isn't it?" she whimpered at his ear, shivering again and again as he moved helplessly inside her. "It's so good, so good . . . please don't . . . don't stop, please, please . . . !"

Incredibly, those soft pleas hardened his body, an experience that was a first in his life. He groaned as he grew even more potent than he'd been before. He drove into her, hard and fast, as hungry as she was. It took longer, but the culmination, when it came, lifted them both off the bed and they cried out helplessly in unison as the world slowly came back into focus in the heated, dark room.

"You okay?" he asked as they lay damp and shivering in each other's arms.

"Okay is too mild a word," she whispered, and laughed wickedly. "Incredibly satisfied is much better."

"I have to agree," he replied, holding her closer. "I should tell you that most men can't go at it twice in a row without a few minutes in between to recover."

"I always knew you were one of a kind," she teased, sliding her long leg against his hairy one.

"You inspired me to unimaginable skill." He laughed. "God, what an experience!"

She arched with pleasure, sighing. "Oh, yes."

He was chuckling to himself.

She rolled over, close, and snuggled against him. "Why are you laughing?"

"I'm feeling very smug."

"You are?"

"You were a virgin, and I satisfied you the first time."

She smiled against his chest. "Abundantly." She smoothed her hand over his hairy chest. "And your arm didn't cause you to fumble, did it?" she teased.

He sighed. "Apparently not." He laughed.

"I told you. People cope."

"What will you do if I turn on the light?" he asked.

"Not notice," she said. "I think I'm boneless now."

While she was wondering what he meant, the soft light of a lamp spread over the bed. He turned back to her and caught his breath. She was pink and cream. Flawless skin, firm, pretty little breasts with their dusky crowns relaxed in the aftermath. Slim waist, flaring hips, long legs. He whistled, obviously spellbound.

She was more inhibited. She glanced down and then back up and colored.

"You'll get used to me," he said softly. "Men aren't as pretty as women without their clothes."

"It's hard," she managed.

He laughed. "It gets easier." He smoothed back her long blond hair, damp with sweat. "I think I dreamed you," he whispered. "You're the most beautiful woman I've ever seen."

She smiled. It wasn't possible to be embarrassed when he was looking at her as if she was the very mystery of life. She stretched, watching his eyes follow the movement up and down her body.

"I thought it would hurt," she said.

He grinned. "I knew a couple of ways around that," he replied, and tried not to look as smug as he felt.

She nuzzled her face against his chest. "And now I'm sleepy," she said, apologetic.

"Me, too."

He reached up and turned out the light. "It's been a long day, Mrs. Matthews."

The sound of her married name made her feel warm all over. "Yes, it has, Mr. Matthews."

"No regrets?"

"Oh, no. Not even one," she replied.

He kissed her forehead and then pulled the sheet over them.

"I need my gown," she began.

"No, you don't," he said easily. "If we have to run out of the house, I'll wrap you up in the sheet first. Okay?"

She just laughed. "Okay."

She didn't mean to go to sleep, but she did.

The light coming in the window woke her. She opened her eyes and her new husband was sitting on the side of the bed, dressed in jeans and boots and a blue flannel shirt, a coffee cup in his hand, just looking at her with pure male appreciation.

She felt the faint chill and realized before she looked that he'd tugged the sheet away.

"Couldn't help myself," he murmured with a smile. "It's like having my own private art gallery. Beautiful."

The soft words eased away any embarrassment or indignation she might have felt. She just smiled. She was getting used to those dark eyes caressing her. And she didn't really mind. It was new, to love, to be intimate, to be married. All those things. With any luck at all, one day his affection for her might suddenly turn to love, just as hers had, for him.

"I'll get older and gain weight and have wrinkles eventually," she said with a teasing expression.

"I won't mind at all. I won't even mind if you get as big around as a pumpkin. I thought about it, somewhere in the middle of our first time."

Her heart jumped. "Did you?" she asked, breathless. "So did I."

He put down the coffee cup and his big hand smoothed over her creamy, flat stomach. "You're still very young," he murmured, and the smile faded.

She put her hand over his. "My mother was eighteen when she had me," she pointed out, smiling.

He drew in a long breath and laughed. "You have a way of chasing my concerns right out the window."

"This one isn't even a concern. I'd love a baby. We could share him."

His heart jumped up into his throat. A little boy who'd follow him around the forest. A little girl who'd look like her beautiful mother. "Wow." The way he said the word made her toes curl.

She smiled up at him. He smiled back.

* * *

They went to the feed store to get grain for the wild animals that couldn't forage in several feet of snow. While they were there, they stocked up on dog food.

"Do you feed it to all the creatures in the outbuilding?" she asked, noting the cases of dog food.

"I do," he replied. He grinned. "It beats sitting out in the woods with a hunting rifle trying to get fresh game for them every day."

She laughed. "I guess it does." She didn't add that she wasn't sure he could manage a rifle anymore. It would have dented his pride, and she couldn't have that. She was so much in love that she felt as if she glowed, just walking beside him around the feed store.

She drew attention. She was pretty, and even wrapped up in the inexpensive shepherd's coat he'd bought her, men looked.

Butch was annoyed a little, but he was proud that she belonged to him. His hand slid into hers as they waited at the counter for the bill to be tallied.

"Here you go, Butch," the clerk said with a grin. "How many critters you got right now?"

"Several," Butch chuckled. "They come and go."

"You got that poor wolf those kids dragged behind a truck?" he asked, and his face went hard. "Hell of a thing to do to even a wild animal."

"They're facing charges for it," Butch assured him. "And the wolf is mending. It never ceases to amaze me how resilient wild things are."

"Truly. I forgot to congratulate you two," he added, looking from Butch to Esther with a smile. "You look good together."

"Thank you," Esther said with a shy smile.

Butch chuckled. "She's turned me into a happily mar-

ried man," he commented, smiling at her. "I like having
somebody who can help with the cooking."

"Only because you taught me how." She glanced at the
clerk. "I couldn't boil water at first."

"Neither can I," the clerk confided. "But my wife, now,
she's one of the best cooks in Benton. I guess I'd starve on
my own."

They all laughed.

"You really do draw men's eyes," Butch mused as they
cooked supper together. "I thought I was going to have to
punch one of those cowboys who were buying feed for
Ren Colter's ranch and gaping at you."

"You did?" she asked, surprised.

He looked down at her and frowned. "Honey, don't you
know how beautiful you are?"

She just sighed and smiled at him. "Not really. I'm glad
you think I am, though. You aren't bad-looking yourself,"
she teased.

He chuckled as he took the biscuits out of the oven and
set them carefully on an oven mitt in their cast-iron con-
tainer. "You make me feel like a man with two arms," he
murmured.

She moved close to him. "You worry about that too
much," she said, and she was serious. "I don't mind it, not
at all. You're just perfect to me, the way you are."

He sighed and smiled. "Blind little woman."

She laid her cheek against his chest, smiling as she felt
his heartbeat. "Love does make people blind to imperfections." She sighed.

He went very still. "What?"

She looked up at him. He seemed all at sea.

"You . . . love me?" he got out.

"Of course I love you, you big idiot," she muttered, searching his dark eyes. "Why in the world do you think I married you?"

"For my abundant worldly goods?" he asked, recovering his poise with humor.

"Absolutely," she teased. "I mean, you have so many!"

He smoothed his hand over her soft blond hair. "I wish I had millions," he said huskily. "I'd deck you out in real diamonds, one as big as that paste one you wear," he added with a chuckle.

She felt those words to the soles of her feet. What would she do? She had millions. One day, her life would get sorted out, Darrin would get what was coming to him, and Esther would inherit her late mother's estate. It was so extensive that even she didn't know exactly how much money was involved. How would her husband react to that? Surely, it wouldn't matter so much . . .

"I know what you're thinking," he teased. "But don't worry about it. We'll have rich kids, but what you inherit won't affect us. Not a bit."

She recalled what he'd said, that he didn't want to be Mr. Esther Marist. She ground her teeth together and forced a smile so that he wouldn't realize she'd lied to him about her background.

"Not a bit," she agreed, and turned suddenly back to the potatoes she'd been cooking, to test them.

They ate lunch quietly. Butch was still recovering from the fact that a woman as beautiful as Esther could love him, when he had few possessions worth anything and he was missing an arm. She was young and gorgeous. She could have had any man she wanted, but she wanted him, imperfections and all, because she loved him. He felt like floating. Except there was the guilt. She was so young. She'd run away from a frightening man and apparently she'd had no experience of men, young men. She clung to Butch because he was the first man who'd been kind to her. But that wasn't love. It was gratitude. He wondered if she knew the difference. He felt guilty, as if he'd pushed her into a relationship before she had time to experience life without the burden of her mother and her mother's lovers. And he'd failed to protect her. They both wanted a child, that was true, but what if she came to her senses too late, after she was pregnant, and she didn't want Butch or a baby anymore? His own worries tormented him.

Esther saw that he was worried. She wondered why. He'd seemed so happy the night before. She flushed, remembering their shared passion. It had been a revelation to her. Butch hadn't said that he loved her, although she'd certainly said it to him. Could he still be grieving for the fiancée who'd thrown him over, who'd had his child in her body but refused to bear it? Men were strange to her, even at her age. Often they seemed to love women who mistreated them. Was he missing his fiancée and regretting his hasty marriage to Esther?

She withdrew into herself, talking as naturally as she could and smiling, but the tension was growing as Butch, too, succumbed to his own tormented thoughts. It moved them apart at a time when they should have been growing closer together.

* * *

After that day, Butch went to bed only after Esther was asleep, and got up before she was awake. She felt inadequate. He didn't seem to even want her anymore, which reinforced her fears that he regretted marrying her.

She went to work every day, and they carried on impersonal conversations, talking about everything under the sun—except themselves.

They were starting to cook supper one night a couple of weeks later when there was a knock on the door.

The sheriff's deputy she knew from the restaurant came in past Butch and tipped his hat to Esther.

"I'm afraid I have some bad news," he said quietly.

They both stared at him.

He drew in a breath. "We did a search on Cameron and found that he had an outstanding warrant, so we arrested him. I should have told you sooner, but we've been busier than usual." He paused. "So Cameron made a phone call this morning, and two well-dressed attorneys from Aspen came and bailed him out of jail."

Esther's heart tried to jump out of her chest. "Oh, dear."

"The attorneys mentioned that they were also representing a Mr. Darrin Ross and that he was planning to have Miss . . . excuse me, Mrs. Matthews here, arrested for pushing her mother down a staircase."

"I didn't," Esther said quietly. "What about the coroner? He said that my mother was thrown down the staircase. I can hardly lift a ten pound bag of dog food, much less a grown woman!"

"I mentioned that. The attorneys said that the coroner had a change of heart and amended his autopsy report." The deputy smiled gently. She did look so frightened.

Esther's eyes closed. "If he can have me charged with

murder and sent to jail, he'll get Mama's estate, won't he, Deputy?" she asked, her blue eyes wide with pain. "If I remember the law, a felon can't inherit, is that right?"

The deputy felt terrible. He hesitated. "Yes."

"Well, that's just lovely," she said, feeling strangely isolated from the world.

"We'll get you the best lawyer we can find," Butch said curtly. "J. L. Denton has a whole firm of them, and he'll help if I ask him to."

She looked up at Butch. He'd been so remote lately that she wondered if he didn't want to see the last of her. But he seemed to care about her fate. "Do you think so?" she asked.

"I know so." He turned back to the lawman. "Pressure was put on the coroner, I'm betting. He's just one man, and if he has a family, they could be threatened."

"Exactly what I thought. I hate to see a man get away with murder, much less try to blame it on an innocent woman," he said shortly. "Not going to happen. I know the chief up in Aspen. I'll talk to him."

"Policemen have families, too," Esther said sadly.

He chuckled. "This one doesn't. He has a mean temper and most people are afraid of him."

Esther felt more hopeful. "Okay. Thanks. What do I do in the meantime?"

"You talk to J. L.'s attorneys," Butch said.

"Good idea. I'll be in touch when I know more."

"Thanks, Deputy," Esther said.

He smiled. "No problem. See you."

Butch walked him out. When he came back inside, his jaw was taut and his dark eyes were flashing. He pulled out his cell phone and pressed a number.

"Hello, J. L.? It's Butch. I have a small problem and I need some help." He went on to outline briefly what was going on. He listened, his eyes on Esther's worried face. He smiled. "Yes, that's what I thought. You will? I'll owe you one. Sure thing. Thanks."

He hung up. "J. L.'s going to contact his attorneys. One of them will be over in the morning to talk to you."

Esther went close. He stiffened a little, but he didn't touch her. She felt a brush of sorrow. They'd been so good together. Now it all seemed lost. "Thanks," she said.

"Thank J. L.," he said, and he forced a smile. "Let's finish lunch, okay?"

She nodded. "Okay, Butch."

CHAPTER SEVEN

The attorney, Barton Frazier, arrived promptly at eight o'clock the next morning. Esther had arranged to come in an hour later at the Gray Dove so that she could talk to him at home. Her boss had been understanding and very kind.

Mr. Frazier accepted a mug of coffee and sat down at the kitchen table with her. Butch had already left for work, so there were just the two of them in the house.

"I want you to tell me exactly what happened the night your mother died," Mr. Frazier said quietly. He was a tall man, dark headed and dark eyed, older than Butch. He inspired confidence.

She sighed. "My mother had lived with Darrin for several weeks. She had no judgment about men at all. He was brutal to her, demanding things all the time, expensive things. She'd refused to give him money to buy an expensive sports car the night she . . . died. He was drunk. She mouthed off at him and he picked her up and threw her down the staircase. She was barely conscious. She pulled off her ring . . . this ring." She showed it to him. "She gave it to me. She'd already pushed her revised will into my purse the day before and told me to hold on to it. She was afraid. She always had some sort of premonition that she'd die violently. I think she knew, the day before, that Darrin was going to do something bad."

He was taking notes. "You have the will?"

"Yes. Darrin sent some man, a Mr. Cameron, down here pretending to be an investigator for the Aspen authorities. Except he wasn't. He saw the ring. He'd have told Darrin that I have it." She looked up. "It's worth millions of dollars."

"And your mother's estate?"

"Probably close to two hundred million dollars." She sighed. "It's mostly tied up in stocks and bonds and land. She owned several houses, many high-ticket cars, a closet-ful of fur coats . . ." She hesitated. "I suppose Darrin has hocked the furs and other easy-to-find antiques to get money for lawyers. He does have some mob ties to minor gangsters. Maybe they're funding him, in hopes of some easy money."

"That's always possible. Did your mother have any living relatives besides you?"

"I have a grandfather, if he's still alive. Mama seldom talked about him. He disapproved of my father." She smiled sadly. "My dad was a wonderful person. Mama ran around on him. He was so sad. He really loved her."

"What was your mother's maiden name?"

"Cranston," she said. "But she never talked about her past, where she was from, even her parents. She didn't like her father at all, though she did tell me of some good times with him, and her mother died when she was small, I think." She smiled. "It's amazing, how much I don't know about my own background."

"We can find your grandfather, if he's still alive."

"That would make him a target, Mr. Frazier," she said

sadly. "I've made Butch one, by marrying him. I'd die to keep him safe from harm. I don't want him hurt, because of me. I love him more than anything."

He smiled. "We'll do our best to keep both of you safe. And your grandfather, if we find him. Was he well-to-do?"

"Mama said he was very rich," she replied. "He lived in some remote place." She frowned, trying to remember. "I think it was Jamaica. She mentioned it once. He left the States when his wife died and his daughter married who he considered the wrong man. Mama said he stopped caring about anything after that."

"What did your father do?"

"He flew airplanes," she said, smiling. "He was a test pilot." The smile faded. "That's how he died, testing a new plane. Mama was off with one of her lovers. Our lawyers had to take care of the funeral, because I was too little to know how to do any of that. When Mama came back and they told her about Daddy, she just shrugged and said there was a big party coming up in Europe and she was taking her new lover there."

"What a life you've had," he remarked, still taking notes.

"We had a wonderful housekeeper. She took care of me all those years." She grimaced. "Darrin made Mama fire her the day he moved in. And Mama didn't say a word, she just did it. I don't think Agnes even got severance pay." She looked up. "Her full name is Agnes Meriwether, and she lived in Billings, Montana, before she came to work for Mama. While you're trying to find my grandfather, do you think you could look for Agnes, too? If we can get my inheritance back from Darrin, I'll have more than enough money to give her a pension and pay your fees so Mr. Denton won't have to."

"We can worry about all that later," he said kindly. "I'm going to get right on it."

He had a few more questions. Esther answered them all. "Just one more thing," she said to Mr. Frazier as he was leaving. "I don't want my husband to know any of the particulars, especially how much I'm worth."

He nodded. "I won't tell."

"Thanks. I told him that Mama had some minor investments that were long-term, and I laughed and said they'd belong to our kids. He said he didn't want to be Mr. Esther Marist." Her eyes saddened. "His pride wouldn't take it. I should have told him the truth up front, but I was so afraid. I'm still afraid."

"You don't need to be. We'll manage this. Trust me."

She looked up into warm dark eyes. "I will," she said.

Butch wanted to know what the attorney had said when they were both home from work later that day.

"He's going after Darrin," she said simply. "I hope he gets what's coming to him."

"So do I," Butch agreed. "When will you know something?"

"Very soon," she assured him.

He made a face and sighed. "I don't like having you in danger," he said abruptly.

"I don't like having you in danger either, Butch," she said softly, and her eyes adored him. "I wish we could go off to some island somewhere and never have to come back again."

He smiled sadly. "That's a pipe dream, honey girl," he told her. "We all have bad times. Best way to handle them is to face them right away."

"Yes, and I didn't do that," she said sadly. "If I'd only gone to the police right then . . ."

His hand slid over hers on the table. "And you might have been lying dead in the snow and I'd never have met you."

"But I'm such a burden," she protested, her blue eyes wide and sad.

"Some burden," he said huskily. "You take my breath away. I can't even believe that you're married to me."

She smiled. "Really? You don't act like you want me around lately."

"I want you around all the time, that's the problem," he said through his teeth. "You're new to marriage, and intimacy. I thought it would be better to give you a little breathing space."

"Silly man," she said, with her heart in her eyes. "I don't need any breathing space."

He drew in a breath. "You don't? Really?"

"Really." She hugged him close. "After supper, I could convince you of that. I mean, if you wanted me to." She looked up at him intently. "You can tell me if there are times when you'd rather not be with me. I can handle it."

"That's the problem."

"What is?"

He cleared his throat. "I want to be with you all the time. Too much."

"Awwww," she whispered, kissing his warm throat. "I want to be with you all the time, too, Butch."

His breath caught. His arm contracted hungrily around her. He felt his body start swelling at once.

"That's really nice," she whispered, and moved closer.

"Esther . . ." he choked.

She reached up and whispered in his ear, shameful things, intimate things that would make her squirm in the aftermath, but all she wanted right now was Butch.

He caught her hand and drew her down the hall, into the bedroom, and locked the door. She went into his arms at once and started kissing him.

A couple of hours later, lying in a tangled, damp mass, Esther looked up at the ceiling and she laughed.

"What's funny?" he asked drowsily.

"You thought I wanted breathing space," she teased. "But I can't even breathe away from you. I was afraid you were having second thoughts, that you might want me to leave."

"I'd do anything to keep you here," he confessed quietly. "You make everything good and sweet. If I lost you, it would take all the color out of my world. I wouldn't even want to go on living."

It was a powerful thing to say. She could literally feel the words. She moved closer to hug him close. "I'm so glad I married you," she whispered. "Even if you weren't the best lover in Colorado, I'd still be glad."

His heart ran wild. She loved him in bed. That meant so much. At the last, his fiancée had noted that he wasn't very good at satisfying a woman. But here was Esther, who had been innocent, and he knew without words that she achieved satisfaction with him every time they were together. Of course, so did he.

"It makes me proud, that you feel that way about me," he said softly.

She smiled, sighing against his hair-roughed, muscular chest. "I'll never leave you," she said gently. "Unless you throw me out," she added, and felt sick to the soles of her feet.

He just laughed. "Fat chance."

He didn't know how rich she was. It was going to be a hard thing to have to tell him. Maybe she should do it now.

"Butch, there's something I need to tell you, something about Mama, and about me," she began reluctantly.

The only answer she got was a mild snoring sound. She lifted up so that she could see his face. He'd gone to sleep. She sighed and sank back down against him. "Well, maybe I can tell you later," she murmured softly to herself. And she drifted off into sleep as well.

J. L. Denton's attorneys lived up to their excellent reputation. They arrived in Benton two days later, loaded for bear. Esther already knew the attorney she'd spoken to, Mr. Frazier. But this time there was another attorney with him, one belonging to the same law firm, and he made Esther uncomfortable. Not that Edward Thornton was unkind. He was simply taciturn, and his pale silver eyes made her nervous.

"Don't let Thorn intimidate you," Mr. Frazier chuckled. "He's hell in a courtroom, but he's mostly kind when he isn't doing a summation."

"Nice to meet you, Mr. Thornton," Esther said gently, and lifted a hand.

He shook it gently and gave it back. "Where can we sit

to discuss our findings?" he asked at once. "And do you want to call your husband so that he can share the news?"

"Mr. Thornton," she said in a low tone of voice, "my husband thinks I'm the daughter of a wealthy woman and I'm hiding from my mother's boyfriend. He doesn't know how wealthy my family is." Her face went hard. "He won't take it well, I can tell you that. So it's better if you just talk to me."

"Very well," Mr. Frazier returned gently. "Now. On to Darrin Ross. A friend of his fenced four very valuable fur coats through a shady acquaintance. The guy who fenced them is known to the Aspen police, and they arrested him for theft. Afraid of going back to jail again, he gave them Darrin's name. So Mr. Ross is sitting in the Aspen jail biding his time until his attorneys can find some way to get him out."

"He'll need money for those attorneys," she said quietly. "And he knows about the ring I wear. Most people think it's paste." She held it out for them to see. "It was valued at several million dollars by the jewelry firm where my mother bought it. Darrin knows about its worth. Mr. Cameron gave it a great deal of scrutiny." She looked up at them. "I should have taken it off and put it in a safe deposit box, but it was the last thing my mother gave me, before she died . . ." She choked up and had to take a minute to get the pain out of her voice.

"If he saw it, someone may try to come and get it for him," Mr. Thornton said quietly. "It would easily pay all his legal fees."

Esther's blue eyes sparked. "He's not getting it. Not if I have to take it out in the woods and bury it somewhere!" She looked worried. "I've put my husband in the line of fire. I couldn't bear it if he got hurt because of me. I love him so much!"

"We won't tell him," Mr. Frazier promised. "But you have to keep the doors locked all the time, even during the day. And be careful where you go. Take your husband with you when you go to work or come home."

"Butch takes me to work and comes to get me," she assured them. "And he's always armed. Poachers and such people can be very dangerous. Butch is a cautious man."

"So he is. Now. Let's go over the case again," Mr. Frazier said, changing the subject.

He wanted to know about the will, how Darrin had behaved just before and just after Terry died. She told them in a choked little voice, about Darrin picking up Terry and hurling her headfirst down the long winding staircase at the Aspen house. She told them of her wild flight, and how she'd ended up in Benton and later married the man who'd saved her life.

"He's such a good man," she told the attorneys, and she was beaming with happiness. "I'd go crazy if I ever lost him." She gave them a sad look from big blue eyes. "He'll have to know what's going on sooner or later. When he finds out what I'm worth, he'll leave me."

"Why? I know I asked you before, but please repeat the reason you think that," Mr. Frazier asked gently.

She sighed and smiled. "I told him there were a few stocks and bonds that we could give to our children. He said that was great because he didn't want to be Mr. Esther Marist," she told them flatly.

Mr. Frazier sighed as well. "There are ways around that, Mrs. Matthews," he replied. "In fact, you could leave what you inherit in a trust for your children, when they come along, and just let the stocks and bonds remain in the hands of your investment broker."

"That would be a fine solution. But what about my mother's bank accounts, and the jewelry she had in the safe deposit box?"

"Your mother's lover might already have that."

She shook her head. "Mama never told him about it. I've carried around a key to it for the past few years. It was something Mama never shared with any of her lovers. She didn't want to be taken advantage of, you see."

"That was wise," Mr. Thornton agreed.

"So Darrin couldn't get to the jewelry and our statements from the broker and the amount of cash she stowed there for emergencies. He doesn't even know which bank the safe deposit box is in," she added with a quiet smile.

"Well, it will keep him busy looking for it, I imagine," Mr. Thornton said, "but I think he has bigger problems than that. He's just about to be charged with first degree murder. One of our criminal attorneys is handling the case for us. He's already out with an investigator—a real one," he added with a twinkle in his eyes, "looking for the witnesses that he swears will point to you as the murderer. This should be very interesting. We're also interviewing people." He smiled smugly. He didn't share why.

"What if they come and arrest me?" Esther asked, frightened.

"They won't arrest you," he promised. "You have to trust us, Mrs. Matthews. This isn't our first walk around the courtroom."

"You sound very certain of that," she replied warily.

He smiled. "I am."

She drew in a breath. "Okay, then. You'll keep me posted, about what's going on?" she added as they started to leave.

"You may count on that," Mr. Thornton told her.

Later, when they were curled up in bed together, Esther hinted about her mother's estate and what Darrin was actually after.

"You said that your mother just had a few stocks and bonds," Butch began.

She drew in a breath. "Yes," she said, retreating. He didn't sound encouraging. "A few minor ones, here and there."

"Then why are the lawyers worried that your mother's boyfriend might send someone down here after you?"

She thought fast. "The will," she said.

"Oh. I see."

She felt him relax. She moved closer with a sigh, resting her cheek on his chest. "That was all I was worried . . . about . . . oh, dear . . . !"

She was on her feet and running for the bathroom. She barely made it. She lost her supper, her lunch—even, apparently, her breakfast.

Butch was right there with her the whole time, a wet washcloth held in his hand to mop her up afterwards.

He kept a strong arm around her, back to the bedroom and eased her onto the bed, dropping down beside her.

He looked very sexy in the soft light of the lamp. Even when she felt nauseated, he was deliciously attractive to her.

She laughed softly. "Even when I'm sick, you're soooo sexy, Mr. Matthews," she teased weakly.

He wasn't laughing. She had the wet cloth over her eyes when she felt his big hand rest lightly above her flat stomach.

She moved the cloth away, her eyes suddenly glued to his pale face. He looked . . . she couldn't decide how he looked.

Her breath drew in sharply. "Do you think . . . ?" she faltered.

"My God." He wasn't swearing. His voice held an odd reverence. His big hand smoothed so tenderly over her stomach. He looked up at her, and there was wonder in his eyes, in his face.

She relaxed. She smiled. She beamed. She laughed with pure joy.

He slid down next to her and cradled her tenderly against him. "Oh, glory," he whispered into her hair. "Daddy Matthews."

She laughed again. "Mommy Matthews."

He nuzzled his face against hers. "We'll have to start thinking about names and a good college, and when she'll get married," he began.

"When he'll get married. I want a boy," she said. "And he has to look just like you!"

He fought tears. His life had been empty, cold, almost savage. Now, suddenly, he was part of a family. He loved it. He wished he could put it into words. He didn't know how.

"Life takes things away from you. Then God gives them back, in the sweetest way," he whispered.

Her arms tightened around his neck. "I'm glad you aren't angry."

"Angry!" He lifted his head and looked down at her. "I've just won the lottery. Hit the jackpot. Climbed Mt. Everest." He looked down at her stomach, concealed by the pretty, thin, blue lacy nightgown she was wearing. "Glimpsed heaven," he added reverently.

She sighed, lying back on the pillow. "It might be a false alarm," she said, and looked worried.

He pursed his lips. "When was your last period?" he asked.

She started, because she hadn't been keeping track at all. She counted. Her eyes widened. "Six weeks!" she exclaimed.

"Almost to the day we married," he chuckled.

"Wow."

"Double wow," he murmured. "You don't mind? We haven't been married long."

"I don't mind at all," she said dreamily. "I never wanted to travel the world or become famous in a profession. I just wanted a man to love, who was a good man, and children, and a real home where I wasn't moved around every month to someplace else." She looked up at him with wonder. "And I found it all, right here, almost overnight."

He bent and kissed her eyelids shut. "So did I. You're my whole life. If I lost you, I couldn't go on," he said huskily.

Her arms tightened around his neck. "You'll never lose me," she said fervently. "No matter what! I promise!"

But life has twists and turns, and fate isn't always kind. Or so it seemed. A few days after Esther had been to the doctor for a blood test and had her pregnancy confirmed, a tall, dignified man in a very expensive suit, with a silver-topped cane, walked into the Gray Dove and asked if a woman named Esther Marist worked there.

Esther was called out of the kitchen, where she'd been helping the cook clean up a minor disaster on the grill.

She stared at the old man, frowning curiously. He seemed to be doing the same, his face bland and his blue eyes blazing. For a few seconds, she was afraid he was one of Darrin's friends.

"I'm Esther," she said hesitantly.

The old man let out a sigh. He moved closer. "Yes, you look like your mother." His blue eyes filmed for just a few seconds and he looked away, clearing his throat. "I don't suppose she spoke of me."

"I'm sorry, sir, but who are you?" Esther asked.

He turned back to her. "I'm Blalock Cranston. Your mother's father. Your grandfather."

She bit her lower lip. She'd thought her whole family was dead, that she had nobody left. And here was the grandfather she'd never known. Tears bled from her eyes.

The old man moved closer, hesitantly, just as Esther flung herself into his arms and bawled.

Luckily, it was midmorning, and only a couple of cowboys were in the restaurant. But Esther wouldn't have cared if it had been full. She'd never been so happy, not since she'd married Butch.

"My girl," the old man choked. "I'm so happy . . . to have found you, at last. Some attorney from here called me. I was on my estate in Jamaica. I had my pilot fly me right over. Damned hard, finding this little town on any map, but the driver I hired seemed to know right where it was." He drew away. "I'm so sorry. I had no idea what sort of trouble your mother was in. We lost touch many years ago." He grimaced. "I didn't know your father, Esther. If I had, well, a lot of misery could have been avoided. I found out many things about his life, after he was gone. He must have been a fine man. The fact that he didn't come from a founding family shouldn't have mattered. Not at all."

She managed a smile. "He was a wonderful father. I mourned him. I still do." She looked up at the old man. "I'm married, you know. He isn't from a founding family, either, but he's a good and kind man and he loves animals."

He smiled back. "And that's not a bad reference."

"He loves children, too, which is a good thing." Her hand flattened against her stomach. "Because we're pregnant. We only found out for certain a couple of days ago." She laughed. "So you'll be a great-grandfather!"

He didn't look displeased at all. He patted her on the shoulder. "I'll try to be a better grandfather than I was a father," he promised. "I'd love to meet your husband."

"He comes in for lunch," she said, "every day."

"Then I'll be back for lunch. We have many things to talk about." He leaned down so that they couldn't be overheard. "Your mother's murderer is in a passel of trouble, and his friends have all deserted him. So the lawyers think he's without means to pursue that will your mother left you."

"Oh, I hope so," she said fervently. "If they came after me, they might hurt Butch. He's a war veteran," she added quietly. "He lost an arm overseas, but it doesn't even slow him down. He's a licensed wildlife rehabilitator."

"A brave man," he replied. "I served in Vietnam. Seems like a hundred years ago," he added, and there was a bleakness about his expression. "So. I'll see you both at lunchtime!"

She grinned. "That's a date!"

The owner of the café and the cook and the other waitress gathered around her excitedly when the old man left to climb into a stretch limousine that was parked at the curb.

"Who is he?!" they exclaimed.

"My grandfather!" Esther told them. "I thought he was dead. I didn't even know who he was! It's just so exciting!"

They all laughed. "Well, he seems to be a gentleman of property, if that's the right phrase," the owner teased.

Esther hesitated. "He has an estate in Jamaica, and I believe he's very wealthy. Oh, dear, what am I going to tell Butch?" she wailed.

"Listen, he loves you. He's not going to say anything," the cook said.

"Absolutely," the waitress agreed.

The owner just smiled gently.

Butch was full of news when he came in to sit at his normal booth right near the door of the restaurant.

"I'm getting a raise," he said. "And just in time! Now we can go shopping for baby furniture . . . what's wrong, honey?" he asked abruptly, because she looked forlorn.

She moved closer, with her pad out, but nobody was close enough to hear. "My grandfather's in town."

"He is?" Butch smiled. "So you do have a little family left, don't you, honey girl?" He caught her other hand and squeezed it gently. His dark eyes were bright with joy. "He'll be our baby's great-grandfather. Did you tell him?"

She nodded.

"Is he nice? Do you like him?"

She took a deep breath. "About that . . ."

"Well, would you look at that?" one of the cowboys remarked loudly as a big black limousine pulled up at the curb. "Must be some rock star in town to film a video. Or maybe a Mafia don." He chuckled.

Esther ground her teeth together.

"What's wrong, honey?" Butch asked, worried when he saw her expression. He looked toward the door, where a tall, silver-haired gentleman walking with a cane came into the restaurant, looked at Esther, and smiled as he approached them.

"Esther, who is that?" Butch whispered.

She drew in a deep breath as the old man joined them. "Butch, this is my grandfather, Blalock Cranston. Grandad, this is my husband, Butch Matthews."

Then she waited for the explosion.

CHAPTER EIGHT

To say that Butch was dumbfounded was an understatement. It didn't take psychic abilities to figure out that the man who'd climbed out of the stretch limo was loaded. The fancy suit, silk shirt, expensive shoes said it all.

Butch looked blankly at his wife.

"So you're my new grandson-in-law," the old man said, smiling as he held out a hand that Butch shook. "Glad to meet you. Very glad. And I hear I'm to be a great-grandfather! Congratulations!"

Butch shifted his shocked eyes to Esther's taut face and moved them back to the old man's. He felt as if he'd been clubbed. "Sure. Nice to meet you, too. Won't you sit down?" he asked, remembering his manners.

"Thanks." The old man grimaced, leaning the cane in the booth beside him as he sat. "Damned leg still gives me fits. I got caught by one of those miserable bamboo traps they laid in Vietnam. Damned near lost the leg, but I told them I'd live with it or die with it, but they weren't taking it off." He sighed. "They didn't listen. But the artificial one works fine. The joint kills me in cold weather, though, which is why I live in Jamaica."

Butch lost the shock and looked at the other man with new eyes. "Where were you stationed?"

"Da Nang," came the quiet reply. "I was there during the Tet Offensive, if you read history. My unit was sent out on a scouting mission and we ran into booby traps. I was the only survivor. Got sent home. I yelled the whole way, cursed everybody I could think of, but they wouldn't let me go back." His eyes were sad. "I lost my best friend, and two guys who'd been in the same boot camp with me. War is hell. Truly hell."

"Yes, it is," Butch agreed solemnly. "I got hit by mortar fire. My best friend ran through gunfire and carried me to safety. He came home with me. A lot of other guys didn't."

"At least we lived, yes?" The old man chuckled. "And that's not a bad thing."

Butch smiled. "Not a bad thing at all."

"Well, I'm here with news," the old man said. "The attorneys who tracked me down are the ones working to put your mother's so-called boyfriend in the jailhouse for the next lifetime or two. Which brings to mind a technical detail. Do you have your mother's will?"

"Oh, yes," Esther said.

"And you've still got that damned ring I gave her," he added, his eyes on her slender fingers. His eyes teared up and he averted them. "She never took it off."

"I haven't, either. I suppose I shouldn't have been wearing it all this time. Darrin's cohort saw it, when he was here posing as an investigator."

"Why is the ring a concern?" Butch asked curiously. "It's just paste . . ."

"Paste?" the old man asked, astounded. "It's worth millions."

The blood drained out of Butch's face.

Esther tried to stop her grandfather, but he was like a car with the accelerator stuck. "Terry owned property and stocks worth almost two hundred million," he continued. "We can't find Darrin, but there's a rumor that he found somebody to forge a new will."

"Why would he do that?" Esther asked. "Oh," she said after a few seconds. "He doesn't know I've got Mama's, unless Mr. Cameron told him."

"Exactly. Hopefully, Cameron didn't have a chance to tell him," the old man said. He sighed. "My poor little girl. She never had much sense about men. Except for your father. I'm sorry I never gave him a chance, girl, sorry I fouled everything up for him."

"You didn't know him," Esther said, her eyes worried as they were riveted to Butch's hard, blank features.

"You have to understand. Your mother was wild even as a teenager. Her mother tried so hard." He sighed. "She was a good woman. She never knew how to handle Terry. Neither did I. I suppose we didn't want to face the fact that she had psychological issues, not until it was far too late. By then, we couldn't convince her that she needed a psychologist."

Esther stared at him. "Psychologist," she echoed.

"Yes. She had an addiction to men. We didn't realize that such things existed. I suppose my wife and I were stuck in the Dark Ages. We moved to Jamaica and lived out in the sticks, where we didn't have much contact with the modern world."

"Isn't it dangerous over there?"

"No more so than here," he said simply. "My family has owned the house there for four generations. We have bananas and cashew nuts and all sorts of tropical fruit. You and your husband should come over and stay with me for a while. You'd love it."

"That would be hard. Butch works for the wildlife service," she said.

"I'd forgotten. Well, he won't need to work once the will's through probate. Speaking of which, you have to come with me to Aspen," her grandfather added. "And don't worry about Darrin. I brought two bodyguards with me. One drives, the other rides shotgun." His eyes, so like her mother's, were like blue flames. "Nobody's hurting my granddaughter."

"Darrin had a contact on the police force . . ."

"Not anymore," her grandfather said. "And most of his cronies are facing prosecution for various and sundry crimes. I've had two investigators on the job. One of them's like a shark. He never quits."

Esther was unsettled. Butch still hadn't said a word. And customers were starting to come in.

"I have to go back to work," Esther said. "I'll talk to my boss about getting off. When do you want me to go with you?"

"Tomorrow. Let's get this thing settled. Are you coming with us?" he asked Butch.

Butch just stared at him blankly.

"We'll talk about that tonight," Esther said quickly. "Are you staying in town?"

"Yes, at the motel." He named it. "I'll give you my cell phone number before I leave here. Now. Since you're working here, I assume that the food must be excellent." He smiled at her. "So what do you recommend?"

* * *

Butch excused himself to go back to work after a meal with stilted conversation. He'd had the shock of his life. He didn't know what to do. He'd expected to live with Esther and have their child grow up in his cabin, the two of them making ends meet, but frugally. And she was wearing a ring that was worth more than every penny he'd make for the rest of his life. He was shellshocked.

"Try not to let this ruin your marriage," the old man said to Butch before he left. "I know it's a shock. But it's not Esther's fault. She can't help the circumstances of her birth. She loves you. She's carrying your child. Don't turn your back on her over money, son," he said gently. "It's so unimportant in the scheme of things."

"Unimportant if you have it," Butch said.

"My wife's parents were caretakers," the old man said. "We had our own hard time when she found out what I was worth. It took me months, but I finally convinced her that she'd be happier with me and the money than she would all by herself."

Butch couldn't find the words. He just looked at the other man.

"Give it time," he advised. "It's like a fresh wound right now. Let it heal for a day or two and then take another look at your situation. It really boils down to this. Is your pride worth more to you than Esther?" He got up, patting the younger man on the shoulder. "And don't worry about her. I won't let anything happen to her. But we can't let Darrin take away everything her mother had without fighting back. The man killed my daughter," he added, and his blue eyes glittered. "He'll pay for it."

"I'm sorry about your daughter," Butch said, finally finding his voice.

"I'm sorry that I had to disrupt your life," the old man

replied. "Things happen. But it's how we react to them that matters. Esther will keep in touch with you while we're away."

Butch managed a smile and nodded as he got up. The old man noted that he took his own slip to the counter to pay for his meal. Esther's grandfather wouldn't have tried to pick up the tab. Butch and his pride were going to have some conflicts before this was over, but he was certain that the man loved his granddaughter enough to overcome the obstacles. What Esther felt was more than obvious. They'd manage.

Esther waited on the curb for Butch to pick her up. He was late—a first, because he'd never been late before. He got out of the truck and helped her into the passenger seat before he got back in and drove them away.

He didn't say a word all the way home. Esther tried to make conversation, but it was so difficult that she finally just gave up and sat quietly beside him until they reached the cabin. He helped her out and went ahead to unlock the door.

"I'll get supper," she said.

He glanced at her. "I'll need to feed the animals out back."

He went out. She changed out of her uniform into slacks and a loose blouse and went into the kitchen to find something to cook.

By the time he came back, she had a nice omelet and fresh biscuits on the table, along with perfectly cooked bacon.

"Please notice that the biscuits don't bounce," she said, trying to lighten the atmosphere at the table.

He didn't seem to notice. He finished his meal and turned on the television set, intent on the news.

Esther cleared the table and washed dishes. One of their future purchases was going to be a dishwasher. She didn't dare mention it now.

She sat and worked on a crossword puzzle, watching him covertly while he settled down with a documentary program after the news went off.

He still hadn't said a word.

When he turned off the television, she just looked up at him with sad eyes. "Do you want me to leave?" she asked.

"If you like," he said. His voice was flat. He looked around. "You're used to crystal and silver and probably half a dozen people to keep up the houses your mother owned. What a hell of a comedown this must have been."

"Actually, I spent most of my life avoiding my mother's boyfriends. I had our housekeeper, Agnes, to make my birthdays special and fix presents for me at Christmas. I don't remember my mother ever being home for any holiday at all." She averted her eyes. "It isn't where you live, Butch. It's how you live, the people you live with, that make it a home. I'm happier here in Benton than I've been anywhere in my life. I don't expect you to believe that." She shook her head. "I should have told you the truth at the very beginning. But you were so kind." Her blue eyes lifted to his cold, dark ones. "I'd never had kindness from a man, or real affection. It was . . . like magic."

He felt guilty. But only for a few seconds. She was rich and he was poor. His pride couldn't get past that. How could any man live with it?

"I'm sorry," he said. He shrugged. "Sometimes relationships just don't work out."

"I'm pregnant," she pointed out.

He swallowed. Hard. "Well, it's early days yet," he said, biting down hard on the agony it cost him to say that. "If you want to do something about it . . ."

She got up from her chair, walked past him into the bedroom, and started filling a duffel bag with her few items of clothing.

He watched her, his mind on fire with doubts and aching loneliness. She was going away, and he'd forced her into that decision. Him, with his pride and his insecurities.

"Your grandfather said to give it a few days," he said curtly.

"Sure. We'll give it a few days." She was furious and trying not to show it. She put the last of her few possessions into the bag and walked back into the dining room. She had her grandfather's phone number. She pushed it in on her cell phone. When he answered, she asked if his car had GPS and when he said it did, she gave him the address. "Can you come get me right now?" she asked, fighting tears.

There was a long sigh. "I can. I'm so sorry, honey."

She lifted her face and looked at Butch, who was quiet and solemn. "Fortunes of war," she said into the receiver, and hung up.

Her grandfather got her a room of her own, next to his, and introduced her to his two bodyguards. They weren't big, brutish guys. One was slender with blond hair and pale eyes, the other was dark with broad shoulders and a cowboy's lankiness. They shook hands with polite smiles and promised to keep her out of harm's way.

"Your husband couldn't face it, I gather?" her grandfather asked quietly.

She didn't speak. She just shook her head.

"Well, we'll manage," he said after a minute.

She almost strangled on her next words. "He said it was all right if I wanted to do something about the baby."

The older man put his arms around her and let her cry. "Men say terrible things when they're upset," he said. "I'm sure he didn't mean it."

She wasn't sure. But it didn't matter. "I'm not giving up my baby," she said shortly. "He doesn't even have to see it. I'll . . . I'll go someplace and live where he won't ever see me again."

"Oh, that's easy," he said gently. "You'll come home with me."

She smiled weakly. "Okay."

He sighed. He'd lost his daughter years ago, but it was almost like having her back. He'd take care of Esther and her child, and maybe it would make up, just a little, for the misery he'd caused Terry by shutting her out of his life when she married Esther's father. He'd failed Terry. He wasn't about to fail Esther.

Darrin had hired a man to get to Esther and kill her, if possible. He had a brand-new will that was forged but looked legitimate.

When the old man showed up with Esther in Aspen, and with the legitimate will, everything was quickly over for the murderer of Terry Marist. It made all the best news shows. It was a big story, a celebrity murder, an estranged wealthy father, a daughter who was press-shy and kept well away from reporters.

Back in Benton, Butch watched the story play out in the

news. His heart ached. He was alone again. He missed
Esther. He was furious with himself for what he'd said to
her, the way he'd treated her. He'd invited her to get rid of
their child. Probably she had, thinking her idiot husband
didn't love her or want her because she had more money
than he did.

He really hated himself. How much became apparent
when he didn't show up for work three days in a row and
his best friend, Parker, came looking for him.

Parker found Butch so drunk that he couldn't even get
words out of him. He set to work, cleaning up the cabin
and then cleaning up, and sobering up, Butch.

After a pot of coffee, Butch was a little more lucid.
"She's in Aspen, facing that trial all alone, and I'm up here
feeling sorry for myself. She'll never speak to me again,
and I deserve it. We were going to have a baby . . ." He
almost choked on the coffee. His voice broke and he had
to fight to steady it. "I told her it was okay with me if she
didn't want it . . ."

"My God," Parker said heavily. "No wonder you got
drunk."

"She's worth millions," Butch said through his teeth. "I
work for wages."

"If she loves you, and you love her, what's the problem?"

"I just told you," Butch said belligerently. "She's worth
millions and I work for wages."

"So have her put all the money into a trust for the kids
and go back to work at the Gray Dove restaurant."

"I can't ask an heiress to wait tables!"

"You never asked her to in the first place," Parker pointed out. "She offered." He smiled. "She loves you."

"She did."

"Trust me, love doesn't wear out just because you have a fight. And I'd know," he added tongue in cheek.

Butch chuckled. "Yeah. I guess so."

"If they haven't fired you for laying off work, why don't you take some of that vacation time you never use and go to Aspen?"

"Oh, sure. Go hat in hand to the door of a mansion dressed like this." He indicated his jeans and flannel shirt.

Parker sighed. "You could call her, you know."

Butch stared at the floor. "She blocked my number." His shoulders moved. "That's why I got drunk."

Parker didn't know what to say. He felt bad for his friend. He wished he knew a way to help him. "I could use some more coffee," he said after a minute.

"I'll go make some," Butch volunteered.

While he was out of the room, Parker took Butch's cell phone and copied Esther's phone number off it. By the time Butch came back, with more coffee, the phone was right where he'd left it, with Butch none the wiser.

"Oh. Hi, Parker," Esther stammered when her unexpected caller identified himself. She didn't usually answer unknown numbers, but she was expecting a call from one of her mother's attorneys.

"Hi, yourself. How's it going?" he asked.

"Well, they've got Darrin in jail, along with that Cameron man, and he's been arraigned. The trial won't come up for several months. In the meanwhile, I've got lawyers trying to straighten out the mess Mother left. I never knew finances could be so complicated." She hesitated. "How's Butch?"

"Drunk."

The single word was shocking. "But he doesn't drink," she said. "He doesn't even keep liquor in the cabin."

"Oh, he bought some," Parker replied pleasantly. "About four fifths of whiskey, actually. He spent several hours throwing up after I found him. He's almost sober now."

"Almost."

"Yeah. His butt's real sore."

"Why?"

"He's been kicking it. Well, metaphorically," he added. "He hates himself for the things he said to you."

"He might have said so," she muttered.

"He said you blocked his number."

She took a sharp breath. "That was just after I left," she said sadly. "I unblocked it . . . He tried to call me?"

"Yeah. That's why he started drinking."

She winced. "He said I didn't have to have the baby," she choked.

"That's why he's kicking himself."

"Oh."

"You might call him. He's pretty broken up. Pride's a damned silly thing, you know. I told him you could just put all the money in trust for your kids and grandkids and go back to work at the Gray Dove."

"What did he say to that?"

"That you probably wouldn't want to wait tables anymore, or ever see him again."

"Idiot."

"Yeah. That's what I called him, too."

She hesitated. "You know, I could really put it in a trust.

I could give away a lot of it, too. My grandfather's absolutely loaded. He doesn't need it. And I like waitressing."

"You could tell Butch that. He might stop drinking."

She smiled to herself. It was the first time she had, since the turmoil had started.

"Think about it," he told her. "And don't tell him I called you, okay? He's my best friend, but he might not like it that I stole your number out of his phone without telling him."

"I won't say a word," she promised. "Thanks, Parker."

"You're welcome!"

It took a little time to get the will through probate. The first thing Esther did was to track down Agnes and give her a pension. Their reunion was sweet, especially when Agnes was told about the baby. Esther promised that she'd be invited to the christening, and she'd send a private jet and a limo to transport her. Agnes was sad about Terry, but she adored Esther and was only happy to have her back again in her lonely life, at least.

Esther's second discovery was the whereabouts of Jack and Glenda Johnson. She found them outside Aspen, where they worked for a trucking concern. She promptly bought them their own private trucking business.

"But you don't need to do this," they both protested when she found them and promised to set them up with their own trucks and a handful of truckers to help haul cargo. They were shellshocked to learn who their mysterious passenger was that night in the past. They were more shocked at the way she repaid them.

She just laughed. "I owe you two so much. I'm married. And pregnant. And so happy. I would never have made it out of Aspen without you two. So just hush. I'm not doing it solely for gratitude." Her face pulled into a mischievous smile. "I have a favor to ask!"

Butch was miserable. He'd been on his own far too long. He'd tried to call Esther, but he'd only gotten a message that her phone wasn't available and after one try, he'd assumed the number was still blocked and he'd given up.

Life was a misery. He was too proud to go to Aspen begging, and too miserable to do much else. He and Two-Toes had the cabin to themselves. Even the wolf looked sad.

It was snowing again. It was the weekend and he was by himself. Parker, the fink, had taken away his last bottle of whiskey, so he didn't even have a way to drown his sorrows.

He listened idly to the weather report while his ears picked up the sound of traffic on the highway. He heard the sound of airbrakes, like on a big rig, and then gears shifting as the truck went along. Probably hit a slick spot, he thought to himself, and went back to the weather.

There was a knock on the door. Probably Parker, keeping an eye on him, he thought absently. He'd been a good friend. Well, except for taking away his liquor.

He opened the door and his heart dropped into his boots. She was wearing a blue fox jacket and dark slacks and a silk blouse, almost the exact things she'd had on when they first met, when he found her outside his cabin.

"I'm all alone and I have no place to go," Esther said, her heart racing. "I'm looking for some cousins of mine that live here; the Crump family."

"No Crumps here, I'm afraid," he said huskily. "Would

you settle for a miserable husband and a handicapped wolf?"

She smiled.

He smiled.

He held out his arms and she ran into them, bawling as he closed the door and shut them into the pleasant warmth of the cabin.

"I'm sorry. I'm so damned sorry," he murmured into her hair as he held her. "I've been a fool!"

"I'm sorry, too. I should have told you the truth, but I thought you wouldn't want me."

"I want you," he whispered. "For the rest of my life!" He drew back and he looked agonized. "The baby . . . ?"

She gave him a sardonic look. "Am I the sort of woman who would do that?"

He relaxed. "No."

She linked her arms around his neck. "My mother's attorneys are working on a trust. The money will go to our children and grandchildren—and probably our great-grandchildren," she added with a laugh. "Meanwhile, I'll go hat in hand and beg for my job back. After all, every penny counts."

"God, I love you," he murmured against her mouth.

She smiled under the devouring kiss. "I love you, too," she whispered.

On the floor beside them, a contented old wolf lay down with his head on his paws and closed his eyes.

Darrin Ross went to prison, for such a nice number of years that the Matthews' firstborn would have gray hair before he got out. Esther's grandfather came to visit from time to time and coaxed them into coming to Jamaica on gift tickets so he could see his great-grandson and two great-granddaughters more often.

When he passed away, and was mourned by his family, his bequest was a shock to his attorneys and his grand-daughter. Because he left his entire estate to Butch.

"Well, darn it," Esther said after the will was read.

"What?" Butch asked, still poleaxed, and deeply touched

"Honey, everybody will think I married you for your money," she said.

He laughed. "Your grandfather would laugh himself sick."

"I'll bet you that he's already doing that, and having a wonderful reunion with my grandmother and my mother," she added.

He drew her close. "I won't take that bet. What a hell of a sweet thing to do."

"He was a sweet man," she replied. "And he was very fond of you."

"Daddy's rich," their son, John, said when they told him.

His sisters were just a little too young to understand that.

"Daddy's sort of rich," Butch said, picking up the little boy with a chuckle. "But that's only with money. Daddy's much richer in love."

"Love is worth more than money," Esther agreed, hugging her husband. "Far, far more."

Butch just kissed her. And that was enough.

THE WOLF ON HER DOORSTEP

KATE PEARCE

CHAPTER ONE

Morgantown
Morgan Valley, California

"Beth? Have you got a second?"

Beth Baker groaned inwardly, released her grip on the door handle of Maureen's General Store, and turned to face the owner. Maureen was a lovely woman, but she did like to chat, and Beth had been hoping to get away without the usual friendly, weekly, interrogation. Not that she minded sharing her business with Morgantown, but there were still things she was reluctant to talk about, and Maureen had a way of extracting information that was almost magical.

"Sure!" Beth smiled. "What's up?"

"That man." Maureen looked at her hopefully. She wore a red T-shirt that clashed with her bright auburn hair, jeans, and well-worn cowboy boots. "The grumpy one."

"You're going to have to be more specific, Maureen," Beth said. "There are quite a few grumps in Morgantown, let alone in the whole valley."

"The one in the cabin."

Beth considered the options. "Do you mean Conner O'Neil?"

"Yes." Maureen nodded eagerly. "Definitely that one."

Beth couldn't disagree with Maureen's description. Her first, and second, impression of the guy who'd come to rent a cabin on the far edge of the Garcia Ranch where she had her day job, was that he was a miserable old grump. Not that he was old. She'd guessed he was in his late thirties like Jay Williams, the friend who had recommended he come to live in the valley for a while.

Beth had met Conner at the Garcias', given him a detailed map of the local area and directions to the cabin, a radio in case the cell network went down, and a week's worth of provisions to get him started. He'd barely said a word to her, so she'd ended up petting his huge dog and chatting to fill the silence while his expression closed down even more. He probably thought she was an airhead. She hadn't bothered to correct that impression on their subsequent meetings because if the gods were kind, after summer ended, she'd never have to deal with him again.

Except now there was obviously a problem and, as the entire Garcia family were away, she was in charge of the ranch and its one isolated guest.

"What's wrong with him?" Beth asked warily.

"He didn't pick up his weekly supplies."

"Maybe he's just been delayed?" Beth suggested hopefully. "It must be hard to keep track of time in the middle of nowhere."

She visited the cabins on a regular basis to keep them clean and aired, and they were pretty basic. They were also about as far away from the town as you could get in Morgan Valley. Conner probably viewed that as a feature, seeing as he didn't like to communicate with anyone—or maybe it was just with her.

"This is the second time he hasn't shown up," Maureen said. "I tried to call him, but I couldn't get through."

Beth frowned. Whatever she thought of the way-too-hot-for-his-own-good grump, that was worrying.

"Do you have the supplies ready to go?"

"Yes, of course." Maureen brightened considerably. "Can you take them up to him? I hate driving out that far with my bad eyesight and ability to get lost in my own backyard."

"I don't see why not," Beth said. "He is our guest, so I am partially responsible for him."

She'd just come back from an early morning visit to the ranch and had been expecting to spend the rest of the day with her kids. There were hands hired to keep an eye on the cattle, but she was definitely in charge of the house. She valued her job and liked her employer way too much not to turn around and go back again.

Maureen went to retrieve the supplies, added fresh milk from the refrigerator, and ice packs to make sure everything stayed cool, and handed the box over to Beth.

"Thank you, dear. Now, make sure you let me know if he's okay, or if you need anything, all right?"

"Will do." Beth picked up the box, went through the door Maureen held open for her, and put everything in her car. "I've got to go home to see the kids, but I'll be up at the ranch again by this afternoon. If Conner calls in before I go, can you text me?"

"Sure." Maureen nodded. "Take care now and thank you."

Beth made sure the passenger door was firmly shut and went around to the driver's side. Her car might be ancient, but having a brother who was a mechanic meant it was still going strong. Not that it would get very far on the roads toward the cabins, which were described as "off the beaten track" for a reason. When she reached the Garcia Ranch, she'd have to borrow one of the trucks.

She drove home, which only took a couple of minutes, and took a left past her family-run gas station to the new homes Ted had built the previous year. There was one for him and Veronica, and one for Beth and her boys. Their father, Kevin, lived in the apartment above the mechanics shop. She insisted on paying Ted rent, which he reluctantly accepted. Her ex might not be sending her money, but she had a housekeeping job up at the ranch caring for Juan Garcia, her private physical therapy clients, and she worked the occasional shift at the gas station when Ted was shorthanded.

Life was good—even with two teenage boys to feed and help navigate through life. She parked around the back of the house and went in through the gate, wrinkling her nose at the smell of burning fat as she opened the kitchen door.

"Oh crap!" Wes, her almost-son, jumped like he'd stuck his fingers in an electrical socket, which was totally something he would do. "You're back early."

"What are you burning?" Beth looked at the frying pan.

"I'm not burning anything." Wes rushed the smoking pan over to the sink and threw it in, making Beth wince. "It's just a little browner than I meant it to be."

She followed him over and watched as he frantically squirted dish soap into the pan and turned on the hot water.

"What was it before you cremated it?"

"French toast." Wes sighed. "It was going really well, and then I got a text, and I forgot about it."

As Wes lived on his phone, Beth wasn't surprised.

"You'd better clean that up properly," she warned. "Or you're buying me a new pan."

"Like I have any money," Wes grumbled even as he filled the pan with cold water and set it to soak.

"You earn money," Beth pointed out. "You have a full-time job as a carpenter's assistant, and you're always busy."

Originally Wes had found the move to a small town from the city suburbs hard. After a series of unsuccessful career choices, he'd ended up working for Kaiden Miller as an apprentice carpenter. Not only did Wes enjoy the work, but Kaiden had managed to knock a bit of sense into his head as well. Wes was now a full-time employee and Beth couldn't have been prouder.

"Where's Mikey?" she asked.

Wes pointed up the stairs. "Sleeping, I think."

"He'd sleep his life away if I let him." Beth sighed. "I need to talk to you both, so don't go anywhere."

"That sounds bad," Wes said as he scrubbed energetically at the pan. "And I'm going to say upfront that whatever it is, it's all Mike's fault."

Beth couldn't help but smile as she climbed the stairs. There was only a year between Wes and Mikey, who shared the same father—her ex—but had different mothers. She'd taken Wes in after the court case that had left him without both his parents. At first he'd been angry and resentful, but years of patience and understanding had paid off, and he was well on his way to becoming an amazing individual.

Her smile died as she knocked on Mikey's door. Her son had come back from college for the summer and barely had time to talk, let alone confide in her. More worryingly, he seemed angry all the time, which set off all kinds of alarms in her head. She'd spent years dealing with his father's unprovoked rages and she dreaded having to deal with them in her son.

She knocked harder and went in to find him sitting at his desk staring at his laptop screen. He was taller than Wes and had darker hair and eyes like his dad.

"What's up?" He didn't bother to turn around when he spoke.

"I need to talk to you. Can you come downstairs for a minute?" Beth asked.

He sighed and swung around like he was doing her a big favor.

"Sure."

She set off back down the stairs. If he didn't want to speak to her, she wasn't going to keep pushing him. The last thing she wanted was for him to get mad, but what he might be mad at her for was a mystery.

Wes had finished cleaning the pan and had made her a cup of coffee, which she accepted gratefully.

"So, what's up?" Wes asked as he also handed Mikey a mug.

"I have to go up to the ranch this afternoon, so I won't be able to get dinner with you guys. I'm not sure when I'll be back, so you'll have to fend for yourselves. I'll leave you pizza money, okay?" She went to find her purse. "The guy who rented the hunting cabin hasn't picked up his supplies from town for over a week, so I have to go and check up on him."

"Why?" Mikey, who had sat on the couch, looked at her directly for the first time.

"Because I offered to keep an eye on things up at the ranch while everyone was away," Beth explained. "I check in on the cabins every two weeks anyway, so I'm just bringing my visit forward a couple of days." Not that Conner O'Neil was ever pleased to see her.

"But why is it your problem?" Mikey shrugged. "It's not like they're going to pay you extra to go traipsing off into the valley to spy on a guy who probably doesn't want to be bothered."

"I don't expect them to pay me extra for doing my job." Irritated by his dismissive tone, Beth held his gaze. "And, by the way, aren't you supposed to be getting some kind of summer job? There's plenty of work up at Morgan Ranch or in town."

"Ranching and waitressing?" Mikey pulled a face. "Not really my thing."

"I don't care if you think those things aren't good enough for you anymore, Mikey, you still need to be contributing to this household." Beth kept her tone even. "I can't afford—"

"You're the one who wanted me to go to college, and now you're complaining about the cost?"

Wes frowned. "Mike, you're being a real jerk right now."

"What's it to you?" Mikey swung around toward Wes. "You get to stay here full-time with *my* mom while I—" He suddenly stopped talking and headed for the stairs. "I'm done with this crap."

Beth set her cup down on the table, motioned for Wes to stay exactly where he was, and set off after her son. This time she didn't bother to knock when she went into his bedroom.

"Michael, that was totally out of line."

He was sitting on his bed, his hands clasped between his knees, his gaze on the floor.

"I know. I'm sorry."

She stared at his bent head for a frustrated minute.

Should she back off, or was it time to have things out with him? She knew she avoided confrontation, but he wasn't his father, she had to remember that.

"You wanted to go to college. It was all that you talked about your whole senior year." Beth leaned back against the door, arms crossed over her chest, and studied him. "Is something wrong? Don't you like it anymore?"

"College is fine." He let out a breath. "It's just . . ."

"Just what?"

"Dad wrote to me."

Coldness settled like a fist in Beth's gut. Of all the problems she had anticipated helping him with, this was not one of them.

"From prison," Mikey added, like she didn't know where her ex-husband currently resided.

"Okay." She managed to nod, even though she was screaming inside.

"He said that he's had loads of time to think while he's been incarcerated, and he realizes what he did was wrong, and he wants me to forgive him."

There were so many words Beth wanted to say, but choosing exactly where to start was proving way more difficult than she'd anticipated. She tried to remember her therapist's advice about taking deep, calming breaths through her advancing panic.

"Do you want to read the letter?" Mikey offered.

Beth shrank back against the woodwork as though he'd thrown a bomb at her. "No thanks."

"Look, I know he was awful to you, but you believe in forgiveness, right? That's what you always told me." He looked hopefully up at her. "He wasn't always bad; you must have had some good times together."

"Mikey, when I was pregnant, he choked me so badly

that I almost lost consciousness and then he kicked me down the stairs."

Pain flickered in his eyes at her stark words.

"How could you expect me to forgive someone who did that to his own wife and unborn child?" Beth asked. "Or is this really about you asking me for permission so you can forgive him?"

"I don't need your permission." He looked away from her.

"You're right, he can be very charming, which is why Wes's mom and I ended up in relationships with him, but he was also controlling and violent when he didn't get his own way." She forced herself to take a breath. "You know what he was like. You were there."

"I wrote back to him."

"Mikey . . ." Beth slowly shook her head, her heart hurting for him so badly.

He suddenly looked up at her. "I just wanted to talk to him, you know? To try and understand."

"Understand what, exactly? That he was a drunk and an abuser?"

"He's trying to change, Mom! He's staying sober and he's working on his anger issues. Why won't you give him a chance?"

"You . . . do what you have to do, okay?" Beth knew her voice was shaking, but she was doing the best she could. "I've got to go. I'll see you later."

She was already halfway down the stairs when he called her name. For once she had neither the intention nor the ability to turn around and talk things out. She pressed her hand over her mouth as nausea rolled over her. If she lost Mikey to Sean, she would never . . .

"Hey." Wes, who was standing at the bottom of the stairs, pulled her in for a giant hug. "Look, he's being a dick. I'll talk some sense into him while you're gone, I promise."

"You knew?" Beth looked up at him.

"Yeah, he told me a while back. I told him he was an idiot, and that Dad would never change." He rubbed her tense shoulders. "Sean tried it with me once, but I saw through his shit." Wes's normally pleasant expression disappeared. "Mike had you to protect him against Dad, whereas my mom"—he swallowed hard—"wasn't very strong."

Beth patted his cheek. "You are a good person, Wes."

"I try to be." He stepped away from her. "I promised myself I'd never end up like my old man, I can tell you that."

"You won't." Beth smiled through her gathering tears.

"If Mike is stupid enough to want a relationship with Dad, you can't stop him, but we both know Dad only wants to use him to get at you." His mouth twisted. "And probably me because I won't have anything to do with him. God, I hate that guy."

Beth nodded and sucked in a breath. "Wes, do you think Mikey used this address when he wrote to Sean?"

Wes raised an eyebrow. "I'm pretty sure Dad knows you would've come back to Morgantown the moment you could, so what's the problem if he did?"

"But not to this specific house." Beth felt her panic rising again. "He doesn't know—"

"Don't stress, okay? It's not like he's getting out anytime soon." Wes took her hand. "I think Mike said our grandma gave Sean his college address. He wrote back when he was there, so you should be fine."

Beth mentally reminded herself to send a stern email to Sean's mom to tell her never to do that again.

Wes squeezed her fingers. "You definitely need a break.

Why don't you go and check on that wolf guy up at the ranch and let me worry about Mike?"

"The wolf guy?" Beth was happy to be diverted into talking about anything other than her ex. "I call him the grump."

"His dog, Loki, is half husky, half wolf."

"How do you know?" Beth forced herself to keep moving by tidying up the kitchen, setting out the pizza money, and chatting to Wes as if she didn't have a care in the world.

"I talked to him one day when he was in town." Wes loaded the dishwasher and put the frying pan away. He'd never met a stranger. "Back in the day, he was in the same Navy SEAL team as that badass Jay Williams."

Beth considered tall, bearded Conner O'Neil anew. "That makes sense."

"It would be really cool if I could find a wolf cub to raise," Wes mused.

"Not in my house," Beth said firmly.

"I knew you'd say that." Wes's expression brightened. "I bet Conner's just gone off hunting and forgotten the day."

"You're probably right, and he'll get all pissy because I came to check up on him." Beth sighed. "But I wouldn't feel right if I didn't go, so he'll have to make the best of it."

She found her backpack, filled it with some basic supplies, and took her warmest coat out of the back of the closet. It was hot in the valley during the day, but at night the cabins at the higher altitude could turn cold.

By the time she returned to the kitchen, Wes had made her a fresh batch of coffee for her travel mug.

"You sure you'll be okay?" Beth asked as she headed for the back door.

"Duh, I'm almost twenty." Wes rolled his eyes. "I'll be fine."

"The cell reception up there can be spotty, so if there's a problem, I'll use the radio to call Nate Turner and he can let you know what's going on."

"Great, that's all we need—the local sheriff turning up in the middle of our wild party." Wes sighed.

Beth went to speak, and he winked at her. "No need to get salty, I was just kidding." He held the door open for her and planted a kiss on the top of her head. "And don't worry about Mike. I'll keep an eye on him, too."

She drove up to the ranch and tried not to think too much about Mikey's choices. Technically, he was an adult now, and she couldn't stop him from forming a relationship with his father, but even the thought of it stressed her out. Sean could be charming as hell as long as he held all the power, but God help you if you disagreed with him. She still had the scars to prove it.

She parked her car in the shelter of the barn and went into the house to pick up a set of keys for Juan's truck. She paused in the immaculate kitchen. Should she let the Garcias know what was going on with Conner, or leave them to enjoy their trip to Las Vegas in peace? Juan hadn't been away from the ranch for five years and had been really looking forward to watching the rodeo. Even as she pictured Juan's excited face, she already knew she wasn't going to bother him.

A scrabbling sound at the back door made her spin around and clutch the keys to her chest.

"Who is it?" she squeaked like some kind of too-stupid-to-live actress in a horror flick.

A low whining sound reached her straining ears. She

rushed toward the door and opened it, only to be bowled over by a huge gray and white wolf.

Even as she shrieked, the wolf licked her face and she recognized Conner's dog. Her trembling fingers found his collar and eased him off her chest.

"Hi, Loki, what's up with your master? Have you come to get help?" she whispered as she crouched beside him and stroked his head. "Or maybe I should start calling you Lassie?"

Chapter Two

Where the hell was the rest of his team? Conner O'Neil peered through the thick, choking smoke and tried to make out anything that looked like a person. Even as he started to retreat, the oil refinery blew up, sending him up into the air like he weighed nothing and slamming him against the cliff wall. His whole body shuddered as the screams of his fellow soldiers reverberated in his ears and he desperately tried to work out which way was up again.

"Mr. O'Neil?"

He jerked upright, his heart pounding so hard it was about to crawl out of his chest, and stared blankly around. The sound of his panicked breathing smothered everything until he forced himself to control it. He wasn't in Afghanistan, he wasn't in danger, and he wasn't at war.

He focused his wavering gaze on the cabin door and the constant knocking sound. Did he have the energy to get out of bed, walk over to the door, and tell whoever it was to have some respect and shut the hell up? He decided he did and swung his legs over the side of the bed.

Even as he struggled to right himself, the door flew open and Beth Baker came charging in.

"Are you okay?" She rushed toward him.

He put out a hand with the intention to ward her off, but she grabbed hold of it instead.

"Oh my God, you're burning up! How long have you been sick?"

She gently pushed him back down on the bed, which was fine by him as he was about to fall at her feet anyway. He retained just enough energy to glare at her.

"What are you doing here?"

She pulled up the only chair and sat beside him. "You didn't pick up your supplies. Maureen was worried about you."

"So what?"

"As you're on my employer's ranch right now, I decided to come and see how you were doing." She placed a hand on his forehead and frowned. "You've definitely got a fever."

"It's goddam hot in here."

She fixed him with a penetrating stare. "There's no need to curse, okay? I get it."

"Then why don't you turn that pretty little ass of yours right around and go the hell away?"

She blinked hard and stood up. For a second he couldn't decide whether to be elated that she was going, or ashamed of his behavior. He closed his eyes, aware that his strength was disappearing, and contemplated what he'd do if she really did walk out. Loki needed food and water. Maybe if he asked her nicely, she'd take his dog back to the ranch with her when she left.

Even as Conner made plans, he was aware of something being off. Where *was* Loki? He cracked open an eye and looked around the cabin. The door was open, and sunlight was streaming through, but there was no sign of his dog.

He tried to remember when he'd last seen Loki. Had it been last night when he'd managed to stumble over to the door and let him out?

He jumped as Beth came back into the cabin carrying a large box and set it on the kitchen countertop.

"Hey." He forced himself to sound reasonable. "Have you seen my dog?"

"Yes, he's in my truck."

"You'll take him back with you? Great. Thanks." He let out a shuddering sigh. "I was just going to ask you—"

She walked over and looked down at him, her usual smile absent, her gray eyes filled with concern despite his behavior. "Actually, Loki came to find me at the ranch."

"*What*?" Conner croaked.

"He's obviously a lot smarter than his owner because he knew to ask for help. I'll go let him out of the truck."

Before he could even think of a way to reply, she turned on her heel and marched away from him. He lay still, listening intently, until Loki bounded into the cabin and leapt up on the bed right onto his chest, making his breath whoosh out.

He wrapped his arm around the dog's massive neck and hugged him hard.

"What were you thinking, bothering our neighbor for nothing, buddy?"

As Loki licked his face, Conner thought he heard Beth mutter something about fools, but he couldn't be sure. Eventually, Loki settled down beside him and Conner was forced to turn his attention back to his unwelcome visitor. She was now in his kitchen putting the supplies away. While she wasn't looking, he had time to appreciate the way she filled out her jeans, the indent of her waist, and the lush curve of her breasts. Not that he hadn't noticed them before, but seeing her here in his personal space somehow made it way more intimate

"Would you like something to drink?" she asked without turning around.

Conner glanced over at his bedside table where his empty water glass stood, and swallowed hard.

"Yeah, that would be great."

She brought over a clean glass filled with water, and a mug of coffee, which made his mouth water. How long was it since he'd been upright enough to make his favorite beverage? He went to sit up and she placed a hand on his chest.

"Before you drink anything, stick this in your mouth." She slipped a thermometer under his tongue. "I need to know if you can stay here, or if I need to take you down to Morgantown to see Dr. Tio."

He went to speak, and she gave him such a look that he clamped his lips together and endured the endless minutes until the thermometer beeped and she deftly removed it.

Her eyebrows shot up. "One hundred and two. That's high."

"I'm fine. I always run hot."

"Why do men do this?" She rolled her eyes. "You either act like every sniffle is the man flu or pretend you're fine when you're dying."

"I'm not dying," Conner insisted. "It's just a temporary thing."

"So temporary that you haven't managed to get down to town to pick up your supplies for two weeks?"

"Eight days. Maureen shouldn't have bothered you." Conner wasn't giving in. "If you just leave me here with the supplies, I'll do great."

"Why did you end up with a fever in the first place?"

Beth continued talking as though he hadn't objected to anything, her gaze moving over his body. "Is it the flu?"

He set his jaw. "I might have got an infection when I was out hunting. I tripped over some barbed wire and it ripped through the leg of my pants. I cleaned it up when I got back, but I guess it might have gotten worse."

"You guess."

He glared at her. "Will you stop treating me like I'm five?"

"Maybe if you stop acting like it, I will." This time she didn't even attempt to hide her annoyance. "Let me take a look."

He grabbed hold of the covers like a spinster aunt and held them to his chest as she sighed.

"Conner . . ."

Beth shook her head at her reluctant patient, who was currently acting all outraged because she'd dared to ask to look at his leg.

"*Seriously*?" Beth asked.

"Look, just let me get washed up before you start on me, okay?" Conner's voice was hoarse. "I stink like the devil's armpit."

Beth wrinkled her nose. "I currently live in a house with two teens. I don't smell anything new." She rose from her chair. "Let me get my medical kit."

"But—"

Man, he was as argumentative as Wes on a bad day. Beth went back into the tiny kitchen, poured what remained of the boiled water into a bowl, added soap and a towel, and brought it back to Conner.

"I'll help you get comfortable first, okay?"

He opened his mouth, probably to disagree with her, and she held up one finger.

"Just stop and admit that you need help, dude. I promise I won't tell anyone in the big manly man club." She set the bowl down, dropped the washcloth in it and wrung it out. "I won't hurt you. I do this for a living."

He slowly shoved the rumpled covers down to reveal himself. Apart from his sweaty T-shirt he wore black boxers and nothing else. She persuaded him to take the T-shirt off.

"You wash men for a living?"

"Only if they ask nicely." She gently pressed the cloth against his neck and let the water trickle down over his lightly haired chest. "I originally trained as a physical therapist, so I know my way around a human body."

His faint sigh as she soaped his chest made her want to smile, but she quickly repressed it. She felt like she was taming a wild animal and she definitely didn't want to scare him off.

She rinsed out the cloth and went for his armpits, which were definitely ripe. He lay back against the pillows, his eyes half-closed as she continued her work. She might be used to dealing with bodies, but she rarely saw such a ripped and splendid specimen of manhood. If she had any criticism it was that he was almost too thin and could do with a few hearty meals inside him.

She also noted the scars and nicks his previous career had left on his flesh. If he had served with the Navy SEALS alongside Jay Williams, he was one tough nut. The fact that even when he was exhausted and unable to get out of bed he couldn't completely relax his guard, told her all she needed to know. She wondered what he looked like under his black beard and whether he ever smiled.

His hand closed over hers and, startled, she looked up at him. He had vivid blue eyes just like his dog.

"I can take it from here, thanks."

She glanced down at her fingers, which were perilously close to the bulge in his boxers.

"Sure." She eased her hand free, aware that she was blushing. "Let me fetch my medical kit and then I'll get you something to eat."

She helped him sit up against his pillows and set the bowl of water and towel on the bed where he could easily reach them.

"Do you have any fresh clothes?" she asked.

"In the top drawer."

"Then I'll get some out for you." She glanced at the rumpled bed. "I know there are clean sheets in the closet because I brought them last time I was here. We'll have you feeling much better in no time."

He didn't respond to her smile. They might be pretty, but he had the coldest blue eyes she had ever seen. She repressed a memory of her ex in a blind rage when it had been like staring into the black pits of hell. During her work at the women's shelter she'd learned that the quiet ones were often the most violent. With Conner's elite military background, she would need to be extra vigilant. She reminded herself to stop obsessing. In his current state she'd easily be able to outrun him.

After locating the clean sheets, she turned her attention to his clothing. He had four T-shirts, two black and two green, and four pairs of black boxers. In the closet he had a camo hunting jacket and pants, a fleece, two pairs of jeans, and two plaid shirts. Seeing as he'd rented the cabin for three months, she could only admire his economic packing skills.

When she returned to the bed, he had his eyes closed and his head was back against the pillows. His skin was covered in a fine sweat and he was shivering.

"Okay, what do you want to do first?" she asked briskly. "Shall I take a look at your leg, or do you want to change the sheets?"

"I don't want to do either of those things," Conner murmured. "I just want you to go away and leave me alone."

"For goodness' sake. Don't be such a baby." She put her hands on her hips. "You're on ranch property. If you die up here, I'm going to be the one explaining your corpse to Nate Turner!"

His eyes snapped open and he turned his head to look at her. "Who's that?"

"The deputy sheriff." She held his gaze. "And your family would probably sue us for negligence or something, so it's just not going to happen."

"I don't have any family."

"Which makes it even worse because you'd probably expect me to dig your damn grave for you."

He stared at her for a long moment and then the side of his mouth kicked up. "Who's cursing now? You look quite sweet, but you're tough, aren't you?"

"As I mentioned earlier, I have two teenage boys living in my house right now. It's like pushing a huge boulder up a steep hill every single darn day." She pointed at his leg. "Now, let me take a look at this."

He sighed. "Okay, fine."

"Thank you." She glared at him, unwilling to be gracious even in victory, and pulled on a pair of gloves from her medical kit. "Let me know if I hurt you."

She placed a towel under his leg and took her time peeling away the bandage he'd wrapped around his calf. There were four or five ragged puncture wounds and all of them were red and inflamed.

"Ugh." Beth said.

"Yeah. I was taking care of the wounds, but the last couple of days I've been sleeping a lot and I didn't get to it."

She wanted to ask him why he hadn't called for help, but now wasn't the time. From what she could see, the infection hadn't progressed too far, and he was a good healer. Although his leg was pouring out heat there were no ominous streaks stretching away from the wounds.

"Can you wiggle your toes?" she asked.

He obliged and she felt her way down to his foot, checking the temperature as she went. His circulation appeared to be holding up well. She carefully cleaned out each ragged cut, making him curse quietly under his breath, applied a lavish dose of antibiotic cream, and wrapped a light layer of gauze around his leg.

"That looks a lot better already." She stripped off her gloves and studied him carefully. She knew she must have hurt him, but he had hardly moved an inch. "Would you like me to help you sit in the chair while I change the bed?"

"Can you give me a minute?"

He looked absolutely terrible, his teeth set in his lower lip and his hands clenched into fists. Maybe the strain of pretending nothing was wrong had finally gotten to him. Aware that her sympathy would be unwelcome, Beth resorted to briskness.

"Sure." She picked up the bowl of bloodied water. "I need to clean up anyway."

She also needed to check in with Dr. Tio and Nate, but she'd do that when she was outside the cabin. There was no need for Conner to hear her airing her concerns. Knowing him, he'd insist there was nothing wrong with him and that she should wave him a cheery goodbye and leave.

She threw the water away, rinsed out the bowl, disposed of her gloves, and checked the bars on her cell phone, which were nonexistent. It was already late in the afternoon and the sun was throwing out enough heat to make the air shimmer and crackle over the barren golden hills like a living thing. The radio she'd brought with her was working and she checked in with Nate Turner, who patched her through to the doctor.

"So, should I bring him into town or not?" Beth asked after explaining what had happened to Conner and detailing his symptoms. "To be honest, he looks like he's over the worst of it, but I'm not a medical expert."

"If you're okay to stay with him, I'd leave him where he is overnight," Dr. Tio said. "And see how he is in the morning. You've got pain medication with you?"

"Yes, I've got my full medical kit."

"Then make sure he takes anti-inflammatory pain pills, acetaminophen for the fever, and get lots of fluids inside him. You know the drill. If he suddenly gets worse, call my emergency service and we can airlift him out to Bridgeport."

"Okay, got it, but I think he's healing up nicely." Beth turned away from the glare of the sun and looked at the cabin, which was still in the shadows. "Can you put Nate back on the line?"

"I'm still here," Nate said. "What's up?"

"I need to let the boys know I'll be staying at the cabin tonight."

"Not a problem, Beth. I'll pop around and tell them."

"Or you can call Ted," Beth suggested. "I don't want them getting the wrong idea."

The last time the police had come to Wes's front door had been in response to his frantic 911 call about his parents. Beth didn't want him worrying unnecessarily about her or freaking out if Nate suddenly appeared on the doorstep.

"I'll see if Ted's around."

"Thank you," Beth said gratefully. "If Conner is feeling well enough to travel tomorrow, should I bring him to see you, Dr. Tio?"

The doctor chuckled. "Good luck getting that man to come anywhere near me, but if you can persuade him to come in, I'd definitely like to check him over."

"What if he won't come with me?" Beth asked.

"Then you just leave him there and go home. Dr. Tio and I will keep an eye on him," Nate said firmly. "You've already gone over and above."

"Okay." Beth eyed the cabin and considered its obstinate occupant. "I'll do my best."

She ended the conversation and walked slowly back down the slope, enjoying the hint of a breeze rustling through the dried-up grass. If she wanted something to do to keep her away from Conner's grumpiness, she could always wash the sheets. It was so hot they'd probably be dry by morning.

She reentered the cabin and stopped dead. He'd somehow managed to get himself into the chair, dressed himself, and was looking right at her. She fixed a bright smile on her face.

"Good, you're up!"

"I couldn't manage to get the sheets off," he said gruffly.

"That's fine." She dealt with them and eyed the mattress. "If you're okay sitting up for a bit, I'll let the bed air out before I put the new sheets on."

"Is it that bad?" He grimaced. "I lost my sense of smell a long time ago, which is probably why I didn't notice my leg wasn't doing too well."

Beth went into the kitchen and set the radio down on the wooden countertop. Was that the first time he'd actually admitted he might have been at fault for not asking for help earlier? Maybe he was thawing toward her a little.

"When did you lose your sense of smell?" she asked.

His expression closed in again. "Some kind of explosion."

Yikes, so much for him easing up. Beth turned her back and opened the newly stocked cupboard. "What would you like to eat?"

"I'm not hungry."

Her shoulders dropped. He was sounding more and more like Mikey every second. If he wanted to be salty, she'd treat him like a sulky teenager and tell it to him straight.

"It's too hot for soup, so you can either have eggs, or some kind of sandwich. Which would you prefer?"

While she waited for him to get over himself, she checked out the small refrigerator and made some more coffee, her indignation rising. If he couldn't be bothered to reply, she'd make her own damn sandwich and leave him to get something for himself.

She grabbed a can of tuna and a jar of mayo and found the loaf of bread she'd brought with her from Maureen's. There was also fresh lettuce and tomatoes from Victor's organic farm. She hummed as if she didn't have a care in the world as she constructed her sandwich. If he didn't want to talk to her, so be it. She was done rushing around trying to make the men in her life comfortable.

Eventually, he cleared his throat.

"I'm not trying to be rude, here, Beth, but shouldn't you be getting back? It'll be dark before you know it."

She sat at the small table with her plate and mug. "I'm fine, thanks."

"I mean, I appreciate you coming out here, but—"

"No, you don't." She raised her head and looked him right in the eye. "You couldn't have made that any clearer if you'd tried."

He shoved a hand through his hair. "Look, I'm not at my best right now, and I probably could've been nicer, okay?"

Beth snorted and returned her attention to her sandwich and her cell phone. "Let me know when you're ready to eat and I'll make you something."

"I'm *not*—" He inhaled slowly and shook his head. "I'll make my own sandwich when you're gone."

"Oh, I'm not going anywhere." Beth offered him her sunniest smile.

"What the hell is that supposed to mean?" Conner growled.

"I've already spoken to Dr. Tio. He said to keep an eye on you overnight and to check in with him tomorrow morning."

He stared at her like she'd grown another head and slowly rose to his feet. She set her mug down and warily watched his stumbling approach.

He placed both palms flat on the table and leaned toward her, rocking slightly.

"You are not staying here."

"Yes, I am."

His expression narrowed and she rose to her feet, suddenly aware of how tall he was, and automatically calculated his reach.

"Go home, Beth."

She raised her chin. "I am not a dog."

His right hand fisted and he hit the table hard. "And I do not need a goddamn babysitter!"

Even as his words reverberated off the rafters, Beth was already ducking, her arm held up to protect her face as she stumbled backward.

CHAPTER THREE

Conner blinked hard and tried to straighten up, as Beth recoiled as though he was going to hit her. She ended up on the other side of the kitchen, her intention to run as clear as the flash of fear in her gray eyes. He took a moment to get his breath before he made himself look right at her. He went to speak but she cut across him.

"Sorry about that."

"You're apologizing to *me*? I'm the one who frightened you!"

"Who says I was frightened?" She shrugged unconvincingly. "Maybe I just don't like being shouted at when I'm trying to help you."

Conner considered his options. Whatever she was saying, he'd seen her fear, but if she didn't want to talk about it, he wasn't going to push her. It wasn't as if they were friends or anything. Even as he made his decision, his stupid brain was still asking a million questions. Who had put that look in her eyes and what kind of person hit a woman like Beth Baker?

Aware he was near the end of his strength, he pulled out the second chair and sat down on it.

"If you pass the sandwich fixings over, I can make myself some lunch."

"No worries, I'll get it for you."

He wanted to argue, but after his last attempt to dictate to her he was too wary to try it.

"Thanks."

He sat in silence watching her move competently around the kitchen, her calm good humor restored, and began to wonder whether he'd imagined what had just happened. But no, he knew what terror looked like—had seen it in his own reflection more than once after a nightmare— and he couldn't forget.

She put a plate in front of him with two halves of a sandwich on it and his stomach growled.

"Take it slowly, okay?" She placed a couple of pills on the table. "And take these after you've eaten. Dr. Tio's orders."

He studied the pills suspiciously "What are they?"

"Just over-the-counter anti-inflammatories, nothing special."

"What else did Dr. Tio say?"

"That he'd love you to drop in and see him at some point, but that he wasn't holding his breath."

Conner started on the first sandwich and devoured it in three bites. "He's a good guy for a medic. He doesn't get bent out of shape when you don't follow his every word."

"That's because he's used to dealing with stubborn cowboys and ranchers who only come and see him when they're practically dying."

She set a glass of water beside the mug. He noticed she wasn't retaking her seat and wondered whether she didn't want to get close to him again. He gestured at her unfinished food.

"You should eat. I'm good for a while."

She chuckled. "Seeing the speed that you ate that first sandwich, I suspect you're going to need another one. It feels just like home. I'll bring it over."

"Thanks."

She delivered his second sandwich and sat opposite him, her chair pushed slightly away from the table and angled toward the open door.

"You don't have to stay here," Conner said quietly. "I'm doing good. I've got Loki for company, and I'm sure you have better things to do than look after a miserable jerk like me."

"Dr. Tio said it would be better if I stayed to keep an eye on you overnight. If you're fine in the morning, I'll leave as soon as I can, okay?"

"But what about your kids?"

"They're old enough to take care of themselves, and a night without their mom nagging them to clean up, get out of bed, and stop gaming will be a treat for them. My brother and his girlfriend live right next door, and my dad has an apartment over the workshop, so I think they're okay." She sighed. "Sometimes I need a break from all that testosterone."

"You're a single parent?"

"Yes. I'm raising my son, Mikey, and my stepson, Wes."

"Wes . . ." Conner took a long drink of water. "I think I met him in town. He works with Kaiden Miller."

"You did. He loves to chat to everyone. He really liked Loki." She looked over at the hearth where the huge dog was sleeping. "Of course, I had to talk him out of trying to find a wolf cub of his own."

"I found Loki when I was in Alaska working on a fishing boat." Conner tried to remember the last time he'd held an actual conversation with someone and came up blank. For some reason, talking to Beth came easily. "He'd been left in an alley behind the hotel. I brought him back with me and we've been together ever since."

Sometimes he thought finding Loki had saved his sanity. Taking care of his dog had finally given him a purpose and a reason to keep getting up in the morning.

"You're a fisherman?" Beth asked.

"I drift around and take seasonal jobs." He shrugged. "I like to try new things."

"How long since you were in the military?"

Even as he tensed, he was also aware of her instant response to a potential threat by the way she eased fractionally away from him. She reminded him of his SEAL team or a boxer bouncing on the balls of his feet, ready to defend himself. He deliberately sat back and tried to look relaxed.

"I retired five years ago." He grimaced. "It's been hard to find my place in the world. I don't have a family; I don't have a base, and most of my military friends are scattered all over the country."

"That's tough."

The sympathy in her voice made him feel uncomfortable. "It's fine. I'm not exactly what you'd call a people person anyway."

"Really?" She shook her head, making her braid bounce. "I would never have guessed that."

"Yeah, I'm real warm and cuddly."

She hid a smile as she sipped her coffee, and he couldn't look away from her mouth. He wanted to lean in and trace the curve of her lips to see if they were as soft as they looked, but he didn't want to invade her space again. That hadn't gone well.

"Don't forget to take your pills," Beth reminded him, drawing him out of his tangled thoughts, which was something of a relief.

He picked them up, put them in his mouth, and chased them down with the entire glass of water. A yawn shuddered through him and he instinctively covered his mouth.

"Not sure why I'm so tired all the time," he murmured, aware that she was studying him closely.

"Your body is busy fighting off an infection. That takes a lot of energy."

She rose from her seat, gathered up both plates and her mug, and took them through to the kitchen.

"Give me five minutes and I'll get those clean sheets on the bed and you can get back in."

He frowned as something occurred to him. "If you insist on staying, where are you going to sleep tonight?"

She pointed at the couch. "It's a pullout bed. I've got my sleeping bag in the truck. I'll sleep in that."

"It doesn't look very comfortable. Maybe you should take my bed."

She swung around to look at him, her eyebrows raised. "Dude, you're way too tall to sleep on there. I'll be fine. It's only for one night."

He went to argue and was caught in another huge yawn.

She went over to the bed and quickly dealt with the sheets. She threw the two pillows at him to put on the fresh covers, but he suspected it was only to make him feel like he was being useful. He turned in his seat to watch her work and meekly handed over the pillows when he'd finished with them.

"Thank you." She hesitated. "Do you need to go out and use the bathroom?"

He wanted to say no, but he wasn't that stupid. She probably wouldn't appreciate his alternate method of pissing in a bottle and dumping it down the sink.

She regarded him doubtfully, her teeth worrying her lush lower lip in a way that drove him crazy. He'd obviously been alone for way too long this time because all he could think about was replacing her teeth with his own. "Or I can get you some kind of receptacle if you don't think you can make it that far."

"I'll make it." To prove his point, he stood and braced one hand on the countertop. He'd dug himself and two team members out of the ruin of an exploded oil refinery, he could get to the damn bathroom.

Conner set his jaw, and Beth knew that however bad he was feeling he would get himself there and back with her help. She'd been trained to support bodies and knew the best way to get him moving and keep him moving, but he was a big guy. She was tall for a woman, but he topped her by at least four inches. She thrust from her mind the uncomfortable thought of being that close to him and not being able to get away.

She reminded herself that not all men were like her ex and that even if Conner turned violent, she was strong enough to deal with him. Despite his military background she instinctively felt safe with him, which made no sense. She had her own truck, she could move faster than he could, and as long as she remained aware of her surroundings and didn't let him trap her in a corner, she'd be fine.

The very basic bathroom facilities backed onto the cabin and were accessed from the outside. There were plans in the works to remodel the cabins and make them more user-friendly, but nothing would happen until Conner moved out. Luckily, the overhang from the roof protected guests from the rain, but that was about as good as it got.

Even before they made it through the door, Beth realized they had a balance problem.

"Stay there."

She propped Conner up against the doorframe and ran to her truck to retrieve the walking stick Juan had left in the passenger seat. She offered it to her patient, who looked affronted.

"I don't need that."

"Yes, you do. Use it to balance your weight on the other side," Beth advised. "Otherwise, if you go over, you'll probably take me with you and then I'll never be able to leave in the morning because I'll be very flat and two dimensional."

He grunted, but did as she suggested, making her job way easier.

"Awesome." She eased him along the path, his arm slung over her shoulder. "Almost there."

"Great," he muttered. "And don't even think about coming in with me."

"Like I'd dare." She offered him a sweet smile as she pushed open the door. "Holler if you need help, okay?"

"I won't."

He shut the door firmly in her face and she turned back to the cabin, grinning. Knowing that men loved to spend hours in the bathroom, she left him alone and went to set the cabin to rights. The sun was beginning its descent now and the shadows were lengthening. It was still hot, which was unusual for this end of the valley. She certainly wouldn't need her warm coat. Beth considered what a night without air conditioning would be like. It wasn't as if she could strip off her clothes and sleep naked like she did at home.

She glanced down at her boobs. Not that Conner would care. She could probably run around the place nude and all he'd do was stare at her like she was nuts. She hadn't been naked with anyone for years. Trusting someone to see her in such a vulnerable state hadn't happened with any of the men she'd cautiously dated over the past five years.

But Conner O'Neil was different. For some strange reason she was attracted to him, and there was nothing she could do about it. With a sigh, she gathered the dirty sheets, pulled out the old washtub and soap, and dragged everything outside. She was too tired to wash the sheets now, but she could at least let them soak overnight and deal with them in the morning.

There was dinner to fix, Conner's injuries to check, and a whole evening ahead trying to make conversation with a man who gave her lustful thoughts and who wished she'd just go away and leave him in peace.

Conner had considered shaving off his beard while he was in the bathroom, but he hadn't had the energy. Despite insisting to Beth that he was one hundred percent fit, he knew he wasn't. He also knew he should be grateful to her for showing up and taking care of him, but after the way he'd behaved he doubted she'd believe him even if he told her.

"Is the chicken okay?" Beth asked.

He looked across the table at her. "It's great, thanks."

She smiled and he was struck yet again by the openness

and strength of her expression. She wasn't beautiful by any standards, but he'd never seen a more interesting and mobile face. He kept wanting to touch her, to reassure himself that someone as vibrant as Beth could exist in his cold and lonely world. But why would she be interested in a man like him? She deserved so much better.

"It's my son Mikey's favorite." Her smile dimmed slightly. "Or it used to be. Ever since he came back from college, he's been making his own meals, taking them up to his room and shutting the door."

"And you let him get away with that?"

"I suppose I do." She studied her plate. "I guess I'm afraid of confronting him right now."

Conner slowly put down his fork. "You're afraid of your own son?"

"No, of course not, it's just . . ." She hesitated. "It's hard to explain."

"Try me." Conner wasn't letting it go. The vibe he was getting off her was all wrong.

"It's stupid."

"If he's making you feel afraid in your own home, that's not cool."

"He's not." She finally raised her gaze to his face. "I don't want you getting the wrong idea, here."

"Then tell me the truth."

She took a sip from her water glass. "Why have you suddenly decided to become all chatty right now?"

He picked up his fork and ate more of the creamy chicken and mashed potato. He felt better than he had in days, and if he could somehow help the woman who'd stepped up for him, he'd do it.

"Do you need me to come and talk to your son?"

"What's that got to do with anything?" She frowned.

"My brother and my father live right next door. Mikey's got plenty of good male role models in his life already."

"Maybe he needs to hear from someone who's not so nice," Conner said.

"Like you?"

He shrugged. "Sometimes boys need to hear things differently for them to get through."

"So, you'd what . . . beat the shit out of him because he's disrespecting his mother's cooking?" She wasn't smiling now. "Like I need another man offering him violence. Why do you think I left his father in the first place?"

"Ah, right. Got it." After a stunned moment Conner nodded like the fool he was. "It still doesn't explain why you won't confront him."

She stared at him for so long that he almost forgot how to breathe.

"Mikey looks like his dad."

"And?"

"He hardly talks to me and I'm reluctant to ask him what's wrong."

"Because you're scared he's going to react to confrontation like his father did." Conner made it a statement rather than a question. "If it's any consolation, I look just like my dad and he never believed in sparing the rod. I promised myself I would never, ever be like him."

She nodded but didn't speak, her gray gaze fixed on his face.

"Have you asked Mikey how he feels about looking like his dad?"

"Of course I haven't. What do you think I could say? Like, hey, Mikey, you look just like Sean, how violent are you feeling today?" Beth snorted. "He's a teenager. I can't even ask him what kind of cheese he wants in his sandwich without worrying how he's going to answer me right now."

Conner finished his glass of water. "Maybe you guys need some kind of therapy or something, because this doesn't sound healthy."

"You think?" She glared at him. "We've been to therapy."

"Then you should keep going." Conner wasn't backing down. "It did me the world of good."

"So good that you drift around the country taking seasonal jobs and hide up here in a cabin all summer?"

"Wow." He opened his eyes wide at her. "Did I hit a nerve or something?"

"I think I liked you more when you didn't talk," she muttered. "Would you like some more chicken?"

"I'm good, thanks."

Aware that he'd pushed way too many of her buttons for one evening, Conner offered to help clear up. She waved him away like the nuisance he was and banged around in the kitchen for a while, which he hoped helped her release some of her feelings. Eventually, he got into bed and sat back against the stack of pillows that now smelled like a spring meadow rather than him.

So, Beth's ex-husband was the jerk who'd hurt her.

Conner's hands flexed into fists as he fondly imagined meeting the asshole in a dark alley somewhere and making him beg for mercy. Yeah, he knew violence wasn't the answer, but sometimes it was the only way to get your point across. He wasn't naïve. He knew how to kill in a thousand different ways and had the nightmares to prove it.

"Would you like another drink?" Beth called out to him from the kitchen.

"Not unless you want me waking you up to go to the bathroom at the ass crack of dawn."

"As to that." She brought over a large glass jar. "This should work if you really get caught short."

"Thanks." He placed it under the bed. She didn't need to know that it was the very jar that he'd been using for the last few days. "That's a great idea."

"Lucky you, having the plumbing to use it." She wiped down the countertops. "I guess I'll still need to fight my way through the spiders."

Jeez, he almost smiled at her, his relief that she'd gotten over his intrusive comments far greater than he'd antici-pated.

She took his temperature and then brought him over a large glass of water and some more pills. "Take these, and hopefully you'll have a peaceful night and feel much better in the morning."

He made himself look her in the eye. "Thanks for help-ing me out. I really mean it."

She shrugged. "You're welcome."

"Are you sure you don't want to take the bed?" he of-fered again.

"Nah, I'm good." She pointed at her sleeping bag, which she'd left on the back of the couch. "I'll just fold out the bed and I'll be fine."

CHAPTER FOUR

Beth lay in the darkness and listened to the even sound of Conner's breathing. His temperature had gone down and he was no longer sweating and shaking, which had to be good. She'd checked his leg just before turning out the lights and everything looked a lot less angry.

She turned carefully onto her side, aware that the sofa bed creaked, and studied Conner's outline in the moonlight. She still couldn't get over how he'd suddenly decided to weigh in about how she should manage her own son. The fact that he had made some good points didn't help. She knew she was avoiding talking to Mikey about a lot of important things and that they needed to go back into family therapy.

She'd hoped that Mikey being away from home and forging his own life would've changed things for the better. Sean deciding to write to Mikey and ask for his forgiveness hadn't been on her radar, but it should have been. Her ex never gave up on an opportunity to pursue his vendettas, and never forgot a slight. If you weren't one hundred percent on team Sean, you were the enemy and were offered no mercy.

Beth sighed and cautiously unzipped the sleeping bag. She was way too hot. Even though she'd left the windows open and Loki was outside guarding the door, she still felt vulnerable. Talking about Sean brought back all the bad memories. The fear that he'd suddenly turn up and upend her life again never quite went away. And now that she knew what he was capable of, that dread had only intensified. She determinedly closed her eyes and told herself to go to sleep.

A slight noise alerted her to the window, and she froze in place as a shadowy face pressed itself against the glass. She knew who it was and went to scream but could make no sound. She tried to sit up, but it was as if her limbs were made of jelly.

"Beth."

He spoke her name and she whimpered, trying to turn her head away from the hot breath on her cheek.

"Beth, honey, you're having a bad dream. You need to wake up now, okay?"

As if she'd suddenly been released from a vise, Beth sat up and threw herself against Conner. His arms closed around her and he rocked her back and forth.

"It's okay, it's okay."

She pressed her ear against his chest and concentrated on the steady sound of his heartbeat, counting each strong beat as she struggled to control her breathing and bring her world back under control.

He slid one hand into her hair and stroked her with the other, his strong, low voice murmuring nothings as she shook and cried.

Eventually, she eased away from him, shoved a handful of hair behind her ear and addressed herself to his bearded chin.

"God, I'm so sorry. I'm the one who's supposed to be looking after you!" She tried to laugh, aware that she was basically sitting in his lap. "I don't usually behave like this."

"As I said, it's no big deal."

He still had his arm around her, and she didn't want him to let go. She only realized she was hanging on to his shoulder when he tried to straighten up and she clung onto him like a limpet.

"I'm sorry," Beth repeated helplessly. "I don't know what's wrong with me."

He hesitated. "How about you come and lie down in my bed? We can talk, or maybe you'll just sleep better?"

She wanted to say no, to assure him that she was fine, but she just couldn't do it.

"I'd like that—if you're okay with it, I mean."

"I wouldn't have offered if I wasn't." Conner took hold of her hand and maneuvered himself back across to the bed. "I'm no stranger to nightmares myself."

"I bet." God, her voice was still shaking. What must he think of her? "I can't even imagine . . ."

"Best if you don't try." He held back the covers, the note of steel back in his voice. "You okay on the inside so you're not close to my bad leg?"

Beth crawled past him and lay back against the pillows until he climbed in beside her and slid his arm around her shoulders.

"You good like this?"

"Yes." Beth turned on her side and curled against him, her hand coming to rest on his chest. She had her panties and T-shirt on, so she was decent.

He murmured something and went quiet, allowing her

the time and the space to regain her composure. She wished she could go back to sleep.

"Every time I closed my eyes, I saw him at the window again," Beth whispered.

"Your ex?"

She nodded.

"You know that even if he was here, I wouldn't let him hurt you again."

"That's not your job. I can take care of myself," Beth stated.

A low chuckle reverberated through his chest, surprising her.

"I'm sure you can, but I'd be more than willing to help out, and why not use all the resources on hand?" He paused. "It's a lot harder to kill someone than you realize."

"I know." Beth shivered. "There was one time when Sean came home drunk and tripped up on the kitchen rug when he lunged at me. He went down like a stone. I stood over him for what felt like an eternity with my cast-iron pan shaking in my hands, but I couldn't do it."

"Because you're a good and decent person."

She frowned up at him. "So are you."

"No, I'm not." She went to speak but he kept on talking. "It's okay, Beth. The way I look at it is that some of us have to be prepared to take on the dirty work to keep everyone else safe." He shrugged. "It was also a way to channel my natural aggression and learn how to control it rather than let it control me."

She rubbed her palm over his biceps. "It still left its mark on you."

"Yeah, but I can deal with it."

Beth had her own thoughts on that, but now wasn't the time to get into it, when he was being so kind.

"Sean's unlikely to turn up here, so I'm not sure why I dreamt he could."

"The human brain is weird like that," Conner murmured, his eyes slowly closing. "I know I won't get blown up again in a war zone, but it still keeps happening in my dreams." He sighed and drew her closer against his side. "I assume Sean's still alive then?"

"Yes. He's in San Quentin."

His fingers tightened on her skin. "Good riddance. I hope he never gets out."

"I'd kicked him out, so Sean was living with Wes and Wes's mom, Sharon. He came home drunk and took a swing at her. When she backed up to avoid him, she fell, hit her head on the marble fireplace and lost consciousness." Beth swallowed hard. "Wes hid in the closet and called 911, but by the time they got to the house, it was too late to save her life, but they did arrest Sean. I kept thinking it could've so easily been me and Mikey."

Conner didn't say anything, but he continued to hold her tight while Beth couldn't stop talking.

"Sean and I were divorced by then, but he kept coming to the house because he had visiting rights with Mikey. I was always afraid he'd get back at me for daring to divorce him. I got my brother Ted to come and hang out with us whenever Sean was expected."

"Ted's the mechanic in town, right?" Conner asked. "He's a big guy."

"Who wouldn't hurt a fly, but Sean didn't know that. When I found out what had happened to Wes's mom, Sharon, I was physically sick." Beth shuddered. "I took

Wes in as soon as the courts would let me, not that he wanted to be anywhere near me at that point. He hadn't known Mikey and I existed until Sean and I got divorced and Sean went to live with Sharon full-time."

"Wes seems to be doing okay."

"He is." Beth smiled for the first time in what felt like ages. Not having to look directly at Conner and the darkness around them was encouraging her to talk about things she normally kept locked deep inside her. "I'm so proud of him."

"He's lucky to have you," Conner said gruffly.

"I think it goes both ways. He and Mikey get on really well now, and they're company for each other when I'm working." She absently smoothed her fingers over Conner's furred chest. "Am I making you too hot, pressed up against you like this?"

He didn't speak for a moment and then he cleared his throat.

"You're definitely making me hot."

"Oh!" She went to move away from him. "Do you need more pain medication? I can get you some."

In reply he came up on one elbow and looked directly down at her.

"Beth, I'm not in pain." His smile was crooked. "And I'm hot because being close to a beautiful woman like you is making me hard and horny."

"Beautiful?" Beth stared at him.

"Yeah." He licked his lips. "Absolutely."

She reached out, cupped his bearded chin and stared into his pale blue eyes for what felt like forever.

"You're very sweet but obviously still feverish. I'm too

tall, too broad, and I have too many freckles to be beautiful. My dad always says I'm built like a Clydesdale."

"And?"

She sighed. "Okay, I'm not going to argue with you about something so silly."

"Good."

She realized she was rubbing her thumb along the hard line of his jaw.

"Have you ever wanted to do something really stupid?" Beth asked softly.

"Like take on hell week and become a Navy SEAL?"

"Yes." She took in a slow breath. "Or kiss a guy who is usually grumpy as hell, but thinks you're beautiful?"

He raised an eyebrow. "You know this is the adrenaline talking, right? Next comes the big crash, so don't do anything you'd regret."

"I don't care if I'm being stupid," Beth retorted. "I'm sick of always doing the right thing and being the good person."

"What if I don't think that's stupid at all?" Conner murmured, slid a hand around her neck and rolled onto his back, bringing Beth with him. "Kiss me as much as you like."

Beth righted herself, aware that she was now straddling his hips and that he was definitely horny.

"Before we get into anything, I just want to remind you that I'm not the kind of guy who sticks around," Conner said.

Beth snorted. "That's why you're so perfect. Like I could have a relationship with anyone with two teenage boys in the house, who would react like Victorian maiden aunts if they thought their mom was having sex."

"We're having sex now?"

Beth smiled down at Conner. "Maybe. Let's see how good you are at kissing first."

Conner gently drew Beth's head down toward his and touched his mouth to hers. She tasted of coffee and tooth-paste, which struck him as just about right.

"What about your leg?" Beth asked.

"It'll be fine," he reassured her. "It's feeling a lot better already." Mainly because all the heat and blood in his body was currently heading for his dick. He wasn't about to complain. If there were any consequences, he'd gladly deal with them in the morning.

She kissed him again and, deep inside him where the last remnants of the decent guy he'd once been resided, something stirred.

"You sure you're okay about this?" Conner forced him-self to ask.

"Yes." She frowned at him. "Do you know? I liked you a lot better when you weren't talking all the time."

Conner obediently shut up and let himself enjoy explor-ing her mouth as he slid his hands over her body. She felt amazing. He murmured his approval as she touched him, rocking his hips against the heat pressed against his groin.

"I'm going to take my T-shirt off," Beth said.

Conner lay back as she did just that and presented him with one of his most favorite views ever. She leaned back over him until her nipples touched his chest and he groaned.

"May I touch?" He knew she didn't want him talking, but he had to be sure they were both still on the same page.

"Please."

He cupped his hand and eased it around her breast, bringing her nipple to his mouth. All thoughts of being gentle and respectful went out of his head when she gasped and writhed against him. He settled his other hand on her hip, holding her down over his hardening dick and let her roll her hips.

"Wait!" She tore her mouth away and he tried to catch his breath.

"Having second thoughts?" He immediately took his hands off her body. "Adrenaline finally crashed? It's all good."

"No! I need to go and get a condom out of my medical kit." She grinned at him. "At least you know this wasn't premeditated."

As she crawled over him and off the bed, he decided it wouldn't be a good time to tell her that he'd been imagining having sex with her for weeks. From their first meeting when she'd ignored his grumpiness and radiated sanity and light, he'd been captivated by her. Of course, realizing that had made him behave even more badly every time they'd met up over the past few weeks, when she'd brought him new sheets or deep-cleaned the cabin.

"Got it." She waved a foil-wrapped packet at him. "I even checked the date, because if it was the one I usually carry in my purse it would definitely be suspect."

He couldn't believe she wasn't in a long-term relationship, because if he was the kind of guy who stuck around, he would be all over the opportunity.

"You don't date?" The question popped out before he thought it through.

"I do occasionally, but sex is another thing altogether."

He just looked at her and she sighed as she got back into bed.

"I know. This is a complete anomaly for me. If I stop

and overanalyze myself, I'll probably end up sleeping in my truck."

Conner moved swiftly to put an end to that kind of negative talk, drew her back into his arms, and kissed her soundly. She responded with an enthusiasm that quickly had him sliding his hand under her cotton panties to caress her rounded ass.

"Mmm . . ." she breathed into his mouth. "That's so nice."

"Can I persuade you out of those panties?" Conner asked. "Because—"

She was already wiggling out of them before he'd finished his sentence and was now completely naked in his arms.

With some effort, he raised his gaze to her face. "You still good?"

In answer she pointed down at his boxers. "Take them off."

"Yes, ma'am."

Conner totally forgot about his wounded leg as he rushed to comply. Not that he cared about any damage he might do. It was all relative and he was good at assessing risk. He cupped her between the legs, found she was already wet for him, and almost lost it like some teenage boy.

"You okay being on top?" he murmured as he touched her intimately.

"Like we could do this any other way right now." She rolled her eyes and straddled his hips again.

"Can you do one more thing for me?" Conner asked.

"Be careful of your leg?" She nodded. "I'll do my best. Are you sure you're okay doing this?"

Now it was his turn to roll his eyes as he opened the condom packet and covered himself.

"What I meant was, can you let your hair out of the braid?"

Beth considered him. "If you like getting hair in your mouth and stuck all over you, then sure."

He held his breath as she raised both arms and let down her hair. It was long enough to curl around her breasts.

"Beautiful."

She met his gaze, hers a little shy for the first time. "Thank you."

"Come here." He drew her over him. "I want you right now."

When Beth woke up, she was pressed up against Conner's right side, her hand on his chest and her knee riding his hip. She allowed herself a moment to just enjoy the sheer pleasure of being so close to another person. To her surprise she didn't feel an ounce of guilt. They'd both gone into their night together with the same desire and honesty, and she still felt the same. She doubted Conner would have changed his mind either. He was one of the most straightforward guys she'd ever met. Maybe that was why she'd been able to let her guard down with him. He wasn't a charmer or a liar. What you saw was what you got, and she craved that kind of honesty so badly.

His skin was a lot cooler than it had been the day before and he wasn't sweating. She angled her gaze down his body to his wounded leg and could detect no signs of further swelling or excessive seepage from the wounds. Would she be able to persuade him to come down to Morgantown and see Dr. Tio? He was as stubborn as all the other men in the valley, so it seemed unlikely, but she didn't want to leave him here alone.

Beth decided that was a battle to be faced later in the morning after she'd dealt with the more basic stuff, like getting to the bathroom. She contemplated her escape route. There was no way around it. If she wanted to get out of the bed, she'd have to climb over Conner. She eased the covers down, grabbed the first T-shirt she found and carefully knelt up.

"Running out on me?" Conner murmured as she climbed over him. He didn't even bother to open his eyes. "Was I that bad?"

"Way to make it all about you." Beth had known getting past a Navy SEAL would never happen and carried on moving. "I need to use the bathroom. I promise I'll be back."

He nodded but didn't move, so she grabbed her backpack and hurried outside. It was way colder than she'd anticipated and completely, stunningly quiet. Loki rose to greet her when she emerged on the steps and she stopped to pet him. The sun was just peeking over the heights of the Sierra Nevadas, throwing an ever-increasing circle of light over the shadowed valley. Beth paused to appreciate the sight. Living in the town meant she rarely had such a view of nature's amazing bounty.

She hurried into the bathroom and took a very quick shower in water that was barely tepid. She didn't attempt to wash her tangled hair. That would take time, expensive conditioner, and an hour of combing when she got home. Her body felt different, the roughness of Conner's beard evident on her skin, the slight bruise on her throat where he'd nipped her when he climaxed. Beth hadn't felt so gloriously female in years.

She went back into the cabin to find Conner was up

and ready to take her place in the bathroom. She smiled foolishly at him and offered her hand.

"Do you need help to get out there?"

"No, I think I'm good." He gestured down at his leg. "If you give me the medical kit, I can take care of this after I shower."

"Sure." She opened up the box, found the necessary supplies and handed them over. "I'll start breakfast while you're out there. Do you want me to feed Loki?"

He limped over to the door and turned to look at her.

"Thanks. His food's in the pantry, bottom shelf. Just fill up his bowl."

After she fed Loki, Beth put on a pot of coffee. Conner was back to his gruff self, but she didn't mind. It wasn't as if she'd been expecting him to change overnight. They were both responsible adults who knew what they'd been getting into and could still remain friends.

She checked the refrigerator and took out some of the eggs she'd brought with her the day before. If Conner had ordered them from Maureen's store, then he had to like them. She took a moment to wonder how Mikey and Wes were doing at home and reassured herself that if there had been any problems, Ted would've contacted her immediately. Just to make sure, she checked both her phone and the radio, but there were no messages or attempts to contact her.

When Conner came back and sat down heavily at the kitchen table, she offered him fresh coffee, half a cheese omelet, and some toast. She didn't point out that the trip to the bathroom had obviously exhausted him, and concentrated on small talk about the valley and Loki as he ate his way steadily through the food. After topping up his mug for the second time she finally asked a question.

"How was your leg?"

"Much better." He observed her over the rim of his raised coffee mug. "You can take a look if you don't believe me."

She shrugged. "You're neither five nor one of my kids, so if you say it's healing nicely, then I believe you." She paused. "Dr. Tio will still want to see you, though, just to make sure."

"And what if I don't want to see him?"

"Why wouldn't you?" She met his gaze. "He's a good guy."

"I don't like being . . . fussed over."

"I'd never have guessed that." Beth shook her head. "I know you like your hermit lifestyle up here, but what if you don't get yourself checked out, and you get sick again? Do I have to come up here every other day just to do a wellness check on you?"

His slow smile was a revelation. "That's supposed to make me want to leave?"

She mock-frowned. "If you make me have to come out here, I can guarantee you would not be getting any sex at all."

"Oh, I think I can make you come all right." His wicked grin took her breath away. He leaned forward and tucked a strand of her hair behind her ear. "Like you'd be able to resist me for long."

She grabbed hold of his wrist. "*Please* come and see Dr. Tio. I'll drive you down there and right back again today. You'll hardly miss any hunting."

"Like I can currently hunt anything." He eased free of her grasp. "You trying to guilt me into going?"

"No." She refused to look away. "I'm asking you as a friend."

He considered her for a long moment and then nodded once. "Okay."

She let out her breath. "Thank you."

Chapter Five

Conner didn't like other people driving him, but he was way too tired to do anything but buckle up and let Beth take him to town. She was a good driver, her gaze everywhere as they bumped down the uneven track toward the more regularly used ranch road. He still held on to the strap because it wasn't exactly a smooth ride.

He'd braced himself for Beth to get weird on him that morning. He'd found that even after he tried to be honest and upfront about his lack of availability, some women read way more into sex than he did. But Beth was her usual cheerful self, which didn't explain why he was now the one feeling disappointed. If he was honest, he'd enjoyed everything about her unexpected visit—her humor, her determination to do the right thing by him, and the way she'd thrown herself into having sex.

She was a bright light in his miserable existence, and just being with her made him want things he'd sworn off years ago.

"You okay?" She glanced briefly over at him. "We're only about fifteen minutes out from town now. I radioed ahead to let Dr. Tio know we were coming in."

"Great," Conner said. "Can't wait."

She chuckled as she turned the wheel to the right and the truck finally hit level ground. He noticed she'd tied her hair up in a messy ponytail rather than her usual braid. He imagined her combing it out as he watched, and then letting him slide his hands into it, and . . .

Jeez. He really needed to get away from her before he screwed things up. She didn't want a guy like him in her life, a man hardened to violence. Hadn't she suffered enough from her abusive ex?

"You can just drop me off in front of the doctor's office. I can call you if I need a ride back," Conner suggested.

"*If*? You planning on walking home or something? *So* not happening." She increased her speed as the road flattened out. "I promised Dr. Tio I would come in and give him my report."

After that, Conner shut up and just watched the scenery fly by. The summer heat had scoured most of the color out of the landscape, leaving it dirt brown, gold, and brittle-looking. He imagined the risk of fire was high and that getting water to the cattle grazing on the hillsides was a full-time job.

Morgantown was a thriving little place with an old-fashioned look to its downtown that harkened back to its roots as a gold rush town. The valley also had an abandoned silver mine and a ghost town called Morganville up on Morgan Ranch. Just before he'd injured his leg, Conner had accepted an invitation to a trail ride to those sites from BB Morgan, a retired marine who was good friends with Jay.

BB had also offered him a job as a trail guide, something Conner had done in the past and enjoyed. He tried to imagine his life if he settled in Morgan Valley and still couldn't get his head around it. He was a loner, a man who made few friends and who didn't need anyone. Even as he reminded himself of that, his gaze kept sliding back to Beth and how good it felt to get close to her.

But she didn't want a relationship. She'd made that very clear. She had teenagers to bring up and a secure loving family around her. Why wasn't he simply able to enjoy that fact and move on like he normally did?

After checking in with Dr. Tio, Beth spent a few minutes chatting with his office staff about potential clients for the physical therapy business she ran in tandem with her job up at the Garcia Ranch. It gave her some additional income and she enjoyed helping people recover their strength and physical abilities. Most of her clients tended to be older, which suited her just fine.

"Do you know Craig Cameron?" Meghan, one of Dr. Tio's admins asked.

"I know there's a Cameron Ranch right out near the boundary of the valley, but I don't know Craig personally, why?"

"He called yesterday looking for someone to work with his mother, Esther. She slipped and broke her arm last month and she needs some physio." Meghan lowered her voice. "He was super bossy on the phone. In all the years I've lived here, I can't say I've heard anything good about the man or his family. My dad worked for him at one point and he didn't even stay a month."

Beth frowned. "I don't need the work right now, but if there's no one else available, I'd be happy to give it a shot."

"Thanks for that." Meghan wrote herself a note. "You

obviously have a way with the difficult ones. I never thought we'd get Conner O'Neil back in here."

"I threatened to go and check up on him every day if he didn't come in. I guess that scared the crap out of him," Beth confided, making Meghan chuckle.

"I doubt he's that easy to scare, but he certainly is easy on the eye." Meghan winked. "I've always had a thing for retired military guys."

Beth tried not to blush as she looked back toward the interior door of the clinic. How long was Conner likely to be? If she was quick, maybe she could nip home, check on the boys, and be back before he even realized she'd gone.

Neither Wes nor Mikey had replied to her text telling them she was on her way home, but that wasn't unusual. They both tended to sleep in, and it wasn't yet time for lunch.

"Meghan?" Beth made a decision. "I'm going to check on Wes and Mikey. If Conner comes out before I'm back, can you tell him where I've gone?"

"Sure." Meghan looked up from her keyboard.

"He has my cell number, or if he wants to get moving, show him how to get to my place, okay?"

She went back out and headed across the street to where the town's only gas station was located. There was no sign of her brother Ted, but she waved at Mano, who was working his shift, and walked on. Even as she approached her dearly loved house, her smile dimmed. She'd allowed herself to forget her problems with Mikey for a short while, but it was time to face them again.

When she went back to the clinic, she'd ask Meghan for some referrals to family therapists and would make sure that she, Mikey, and Wes went to get some help. Sean's reappearance in Mikey's life was too disruptive to ignore. Mikey was an adult now and free to make his own decisions, but as his mother she would do everything in her power to help him make good choices.

As she delved into the pocket of her jeans to find her house keys, she yawned so hard she almost cracked her jaw. After she'd dropped Conner back at the cabin she would come home and sleep for a week. The Garcias were due back in two days and she hoped everything would be back to normal by then. Conner was leaving at the end of August, which meant he'd still be around for another month or so. Not that she would be seeing much of him; she only went out there every second week. If she asked Kaiden Miller, the part-time ranch foreman, he'd probably deal with Conner's needs at the cabin, leaving her with no contact with him at all.

She fitted her key in the lock and went through the front door. Would that be for the best? She didn't want to spoil their amazing night together or make him feel like she wanted a repeat or something . . .

Not that she'd say no if he was interested.

Beth grinned as she walked through into the family room. An open pizza box sat on the floor by the couch along with an abandoned game controller and two cans of soda. The drapes were still shut and the whole room smelled like essence of teenage boy. Wrinkling her nose, Beth opened the drapes and the window and set the empty pizza box back on the countertop.

Apart from the humming of the various appliances and the ticking of the kitchen clock, the house was silent. She checked the time and decided to go upstairs, stick her head in both of the boys' bedrooms and let them know what was going on.

Wes's door was slightly ajar. He'd made his bed and his laptop and backpack were missing, meaning he'd either gone to community college for his advanced carpentry course or to work with Kaiden. Beth mentally replayed what day it was in her head and realized he was definitely headed to Bridgeport for college and would be back late in the afternoon.

Beth went along the hallway to Mikey's room and knocked on the door. There was no response, which was typical, so she went in. To her surprise, Mikey's bed was also made, and his blinds were up. As Beth paused to consider where he might have gone, her gaze fell on his desk where a note with her name on it was propped up against his lamp.

She picked it up, her fingers suddenly shaking, and started to read, only to have to stop and start twice over because her brain refused to make sense of what she was seeing.

"No," she whispered. "Mikey . . ."

A knock on the front door had her sprinting down the stairs and rushing to open it.

"Mikey?"

Conner frowned at Beth. "Nope." He took a second look at her panicked face and reached for her. "What's wrong?"

"He's gone."

"Gone where?" Conner took hold of Beth's elbow, gently led her back inside the house and closed the door behind them.

"To his father." She thrust a piece of paper at him. "But

how does he think he's going to get there? Is he going to hitchhike?"

Conner read the short note and looked up at Beth, who was pacing the room, her hands twisted together.

"Mikey's gone to see his dad?"

"So he says."

He'd never seen her so agitated, but he could only imagine what she was going through, worrying about her kid.

"Does he have any money?" Conner asked.

"He has his own bank account and he has a job at a pizza place near his college, so he might have some. I try not to pry into his finances. I only get a notification if he goes overdrawn, and he's never done that yet."

"Okay, so he could've bought a bus ticket online?"

"Yes, that's how he got home after the last semester. I picked him up in Bridgeport. But how could he have gotten there this morning?"

Conner shrugged. "Taxi, Uber, someone at the gas station he could hitch a ride off."

She went still. "Or Wes took him."

"Would Wes do that if he knew where Mikey was headed?"

"Probably not, but Wes does go to Bridgeport for college, so if Mikey came up with a reason to tag along, Wes wouldn't have said no."

"Why don't you text Wes?" Conner suggested. "And, as your ex is in San Quentin, how does Mikey think he's going to get in and see him anyway?"

Beth made a face. "Mikey probably thinks you can just turn up and ask to see someone."

"What *do* you have to do?" Conner asked, intrigued, and she threw up her hands.

"I don't know! Maybe you could google that while I'm texting Wes."

"Sure." He got out his phone, pulled up the website and started to read. "Wow, there's a lot of stuff you have to go through before they'll let you visit." He looked up. "Do you know if he submitted a visitor application?"

Beth didn't answer, her attention fixed on her cell as she typed fast with her thumbs. Eventually, she looked up.

"Wes gave him a ride this morning. Mikey said he had a job interview in Bridgeport and that he'd hang around until Wes finished his class, and they'd come home together."

"And are you sure that Mikey won't just do that?"

Beth stared at him like he was stupid. "If he was going for an interview why wouldn't he have mentioned it in his note? He *said*, he's going to see his father."

"Okay." Conner nodded. "So how do you want to play this? Do you want to head out to Bridgeport and see if Mikey's hanging around waiting for a bus? Or do you want to stay here, call San Quentin, and give them a heads-up that he might try to get to speak to his father, and let him learn by his own mistakes?"

"Conner . . ." Beth came over and put her hand on his arm. "You don't have to worry about any of this. I'm sure that when I explain the situation, Nate will take you back to your cabin, or I can call Ted and ask him—"

"Not happening." He put his hand over hers and squeezed hard. "I'm coming with you. I can't let you do this alone."

"But . . . you're still not one hundred percent fit, and this has nothing to do with you, and—"

He stared her down. "And I'm still coming. Think of it as repayment for all you've done for me over the past twenty-four hours."

"You don't need to pay me back for any of that." Beth looked steadily back at him and he couldn't resist dropping a kiss on her nose.

"Not your decision." He took a step back. "Now, do you need to grab anything before we go, or shall we move out?"

She sighed as if finally giving up the fight. "We should let Ted know what's happening just in case Mikey gets in touch with him rather than me."

"If you give me your phone, I can text him and Nate from your truck while you drive," Conner said. "Do you need ID, cash, or supplies for the journey in case we've missed him in Bridgeport?"

"Seeing as he left here about three hours ago, he's probably already gone." She bit her lip. "Are you *sure* about this?"

"Yeah." He took her by the shoulders and pointed her toward the stairs. "Why don't you get ready while I make some coffee for the trip?"

Fifteen minutes later they were back in the refueled truck and heading out on the county road. Ted had arrived back at the gas station just as they were leaving, and Beth had filled him in on what was going down. He'd promised to tell Nate and keep an eye out for Wes if he came back before them. He'd also said he'd ask one of the hands up at the Garcia Ranch to check in on Loki.

As Beth drove toward Bridgeport, Conner looked up the route Mikey would have to take to get to San Quentin using public transport.

"Basically, Mikey will have to take a bus to Gardnerville, then one to Reno, then a Greyhound to Oakland. After that he'll have to get on the BART to San Quentin and walk the rest of the way to the prison." Conner whistled. "Google says that's going to take him around one day and four hours. It would be quicker for us to wait, get on a plane tomorrow, and meet him there."

"You're probably right." Beth overtook a truck full of tomatoes. "Any idea what time the bus leaves from Bridgeport?"

Conner consulted his phone. "There are a couple of buses a day. One at nine thirty and the other at one thirty. Do you think he might've made the first one?"

"It depends what time Wes got them there this morning. His class doesn't start until ten and he usually arrives about a minute before it begins."

"Sounds just like me." Conner set his phone in the center console.

Beth glanced over at him. "I know I haven't said this yet, but I really appreciate how calm you're being."

He shrugged. "I learned patience and strategy in the SEALs. No one wants you panicking in the middle of a battlefield."

"Well, I appreciate it." She half laughed. "It's not like me to get all agitated."

"I know." He put on his sunglasses and sat back. "But, if my kid had done a runner, I guess I'd be a little upset, too."

When Wes sent her a text, Beth handed her phone over to Conner to read it out and type in her reply. Despite her earlier words, she was really glad he'd decided to come with her. She was definitely capable of dealing with Mikey on her own, but having Conner's quiet support was more reassuring than she'd anticipated.

"Tell Wes not to hang around if he's done for the day, and to go home," Beth said as Conner typed.

"He says he's on his lunch break and he'll meet you at

the bus station," Conner reported back. "It might be worth talking to him before you send him on his way. He could have some additional intel we're missing."

"Good point," Beth conceded as they came close to the outskirts of Bridgeport and she headed for the parking lot behind the bus station. "But then he definitely will be going home."

Even as she was parking the truck, she saw Wes approaching, his expression uncharacteristically grim. She knew he'd be blaming himself for what had happened. His loyalty to her and his half brother was central to who he'd become as a person and he took his big brother responsibilities very seriously.

"What's up?" Wes asked as she and Conner got out of the truck. "I haven't heard a peep out of Mike since I left him in the college parking lot."

"He left me a note saying he was going to see your father in San Quentin," Beth explained. "Did he say anything about that to you?"

Wes recoiled. "Hell, no, because if he had I would've sat his stupid ass down and told him all the reasons why that was the dumbest idea on earth!"

Beth noticed Conner fighting a smile.

"Did he seem okay on the drive in? Did he say anything that sounded weird?" Beth asked.

"No more than usual," Wes said. "Although he wasn't saying much at all, to be honest."

"What time did you get here?"

"Earlier than I like, because I had to pick up a book from a friend, so just after nine."

"What was Mikey wearing?" Conner asked. "And did he bring a backpack?"

Wes glanced over at Beth as if asking her permission to answer Conner's question, and she gave him a tiny nod.

"White T-shirt with his college name on it, black and orange baseball cap, jeans, and red sneakers."

"So pretty much the same as every other person getting on the bus," Conner muttered.

"Pretty much." Wes nodded. "He had his black back-pack with him. He definitely had his laptop because he had a hissy fit when I tried to throw his bag in the trunk of the car."

"And he didn't say anything at all to you about not waiting around for him, or where exactly this job interview was taking place?" Beth asked.

"Nope, but I didn't ask for details. I was just glad he was looking for work after being such a jerk about it to you."

Conner glanced briefly at her but didn't add to the conversation.

Beth shielded her eyes and looked toward the ticket office. "I suppose I can ask if they saw Mikey this morning. At least we think we know which bus he was trying to get on."

Conner patted her shoulder. "Maybe he'll still be sitting there, and you can just take him home."

"I didn't see him when I walked through," Wes said dubiously. "But I guess he might have been hiding."

The sun was at its highest point in the clear blue sky and the heat from the sidewalk was blistering. By the time she'd traversed the parking lot, Beth was already sweating. She was genuinely amazed to see an actual person sitting in the air-conditioned stillness of the tiny office behind the thick glass.

"Hi!" she said brightly. "I'm trying to check if my son got on the bus to Gardnerville this morning at nine thirty?"

The elderly lady smiled at her. "I'm afraid I'm not allowed to give out information about our passengers, ma'am."

"Even to their mothers who are worried about their babies going out into the world?" Beth asked. "I mean, I know you can't tell me 'officially,' but maybe if I show you his picture you could just nod if you saw him, set my mom's heart at rest, and I can go home happy without him having any idea I was checking up on him?"

Even as the woman hesitated, Beth noticed her name badge.

"Are you by any chance related to Andy Ferraro, Dorothy? I went to school with Andy when he lived in Morgantown, and you look just like him."

The woman beamed back at her. "He's my great-nephew."

"That explains it. I'm Kevin Baker's daughter. My dad and brother own the gas station in town." Beth offered another friendly smile. Sometimes living in a small town had its advantages. "I heard Andy's living in Bridgeport now, but I've seen him at church with his parents on Sunday in Morgantown."

"He's a good boy." Dorothy hesitated and then gestured at Beth's phone. "Show me the photo, then."

Beth held it up to the glass and Ms. Ferraro nodded. "He definitely got on the bus to Gardnerville."

"Thank you so much." Beth put her phone in her pocket. "I feel so much better now. Give my regards to Andy when you next see him."

"Will do."

Beth turned away to find Conner watching her intently

while Wes stared down at his cell. He met her gaze and she walked toward him.

"He's on the bus?"

"Yup." Beth took a shaky breath and turned to Wes. "Look, after you finish up classes for the day, I want you to go straight home."

Wes frowned. "It would be way better if *you* went home and I went to look for Mikey."

Beth put her hand on his arm. "Wes, I need your help on this. If Mikey comes back by himself, I want someone there to let me know he's safe, and I trust you to do that."

"What about Uncle Ted?"

"If Mikey's failed to get to see his father, the last thing he'll want is an adult telling him all the things he's done wrong. He's way more likely to confide in you, and I want him to stick around until I can get back and talk to him, okay?" Wes looked unconvinced, so Beth kept talking. "*Please*, Wes."

"Okay." Wes glanced over at Conner, who had been listening quietly. "But only if you take this guy with you."

Beth tried not to roll her eyes. "I'm perfectly capable of traveling on my own, Wes."

"Sure you are, but I guess if I can't be there, Conner's a good man to have your back." Wes turned to the man in question. "You'll keep an eye on her, won't you?"

"I absolutely will." Conner nodded. "I give you my word that I'll do everything I can to make sure she and Mikey make it home safely."

"This isn't some kind of disaster movie," Beth reminded them both. "All I have to do is locate Mikey and bring him back. It's not exactly rocket science."

"I know." Wes grinned. "It's just way more fun and dramatic my way."

Beth poked him in the arm. "Get along with you."

She watched as he sauntered out of the building and disappeared in the direction of the college.

"Do you think he'll do what you asked?" Conner asked.

"Yes," Beth said. "He's a smart kid." She hesitated. "Can we talk about what to do next?"

"Sure." Conner got out his phone. "The bus to Gardnerville takes a very circuitous route, but I still think he'll arrive before we can make it. Our best bet, in my opinion, would be to drive directly to Reno, which is roughly two-and-a-half hours away from here, and meet him there before he boards the Greyhound to Oakland."

"You've already worked it out?" Beth stared at him.

He shrugged and showed her the information on his phone. "You don't have to do it that way if you don't want to. We can stop off in Gardnerville to make sure he didn't get stranded there, and still get to Reno before he will. The bus is that slow."

"Okay." Beth nodded. "If you're still willing to come with me."

"I promised Wes I'd keep you safe. I'm not the kind of person who breaks his word." He glanced down at her as they headed for the door. "Do you want to find someplace we can have lunch or get takeout? We've got time."

Chapter Six

There was no sign of Mikey in sleepy Gardnerville and no one around to ask if he'd gotten on his next bus. The town was so small they only spent twenty minutes checking out every possible place he might be. Beth topped up the gas tank and settled in for the drive to Reno with Conner at her side. For once she really appreciated his disinclination to chat, as inwardly she wrestled with a thousand questions and increasingly scary scenarios.

"Would you like me to drive?" Conner finally broke his silence about an hour into the journey.

"I'm good at the moment," Beth said. "It gives me something to concentrate on rather than wondering if Sean set up a prison visit for Mikey and neither of them bothered to tell me."

"It's possible." Conner nodded. "From what I read on the Department of Corrections website, the inmate has to send the visitor a questionnaire to fill out and return before they can be approved to come in."

"So, Sean would have instigated this." Beth nodded. "Of course, he would. What gets me is that Mikey didn't mention it."

"Maybe he just heard back that he'd been approved and grabbed the opportunity to go for it when you were out of the house?"

Beth groaned. "Don't make me feel even worse."

"I'm the one who dragged you away," Conner reminded her.

"You didn't ask me to come and interfere in your life. That's totally on me."

"True." Conner stared out of the window for a long while. "But I'm glad you did."

Beth snorted and used the opportunity to check her route on the navigation system.

"If Sean is in general population, and Mikey has his visitor clearance, he can visit over the weekend," Conner added.

"I don't know where Sean was placed," Beth said. "I've tried not to have anything to do with him or his mother since our divorce and when I formally adopted Wes."

"I can see why." Conner shifted in his seat. "If you don't need me to drive, do you mind if I take a nap?"

"Sure, why not?" Beth said.

He set his coffee down, leaned his seat back and instantly fell asleep, a skill Beth could only envy. She rechecked where she was in relation to the outskirts of the city, mentally plotted the best route into town to avoid any crowds, and settled in to finish the journey.

"We're here."

Conner woke up as Beth spoke and cast a bleary eye over the flashing lights of Reno. He'd been there many times during his navy career, and couldn't really distinguish one visit from another. He'd gambled, drunk too much, watched some dubious shows, and occasionally gotten laid, but none of it had really helped with the stress of his job. He hadn't been back for about ten years, but it didn't look like much had changed.

"Where exactly is here?" Conner reset his seat to the upright position.

"I'm parking in the Greyhound bus station lot." Beth checked her cell. "Wes and Ted say Mikey hasn't turned up at home, so we'll just have to assume he's still on his way."

She turned toward him, and he could see the worry in her eyes.

"He's going to be mad at me, isn't he?"

"Probably." Conner wasn't into lying. "But you're still his mom and he lives in your house, so he needs to hear what you have to say." He paused. "What *are* you going to say?"

"I don't know." She grimaced. "I suppose it depends on what exactly he'd planned to do when he got there and whether the idea came from Sean or is something Mikey totally thought up by himself."

Conner nodded.

"If he really did just decide to take off, I'm still going to be mad," Beth continued. "But if Sean manipulated him . . ."

Conner reached out and cupped her chin. "You've got this."

"I don't, but that's okay. One thing I've learned as the mother of teenagers is that you have to think on your feet and be prepared to hear the dumbest reasons for doing things ever invented." She sat back and fumbled with her seat belt. "Shall we head out? The Gardnerville bus is due in soon."

Conner followed Beth to the center of the bus station,

checking the arrival time for Mikey's bus as he walked. It was due in way earlier than he'd anticipated and they wouldn't have long to wait. When the bus swung into its berth, he took a step back into the shadows as Beth went to stand by the opening door. He spotted Mikey at about the same time the kid spotted his mom and tried to back up.

"Mikey?" Beth spoke up clearly. "I need to talk to you."

Her son sighed, hoisted his backpack higher on his shoulder, and came toward her.

"I suppose I should've guessed you'd tried to stop me."

"Why wouldn't I?"

Mikey shrugged. "Because I'm an adult and I can make my own decisions?"

"Such an adult that you couldn't even sit down and tell me to my face what you intended to do?" Beth asked.

Conner winced at Mikey's stubborn expression.

"I didn't tell you because I knew you'd make a scene—and I'm right because here you are, doing it in public anyway."

Conner took an instinctive step forward and then restrained himself. This wasn't his fight, but the disrespect in Mikey's voice grated on him. Instead he cleared his throat.

"Beth, why don't we head to the nearest place where we can get coffee and you can talk it out there?"

Mikey's attention swung to Conner.

"Why are you here?"

Conner met Mikey's indignant gaze. "Because your mother was worried about you and needed some support. I'm Conner O'Neil. I've been renting a cabin up on the Garcia Ranch."

"I know who you are. I've seen you in town. What I

don't understand is what you're doing hanging out with my mom."

"That's none of your business, Mikey." Beth stepped in between them. "And if you really want to know the truth, I'm damn glad he stepped up to help me."

She looked over at Conner. "That's a great suggestion about getting a coffee. There's a place right on the corner."

Even as Mikey opened his mouth to object, Conner spoke over him.

"You've got two hours until your next bus leaves, son. You can spare the time to talk to your mother."

Without a word, Mikey followed Beth out of the bus station with Conner bringing up the rear. None of them spoke until they were in the air-conditioned interior of the coffee shop. Conner located a table and indicated to Mikey that he should take a seat.

"What can I get you both?" Conner asked.

Well aware that he was a spare wheel, Conner was keen to give them as much time together as possible. His leg was aching; his temperature was climbing, and if Beth's son continued to disrespect his mother, Conner might just have something to say about it.

He joined the line, mentally repeating the coffee orders, and waited patiently for his turn, one eye monitoring the intense conversation going on at his table. Even from a distance he could tell that things weren't going well. Mikey had crossed his arms over his chest and was leaning back in his chair while Beth was gesticulating wildly and getting pink in the face.

Man, he was glad he hadn't had kids.

By the time he reached the table, a frosty silence had descended. He sat down and distributed the drinks.

"Thanks, Conner." Beth offered him a tight smile. "Mikey says Sean set up the visitor approval thing and that he's planning on visiting him Saturday."

"Okay." Conner sipped his drink and let the caffeine roll through him before taking a couple of painkillers.

"Why are you telling him?" Mikey asked. "He's not part of our family."

Beth opened her mouth and then abruptly stood up. "Excuse me. I've got to let everyone back home know that we found you, and I really need to use the bathroom."

Conner looked up as he caught the hint of tears in her voice. From the stricken look on Mikey's face as she turned away, so did her son.

As Mikey added way too much sugar to his coffee, Conner considered what to do. It was none of his business, but seeing Beth upset hurt his soul.

"She's really mad at me, isn't she?" Mikey broke the silence.

"I think she's madder at your father for putting you both in this position."

"He's trying to change and all she can say is that he's a bad guy and a loser."

"That's her truth." Conner shrugged. "Just because you don't feel the same doesn't make it wrong. She lived with the man, she protected you from his rage when you were a kid and she's trying to protect you now."

"So, you think I should just go back home like some kind of loser just to make her happy?"

"Not my job to tell you what to do." Conner raised an eyebrow. "I'm just asking you to show some respect for the woman who raised you."

Mikey's cheeks reddened and he looked down at his drink as Beth returned to the table.

"Ted and Wes were pleased to hear you were okay," she reported as she sat down, her voice unnaturally cheerful. "Wes said several other things, but most of them aren't repeatable in polite company."

Mikey checked his phone. "Is it okay if I go use the bathroom before I return to the bus station?" He pointed at his backpack. "I'll leave this here so that you know I won't run out on you."

When Mikey was out of earshot, Conner reached across the table and took Beth's hand.

"You holding up okay?"

"Not really." She grimaced. "Legally he's an adult, so I can't force him to come home with me."

"You know I could knock him out without anyone noticing."

"Thanks, but I don't think that will work." She straightened her spine. "I guess I'll just have to try the begging and mom guilting again."

Conner studied their linked hands and then looked up at her.

"How about you just let him get on the bus?"

She stared back at him, her eyes widening. "I thought you were on my side."

"I am."

She tried to ease her fingers free and he held on to them. "Let him meet the guy, let him make his own mistakes."

"You just don't get it, do you? When he wants to be, Sean is really persuasive and charming. What if Mikey falls for that?"

Conner frowned. "Do you think he will?"

"*I* did." This time she managed to pull out of his grasp and sat back, her arms folded. "Mikey's at a very vulnerable age, he—"

"But you brought him up, and he's had great role models since you moved back to Morgantown." Conner wasn't willing to back down. "Why won't you give him a chance to prove it?"

She raised her chin and glared at him. "I know I've said this before, but I'm really starting to prefer it when you don't talk to me."

An unaccustomed stab of hurt hit his heart. "Okay. I'll shut up and keep my nose out of your business." He picked up his coffee. "I'll meet you back at the truck—unless you want me to find my own way home?"

"You're really going to act all butt hurt *now*, when I'm dealing with my runaway son?"

There was a lot he wanted to say about that, but she was right that this wasn't the time. He pointed at his cell. "Text me when you're ready to leave."

She flung up her hands and muttered something uncomplimentary as he walked out into the sticky afternoon air. If Mikey's bus left on time, she had just over an hour to convince her son to come home with her. Conner's gaze fixed on the flashing lights of the nearest casino. As he definitely wasn't needed, maybe he'd go and chance his luck somewhere else.

Beth followed Mikey all the way back to the bus station, still arguing, until Mikey refused to even answer her. She waited with him as the bus pulled in. He set his backpack on his shoulder and looked at her, his gaze determined.

"I'm going, Mom."

"Mikey . . ."

She reached for him but forced her hand to fall to her side. She nodded, let out a shaky breath and took a step back.

"Okay, take care and let me know that you got there safely."

She turned and walked away, her eyes filling with tears, and refused to look back. She didn't wait to see the bus pull out, but made her way back to the parking lot to find Conner sitting in the bed of the pickup truck, his expression unreadable.

She opened the truck, got in, and started the engine. Conner climbed in and settled into his seat, his gaze straight ahead. Neither of them spoke as she paid the parking fee and they set off back to Morgantown.

Beth waited for Conner to make some comment about her inability to make her son come home, but he didn't say anything, which somehow made her feel even worse. But what could he say? He'd made his position clear and so had she, and that was the end of it. Sure, she'd alienated her son and the man who'd gone out of his way to help her on her frantic journey, but that was on her.

She'd told Conner to keep his opinions to himself and he'd done what she'd asked, so why was she still upset? She cleared her throat.

"Let me know if you want to stop for coffee or anything. There are a couple of places along the way that stay open late."

"I'm good, thanks."

He didn't bother to turn his head to reply, his gaze fixed

on the road ahead. He looked even more exhausted than she felt, which made her guilt kick up.

"You look terrible."

"Thanks."

"I told you it wasn't necessary to come with me."

"I heard you the first time and I came anyway."

Beth sniffed. "If you get sick again, Dr. Tio's going to blame me."

"I doubt it. He knows how stubborn I am."

"I'm surprised you didn't think I should force Mikey to come back with me, because that's what a good mother would do, wouldn't she?" Beth said.

"Actually, I'm the one who suggested you should let him go."

"Well, of course you did, and you're probably secretly gloating that he made me look like a fool."

He slowly turned his head toward her. "Beth, what exactly are you trying to do here?"

"*Nothing.*"

"It sure sounds like you're trying to drag me into an argument."

"Why on earth would I do that?"

"Because you're mad as hell about everything and spoiling for a fight?"

"I am *not*—"

He spoke over her. "It's not going to work. Your fight is with Sean and I'm not going to act as his substitute."

"That's ridiculous!"

All Beth really wanted to do was burst into tears and let him hold her. If he was too stupid to realize that, then more fool him.

"Whatever you say." He looked out of the window. "Wake me up when we reach Morgantown."

Conner opened his eyes as they pulled up in front of Beth's house. He hadn't slept much, but pretending was far easier than trying to work out exactly how to deal with Beth. How was it possible for someone to be furious about something and yet almost in tears? How was a guy supposed to handle all that being thrown at him at once? And more importantly, why did he suddenly care?

"We're here," Beth announced.

"Yeah, thanks for the ride." Conner opened his door and got out into the coolness of a Morgantown night. "Let me know how things shake out." He paused. "If you want to, otherwise forget it."

"Where exactly do you think you're going?" Beth demanded.

He pointed vaguely toward the dark slopes of the valley. "Home."

"There's no one to take you at this hour except me." She took out her keys. "Just let me check on Wes and get some more coffee and I'll drive you up there."

"I don't expect you to do that, Beth," Conner said firmly. "I can ask—"

He was speaking to thin air. He followed her into the house because she obviously wasn't in the mood to stop and chat. She still hadn't answered him as Wes came toward them and gave her a huge hug.

"Did you get him? Is he sulking in the truck or did Conner tie him up nice?"

Beth gently detached herself from Wes. "He decided he wanted to go through with his plan to see your father."

"And you let him?" Wes's startled gaze flicked toward Conner. "Like he's on a bus right now?"

"There wasn't a lot your mother could do about it," Conner spoke up as Beth went into the kitchen and started fussing around with the coffeepot. "Mikey's an adult and he made his choice. Your mother chose to respect that decision."

Wes opened his mouth again and Conner shot him a pointed look.

"I've got to take Conner back to Garcia Ranch, but I'll come straight home after that." Beth spoke from the kitchen. She looked absolutely wiped out and miserable and Conner wished he could go to her. "We probably won't hear anything from Mikey until tomorrow, so if you want to head up to bed that's okay."

"It's way too early to sleep, Mom." Wes shook his head. "How about we do this? I'll take Conner, and you go to bed."

"That would be great." Conner turned to Wes. "I'm ready when you are."

Beth looked at them both and set her keys back on the countertop. "Fine. Okay." Her gaze flicked toward Conner but didn't reach his face. "Don't overexercise your leg."

"I won't." Conner's hands flexed as he resisted the urge to stride over and take her in his arms. "I hope Mikey works out who the good guys are soon."

Rather than driving his own car, Wes took Juan's truck so he could pick up Beth's car from the ranch and bring it home. Conner relaxed as Wes drove him up through the darkened streets of the town and out on the county road toward the foothills surrounding the valley. He'd grown fond of the area with its extremes of weather and stunning scenery and already felt quite at home.

"Mom's just tired right now." Wes suddenly spoke up. "So, like, don't take anything she says to heart."

"She has a right to be upset," Conner responded. "I totally get it."

"Mikey doesn't really understand what Dad is like because he's younger than me and doesn't remember the worst of it. And Beth, like, really protected him. My mom wasn't so strong, and Dad treated her like shit."

There was a hard note in Wes's voice, the sound of a survivor Conner immediately related to.

"Dad might be able to charm Mikey for a while, but eventually, when he doesn't get what he wants, he'll turn on him. I tried to tell Mikey that, but he didn't believe me." Wes sighed. "Some people just have to work things out for themselves, right?"

Conner grimaced. "I certainly had to learn everything the hard way."

Wes cut him an amused glance. "You're like a fricking Navy SEAL. You're, like, a number-one badass."

"It's nothing to be proud of." Conner shifted in his seat. "And it took a long time for me to learn how to channel my anger with my own father into something positive."

"Mikey doesn't think he's angry, but he is," Wes said slowly. "Maybe seeing Dad will make him realize where that anger should be directed."

"Man, I wish I'd worked that out when I was nineteen," Conner said, which made Wes smile.

They completed the rest of the journey in silence as Conner struggled to stay awake and deal with the throbbing in his wounded leg. As the truck approached the cabin, he heard Loki barking.

"Thanks for the ride, Wes." Conner opened the passenger door. "I can take it from here."

"Okay." Wes nodded. "Have a great night."

Conner got out with some difficulty and stood still as Loki bombarded him with love and almost knocked him on his ass. His dog had obviously been well taken care of by the ranch hands as his bowl was full of fresh water and he'd been fed. As Wes drove away from the cabin, Conner couldn't quite believe everything that had happened in the last thirty-six hours. He managed to make it up the steps and opened the front door.

The faint smell of coffee and Beth's flowery perfume drifted out to greet him and he swallowed hard. Without her the cabin felt both too big and too lonely.

"Stupid fool," Conner muttered to himself as he felt in his pocket for the painkillers and antibiotics Dr. Tio had given him that morning. "Get over it."

It wasn't like him to be sentimental, but maybe he was just worn out and needed a good night's sleep to set his mind at rest. He swallowed down the pills with a glass of milk and the rest of Beth's chicken, used the bathroom, and got himself ready for bed. Dr. Tio had dressed his wounds and told him to leave them alone until the morning.

He lay down and listened to the sounds of the night— the distant howls of a coyote pack and the much louder song of the grasshoppers. In the all-encompassing silence he tried to work out when things had gone wrong with Beth and still couldn't put his finger on it. For the first time in his life he didn't know how to fix things because in the past he'd never bothered and had just shrugged his shoulders and moved on. But something about Beth had changed him.

He had only known her for a couple of months, but everything inside him was yelling at him to stop dicking around and pay attention. And he'd learned to listen to his gut in the military. There was something there—something tantalizing and new. He wanted to reach out his hand and find Beth's waiting for him.

Even as he considered what to do, the painkillers kicked in and he was suddenly asleep.

"You didn't need to wait up for me," Wes said as he came into the kitchen and found Beth sitting at the table.

"I know." She shrugged. "I made the mistake of having more coffee and now I'm wide awake again."

That was partially true. Wes didn't need her to spell out that she'd *needed* to see him return safely unlike his half brother.

"Mikey will be okay," Wes said.

"I'm sure he will," Beth agreed.

It was rapidly becoming clear to her that her boys didn't need her as much as they used to, which was both a blessing and a curse. Her father always said that the best thing a parent could do for their child was give them the tools to become responsible functioning adults, so she supposed she'd done her job. She'd always be there for them, but she definitely needed to let them live their own lives and make their own mistakes.

Which sounded great in principle, but was obviously a lot harder to put into practice than she'd realized.

"Are you mad that he wouldn't come home?" Wes asked.

Beth sighed. "Yes. I wish I wasn't and could be a better person, but I can't seem to manage it right now."

"Maybe Mikey just needs to work things out for himself," Wes suggested.

"That's what Conner said."

Wes paused at the bottom of the stairs. "I know it's none

of my business, but you were pretty salty with Conner, considering what he did for you today."

"I didn't ask him to come with me," Beth said. "And I did say thank you when we arrived back here."

"I kind of told him you were probably overtired."

"Why?"

"Because he was obviously worried about you and trying not to let you know."

Beth snorted. "Conner O'Neil doesn't worry about anyone. He's a tough guy who likes to keep people at a distance and that suits me just fine."

"But he didn't keep you at a distance," Wes said slowly. "In fact, he went out of his way to help you."

"Wes." Beth rose to her feet. She really wasn't going to discuss everything that had gone down between her and Conner, but she could see from Wes's perspective that she might have come off as cold. "I don't need a lecture from you right now. I'll call him up in the morning and apologize, okay?"

She moved toward Wes, who was blocking the stairs.

"You *like* him, don't you?"

She rolled her eyes even as her cheeks heated up. "Sure, like a woman who has two teens in the house would have time to get involved with anyone right now."

"Mikey and I wouldn't care."

She cupped his chin, aware of the softness of the new stubble he was so proud of. "I was just kidding."

"Okay." Wes stepped out of her way. "Let me know if you hear from Mikey."

"Same." Beth went up the stairs feeling like she'd aged a hundred years. "He's way more likely to contact you than me."

"Maybe." Wes didn't sound convinced. "Night, Mom."

Beth dragged herself to the bathroom, brushed her teeth, and took herself to bed. The desire to cry constricted her throat and made her chest hurt, but she couldn't seem to let her tears flow. Mikey was on a bus in the middle of nowhere, she'd chased Conner away, and even Wes wasn't completely on her side.

Was she wrong about everything?

She was so used to having to deal with what life threw at her by herself and protect those she loved, that the idea of letting anyone go it alone was frightening. She turned onto her side and looked out at the moonlit sky. Up at the Garcia Ranch, Conner was probably already sleeping without a thought in his head. She'd told him she didn't want a relationship and to butt out of her personal life.

And Conner, being a man who was used to taking orders and following them through, would definitely leave her alone, just as she'd asked.

CHAPTER SEVEN

Beth took another unnecessary tour of the house, making sure everything was in order for Mikey's imminent return. To her great relief he'd contacted Wes on Sunday night and asked if he would mind picking him up from Bridgeport after he got off the bus Monday afternoon. Wes had asked Beth what she thought, and she'd been happy to relinquish the task. She had no idea what she was going to say to Mikey, so the longer she had to think about it the better.

She checked through the front window, but there was no sign of Wes's car. As promised, she'd called Conner and had immediately been put through to his voicemail. She assumed he was sleeping in, and she couldn't blame him. She'd offered him her thanks for helping her out, apologized for being short with him, and explained that Mikey had arrived safely at San Quentin. She'd wanted to say a lot more, but talking to thin air had never been her favorite thing, and how could she express what she was feeling when he'd be leaving town in a few weeks anyway?

Even as she continued to worry about Mikey, part of her was thinking about Conner, how it had felt to be herself for a few hours, to be *desired*, and free to share an intimate moment with an incredibly hot man. The idea that she deserved that—that for the first time in her life she had the opportunity to move beyond parenthood and think of herself—was both terrifying and alluring,

Beth forced herself to focus on Mikey. She'd see Conner if he came down to Garcia Ranch or if she went out to service the cabin, and she'd treat him just the same as she always had. Her cell buzzed and she went over to where it was plugged in on the kitchen countertop.

Back in 5

Beth put on some fresh coffee and headed upstairs to her bedroom. The last thing she wanted was Mikey thinking she'd been so desperate to see him again that she was lurking behind the front door ready to pounce. She'd go for calm and casual and not ask the thousand and one questions that had kept her awake half the night.

"We're back!" Wes called up the stairs.

Beth waited another three minutes and steeled herself to go down to the kitchen, where Mikey was taking off his jacket and setting his backpack on the countertop.

"Hi!" Beth said, and immediately couldn't think of anything to say as she anxiously scanned her son's tired face. She grabbed her keys from the hook. "Sorry I can't stop to chat. I've got to go up to the ranch to make sure everything is okay for Juan's return tomorrow."

"I'd really like to talk to you, Mom," Mikey said.

"Then we can do that when I get back and you're all settled in, okay?" She gave him a bright smile and turned to Wes. "There's half a chicken pie in the refrigerator if you guys get hungry."

"Mom . . ." Mikey blocked her exit. "Is this how it's going to be? You're too mad at me to even discuss things?"

She forced herself to meet his gaze. "You know what, Mikey? I'm just as entitled as you are to be given space to work out how I feel about things. Maybe it's your turn to back off and not expect me to instantly be ready to do what you want when you want it."

He blinked and swallowed hard. "Okay, I mean I'm sorry, I just . . ."

"Thank you." She nodded and went past him, her keys clenched in her fist. "I'll see you both later."

Even as she drove up to the ranch, she began to doubt herself. She'd always gone out of her way to make sure her kids felt listened to and validated, like her parents had done for her. When she'd first told her dad about Sean's abusive behaviors, he'd believed her one hundred percent and done everything he could to make sure she felt safe and could get out.

But maybe Mikey needed to learn something, too; that his actions had consequences, and that she wasn't a machine but a real live human being who had a right to feel hurt by his behavior. She wasn't mad at him anymore. She just needed some space.

She pulled up outside the ranch and went inside to make sure everything was ready for Juan's return. She'd stopped at Maureen's and gotten fresh milk and produce so Julia, Juan's daughter, wouldn't have to stop in Morgantown after the long journey home. Cleaning had always soothed her. Her therapist said it was a way of maintaining control over something when everything else was in chaos, and she couldn't disagree.

Eventually there was nothing left to do. Beth sent a text to Julia to let her know she'd come by at the end of the week. In return, Julia sent her a picture of Juan watching the rodeo and grinning like a fool.

Beth was still smiling as she locked up the house and went toward her car. The sound of a horse neighing made her look over toward the barn and the paddock behind it. She stuck her keys in her jeans pocket and marched over to the fence, shading her eyes against the sun.

"What the heck are you doing here?" she called out.

Conner turned the horse around, his face shadowed beneath his hat, and came slowly toward her.

"It's okay. I asked Mr. Garcia for permission."

She pointed at his leg. "You're supposed to be resting up!"

A smile kicked up the corner of his mouth. "That didn't seem to bother you a couple of nights ago."

She felt her skin heat up and it wasn't entirely due to the sun. "I didn't know you could ride."

He shrugged. "I worked as a hired hand in Texas one summer. I was just trying to see if I remembered how it all works."

As usual he was underplaying his ability. He looked damn good on a horse to her. Suddenly aware that she was chatting away with him like nothing had happened, she straightened up.

"Okay, I have to go now. Mikey came back."

"And you came out here?"

His penetrating gaze cut right through her and she sighed.

"I didn't know what to say to him. I needed to think."

"Understandable."

"So, I'd better get back there and try, I guess." She smiled. "See you around, Conner, and thanks for your help the other day. I really appreciated it."

She turned toward the barn. Man, he looked good on a horse, but why wouldn't he? He looked good all the time. She wanted to lick him all over like an ice cream.

"Beth?"

She wished she had the resolve not to turn around, but she didn't.

"What?"

He gestured at the gate. "Could you open that for me?" He rubbed his injured leg. "I'm not sure I can lean over right now without falling off."

She stomped back toward him and unlatched the gate. "I told you this was a stupid idea. If you can't bend down to reach the gate, how the hell are you going to dismount?"

His smile was crooked. "Er, I was hoping you'd help me with that, too."

He didn't sound very apologetic, but as Beth already knew how much it cost him to ask for help for anything, she didn't take offense.

"Fine. Come over to the mounting block."

He clicked to the horse and walked over to the newly renovated barn. Beth waited as he lined up the horse and then took hold of the bridle.

"You've got this."

"I damn well haven't." He grunted as he slid his booted feet out of the stirrup. "Me and my big, stupid ideas."

"What would you have done if I hadn't come up here?" Beth asked as he placed one heavy hand on her shoulder and attempted to swing his leg over the saddle.

"Ridden around until one of the hands came back to the barn or I found a hay bale or a grassy patch to fall off onto?"

"Idiot." Beth sniffed as she braced herself to help him down.

"Yeah, well, you already knew that." He reached the ground, one arm still anchored on Beth's shoulder, and buried his face against her neck. "Damn."

She was in no hurry for him to let go as her knees wobbled not with tiredness, but with complete lust.

He kissed her throat and she sighed. "That's so unfair."

"Can't help myself." He did it again. "Here you are again, saving my ass when I don't deserve it."

"Seems to be becoming a habit," Beth whispered against his cheek. "I really should stop—"

"Don't." His mouth covered hers and she kissed him back without reserve.

After a long while he framed her face with his hands and looked down at her, his expression serious.

"I want to tell you something."

"Okay."

"I think we could be good together."

Beth frowned. "We were—unless you're saying you didn't have a good time the other night because—"

"Not just sex—although that was awesome. I mean all the other stuff, like hearing you laugh, seeing you with your kids, or getting you mad enough to tell me off."

"Like everyday stuff?" Beth asked suspiciously.

"Yeah, exactly."

"What are you saying here?" Beth realized she was trembling.

"BB Morgan offered me a trail-riding job at his place."

"And?"

For the first time he looked down at his boots rather than at her. "I was thinking I might take the job. It comes with accommodation and everything."

"And . . . does that mean you'll stick around?"

"Yeah. I mean, only if you were okay with it, because you said you didn't want a long-term thing—"

She put a finger against his lips. "You said you were leaving at the end of the summer. I didn't want you to feel like you were beholden to me."

He looked deep into her eyes. "Maybe I want to be."

"You do?" Beth whispered.

"Yeah." He hesitated. "You make me feel like I've finally found my home."

Even as she went in for another kiss, he stiffened and raised his head.

"We've got company."

She turned in his arms and saw Wes's car coming to a stop behind hers.

"Dammit!"

"Talk about bad timing," Conner said dryly.

"This is the problem with living with teenagers and trying to have any kind of relationship," Beth muttered as Wes and Mikey emerged from the car, arguing so fiercely that she hoped they hadn't noticed what was going on right in front of their eyes.

"Mom!" Mikey's shocked voice made her clutch onto Conner's arm. "What the hell? I thought you were coming up here to clean the house!"

Wes stepped forward. "How about we put the horse away before this gets too dramatic?" He frowned at Conner. "You look like shit."

"Thanks." Conner removed his arm from around Beth's waist. "Why don't you guys talk while I put the horse back?"

"I'll help you," Wes offered. "You look like you're about to face-plant the ground. Aren't you supposed to be resting up?"

Conner sighed as he held on to the bridle and limped toward the interior of the barn. "Man, you sound just like your mom."

Beth waited until Wes and Conner were safely out of earshot and turned back to Mikey.

"I asked you to give me some space," Beth said evenly.

"I know." He shifted his feet.

"So why did you drag Wes up here to bother me?"

"I didn't know you'd be cuddling up to Conner O'Neil, did I?"

"That's got nothing to do with it and you know it," Beth retorted. She gestured toward the house. "Seeing as you're here, why don't we get out of the heat and you can tell me what you want to say."

She led the way into the quiet house, knowing that the Garcias wouldn't mind her using their space for something so important. Family was essential to Juan and Julia and they were both very fond of Mikey.

She fixed two tall glasses of ice water and pointed to the kitchen table. "Do you want to sit down?"

"Not really."

Beth took a seat anyway. It meant he'd be towering over her, but she was too tired to worry about that.

"I saw Dad," Mikey said.

"Okay."

"He was super pleased to see me. He said he doesn't get any visitors."

Probably because he's alienated everyone in his life who's tried to help him, and beat up his girlfriends, Beth thought, but didn't say the words out loud. Sean was still Mikey's father.

"He looked a lot thinner and older." Mikey took a slug of his water. "He said he wished things had gone differently, and that he was learning to deal with his rage issues, and was in therapy."

He looked at her as if seeking approval, which she wasn't prepared to give him. It dawned on her that she really didn't care what Sean thought or did anymore. Sometime over the past few years he'd lost his hold over her. The only concern she had right now was how he would influence Mikey.

"Don't you care?" Mikey asked.

"Not really." Beth decided to be honest. "Do you?"

"Of course, I do. He's my dad." Mikey set his glass down on the countertop. "You taught me that everyone is redeemable."

Beth had nothing to say to that, and Mikey took a quick lap around the extensive kitchen, his expression troubled.

"I went back on the Sunday morning before I had to get on the bus. He tried shit-talking about you and Wes's mom and I shut him down. He didn't like that."

"He wouldn't."

"Then he asked if I had any money to spare."

Beth bit her lip and looked up at her son, who swallowed hard.

"He got all salty when I said I was at college and not earning much. He said that if I had nothing to give him, then he didn't really need to see me again."

Mikey finally sat opposite Beth. "He was like two different guys. He was so funny and charming the first day, and then when I wouldn't agree with him about you being a bad person, or give him money, he just flipped and got real mean."

Beth instantly wanted to reassure him that maybe Sean had just been having a bad day, or . . . and remembered that she was done making excuses for her ex.

She nodded and Mikey frowned at her.

"Haven't you got anything to say about any of this?"

"It's not my place to comment on your relationship with your father," Beth said.

"Why not? You commented about it plenty at the coffee shop in Reno."

"Which was wrong of me." She paused. "You're an adult now. If you want to see Sean that's entirely up to you." She reached over and patted his clenched fist. "I trust you to make your own decision about this, Mikey. I'm happy to listen if you want my opinion, but I'm no longer going to tell you what you should or should not do."

Mikey didn't look any happier, so she continued talking. "I've spent so long protecting you that it's been difficult for me to let you make your own choices, because I get scared. But when you got on that bus to Oakland, I finally realized I had to let you find your own way. I could've forced you to come home with me, but what would that have achieved? Just more resentment and misunderstandings, and I don't need that in my life again."

"So, what happens if I want to see Dad again?" Mikey asked.

"You do what seems right to you. I'm certainly not going to stop you." She smiled at him. "The only thing I'd ask is that you don't tell me anything you talk about. Keep it between yourselves."

"But what if I need your advice?"

"Then, as I said, within reason I'm willing to listen to you." Beth met his gaze. "You need to understand that I have boundaries, too, Mikey. It's taken me years to deal with the impact Sean had on my life, and I'm no longer willing to immerse myself in his chaotic existence."

"Boundaries are good." Mikey nodded. "I remember my

therapist talking about those. Maybe I should go get a refresher course."

"Maybe we all should go." She squeezed his fingers. "I love you, Mikey."

He offered her a hesitant smile. "Wes said I could talk to him about Dad whenever I liked because he remembers him way better than I do."

"Wes saw a completely different side of Sean, the side I tried to keep from you," Beth reminded him.

"I still remember him yelling and breaking things and us hiding in my bedroom until he passed out on the couch." Mikey shivered. "It was terrifying, but even then, I knew you'd protect me."

Beth winced at the pain in his voice.

"Wes said his mother died protecting him from Dad," Mikey said. "I never knew that until today, did you?"

Beth nodded. "If Sharon hadn't confronted Sean, he could easily have turned on Wes, so I get what he's saying."

"Wes said Dad started beating him, and Sharon got in the way and told Wes to go upstairs and hide until she called for him. Wes hid in the closet, dialed 911 and stayed on the phone so the cops would believe him and come quick."

Beth met Mikey's anguished gaze. "I always thought what happened to Sharon would happen to me. The first time Sean turned on you, I realized it was time to leave. I was lucky enough to have family who believed me and gave me somewhere to run to. Sharon didn't have that."

Mikey reached out and grabbed her hand. "Thanks, Mom. I probably don't say it enough, but I really am grateful."

She shrugged. "It's what good parents do." She squeezed

his fingers. "I think we should definitely all go back to therapy and talk this through, don't you?"

Conner leaned against the side of his truck and prayed to God his leg would hold up. Wes had taken one look at him and decided to deal with the horse himself, which was highly embarrassing but well deserved. He had no business being out here trying to ride a horse. He should've stayed in his cabin and rested up like Dr. Tio had told him.

Wes came to find him. "You should go home."

"Yeah." Conner agreed, even though he wasn't moving an inch until Mikey and Beth emerged from the house.

Wes nodded at the house. "They'll be okay. Mom is an awesome person and she really gets Mikey and me."

Conner grunted. "Not sure Mikey appreciates that right now."

"He does. He was gutted when she wouldn't talk to him. It made him, like, think about her as a real person for the first time, as apart from his mom."

"About time," Conner said.

"We're also both good about you dating her."

"I didn't realize I needed your permission." Conner raised an eyebrow.

"Well, you kind of do because Mom won't do anything if me and Mikey have a problem with it."

"You might be surprised about that," Conner said. "And, as I'm getting my own place out on Morgan Ranch, we won't be cramping your style."

Wes looked at him. "What does that even mean?"

Conner sighed. "Stop making me feel old."

"You are old." Wes straightened up. "Hey, they're coming out. Try not to look like we've been talking about them."

Beth's gaze went straight to Conner and she frowned. "Why are you still here?"

"Wow, nice," Conner said. "I feel really appreciated now."

"It's okay, Mom, you don't have to pretend anymore." Wes intervened. "We know you've hooked up with him and we're okay with it."

"Not that I asked you, but fine." Beth's cheeks flushed. "Would you like to come and eat dinner with us, Conner?"

"Sure." He nodded. "That would be great."

"And you can stay the night if you like." Wes winked. "Mikey and I won't hear a thing while we're playing *Death Avenue Seven*."

Conner didn't think it was possible for someone to get that red and not expire, but somehow Beth was managing it.

"You can drive down with me, Conner," she said repressively. "And pick your truck up later."

"Great idea." He rubbed a hand over his leg and limped over to her car. "I'm not sure I can drive anyway."

She snorted as she got into the car. "I have no sympathy for you at all."

He waited until the boys had driven off in a cloud of dust and put his hand on her thigh. "Not so fast."

"What now?" She turned to face him, her expression suddenly apprehensive. "Oh God, have you changed your mind already? Did Wes say something truly awful? Do I need to kick his—"

He wrapped a hand around her neck and drew her in

for a kiss. Eventually, she stopped spluttering and kissed him back. When he had her attention, he cupped her chin.

"I haven't changed my mind. I still want to be with you, and I have no intention of sleeping with you at your house with two teens in it."

"Okay."

"You good with all that?"

"Yes."

He smiled. "We've both got good reasons to be gun-shy, Beth, and we're old enough not to have to rush into anything. Let's take our time, get to know each other, and enjoy the ride." He paused. "And I want you to know that I will never, ever lift a finger against you or your kids."

Beth's smile was both sweet and full of teeth. "If you did, I'd kick your ass out the door so fast and so hard you'd think you were flying."

"Noted." He nodded and kissed her nose. "I think I could fall in love with you."

"Really?" She raised her eyes to meet his. "That's amazing."

"Beth . . ." In this new landscape, he struggled to find the right words, but he didn't need them as she carried on talking.

"I love your strength and the way you offered me your support without question. I love the way you get along with Mikey and Wes and what you'll teach them and me about how to be a good man."

His conscience stirred. "I'm not—"

"Yes, you are." She refused to let him look away from her. "Okay, you're also grumpy, stubborn, and inclined not to listen to good advice, but I can live with that because according to my sons I can be that way, too."

Conner shook his head. "Can't say I've noticed."

She beamed at him. "Which is obviously why I like you." She glanced at the exit. "Shall we head out before Wes decides to come back and look for us?"

"It's just the kind of thing he'd do, isn't it?" Conner commented as Beth set off down the track leading to the county road.

"Wes likes to be in the center of the action and he really does look out for those he considers family." She looked both ways before easing out on the main road. "When do you start your job up at Morgan Ranch?"

"Whenever I want. BB had someone quit unexpectedly, so the sooner the better."

"You'd better wait until your leg is healed." She gave him a hard stare.

"Yes, ma'am."

Conner sat back with a contented sigh. He'd found a woman who cared about him and wouldn't take any shit, a place to settle down, and an occupation he enjoyed. What more could any man ask for? Everything in his past life had brought him to this place and to this woman, and he was no fool. When it felt this right, it was time to reach out, grab hold of his chance of happiness with both hands and hold on tight for the rest of his life.

RESCUE: COWBOY STYLE

REBECCA ZANETTI

This one's for my family, Tony, Gabe, and Karlina. The pandemic has been tough, but being able to spend more time with you has been a blessing.

CHAPTER ONE

There was nothing Trent Logan liked better than getting a city girl out of her clothes.

The dark-haired beauty at the doorway wore a silk shirt with still-creased pants—definitely city. Considering this one was sopping wet and shivering, the night was about to go a lot better than he'd hoped. Even across the clubhouse, dancing bodies, and loud noise, he clocked her before anybody else did. "Finish pouring these." He handed the tequila bottle off to another cowboy, nodding at the empty shot glasses on the bar.

Then he wound through the crowd, evaded the grasping hands of a couple of buckle bunnies, and reached the still-open doorway. "You parked too far away, darlin'," he noted, motioning her inside before shutting out the desperate wind and devastating rain that was starting to turn into sleet. He hadn't seen her before—was she someone's date? As far as he was concerned, if her date had left her to navigate the storm by herself, the woman was fair game. Friends or not. Brothers or not. Then she looked up, and the sight of her deep blue eyes nearly knocked him back a step.

She gulped.

His gaze narrowed.

"Um." She looked around at the crowded, noisy party. "I followed a dog here."

Oh. He opened the door again, and Harley sat, looking at him but not coming closer. Trent paused and studied the animal. "He's a wolf, darlin'. One who usually watches from afar." Interesting.

She blinked, her eyes widening. "I followed a wolf?"

Apparently so. Harley rarely let anybody get that close. Maybe he just liked women and not the men in the lodge. "Yep. His name is Harley, and best we can figure, some-body raised him from a pup and let him go. Or maybe his owner died. Either way, he's welcome here and we make sure he's fed. If for no other reason than it keeps him from eating our cattle." Trent took the time to actually look at her. No coat, no purse, wet clothes. The bottom half of her was muddy. "What happened?" That quickly, he switched from party mode to protection mode.

She wiped rain off her face, and her dark hair tumbled out of whatever clip had tried to hold it. The mass started to curl around her heart-shaped face. "I got lost. Ran off the road."

Well, crap. There went his plans. "You hurt?" He gin-gerly ran his hands down her arms and bent several inches to look closer at her eyes. Clear, not dilated. Stunning. Her face was pale, her skin smooth. And damn, she was curvy. He liked a full-bodied woman—always had. "Talk to me, sweetheart. Are. You. Hurt?" He put enough bite into his voice to catch her attention.

She coughed. "No. My car hit a fence and got stuck in the mud. Near the downed tree with the huge roots."

He paused. "That's three miles down the lane. You walked three miles in this storm?"

She swallowed and pushed wet hair back from her face. "I thought I saw lights." Her voice was soft. Cultured and smooth. "Then I saw the dog or wolf, and I followed the road."

Smart move. "All right."

She looked around warily and caught sight of Jesse making out with some blonde on the sofa, having reached second base. Maybe third. "I, ah, should probably go. Can I borrow a phone? You must have a landline out here, because I couldn't get any service on my cell phone. Still can't."

He cocked his head, not liking the blue tinge of her lips. "Who are you going to call?" It was the first early spring storm, and nobody with a lick of sense would be driving in it right now.

Her mouth opened and then closed. "A tow truck?"

He grinned, and she blinked. Once and then again. "Unless there's a kid or animal in your car, or medicine you need to stay alive, nobody is going to head out that way until the weather gives up the fight." He lifted an eyebrow.

Slowly, she shook her head. Probably reluctantly. "No kids, animals, or medicine." She shifted her feet and instantly lost her balance as her muddy shoe slid across the floor.

He caught her, steadied her, and then took her hand. "All right then. Follow me."

She tried to pull back, and he didn't blame her, but the blue lips had sealed her fate. Being well over six foot with a broad chest, he easily parted the crowd in the clubhouse and guided her to the wide hallway leading to the rooms.

There he paused, turned again, and drew her the other way, reaching a door that had a metal cowgirl on it. He pounded on the door and then opened it slightly. "Man coming in. Yell now if you object."

No sound—except for a soft one of distress behind him.

He liked the feel of her hand in his, except for the trembling. So he drew her into the women's bathroom, walked past the ugliest pink couch ever made, a set of vanities, a wall of stalls, and stopped at the shower area. "Sometimes there are clean towels." He ducked down and yanked one off the shelf. Then he turned and handed her the towel.

She took a step back. "I, er—"

He stepped toward her; she'd gone even paler. "You're cold, and you need to get rid of that chill. This is a nice, warm shower, it's the ladies' room, and I guarantee you're safe."

She clutched the towel and her shaking increased.

He drew air in through his nose. "I'm not the most patient of men, Blue Eyes. Here it is. Either you get your butt in that shower and warm up, or I'm putting you there." He paused. "And the clothes aren't coming."

Her chin firmed and those eyes finally focused. "Then get out of the bathroom."

Amusement filled him. "Good choice. I'll have somebody bring you in something to wear. Leave the wet clothes on the floor, and we'll figure out what to do with them." He reached in and started the shower, striding out of the restroom to the hallway and down to what functioned as his suite in the club when he needed or wanted to crash there. Something he hadn't done in so long, he wasn't sure there were clean clothes, considering he lived in the one ranch house they owned at the moment.

He found the best clothing he had and asked a couple of women heading into the restroom to take them in.

Then he waited.

She emerged, wet clothing in hands, looking delectable in his very faded Metallica T-shirt and the only pair of loose-fitting boxers he could find. Her legs went on forever to bare feet with bubblegum-colored toe polish. "I can't wear these things," she whispered.

"They're all I have." He paused, those legs causing thoughts they shouldn't. "You can join the party or get some shut-eye while the storm plays out."

She faltered. "No party."

"You hungry?" he asked.

"No."

"Okay." He took her hand again, drawing her down the hallway and nudging his door open with his hip. She followed and partially turned, her eyes wide, her shoulders back. "I'm locking the door."

He grinned. "Good plan." Then he nudged her farther inside and shut the door with him on the other side, barely holding back a chuckle when the doorknob, indeed, was locked with a loud click.

Rain pattered against the wide sliding glass door that looked out onto rows of fields on the other side of a spacious living area. Hallie woke up and stretched, warm and sated. Comfortable. A smell surrounded her—masculine and forest-y. She blinked, her back against a very firm front. A male one.

She swallowed and looked around, not moving. The night came back to her. The storm, the crash, the cowboy. The one bracketing her from behind, spooning her within a cocoon of safety that *so* was not safe. But it felt good. So darn good and warm and tempting. She started to slide toward the edge of the bed.

The arm resting casually at her hip moved and banded around her waist, tugging her back into ripped male muscle. "Mmm." The low sound was sleepy, and firm lips skimmed along the back of her neck.

She shivered, and her body did a slow roll. The lips nipped near her ear. Yep. He'd felt the shiver and roll. "Wh-what are you doing in this bed?" Her voice was breathy, and fear wasn't any part of it.

"It's my bed." The slow drawl, all cowboy, came from the man she'd met the night before.

"You said I was safe." Why did he have to feel so good?

He placed the softest of kisses square at the nape of her neck. More shivers, more body rolls. "You are." When she didn't answer, he commenced kissing her shoulder.

"Stop," she said.

He stopped.

"Let me go."

He let go.

The oddest feeling of loss swamped her. She had to bite her tongue, hard, to keep from seeing if he'd follow other orders . . . like starting again. Instead, she scooted to the edge of the bed, stood and turned around. She shouldn't have.

He lay in the bed, the covers at his waist, his bare chest revealed. Smooth, hard muscle with jagged scars and one that looked like a bullet hole above his heart.

His eyes were green—even darker in the morning than she'd noticed the night before. A manly scruff covered his jaw, and the hollows and angles of his rugged face went well with the cowboy drawl. His hair was dark, not quite black but a deeper shade than brown, and it was a little shaggy, as if he didn't have time for a haircut.

Not that he wasn't perfect to start with.

She swallowed. "What's your name?"

"Trent." His gaze wandered down her T-shirt. Rather, his T-shirt that was covering her. The guy was big enough that his shirt was loose on her, a fact she appreciated since she had more curves than a mountain road. "You're called—?"

She tried to stand taller, but it was difficult in her bare feet. "Don't you usually know the names of the women in your bed?" Yeah, she sounded stiff. But at least not turned on, which she definitely was. Darn it.

"Sometimes." He rolled a shoulder in a tough-guy shrug.

The saliva increased in her mouth, and she tried not to drool. That was one heck of a shoulder. Two, really. Muscled and strong and tan. Even the tattoo that covered his right shoulder, of a snarling wolf with sharp claws surrounded by intriguing designs, called to her. But nothing compared to that drawl. So not fair. "I locked the door last night."

"I picked the lock." He levered himself up on one elbow, and the covers fell farther. Not quite far enough.

Finally, she was awakening . . . along with her temper. "You had no right to sleep in the same bed with me last night."

"Baby, I told you it was my bed." He yawned, not nearly impressed enough with her temper. "I didn't touch you, and truth be told, you're the one who rolled your sweet butt into my body, sighed in a way that nearly killed me, and went right back to sleep."

Baby. Nobody in her entire life had called her baby. Her

abdomen heated. She shouldn't like it. Oh, definitely not. In fact, she did not like it. She opened her mouth to tell him so, but his words cut her off.

"I even put a pillow between us, being a perfect gentleman," he complained, his grumpy look too sexy for her peace of mind. "You trapped it with your knees, rolled over, and shoved it to the floor in a gymnastic move I'll be seeing in my dreams for a decade. Then, you *again* snuggled into me."

She pushed her hair out of her face. There was nothing to say.

He didn't let her silence stop him. "You gettin' back in this bed so we can both relieve some tension?" His eyes flared, and his gaze skimmed the tops of her thighs.

She took a step back, when what she really wanted was to relieve tension. Tension was bad for a body. Definitely bad for a woman who needed to be vigilant. In fact, tension could cause heart disease, couldn't it? Her internal debate didn't last. "I need to go pick up my car." She had to get away from Trent, who hadn't bothered with a last name. Most women in his bed probably weren't told his last name. The fewer people who saw her, the better. "Listen, er, Mr. . . ."

"Logan. Trent Logan." He threw back the covers, and thank goodness he was wearing boxer briefs. But they were much more formfitting than the ones he'd given her, and they didn't hide anything. Not at all. He really was all male.

"Trent Logan?" she murmured, rolling the name around on her tongue.

He paused and looked at her over the bed. The one they'd apparently shared all night. "What?"

"It's the perfect cowboy name. One strong syllable

followed by two. Cowboy charm." She grinned and shook her head. "Seriously."

He cocked his head, those intense eyes appraising her. "Word to the wise, Hallie?"

Her breath sped up, and her lungs did some sort of jumpy thing in her chest. "What?"

"You can be grumpy, you can be spunky—you can even be sweet. But the one thing you do not want to be right now, in the bedroom with that bed so close, is cute. Got it?"

She looked for the joke. Looking for the humor in his eyes. Nope. No joke. "Got it," she said, even though she didn't. Not even close. But she also wasn't dumb.

"Good." He reached down and yanked up a pair of faded jeans with holes in them. "Coffee. I need coffee." He led the way to the door and freedom, walking out and not looking back. The atmosphere relaxed with him gone, and she jumped into action.

"Did you say coffee?" she called.

CHAPTER TWO

The only thing that hurt worse than his pounding temples was his groin. The woman in his bed was soft and lush, and walking away created a pisser of a morning. But she'd refused, and that was that. Trent loped, barefooted, into the now vacant clubhouse party room, kicking a couple of red coolie cups out of his way.

The place was a mess. The sofa had been pushed against the far wall, several chairs were overturned, and tequila, beer, and who knows what else covered the floor. At least it was quiet. Harley sat at the sliding glass door at the other end, looking in, his eyes seeking.

Trent cocked his head. The animal had dogged them from afar for almost three months, never coming close until last night. Until the woman needed help.

Trent set the coffee to start and began tossing empty tequila bottles into the large trash can at the end of the bar.

"Are you all reliving your frat days?" Hallie asked dryly, tugging a stool closer to the bar.

He grinned. The woman really was cute. Her hair was now full-on curly around her face, and her blue eyes were still a little sleepy, but she no longer shivered or looked chilly. Instead, she looked tempting in his shirt and older boxers. "It's the end of calving season, darlin'. A party was needed."

"Of course. End of calving season. Everyone needs a party then." Her gaze cut to the dripping coffee as if she could hurry it up.

He chuckled, turning to see that Harley had disappeared from view. "We plan the calving season, hoping against hope we can squeeze it in between the really bad winter weather and the really bad spring weather. Pretty much everyone nailed it this year, and that's that." The coffee finished and he leaned down for two mugs, double-checking they were clean. Close enough. He poured and then nudged one toward her. "I doubt there's cream, but there's probably Baileys in the fridge."

"This is good." She blew on it, her hands curving around the mug.

Lucky mug. A city girl who drank it straight. Interesting. He took several gulps, letting the hot liquid hit his system with a jolt of power. "You a tease?" he asked.

She blinked. "Because I wouldn't have sex with you this morning?"

"Just askin'." And he was. She had wanted him, and he sure as heck had wanted her. "I don't have time for games or lies, so I figured I'd get the scoop." Then, maybe, he'd ask her out that night.

She swallowed some coffee and set the cup down, spinning it gently in her hands. "It's like this." She looked up, her eyes earnest, her face without makeup so pretty it was hard to concentrate on her words. "I'm soft, Trent."

He took another drink of the strong brew. "I noticed, baby." Her soft and sweet body was a temptation. Hopefully she wasn't one of those girls who thought stick-thin was the only way to be. He'd never understood that line of thinking, because women were supposed to be soft and curvy and a handful.

She smiled. "No. I mean, yeah. My body is soft and so is my heart. Very. I can't let you into one without letting you into the other, and I don't know you."

He had been wrong. It wasn't cute that slayed him. It was sweet. He settled back, deciding what to do with her admission. "How many have gotten in?" The question escaped him before he could mull it over.

"You want numbers?" she challenged.

He should definitely not go there. "Yeah."

"One."

He coughed into his coffee and quickly regained control. "How old are you?"

"Twenty-four. You?"

"Thirty-two." Truth be told, the woman looked younger than that. "When?" He didn't elaborate, because she obviously had a brain in her head.

She sipped again, a slight veil coming down over her eyes. "It ended three years ago. I was married." Her voice remained level—too much so.

"When did it start?"

Her grin was quick. "When I was seventeen."

Ah, crap. This wasn't going to be a jilted-lover story. "How'd he die, Hallie?"

She blinked. "I don't know how. Just where. Afghanistan."

Just the word shot him right back there to the desert. He took a bigger gulp, hoping to burn the acid taste out of his mouth. He was settled, he was alive, and so were his brothers. Most of them. Tragedy was over, and he shouldn't share hers.

Then challenge lit her expression. "Shall we talk about your numbers now?"

"Not a chance." He didn't tomcat around like a lot of his brothers, but he hadn't been a monk, either. "What are you doing getting lost in Wyoming in the middle of a storm?"

She stiffened and then settled, her smile lacking something. "I'm just driving through Wyoming to meet some friends in Montana for a girls' week. Fun and wine and gossip."

He leaned in, his interest piqued. "Well now, Hallie. I'm thinkin' that's the first time you've lied to me."

She jolted, emotions scattering across her face, and then settled. "I'm thinkin' my life is none of your business."

Those words rolled right through him with a heat he'd never felt before. He'd known her less than twelve hours, and so far, she'd given him cute, she'd given him sweet, and now she'd hit him over the head with sass. His grin, when he let it loose, was slow and full.

The look in her eyes went from sass to *oh shit*.

Yep. She got him.

It wasn't the first time in Hallie's life she'd felt off-balance, not by far. But the hottie cowboy taking her measure had more brains to him than she'd thought the night before. Oh, he had the good-ole-boy thing down, but something flashed in those dark green eyes. Not for long, but it was there. Alert and predatory.

He shut it down fast, the charm returning.

She had to get out of there, but she needed another cup of coffee first. So she held out her mug for him to refill. Then she looked at the disaster of the room in the light of day. "What the heck is this place? Some sort of party lodge?"

"Yes and no." He leaned against the tall, stainless steel fridge, his torso bare and the top button of his jeans unclasped. His hair was mussed and his jaw a couple days past needing a shave. "Wyoming is a big state, and you're in cattle country. Neighbors are separated by miles . . . and I mean *separated*. My family bought acres of ranch land about six months ago, and we created this lodge to live in as we figured out the best way to work the land. We have one ranch house already, that I've lived in since I supervised the construction of this lodge, the barns, and garages, and now we're mapping out the rest of the property."

Well, that made sense. "So this lodge is kind of like a country club?"

He snorted, looking into his coffee cup. "No. We have country clubs and golf courses . . . somewhere. This is a lodge for us. We haven't named it. So far, we've come up with Cattle Club, Ranch House, or The Lodge. But Wyatt thinks those all sound like cathouses, so . . ."

"Oh." The place looked more like a fraternity house with suites to her. "All right. So you ride horses and party. Makes sense." Then she shook her head. "It's kind of like one of those motorcycle clubs with rooms and patches, but you guys ride horses instead of motorcycles?"

"Baby." That tone. When he spoke with that drawl, it just wasn't fair, and he seemed to know just how good it sounded. "We ride horses, motorcycles, dirt bikes, Razors, four-wheelers, and snowcats. If it can be ridden, we ride it." He jerked his head back.

She looked above the bar, where a hand-carved sign held that very motto. Heat slid into her face. Was that supposed to be an innuendo?

The outside door opened and two extra-broad men walked inside, along with plenty of rain and wind. They were nearly identical—definitely twins. The first guy held her suitcase along with her purse.

"It's crap out there," he said, setting them down on a chair. He paused, his gaze flicking down Hallie's bare legs. "Hello."

Trent's sigh was loud. "Hallie, meet my brothers Zachary and Zeke Snowden."

"Brothers?" she asked, tilting her head.

"We bonded and became family in the . . . military," Trent said.

"I'm Zachary. The good-looking one." Zachary stepped forward to shake hands. He was tall with twinkling brown eyes and even darker hair, and he had to be early thirties? His rugged face showed open affection, and with the brown Stetson on his head and a beige jacket, he was all cowboy. An old scar ran from beneath his right ear, down his neck, to disappear under his shirt.

Zeke gave her a nod, his eyes not twinkling, his hat black. He had a couple of scars across his right temple that looked like a blade had cut deep. Even so, serious hottie, and she couldn't tell them apart except for the scars and differing expressions.

That was one heck of a gene pool.

Zeke tossed keys at Trent, who snatched them easily out of the air with one broad hand. "Pulled the car out early this morning and took it to Mac's Garage in town. The control arms are mangled," Zeke said.

Hallie swiveled. "On my car?"

Zeke's eyebrows rose. "Yeah."

"Why are you telling him and not me?" She didn't have

a lot of power there in a borrowed T-shirt, old boxers, and bare feet, but come on.

Zeke actually focused fully on her this time. His eyebrows returned to their normal spot on his hunky face, and his eyes warmed. "Trent texted me this morning and asked us to pull the car out of the mud and check it out. So we did."

She cleared her throat. "That was kind of you. What do I owe you for towing services?"

The warmth spread from Zeke's eyes to his full mouth, which tipped in a grin. "It's on the house, darlin'."

She'd never been called so many endearments in her entire life. "Thanks." Then she glanced at Trent, trying to stay calm. Somewhat. "Do you know what control arms are and where I can get some?"

His grin tugged something unidentifiable low in her belly. "I'm sure Mac ordered some."

"Yep," Zachary said, looking around the demolished room. "Said he'd have them in a week and be able to install them in a day or so."

Panic slid down her throat. "Oh." She had no car, no money, and no control arms. What the heck were control arms? She stared into her nearly empty mug, her mind spinning.

"When does Wyatt get home? We need to take care of stuff around here," Zeke said.

"Soon," Trent said, his gaze on her.

Zachary lost the grin. "Is everything . . . okay with him?"

"Affirmative," Trent said. "We have enough business to worry about around here. For example, the Newberys had a low calving season—they lost heifers in that slide, and we can do a Zoom vote on it."

What were they talking about? She lifted her gaze and watched him, curiosity rising.

Zachary nodded. "What's the donation?"

"Just a calf each," Trent said. "That'll put them in good shape. By Tuesday."

"Got it," Zeke said. "Let's go, Z." He nodded to his brother. "We have several fences down from the storm, and daylight's burning."

Zachary winked at Hallie and followed his brother. "See you soon."

She finished her coffee, thinking this through. Okay. She probably had enough money for one night at a hotel, and maybe there was a job in town that she could do. It was a small town, so she'd be safe. For a while.

"Babe? What's goin' on in that head of yours?" Trent set his mug in the sink and reached for hers.

She hopped off the bar stool and reached for her suitcase. "Um, nothing. I'll go get dressed. I hate to impose further on you, but would you give me a ride into town? To a hotel?" Then she looked around at the room that so badly needed cleaning. As did the women's restroom. Her head shot up and hope filled her. "Um, who usually cleans this place?"

He looked around. "Well, we had a cleaning lady, but she got irritated and quit. That's one of the items we need to discuss via Zoom. You offering?"

More heat slid into her face. He could tell she was broke, and he was being kind. Man, she hated pity, but she was also desperate. "I'm offering. Twenty dollars an hour, cash, and I stay in one of the rooms until my car is fixed." She held her breath, waiting.

"Twenty dollars an hour, cash, and you're staying at the ranch house."

Her head jerked up. "No."

"Yes." He swept an arm out. "Sorry. No way are you staying out here by yourself—club rules."

Her chin lifted, and she narrowed her gaze. "You're telling me that you couldn't stay out here by yourself one night if you wanted to do so?"

"No. I'm tellin' you that you're not staying out here alone. I promise you'll be perfectly safe at my ranch—I didn't take advantage of you last night, and I never would. Take it or leave it, baby."

Did she have a choice? "Fine, but stop calling me baby."

CHAPTER THREE

When Trent walked into the drizzle outside the clubhouse, the light rain turned the dried mud on his boots to wet mud. Harley stood in the middle of the nearest field, watching him. Man, that wolf was getting even weirder.

The twins were double-checking the various garage doors before heading out. Zachary looked up. "Does Wyatt need backup?"

"No. He checked in, and the mission is good. He has enough backup." Trent didn't have time to talk about this. "It's his last mission, and then we're free." Probably. Wyatt had one more job to do to repay a favor from his past, and then their soldier days would be behind them. Would ranching be enough for all of them? He wasn't sure.

Zach grinned now, his body relaxing. "Good. Where's the city girl?"

"Wanted to take a shower and change into clean clothes," Trent said, eyeing the fences lining the property. He tugged a cell phone from his back pocket. "Has service returned?" It went out often, and it was hit-or-miss whether the call would go through. He had a satellite phone in the clubhouse but didn't want to dig it out of one of the safes.

Zeke nodded. "Zachary already has three dates lined up for the weekend, so we have service."

Zachary pulled down a door and locked several snow-cats safely inside. "I'm a lonely guy."

Trent rolled his eyes and dialed quickly.

"Simpson," a low voice rumbled over the sound of wind in the background.

"Hey, Greg, it's Trent. What time do you have your kids heading out to clean the clubhouse?" Trent might have to cut them off at the main road. The Simpson kids were two boys and a girl, all teens, and they liked to earn going-out money. Considering he'd lied to Hallie that they didn't have anybody to clean the clubhouse, he hoped he'd timed this right.

Greg sighed. "I have two fences down and the kids are helping right now. I'll send them out this afternoon."

"Tell 'em I got it covered this time and not to worry about it for the next week. I know they're trying to earn money, so send them to the ranch house for work if they have extra hours. We have plenty for them to do." Water dripped from the rim of his hat onto his shirt.

"You got it. Bye." Greg disengaged the call.

Trent looked up to see both of his brothers staring at him, Zachary with a shit-eating grin and Zeke with his usual frown. "What?"

"I thought you were moving back to the club and forcing Wyatt to take over the ranch house. Said it was too quiet out there." Surprisingly, it was Zeke who spoke first.

Trent shrugged. "It's a better environment for Hallie than this party place, at least until I figure out what's going on with her and send her on her way."

"Is the city girl in trouble?" Zeke asked.

"Yeah," Trent said softly.

Zachary tested the lock on the entry door to the second garage. "Our kind of trouble?"

"I don't know. Yet." Trent glanced up at the rolling black clouds.

Zachary grew still, his amusement disappearing. "We don't bring trouble home. You know that."

"No kidding, Zachary," Trent returned, looking around. "That's why I'm taking her to the ranch house and away from our home here." Now wasn't the time to discuss any of this. "We'd better get on those fences."

"Affirmative." Zeke headed for a silver Dodge truck with Zachary on his heels. "Give us a call when you hit the south pastures, and we'll meet up there. Midafternoon."

Zachary climbed into the passenger's seat, his limp barely noticeable even though he'd taken a knife to the leg just a few months ago. "Tell the city girl I have a couple hours free this weekend if she wants a tour of town." He shut the door before Trent could tell him where to put his free hours.

Zeke paused with his arm on the door. "You have to stop takin' in strays, brother. Zachary, in his smooth way, is right. We don't need missions close to home. In fact, we agreed there would be no missions touching this place— remember?"

True, but Zeke hadn't seen the panic in the woman's blue eyes that morning. Or the night before. Trent sobered. "I know. I'll sort her out fast." Then he'd get back to his casual and easy life. Alone.

Zeke's eyes remained perfectly blank. "If you need help, let me know." On that note, he stepped into his truck and ignited the engine, spinning around.

Yeah, his brother, all of his brothers, would have his back no matter what—even if he was screwing up what they'd so painstakingly built out of blood and death. Trent watched the taillights through the rainy day before making another call, this one to the ranch-house housekeeper. "Hi, Mrs. Leiton."

She harrumphed through the line. "Trent? What the heck did you get on this white shirt the other day? I swear by all that's holy, you're not a teenager any longer. The last thing I need is to try and get"—she sniffed loudly—"dark rum and Coke out of a white shirt. Why can't you be a normal man and drink clear liquids? Rum is for girls. For the love of Pete. Turn to gin or vodka."

"I think that's actually Bart's barbecue sauce." It had tons of rum in it. He looked around at the now quiet and lonely clubhouse. "You know, I think you have a point."

She paused. "Excuse me?"

He rolled his eyes. Despite her sixty years, his house-keeper was more of a drama queen than anybody he'd ever met. "I have been overworking you. How about I pay to fly you to visit your sister in Arizona for a week? You could get out of this rain and soak in some sun."

Quiet spun for a moment. "What the heck have you gotten yourself into now?"

He leaned against the garage door and knocked his head against the metal several times. "Would you believe I'm actually trying to do the right thing?"

"I would, but that doesn't mean you have a lick of sense." She'd worked for him the last few months, and she was good at her job. The woman was also a menace when she held a wooden spoon in her hand, and she'd whacked him more than once with it. "What is going on?"

"First class," he said, sweetening the pot. "And a rented convertible the second you land."

She gasped. "I adore you, but there's no way I'm refusing

that offer. I have to go home and pack. I can be on the seven o'clock flight tonight, and Muriel is having a pool party tomorrow. She's been holding it over my head for a week, considering we're in a tsunami here, and if I show up in a convertible, she'll lose her mind."

He chuckled, scouting the surrounding area for any threats. "Good. Go. I'll take care of the ticket and the car."

"But—" Movement sounded. "I've started the spring cleaning, and the place is torn apart in every direction. Even the laundry—and I know not all of those clothes are yours. Zeke keeps dropping stuff off. It looks like a disaster."

"Perfect," he said, straightening as Hallie walked out of the clubhouse.

Mrs. Leiton sighed. "Just don't do anything crazy, okay?"

It was too late for that. "Have a nice trip." He disengaged the call and watched the city girl look warily around the vacant parking area. Her shoulders were stiff and her fists clenched. Today she wore dark jeans, a blue sweater that matched her eyes, and a silver clip in her hair, keeping tendrils off her pretty face.

Her gaze landed on him, and relief filled them before being quickly banked.

Yeah. Definitely too late.

Hallie tried to hide her reaction to seeing the big cowboy near the black truck. Then she looked around and really took in her surroundings. The clubhouse and bedrooms were in one building, while huge matching buildings flanked it on either side, making a square-shaped parking area in the middle. Unlike the main building with its many wide windows and sliding glass doors, the metal buildings held normal windows, wide garage doors as well as people-sized doors.

Beyond each structure, fields and hills rolled away to the mountains that rose all around them. The wind picked up and she shivered.

He watched her from beneath his weathered brown cowboy hat, those dark eyes hooded.

They were alone. Completely.

She hesitated and studied the wolf, who had run across the field to sit on the concrete near one of the garage doors the second she'd walked out. He was a real freaking wolf. His thick fur was a myriad of colors—white, gold, black, brown, even red—and his eyes, a deep golden yellow, were focused on her. His muzzle was white, while darker colors spread up between his eyes and flowed throughout his coat. He yawned, revealing shockingly sharp canines. "He's real," she whispered.

Trent nodded, surprise lifting his eyebrows. "Yeah. Full-bred wolf—and he rarely comes this close. I think he likes you."

"How old is he?" She wasn't sure which looked more dangerous—the wolf or the cowboy.

"Around two, I guess." Trent moved toward his truck, long and lean with a natural grace. He opened the passenger-side door. "Hop up. Another storm is coming."

What in the world was she doing? She'd jumped from one disaster to another, and now she was alone with a guy twice her size and a *wolf*. "I'm not usually so stupid," she admitted, hesitating.

Trent smiled, the flash of white teeth somehow reassuring. "Hallie? You left stupid behind at the interstate."

Laughter bubbled out of her before she could stop it.

His smile slid away, leaving an intensity in his gaze that fluttered through her abdomen. "I like your laugh."

She shifted her stance. "Thanks." Then she pushed a wayward curl away from her face. "I didn't mean to go so far from the interstate and am still not sure how I ended up so lost." The storm had come up suddenly, and visibility had been nil the night before. "I was trying to find a place to pull over for the night."

He gestured her toward the truck. "I could be wrong, but I'm figuring you were already in a mess before the storm took over."

Oh, he had no idea. She plastered on a bright smile and strode forward, letting him assist her up into the truck, his easy strength stealing her breath. "Nope. Just heading for a fun girls' weekend."

He leaned over her to fasten the seat belt, his elbow brushing her arm. "It's odd you haven't tried to call *the girls* to let them know you aren't going to make it." Electricity ran over her skin at his touch, and that scent of male and leather was going to destroy her. He leaned back.

She blinked, affected by his nearness when what she really needed was to keep her wits about her. "I called them after my shower." Hopefully the service had been restored.

"Huh." He tugged off his hat and tapped it against his jean-clad thigh, scattering water. Apparently it had been raining earlier. "Darlin', you're a crappy liar. Not that you're crappy and a liar, but that you completely suck at lying. Worst I've ever seen, to be honest."

Heat flowed up and into her face until her cheeks burned. "I am not."

"Are too." He plunked the hat back on his thick hair. "Yep. Your eyes dart to the left, you lick your lips, and your entire body stiffens. Then you make eye contact and don't turn away. Even if I wasn't trained in detecting falsehoods, I could tell you're lying. You should never play poker. Like ever."

She breathed in slowly, meeting his eyes, exactly as he said she did. "You were trained in detecting lies?"

"In my past life," he said, his eyes flat for a second. Then he turned as the wolf stood and shook his fur, padding closer. "Well, this is new." He watched the animal move to the truck and then opened the back door. "I guess he's coming with us?"

She blinked. "You don't make your wolf go with you?"

The flatness disappeared, and the sparkle came back into Trent's emerald eyes. "He's not mine. All wild, all animal, and he goes where and with whom he wants. He hangs out in the distance and watches us, but he's never tried to get close before. I think it's you."

Well, that was crazy. "Why me?"

He shrugged. "I don't know. He watches all of my brothers and seems to stick closest to Wyatt, who's out of town right now. The animal is a mystery."

"Brothers, like you had the same parents?" Somehow, she didn't think so.

"No. Brothers here in the club." Trent watched the wolf jump into the back seat. "Looks like he's coming home with us this time."

Home with us. The words implied an intimacy she craved—for about two seconds. Was she putting this nice cowboy in danger by staying with him until her car was fixed? She was in the middle of nowhere, and she was almost out of burner phones, but it felt as if she was safely off the grid. Whatever the grid was. She only had one more burner phone left, and then she'd need to find another store to buy more.

The truck door shut, and she jumped.

The wolf immediately flopped down across the seat, watching her with one eye.

Trent chuckled. "He doesn't want to scare you. Talk nice to him so he can relax." Then he shut the back door.

How did one talk nicely to a wild wolf? "Um, you don't look wild. Except for the teeth. Your teeth are definitely sharp."

One ear twitched.

She grinned. Okay. For a wild animal that could tear her apart, he was kind of cute. "At least you're exactly what you look like," she whispered. "Some wolves are hidden behind manners and nice suits."

Harley turned his head toward her, both eyes focusing.

Then Trent stretched his muscled form into the truck, taking up most of the space and all of the oxygen. That quickly, she remembered that sometimes wolves were handsome and helpful, too.

What had she just gotten herself into?

CHAPTER FOUR

Trent locked the fourth gate on the way out, driving along pastures and keeping an eye on heads of cattle and the land. He wasn't the most patient of the brothers, but he was close. The woman was safe in his truck, so he could wait her out.

She watched the hills roll by outside. "Why are the fences locked so securely?"

It was a good question. A smart one. Fences were common but locks few in cattle country. "We keep high-powered machines in the shops at the clubhouse," he said, which was partially true.

"Oh." She leaned closer to the window as a couple of young calves scampered on the other side of the fence. "Those little cows can get through the fences to the road."

"Yeah, but they won't go far from their mamas quite yet," he said, keeping an eye on them anyway. "Wyoming is an open-range state, so we're always careful."

"Open range?" she asked.

His assessment of her as a city girl had been spot-on. There were several states that were open range, and apparently she'd never heard of the concept. "Yeah. Cattle have the right to go wherever they want, and if you hit them, it's your fault. In fact, we don't even have to build fences to keep them in."

"What if you live here and don't want cows in your front lawn?"

"You build a fence to keep them out." He rubbed the scruff across his jaw. "Of course, you can charge the cattle owner for half of the fence, maybe." He kept to the range, avoiding town for now. "You never said where you're from."

She stiffened just enough for him to notice. "Oh. Well. I'm from Denver."

Right. Sure, she was. "Really? Which neighborhood?" he asked, reaching the first fence on the ranch house property. He stopped by the gate and waited.

"Sloan Lake," she said instantly.

He pressed the remote control and the gate unlocked, swinging open. "That's a nice area in Denver," he said calmly. One that'd be easy to confirm on the Internet.

She watched the gate swing inward. "You're awfully high-tech. I take it we're on your ranch?"

"It's not mine. It's the only patch of the land that already had a house on it, and since I was the first in town, I stayed there while having the clubhouse built. I keep meaning to move out but just haven't gotten around to it." He didn't need a home, since he liked his life the way it was right now. He drove through and waited for the gate to engage behind them.

She looked past the wolf and out the back window as the gate swung shut and locked. Slowly, the color began to drain from her pretty face. She studied the rolling fields, cows, and surrounding mountains.

Although it was a little late for her to realize her

precarious position, her current predicament wasn't all her fault. Though she should've been a lot more aware of her options the night before. "If you were mine, we'd be having a difficult conversation right now, sweetheart."

She jumped, her blue eyes wide.

He sighed and pointed to the glovebox. "There's a loaded Glock 19 in the glovebox. You can have it if you want."

She jerked and looked at the glovebox as if something might jump out at her. "Glock 19? Does it have the safety on?"

His chin almost dropped to his chest. "Honey, the Glock doesn't have a manual safety. Have you ever shot a gun?"

"No," she whispered.

He exhaled slowly to keep his temper in check. "Then don't take that one." What were his options with her? If he took her to town, she'd try to find money to pay for her car and then she'd run. Every protective instinct he had wanted to tuck her away from danger at the ranch, but he didn't know her. Oh, he knew she was being chased, but by whom? Then she turned toward him, those eyes so blue and terrified.

He was lost. Completely. "All right. Here's the deal. We're going to the ranch, you're going to be safe, and you're going to tell me what is going on. All right?"

She blinked. "Nothing is going on."

Terrible liar. Seriously. She couldn't stop fidgeting. "Who are you running from?" He sped up, and the truck bumped across the muddy road.

"Nobody," she whispered, still looking pale.

This wouldn't do. Though he couldn't blame her for being afraid of him, considering they'd just met. He pulled over and whipped out his phone, opening a video call.

"Trent? Is Wyatt okay?" Austin asked, his face too close to the camera.

"Yeah. He checked in and all is well. Sheriff Austin McDay, this is Hallie. I don't know her last name, and she's being stubborn about telling it to me." He handed the phone over to Hallie.

She swallowed, looking at Austin, who wore a black cowboy hat and a badge hanging from his neck. "Hi."

"Hi. Do you have something to report?" Austin asked.

"No," she said, her dark brows drawing down as she looked at Trent.

"What are you doing?" Austin's question was for Trent.

Trent reclaimed his phone. "I'm taking her to the ranch house, and she seems nervous about it, so I thought I'd let the law know what I was doing. You can call and check on her periodically." He studied the woman. "Listen, Hallie. This is up to you. If you want me to take you to town, I will. However, I could use some help at my place, as well as the clubhouse, and I'll pay you. Either way, it's your choice. I'm not going to force you." If she refused his help, he'd put some security on her in town until he figured out how much danger she was in.

She swallowed. A slight smile tugged at her bow-shaped bottom lip. "Maybe you and the local law are in cahoots. How do I know I'm safe now?"

Cahoots? Who used the word *cahoots* these days? Everything in Trent warmed and then heated. If she got any more adorable, he'd just go down on one knee and propose right now—something that was so not going to happen. He had to help her and get her out of town before that kind of idea took root. He needed freedom, after his past. "Huh. Austin? Are we in cahoots?" he asked, unable to keep the amusement out of his voice.

By the narrowing of Austin's gray eyes, he wasn't in the mood to play. "No. In fact, I believe we have a lot going on right now, brother. Give the phone back to the woman."

My woman. The thought hit Trent before he could stop it. Nope. Definitely not going there. He handed the phone over, watching her carefully.

Her hands were small and her nails natural with a light cream-colored polish. She took a deep breath before looking down at the phone. "Yes, Sheriff?"

"What's your last name, sweetheart?" Austin asked.

She tried so hard to keep her expression neutral that Trent wanted to wince. "Smith."

No way. She hadn't really said *Smith*, had she? Trent barked out a laugh, unable to help himself. She jolted, her wide eyes swinging to him. Then that pretty jaw firmed, and it was all he could do not to take a bite out of it. Her sweetness, maybe even innocence, smashed him right in the heart. But that stubborn challenge in her eyes—well now. That hit him much farther south.

He leaned closer to the phone, seeing the realization dawn across Austin's rugged face.

His brother shook his head. "I take it you don't need me to send Mac out to meet with you?"

While they all could detect falsehoods, Mac was a human lie detector with unreal skills.

"I don't think he's needed," Trent said dryly. Hallie really was the worst liar he'd ever seen. Why did that intrigue him so?

"Cute and sweet are a dangerous combination for you, brother," Austin warned, acceptance already lightening his tone.

Trent grinned. "And not for you?"

"Nope. I just want obedience from my woman," Austin

said quietly. "Pretty much demand it, actually, which is why I haven't found her." He sighed. "I guess this is the next step for us, right?" Then he handed his phone over to his receptionist. "Reassure Miss . . . *Smith* that she's safe with Trent."

Ethel Ryerson grinned into the phone. "Hey there. You're safe. These boys are wild, but they'd never hurt a woman. Or anybody, really." Her white hair was streaked with blue today, which matched her eyeshadow. Her skin was weathered but impressively unlined for a woman over the age of eighty. She ruled the sheriff's office with homemade donuts and an iron fist, and sometimes it seemed she was from an age long gone by. "Although, if you're in trouble, you might as well confess all right now, cause they're gonna want to fix it."

Hallie leaned away from the phone. "I'm not in trouble. Well, except for my car being a mess without control arms."

Ethel frowned. "What are control arms?"

"Right? I have no idea, but apparently they're important." Hallie sighed. "Thank you for reassuring me."

"Sure thing," Ethel said. "Come on into town one day and I'll give you the scoop about everybody."

Hallie plucked at a string on her jeans. "That's kind of you. Thanks."

Oh, it was clear as day that Miss Hallie had no plans to stay in town. Trent rubbed his chest. He had to keep things casual, and apparently that was fine with her. Good. She brought a light to the day that he hadn't realized was dark, and that had to mean something, right? Just temporarily, though.

It was fast and it was crazy, but he'd stopped being a normal guy a long time ago in a rodent-infested cell on the other side of the world. They all had. When he found something good, something he needed, he didn't hesitate to enjoy the moment.

Hallie was good, and something told him she was needed. But she also wasn't casual, and he couldn't take advantage of her. He'd never been friends with a woman—maybe that's what they both needed.

Yeah. He could banish the aching desire he had for her. Well, probably.

Austin came back on the line. "There's another storm moving in tonight, so I'll meet you guys in the south pastures this afternoon to repair what we can. You know what I need you to bring."

Trent took the phone. "I can handle it alone."

"I'm sure you can, but that's nonnegotiable." Austin didn't smile.

Trent nodded. That was fair. Austin was the president of the group, the sheriff, and had a right to protect everyone. "Okay." He'd bring something with her prints on it so Austin could run them through the system. They might as well know what they were up against. He tossed his phone onto the dash. "So, Smith. Do you want me to take you to town or not?"

She settled back in her seat. "No. I'll take the job at the ranch house until my car is fixed."

He made a mental note to ask Mac to take a little extra time with the car. "Ethel has that effect on people." He drove the truck back down the road, looking for the right words. "Is the law after you?" While he seriously doubted it, he needed to ask.

"No." She snorted.

All right. That was the truth. Anything else, anybody else, he could handle. "Hallie—"

She turned toward him and threw her hands up. "Enough. All right? I don't need or want your help, cowboy." Pink blazed across her cheekbones, fascinating him. "I'm not in trouble. I'm not on the run. I'm just trying to start a new life somewhere. Yeah, you're sexy with that drawl and all, and cowboys are intriguing, but I'm not looking for a sweet good-old-boy right now. So butt out of my personal business, and we'll get along just fine this week."

Well, at least she wasn't afraid of him any longer. "You think I'm sexy?" he asked, throwing in extra drawl.

The growl she gave before turning to look outside both amused him and made his jeans too tight. It was going to be a long week, but there was no doubt in his mind that she'd be worth it. He could maintain sexy, but never in his life had he been sweet. That wasn't in the cards for him, or for anybody in his family.

Would the woman still look at him with that intrigue in her eyes if she saw the real him? For the first time since meeting her, the darkness started to edge back in. Reality, as he well knew, wasn't on his side.

But he was on hers. It was a good place to start.

CHAPTER FIVE

The truck was nearly taken out by a woman in a battered SUV taking the corner at the end of the driveway too fast. She had gray hair and honked twice as she sped past.

Hallie caught her breath. "Who was that?"

Trent shrugged. "Crazy driver. Might've been somebody from the county checking the meters. They have the fence codes."

Hallie frowned and looked in her side mirror at the rapidly disappearing vehicle. "Was that a mop in the back seat?"

"Mop? Nope. Looked like a fishing pole to me."

She blinked. "Where is there to fish around here?"

"Rivers?" Trent pulled to a stop in front of a lovely ranch home. "Let's get inside before the rain hits again."

She jumped out and hurried across the stone parking area and then inside when Trent opened the door. The wolf bounded out the opposite direction toward a barn.

The ranch house was a dream come true. Wide and sprawling with more windows than Hallie would've ever imagined, each facing a field, barn, or mountain. Cattle dotted the landscape along with some trees and a winding river. As a kid, alone in government housing while her mother worked, she'd dreamed of homes like this. Places like this. She twirled around in the living room with its masculine leather furniture and stared at the massive stone fireplace. "I can't believe you live here."

"Just temporarily. Whoever settles down first will probably live here if we haven't built the other homes yet." He smiled, dumping her suitcase near the door. His chest exhaled as if he'd been holding his breath. "But I'm glad you like it."

Like it? "I love it." She paused. "Is anybody close to settling down?"

"No."

She looked around again, trying not to let a bizarre disappointment filter through her at his blunt answer. Beauty had always struck her deep, although the home couldn't come close to the beauty of the man. He was almost too good to be real. She had the oddest urge to ask about the scars down his chest or the bullet hole above his heart, but she was the one who'd insisted they stay out of each other's business. "I notice there are tons of windows and sliding glass doors here, just like at the clubhouse." His room there had boasted a wide glass door beyond the sitting area.

He nodded, his eyes darkening with a glitter that made her breath catch in her throat. "I like to see outside and be able to get there quick if necessary."

Her lungs wobbled. There was so much more to his explanation, but she had no right to pry. Yet he waited as if giving her the opportunity. "It'll be a pleasure to clean this place."

"We'll see about that." Letting her off the hook, he

gestured through a wide archway into what looked like a kitchen.

She wandered that way and stopped cold. The kitchen was beautiful, with counters made of rock-brown granite that had silver and gold winding through it, stainless steel appliances, and soft buttercream walls. But every drawer and cupboard was open, with the contents scattered throughout the entire room, over the bar, and on the table in the breakfast nook. "What happened?"

His sigh was exaggerated but kind of cute, like a mountain lion's if it sighed. "In the middle of spring cleaning, my housekeeper had to go see her sister in Arizona. Some sort of family emergency, I guess." He rubbed a hand through his mussed-up hair. "She left a text that my room and the laundry room are even worse."

Hallie turned to study him. His expression was blank and carefully innocent, which put her instincts on alert. But why else would his housekeeper make a mess and leave if not for an emergency? As strong as the attraction was between them, it was nuts to think he'd sent off his housekeeper just so Hallie could have a job to do and a place to stay. It made no sense that the fleeing and happily honking woman from the road was involved. Hallie's ego would never be that big. "I hope your housekeeper is all right and the emergency isn't too bad."

He lifted a powerful shoulder. "She'll check in. I'm sure it's all okay." Then he looked around. "I don't suppose you know how to cook?"

She loved cooking, and this kitchen was sublime. "Yeah, I can cook."

His eyebrows rose and his eyes softened. "I'll double your pay if you cook for the week. Like really cook."

She didn't know the difference between cook and really cook, but she'd take double the pay. "Does your house-keeper cook?"

He grimaced. "Kind of?"

Ah. Okay. "Well, we haven't eaten yet, and I'm sure you have to go do ranch stuff. Why don't I clear a couple of spaces here and make breakfast? I mean, if there's food in the fridge." Her stomach rumbled right on time. She turned, stretched over a bunch of plastic bowls on the floor, and opened the fridge. Yep. Eggs, bacon, cheese, and some decent salsa. Humming, she pulled out the lower freezer and found hash browns. "I can do a country breakfast." Seemed fitting.

He leaned against the thick wood trim of the entryway, his thumbs tucked into his worn jeans. With his green tee stretched tight across his chest beneath a brown jacket, he looked every inch the hungry cowboy. "It's a deal. I'll take your suitcase to your room."

She jumped over a bunch of mismatched pots and pans, already removing her jacket. "I can take my own suitcase."

"Right." He turned and strode to the front door, fetching both her case and her purse. "Follow me."

The cowboy was a gentleman. Guilt flushed through her as she followed him, her steps more hesitant. He was a nice guy just trying to help her, and she might've brought danger to his door. The people after her wouldn't care who else got hurt, and they had found her twice already.

The guest room was peaceful, with a homemade white quilt on the queen-size bed. The furniture was a soft white with a matching thick rug over the wood floor. A wide sliding glass door led out to a quiet alcove with two chairs surrounded by what looked like hydrangea bushes.

He set her suitcase on the floor and her purse on the bed. Her other phone rolled out.

His head tilted and he studied the phone. "Is that a burner phone, darlin'?"

Panic tightened her throat. "Just a prepaid one. Since I'm moving, I thought I'd get a new phone and plan once I figure out where I want to live."

He turned, his gaze piercing. "I thought you were going to visit friends for a girls' weekend."

She gulped, her mind spinning. "Yeah, I am. Girls' weekend and we were going to find a fun place for me to live. I need a change. I think I told you that?"

"You've told me a lot of things." His voice was deep with an edge anybody with a brain would heed. "Hallie, you're safe here. You have time to realize that fact, but time is never endless."

She blinked. "What does that mean?"

"It means that I'm a reasonable man, but you're coming close to exhausting my patience." He looked big and broad in the doorway, and if he wanted to keep her from leaving, he could easily.

She put both hands on her hips. "Why should I care if you run out of patience?" Yeah, she was challenging him.

His smile held a predatory gleam. "That's a stupid question."

She took a step back. Stupid? The hair prickled at the nape of her neck, and she noticed, for the first time, a sense of danger around him. From him. "It is not." Lame. Totally lame response.

He moved then, coming right at her.

She froze.

He was a powerful man, and he moved fast when he wanted. He reached her, lifting her chin with one finger.

Her knees trembled, partly from fear. Partly from something else she didn't want to examine too closely. "Um—"

"No. No more lies." Then he lowered his head, and his mouth took hers.

Trent had never tasted anything sweeter in his entire life. He kissed her, trying to go gentle. Then she opened her mouth, accepting him, and he was lost. He dove in fast, taking more, his thumb sweeping along her delicate jawline. He'd kissed plenty of women in his life, probably more than he could count.

Nobody came close to this one.

She murmured and stepped closer into him, her hands sliding up his chest to tangle in his hair. Her body pressed against his, all of that softness against him. He growled and clasped her hip, moving her into the wall, sliding his knee between her legs.

Her gasp into his mouth only spurred him on.

Then she gave a soft sound of need, and he paused, his hand tangled in her thick hair. He gentled the kiss, releasing her with definite reluctance.

She looked up at him, her blue eyes dazed and her pretty pink lips swollen.

Never, in his entire life, had he felt something so right as Hallie against him. "Would it completely freak you out if I admitted that you're tempting me to actually keep you?" he rumbled.

Need and want and humor rippled through her eyes. "Like an 'I want you' keeping, or a serial killer keeping?" she asked, her body relaxing in his hold.

"I told you not to be cute," he whispered.

She smiled, arousal splashing crimson across her high cheekbones. "I'm afraid it's my default setting."

The woman was killing him. Without question. He released her hip and untangled his fingers from her hair, acutely aware that the bed was right behind him. Her default setting was cute? Yeah, it definitely was, and she was quick on her feet with that cute and a whole boatload of spunk.

He stepped away from her before he could toss her on the bed. Keeping her was out of the question, and it was shocking how much he wanted to, all of a sudden.

She looked at him, her eyes glowing. "How did you get the scar above your heart?"

The question caught at him, and he paused. "I'll tell you my secrets if you tell me yours." Although he wouldn't share that part of himself—his heart—with anybody. He'd left it behind years ago, and whoever wanted in his life had to be okay with that fact.

"Will you?" she murmured, seeing too far inside him. "Somehow, I don't think so."

Smart and insightful. It figured he'd be intrigued by a woman who'd try to look inside him, even though it was mainly dark in there.

The walls started to close in on him, and he turned to stare out the slider. He could reach the door, open it, and be outside in fresh air within 0.7 seconds, and that thought calmed him. There was a reason the ranch and clubhouse had multiple exits.

"Trent?" Hallie asked, bringing him back to the present.

He turned, quickly banking his emotions. "I believe you promised me breakfast. Go ahead and get settled. Then we can eat, and I'll show you the rest of the house before I head out to take care of the fences." He could just secure her purse and license, but that wouldn't foster trust between them. For that matter, getting her prints for Austin was probably in the gray area, too.

She faltered, obviously catching on to his mood. Her fingers went to her bottom lip. "Are you okay?"

"I'm fine." He turned and strode out of the room, heading for the living room with its floor-to-ceiling windows and double sliding-glass doors. Opening one, he walked out across the glossy and fancy stained-cement porch to the end near the lawn. Cool wind whipped at him, brushing his hair back. He took a deep breath.

Freedom. Wind and air, no matter how volatile, would always feel like freedom to him. To all of them. They'd been captured by the enemy and tortured for more than seven years, but that hellhole was far away. He hadn't had a flashback in eons, and it was surprising how close one had just come.

His hands shook, so he shoved them in his pockets. His bar called to him, and he really wanted a whiskey. So he purposely stayed outside, away from alcohol.

No person or habit would ever rule him again. Alcohol was to be enjoyed for fun, not used as a crutch. Period.

He surveyed their land. Rolling hills and cattle stretched out as far as the eye could see, showing fences and waterways that led right up to the brutal mountains around them. They'd build a ranch to the west and another to the east once the weather calmed down. For his brothers. They might've had different parents, but they'd bonded in blood and death. Become brothers. Family. When they'd remade themselves, when they'd *rebuilt* themselves, they'd done so here in the wilds of Wyoming.

Sounds came from the kitchen, and he partially turned to see Hallie setting out fixings for breakfast, her movements economical and smooth. Her lips were pursed as she concentrated. She filled out her sweater and jeans like a bombshell from a fifties movie. Her thick mahogany hair was piled on her head out of the way, and his fingers itched to tug that clip out and let the mass fall wild and free around her shoulders.

He'd survived an unimaginable hell, and he'd made a new life here. Although it didn't make any logical sense, he was starting to want her in it, and he'd never lost a campaign or a battle of wills. But was he fighting himself or her? He had survived hell, and he didn't need any more risks. Any more responsibilities. No matter how special she was—or how badly he already wanted her.

She looked up, her gaze catching his.

He smiled, letting the predator in him show, maybe wanting to scare her off. He definitely expected her to look away.

She didn't. Her lips firmed and her chin actually lowered.

Challenge accepted.

CHAPTER SIX

Hallie finished the fifth load of laundry and stared at the different piles she'd created on Trent's oversized bed. Covered in a deep gray comforter, the bed was so large, it had to be a special order. The room smelled like him—woodsy and wild.

She frowned at the stack of ripped and torn jeans, having started it as a possible throwaway pile. It turned out that almost all of his jeans were ripped or torn.

She'd hung shirts in his oversized closet but didn't want to go through his drawers to figure out where to put socks, boxer-briefs, and the jeans. She bit her lip.

There was something way too intimate about doing Trent's laundry. Especially after that kiss earlier.

Her mind was still reeling. She touched her lips again. Who kissed like that? She'd forgotten everything while his mouth was on hers.

Thunder rolled outside, and she jumped. She was getting in way too deep with the cowboy, way too fast. She couldn't get him killed. And yeah, she kind of liked the way he looked at her—as if she was sweet and smart. She really didn't want him to know what a moron she'd been.

Because he was almost perfect. Tall and strong, tough and kind. More importantly, he had a safe job ranching in Wyoming. Maybe she could head back this way once she'd figured out her life.

Once she found safety. If she became safe. She returned to her room, picking up the burner phone and doing a quick search on the Internet before making her call.

"Mac's," a deep voice answered.

She cleared her throat. "Um, hi. This is Hallie, and I think you have my car? It's red and needs something called control arms?"

"Yep. This is Mac. What can I do for you?" Mac had a low drawl and sounded like he was in his early thirties.

"You can get control arms faster than a week," she said in a rush. "Is that possible?"

Mac was quiet for a moment. "Nope."

She blinked. Just nope? "How necessary are control arms?"

"Well, do you want your suspension system to allow your tires to go up and down in a controlled manner?" Mac drawled.

She sighed. "Only if absolutely necessary."

"It's necessary," Mac returned. "Where's Trent, anyway?"

So the mysterious Mac knew she was at Trent's? Figured. She'd lived in a small town for a short time as a kid, before she and her mom had moved on, and she remembered there weren't any secrets. "He's out doing something with fences," she said. "Is there any way you can put a rush on fixing my car?"

"Nope," Mac said again. "I had to order parts, and I'm working the land while also running the garage. I'm doing the best I can for you." He sounded smooth and earnest.

She had the oddest feeling that he could hurry it up if he wanted. Why wouldn't he do so and charge her double or something? "Is there any reason you can't speed it up?" she asked.

"I just gave you reasons," Mac said easily. "You're safe out at the ranch house for the week, and I know Trent needs the help, so why not make a little cash before you head out?"

Yeah. No secrets. She shook her head. Maybe everything was just as it seemed. "I guess." She could try to rent a car, but she was out of money and she couldn't use her credit cards. They were way too easy to trace.

"Bye." Mac ended the call.

She looked at the phone in her hand. "Well." That was a little rude, but he had answered her questions. There was an office in the ranch house with a laptop, but it was probably password protected. Then she glanced down at the phone. Well, it had Internet. So she looked up control arms, and whether they were actually important. Then she called her mailbox—the one on the phone she used to have.

There were several hang-ups and then a terse message from her former neighbor to call.

She took a deep breath and opened the sliding door, stepping outside to her little alcove. Even the chairs were charming, and she sat, staring at the beautiful foliage that led to more fields beyond. Then she dialed.

"Hello?" Mrs. Planton said before coughing several times. The woman still smoked a pack a day, even though she was in her sixties and said she knew better.

"Hi, Mrs. P." Hallie tried to keep her voice even. "I received your message."

"Oh, Hallie. Hello." Mrs. P's voice lowered. "You said

to call if anything strange happened, and that man has been back several times looking for you. Brad was his name? He finally went to each apartment to see if anybody knew where you'd gone."

Hallie sat back and closed her eyes. "What did you tell him?"

"Just that you disappeared in the dark of night," Mrs. P said, gleeful conspiracy in her voice. "Nobody else knew a thing, either. He doesn't seem to be getting over you, dear."

It wasn't the failed romance that would get Hallie killed, unfortunately. "Thank you for covering for me."

"Always. Are you safe? Do you need money?"

Hallie grinned. "I'm safe and I don't need money." Not that the elderly woman had any to spare. "Take care of yourself, okay?"

"Of course. If you need backup, you call me." Mrs. P hacked away several seconds. "Bye."

"Bye," Hallie murmured, disengaging the call. Then she carefully tore the cell phone apart and crushed every piece of it beneath her shoe before throwing it all away in the garbage.

She had dinner to make.

Trent cut off a section of barbed wire, bent over as the wind smashed into him. The clouds opened and rain started to fall. Just great. He looked up as Zeke headed his way, several fence posts secured over one shoulder. "Show-off," he muttered, grinning.

Zeke let them drop near the battered pickup, his eyes twinkling beneath the brim of his hat. "There's nobody here to show off for, brother." He looked around and then lifted one of the posts. "How's the city girl?" This time, he spoke in his native language.

Trent answered in Russian as well. "She's spooked but kisses like a dream. I need to help her out so she can get going."

Austin looked up from down the line and spoke in his native language. "Maybe you should keep her. I can tell you seem more relaxed than before—maybe she's your key to happiness."

Trent easily switched to the Scottish Gaelic to answer. "She deserves better. The darkness has been coming in, and the nightmares have almost killed me. She stopped all of that with just being here. But she's a nice girl, a smart one, and I have no idea how to live a normal life. None of us do anymore."

Austin leaned against a post and let the rain pound down on his hatless head. "Well. I guess we help you figure it out, then." He went back to speaking English.

Yeah. They might all be screwed up, but his brothers would try to cover him. No matter what. Trent grinned. "She is sexier than any woman I've ever seen."

"Oh, you have it bad. It's time for you to admit it, brother." Mac jumped off the back of the truck with a hammer in his hand. "She called me earlier and asked if I could speed up my process. I'm an artist, man." He chuckled, his face protected by a black hat that matched his eyes.

Zeke snorted. "If she wants to leave, you have to let her."

"I know." Trent would never keep anyone prisoner after the life they'd led. "I've given her an out several times, and she hasn't taken it. If she wants to go back to town, I'll drive her. One way or another, I plan on taking care of whatever problem she's having, and then I can let her leave knowing she's safe."

Zeke shook his head. "You don't want to let her leave. We said we'd move here, work ranches, and start normal lives. That includes family, love, and all that crap for some of us. Definitely for you. Stop being a wimp, take your time, and charm her."

Zachary strode down the fence line, already laughing. "You have no charm. Me? I'm from a long line of Russian royalty, and I'm full of charm."

His twin threw a ball of twine at him. "We're not from royalty, but you're definitely full of something." He cleverly mixed Russian, Gaelic, and English in his retort.

"We could be from royalty," Zachary objected.

"You ain't from royalty," Austin said, going with a Kentucky accent.

Trent nodded. Nicely done. It was Trent's original accent, and Austin had nailed it. One of the ways they'd survived captivity, the mind-numbing sameness of it, was learning each other's languages. Learning about each other's lives and losing ties to any one place. Until now. "It'd all be so much easier if she'd just let me handle everything."

Austin picked up a posthole digger. "You could always let her know the real you, the truth about us, and then let her decide."

Yeah, she wasn't there yet. Trent shook his head. "She may be destroying my demons with that sweet laugh of hers, but I ain't come close to destroying hers. She has to trust me first, and I'm struggling in that area." It felt weird to fall back into his Southern accent, but he did it anyway. It was a game they'd learned to play, just to stay sane. Picking up the last guy's language or accent.

Zeke rolled his eyes. "If she didn't trust you, she wouldn't be staying at your place." He switched to French.

Austin's gray gaze flicked his way. Zachary straightened. Trent paused.

Zeke said it again, his French flawless this time.

Mac relaxed and lapsed into French. "I always thought that Zachary would find a woman first. Would want to settle down as soon as possible."

"Ditto," Austin said, plunging the posthole digger into the damp earth.

Zeke didn't look at his twin. "Nope. He's a player, and he's not going to settle down for quite a while."

Zachary tossed the twine in the air and caught it easily, ducking then to grab another fence post and losing his constant smile. "I don't want to be responsible for another human being besides Zeke right now. It's easier to love them and leave them." He returned to English, sounding as if he hailed from California. "I'd hold on too tight, and I'd lose her. We all know it."

Zeke dropped to his haunches to help direct the post into the hole. "Trent, I think you can do it. I know you just met her, but she's got you wound tight. Why not give it a chance?"

Trent reached for more barbed wire with hands covered by thick gloves. His brother had a point, and the closer he got to the stunning brunette, the more he thought they might have a chance. "I just want to keep her safe right now. So long as she stays within the perimeter of our land, she'll be safe."

Austin grunted as he twisted the post into place. "What if she doesn't want to stay within the perimeter?"

Trent blinked. "We own over half a million acres. Why wouldn't she want to stay within the perimeter?"

Austin paused and then nodded. "I guess that's a good point."

"Though"—Zachary pushed his hat up—"if you get her to fall for you, and admit that she's what you want, she'll be lonely out here. Maybe a few of us should get married. It is the next step." He looked at Mac.

Mac slowly shook his head and tossed wire cutters into the back of the truck. "Don't look at me, brother. I already had the only woman I'll ever want."

Trent wiped rain off his chin and studied him. "You could call her, you know."

"She thinks I'm dead," Mac returned. "She's moved on, and that's good. It was ten years ago, man."

Zachary smoothly switched topics and drew the focus off his brother. Like always. "I think Austin is next."

Austin tucked his badge more securely at his waist. "I haven't found what I need in this town, and I don't see it happening."

Trent moved toward the truck. "Some ladies like a control freak, don't they?"

Zachary shook his head while Zeke nodded.

"Exactly," Austin said grimly.

Trent looked at his watch. "Hurry it up, brothers. I have dinner waiting for me." If it was anything close to the brunch Hallie had cooked for him earlier, he might just have to up and propose to her. He grinned.

"Good. I'll run her prints while you're snacking," Austin said grimly.

Trent lost the smile.

CHAPTER SEVEN

Hallie tried not to get lost in the blissful intimacy of cleaning the kitchen and doing the dishes with Trent after a dinner of pot roast that had him praising her up and down. It was a simple pot roast, but the guy really did appreciate it. He was so sweet.

He poured two more glasses of Opus One cabernet, the good stuff, and motioned her outside to the fire pit to the left of the cement area. He'd already started a fire, which crackled happily into the chilly night. "At least it's stopped raining," he said, waiting until she sat before handing her the drink.

The wind had chased the clouds away, and moonlight glinted off the fields, making the rough grass sparkle like yellow diamonds in the distance. She accepted the glass and looked up at the full moon, its luminous orb brighter than the millions of stars glimmering through the darkness. Though she'd already had a couple glasses of wine, she let herself relax into the buzz. "It's so beautiful here," she murmured, feeling she could breathe for the first time in way too long.

He sat next to her, extending his long legs toward the

fire. "The sky seems to go on forever. Sometimes I grab a sleeping bag and just crash out here, watching the stars until the sun returns." He sounded thoughtful. Comfortable.

She took a sip and let the cabernet warm a path to her stomach. Intimacy wound around them, through her. She should be cautious, but the stark beauty around her, the potent wine inside her, and the handsome man next to her combined into a dream she didn't want to shake. So she took another sip.

"Dinner was fantastic," he said. Again.

She smiled, letting her gaze wander to the glowing fire. "It was okay. I only used what I could find in the kitchen."

"It was the best I've ever had," he said quietly.

The words shouldn't touch her so deeply, but she couldn't help the warmth spreading through her. "Hasn't anybody ever taken care of you?"

"Nope." He crossed his cowboy boots at the ankle. "My folks died before I was two, and I was raised by a grandpa who really didn't want to raise a kid. We did okay, but I enlisted the second I turned seventeen." He shrugged. "Guess I found my family in the military."

"You grew up here in Wyoming?"

"Hmmm. Where did you grow up?" The wineglass looked small in his broad hand.

She swallowed. "I grew up all over, to be honest. My mom didn't like to stay in one place for long, and I'm not sure she even knew who my dad was, so that was never an issue. We traveled a lot, sometimes in a car and sometimes hitchhiking." She shivered.

He reached for her free hand and tangled their fingers. "Sounds scary."

"Sometimes it was," she admitted. "Other times, it was

a great adventure. She died of breast cancer when I was seventeen, and I stayed in a home for a year. That's where I met Paul."

"Ah, Paul," Trent said. "You mentioned he was in the service. Which branch?"

"Army," she said quietly. It had been three years since she'd lost him, and the pain would always be there, but she could appreciate the good times now, too. "We were married at eighteen, and he died three years later."

Trent tightened his hold. "I'm sorry, baby."

She nodded. "What branch did you serve with?"

"Navy," he said, the softness in his voice disappearing. "What did you do after he passed?"

She took another drink of the delicious wine, knowing she should remove her hand. Yet she left it in his. "I went to school and earned an accounting degree. After the childhood I'd had, I just wanted to plant roots with a good job."

He stared at the fire, too. "Then why are you crossing the country and looking for adventure?"

For a moment, she'd forgotten her secrets. "I'm not crossing the country." She tried to pull her hand free, but he didn't let her. She swallowed. He seemed like such a nice guy. Maybe he'd understand what she'd done. "Listen, I—"

"Hello." Zeke came around the side of the house with Zachary on his heels. The twins tugged chairs closer to the fire and dropped into them. A minute later, two other men strode from the other side of the house and did the same thing, both stretching out their cowboy boots to the fire.

Trent sighed. "Hallie? You've met Zeke and Zachary." He pointed to the guy on their left. "That's Austin, our sheriff and the president of our lodge. He's the only one who likes the name 'Cattle Club' for us. You met him on the phone, but he might look different in person." Trent pointed to the other man. "That's Mac. The guy who's supposed to be working on your car."

Was it a law that cowboys were ridiculously good-looking, or what? Hallie nodded her hellos. The sheriff was just as big as Trent, but he had jet-black hair and gray eyes. Mac was like a dark blond Nordic god with blue eyes that looked like glacier ice. She'd seen a glacier once when she and her mom had lived in Alaska.

Mac leaned to the left and opened the compact fridge set in the stone pillar, taking out beer bottles to pass around. "Thought we'd check in," he said.

She tried again to pull her hand free and then gave up when Trent didn't release it. There was no way she was getting in a tug-of-war with his friends watching them. "How's my car?" she asked.

Mac tipped back his head and took several deep pulls of his beer. "The same as it was when you called earlier. I can't do anything until the parts arrive." He turned and nodded at Zeke. "You're right. She is pretty."

"Yeah, and I saw her first," Trent said, not sounding amused.

Warmth blossomed in her face. They thought she was pretty? Not that she cared, but still. No matter how many diets she tried, she never seemed to lose weight. She'd given up being thin years ago and now was comfortable in her own skin. Still, it was nice when hottie cowboys thought she was pretty. She shook her head. Sometimes she was such a dork.

Zachary drank down half his beer. "Has she told you who she's running from?"

She jerked.

"Nope," Trent said.

Austin studied her across the fire. "You're a lot more patient than I would be with my woman."

"I'm a saint," Trent agreed.

She coughed. "I'm not his woman." Were they from the last century, or what?

"Right," Mac said, his gaze on their joined hands.

Her temper started to spike. "Have any of you considered that if I'm running, there's a reason? That maybe I'm bringing danger to Trent? To all of you?"

Zeke showed his teeth in a way that was far from charming. "We like danger."

She rolled her eyes. "For goodness' sake. You're nice country boys. Sure, you deal with downed fences and running cattle, and I know Trent served in the military a while back, but you live peacefully. I'm certain you're tough, but you have no idea about some of the dangers out there."

Zachary choked on his beer. Zeke and Austin held identical expressions of near shock, while Mac just let his mouth drop open.

She chanced a look at Trent, who was staring at her as if she'd lost her mind, his green eyes sizzling. Oh man, she'd insulted them. She squirmed in her chair. "I'm just saying, you're strong and all of that, but . . ."

Trent set his wineglass down, plucked her right out of her chair, and put her on his lap, her legs over his and her butt on one of his thighs.

She yelped, shocked at the speed with which he'd moved.

Calmly, he tangled his hand in her hair, drew her head back, and leaned into her face. "I'm thinkin' we might want to get a couple of things straight."

"Amen," Austin muttered under his breath.

She couldn't breathe. This wasn't exciting or breath-taking . . . it was seriously scary. The easygoing cowboy was suddenly terrifying, and her body refused to move. She froze like a deer frightened by powerful headlights.

The firelight cast harsh shadows over his rugged face, and those eyes glittered raw emerald green. His breath brushed her lips with the scent of wine and mint. "I've tried to go easy on you, to be gentle and give you time to trust me, but I see now that you have the instincts of a pinecone."

She gasped, still afraid to move. A pinecone? And why had his accent changed? He sounded like he was from the South rather than Wyoming all of a sudden. "Trent—"

"No. Don't 'Trent' me with that soft voice and those luminous eyes that beg for gentle. We're done with that." His hold was firm but he was careful not to hurt her. The thighs beneath her butt were rock hard, as was the hand clasping her hip. "I didn't just serve, baby. And I promise, no matter how dangerous you think the person hunting you is, he isn't close to what I've become. I'm a killer, Hallie. You might as well understand that now."

She gulped. All right. "You were in the military—"

"I was a hell of a lot more than that. We all were." He didn't relent. "Now. You're going to tell me who's after you so I can put them in the ground." His expression was implacable and his voice gritty.

She tore her gaze away from his to seek out Austin across the fire. "You're the sheriff," she whispered.

He nodded. "Yep. For this week. I'm just filling in while our sheriff is out of town. So nothing can happen until Sunday, unfortunately. After that, I'm with my brother here. If somebody is threatening you, we end them. It's looking to me as if Trent is claiming you, whether he realizes it or not, which makes you family."

Claiming her? For goodness' sake. "This is crazy," she whispered, looking back at Trent while he held her off balance.

"Probably," he agreed. "Austin's right. I can't get that kiss out of my mind. It felt right and real. Now. Tell me what's going on so I can go back to being gentle and wooing you."

The guy who so calmly said he'd end the threat wanted to woo her?

Trent held her gaze. "Austin, did you run her prints?"

She sucked in air. They'd run her prints? Seriously?

"Yep," Austin said. "They're not in any system I could find. I have Jesse running a deeper and not-so-legal dive on her right now. Guess I'm not sheriff material after all."

Mac snorted. At least, the sound came from where Mac sat, although Hallie couldn't look away from the intensity of Trent's gaze. It was as if he held her captive with his eyes alone.

His hand tightened in her hair and he tugged. Not so gently this time. "Talk."

Her temper spiked again. "I'm not telling you anything."

His smile was slow. Intense. Predatory.

Her abdomen rolled over. The calm cowboy who'd held her hand and watched the fire with her was gone. Had he really existed? She swallowed. There was no way out of this. "Fine, but I want my own chair back."

"No." He released her hair and settled his arm around her shoulders, cradling her in a way she'd never experienced. Even though he had the scary vibe still going, she felt protected. Shielded. Confusion swamped her. "Start talking, Hallie."

She cleared her throat and glanced at Austin. Even though he was only a temporary sheriff, he was still the law right now. She inclined her head toward Trent. "How about we talk, just the two of us?"

"No," Trent said again. "They're family, and I'll tell them everything, anyway. When we have a problem, we work it together. Let's get this done with now."

"You are so bossy," she snapped.

He brushed a wayward curl away from her face. "Yeah, I know. I managed not to be for almost twenty-four hours. You're welcome."

She smacked his chest. "I don't appreciate the humor. The wooing didn't last long."

As if he couldn't help himself, he leaned over and placed a gentle kiss on her nose. "I guess there are different types of wooing. My type is to be nice for twenty-four hours and then take care of any threats against you. After that, we'll make it up as we go."

It was seriously difficult to concentrate while sitting on his rock-hard thighs. She squirmed a little to get comfortable, and he groaned. She grew still.

"Hallie," he warned.

"Fine." She took a deep breath and started from the beginning.

CHAPTER EIGHT

Trent let his body relax now that his woman was safely in his arms finally telling him the truth. Oh, he hadn't made her his yet, but there was no doubt that was going to happen. He'd been lost from the first time she'd flashed those pretty eyes at him, and it was time he manned up and admitted it. Seeing her scared and unwilling to bring harm to his family had shoved him headfirst into being all in with her. She was what he wanted and no doubt needed. He'd go slow for her, but it was going to happen.

Fear filled her eyes as she began to speak, and he knew he'd done the right thing. She needed protection, and that he could provide.

Easily.

She took another deep drink of her wine. "I graduated a year ago with an accounting degree and found a great job with a firm called Montgomery and Sons. It's a cute name, don't you think? Sounds like a furniture store instead of a numbers place."

"Very cute," Trent agreed, reaching down for his wineglass and signaling for Austin to dial Jesse in on the conversation. "Does anybody named Montgomery actually own the firm?"

Austin placed his phone on his thigh, no doubt with Jesse listening in.

She nodded, her head brushing against Trent's shoulder. "Yes. Silas is the dad, and his sons are Brad and Charles. They really seemed like a nice family, Trent."

"But they're not?" Trent encouraged her, noting her very slight emphasis on Brad's name.

She shook her head. "Apparently not. I worked there for a year, mostly getting up to speed and then taking on a couple of clients on my own. It was a good job, pretty much. So-so health benefits," she said thoughtfully.

"I take it something went wrong?"

She sighed, a light pink dusting her cheekbones. "For the most part, we all just worked on our own clients and didn't cross files. I did a good job, and I was steadily building my own accounts. I wish things had just stayed that way, but they didn't."

"Because of Brad?" Trent guessed.

"Yes. How did you know?"

He knew because he'd learned to read small changes in voice, movement, and expression so he wouldn't get his ass killed a million miles away. "It was just a good guess. Tell us the rest of it, sweetheart." So far, he didn't want to kill anybody, but he'd bet anything that was about to change.

"I started dating Brad two months ago. Well, three months, I guess. I've been on the move for one."

Zeke made a small movement.

Heat rushed through Trent but he forced his body to remain relaxed. "You've been running for a month?"

She nodded again. "Yes."

Harley padded out from the field, looked around, and flopped down in front of Trent's chair. The wolf had grass all over his body but didn't seem to mind.

Trent jerked and his brothers stared at the wolf as if in shock. The animal never came this close.

"He's so adorable," Hallie murmured, her voice slightly slurred.

"You were dating Brad," Trent prodded her. He'd worry about the wolf later.

She snuggled closer to his chest, the movement natural and unconscious. "Brad's the youngest and it seems his dad and brother don't take him all that seriously, but I thought he was funny. We went out several times. Then one night, we were supposed to go to a dinner at the mayor's home. Some sort of fancy fundraiser."

She exhaled. "I forgot that I wasn't supposed to go to the office on Fridays after noon."

Austin stilled.

Trent brushed her hair off her pretty face. "You never went to the office on Friday afternoons?"

"No. I figured it was just family or board members on Friday afternoon, and it was actually nice having that time off every week. It really didn't seem like a big deal." She rubbed her nose and settled more comfortably into his arms.

"Until it did?" Trent guessed.

"Yeah. Brad had given me the tickets for the party, and I'd forgotten them at the office, so I swung by right before picking him up at his house."

Zachary leaned forward toward the fire. "You were driving?"

"Brad didn't have a driver's license," she affirmed. "At the time, I thought it was just a quirk, but I later found out he'd been charged with negligent homicide because he'd driven drunk. His family was friends with some high-up officials, and he only got probation and loss of license for a few years."

Now they were getting to it. "Brad was angry you found out about those charges?" Zachary guessed quietly.

"Oh, no." She waved her hand through the air. "He isn't the bad guy here. Well, not the worst of the bad guys. I guess they're all bad guys." She took another big drink of wine, and Trent reclaimed the glass, setting it aside. She'd probably had enough.

"Honey, you're kind of talking in circles," he said gently. "Could you get to the point?"

"It's the wine," she admitted, pressing the heel of her palm against her forehead. "My brain is fuzzy."

"Hallie." Trent put more bite into his tone this time.

She blinked several times. "All right. I went to get the tickets and was just leaving my office when all this yelling came from the conference room. I kind of froze, because the voices were so angry."

"Who was it?" Trent asked.

"It was all three of them and another man who had a really deep voice. He was yelling that he hadn't shot Bixby just for them to, well, eff up the books with the IRS. That they'd helped him and would all go down for murder if they didn't straighten the mess out."

The mere fact that the woman used "eff up" instead of what most certainly had been said sealed her fate. Trent had no clue why the compulsion to keep her was riding him so hard, but it was there, and so was she. The need for her went deeper than he could understand, than anybody would ever be able to understand, but it was soul deep. If nothing else, he now realized he still had a soul, and she was the one to save it. "Tell me you ran," he muttered.

"Oh, I ran." She caressed his arm, her palm so soft he wanted to moan. "I ran as fast as I could. Brad caught me at the door, assured the rest of them that it was okay, and hurried me outside to his brother's car."

Maybe Trent wouldn't have to kill Brad.

"Then we drove away, and he was swearing and so mad. I told him we had to go to the police, and he laughed, saying his dad had help in the police department." She shook her head. "Brad was so upset."

Poor freaking Brad. "What then?"

"He told me everything," she said quietly.

Yep. Brad needed to die. "Telling you everything just put you in more danger, sweetheart," Trent muttered.

"No kidding. The guy yelling was Marc Lewis of Lewis and Bixby, which is a major retailer of sporting goods. He'd been stealing from his partner, had gotten caught, and then had killed him. Silas was in on the theft and helped dispose of the body. And so did his sons." She whispered the last. "I don't think it was the first time they'd stolen from people—or killed."

Probably not. "What then?" Mac asked.

"We were driving, Brad was explaining how I couldn't ever tell anybody, and his phone rang." Her voice trembled. "He talked for a while, arguing and then finally agreeing, although he sounded sad." She bit her lip. "Then he drove the car back to the office and said that I was safe but his dad needed to make sure I'd stay quiet."

Trent shut his eyes, tightening his hold around her.

His brothers crowded closer as if to provide more reassurance that she was safe. They might not understand his feelings for her, but they knew he had them. As his brothers, as the men who'd gone through hell with him, they'd do anything they could to help him get what he wanted. What he needed. Now that the decision was made, it was surprisingly easy to get rid of the illusion that he'd wanted freedom.

He wanted *her*.

She cleared her throat. "I knew they didn't just want to talk, but I pretended to believe him. Then he told me that my name was on many of the papers dealing with Lewis and Bixby, and that I was as involved as the rest of them. He was right, because I did help on that file. But I didn't know they were stealing." She sighed.

Trent kneaded her nape, careful to stay gentle. "What then?"

"Brad parked and jumped out of the car, and he reclaimed his keys. So I slowly exited, smiled, and just ran as fast as I could in the other direction, straight to my car. I had my keys already in my hands. I couldn't think what else to do right then."

Trent swallowed over a lump of pure anger. "It was nighttime by now?"

"Yeah, and I was in heels." She shook her head. "I got into my car, slammed the door, and Brad pounded on the window. He was so angry. I never even imagined he could look like that." She rubbed her fingers along Trent's jaw. The whiskers must be scratchy, but she didn't seem to mind. "I'm not a moron, and I do have more sense than a pinecone. But they seemed so nice, and I had no idea they were stealing or didn't mind murdering people."

"So you ran?" Trent asked.

She nodded. "I knew I couldn't go back to my apartment, so I just started driving as fast as I could away from Boise, since Brad said they had the law in their pockets.

That might not even be true, but I couldn't take the chance. I used my credit cards at a Target for the last time and bought a suitcase and everything else I might need, then kept going."

He brushed his knuckles along her cheekbone. "That was smart."

"They almost caught me in Jackson and then in Denver," she admitted. "I've been stopping along the way at public libraries, using different IP addresses, to log in and try to get more evidence on the bad guys. I've collected a good bit, I think."

Impressive. Dangerous, but he felt a pride in her. "Where were you going?" Trent asked.

She took another deep breath. "I read about an FBI office in Montana that took down a corrupt small town, so that was my plan. Because the Boise local law might be involved, the FBI can get involved, so I figured if I could just get to that FBI office, the one with the good track record, they could at least start a case or something."

It wasn't a horrible plan. What else could a woman on her own do? It wasn't as if she knew Trent and his brothers existed.

"So." She pushed against his chest. "Now you understand why I have to go. If you'd let me borrow a truck, I could go to the FBI in Montana and have this taken care of. There is a chance I might end up in prison, but maybe you could write to me." She tried for a joke, but the laughter didn't reach her pretty eyes.

Austin stood first. "All right. Meet at the clubhouse at five in the morning?"

Trent nodded. Jesse should have all they needed by then. "How many do we have out of town right now?"

While they wanted out of the mercenary business, right now, they had a couple more situations to handle.

"We have four out and eight here," Mac said, standing and gathering the beer bottles. "More than enough to take care of this and keep the ranches in working order."

As silently as they'd appeared, his brothers faded into the night, heading to the clubhouse.

Hallie remained in his lap, idly playing with his hair. "I think I'll have to wait until morning to drive to Montana. The world is really blurry right now."

He finally let himself lean in and take her mouth, all but drowning in sweetness and wine. She was soft, and the ragged sound she made nearly undid him. He tried to make himself stop, to not take her deeper, but she was all heat and fire, pouring down his throat to land somewhere he didn't know he still had. Somewhere deep and real. Finally, he released her just to let her breathe.

She rubbed her cheek against his chest like a little cat. "I wish I'd met you before all of this, Trent Logan."

He didn't exist before all of this. At that thought, he carried her into her room and left her safely there, even though it nearly killed him. She was tipsy and vulnerable, and nothing in him would take advantage of that, no matter how badly he wanted her. Needed her.

Then he turned and stalked back outside to sleep near the wolf beneath the stars.

CHAPTER NINE

Hallie's head ached, but the travel coffee mug felt warm in her hands. Trent drove along the bumpy road as dawn tried to peek through the bruised clouds despite the rain that pounded down, soaking the earth and pinging against the windows. She took a deep drink, trying incredibly hard not to complain about the early hour.

The wolf snored loudly in the back seat as if in perfect agreement. He did seem to want to stay close to her.

She cleared her throat. "So, um, I'll clean the clubhouse today for pay, and then I can head to Montana if you'll let me borrow your truck. Or any truck."

"No." Trent leaned forward and angled his head toward the fields in front of them.

She stilled. "Excuse me?"

He turned her way, his gaze inscrutable. "I said no."

Well. "Fine. If you won't lend me a truck, then I'll rent something in town." She had enough cash to do that, probably.

He turned and studied the field on the left, frowning. "I said no. You're no longer handling Montgomery or sons."

His voice was distracted and tension thickened the air around them.

She nudged him in the arm. "What in the world are you talking about?"

"Ah hell." He jerked the truck to a stop. "Stay inside." Without waiting for an answer, he pulled a shotgun from behind his seat and jumped out, firmly shutting the door. Rain beat down on him, and he'd left his hat in the truck.

She released her seat belt and scrambled to the driver's seat, pressing against the window to take in the darkened morning outside.

Harley jumped up and made a weird growl-bark noise, his nose wet against his window.

Trent leaped over a fence, as graceful as any animal, and landed on the other side with the gun safe in his hand. He turned and made some weird hand gesture before letting out a piercing whistle.

Harley barked twice and dropped to his haunches..

Hallie shook her head and looked over the seat at the prone animal. "Wow. Somebody really did train you at one point, and there's no way they'd just force you out. You must've lost someone, huh? I know how that feels." For a second, she'd been afraid of being in the locked truck with a wild animal. Now he lay as tame as any house dog, and she could identify with him.

She turned her attention back outside. What was Trent doing? Her eyes scanned the area and found a bunch of cattle and . . . holy moly. A mountain lion. A real one with glinting yellow eyes and powerful muscles beneath its wet coat. It circled a dead cow, fur raised on its back, its gaze on Trent.

Panic gripped her, and she froze in place. Weren't mountain lions afraid of people? Why didn't it run? Trent was a dark shadow in an even darker morning, and he moved carefully, lifting his gun and shooting into the air.

The cat snarled, and the sound reverberated across the field and into the truck.

Hallie pressed her hand to her throat, her gaze riveted on the scene. The cat continued to circle, not moving away. Then it bunched its legs and struck, faster than she would've thought possible.

Trent twisted, nailing the animal with the butt of the gun and throwing it several feet. It had to weigh about a hundred pounds and was sheer muscle.

Then he pointed the weapon and fired. Once and then again.

She jumped both times, her heart beating so fast and hard that the truck started to spin around her. "Okay. It's okay," she whispered, maybe to the wolf and maybe to herself.

Trent faced away from her, a massive man surrounded by the perils of nature. He looked down at the fallen cat, his shoulders hunched. He shook his head.

Then he turned and prowled back to the truck, clearing the fence easily again.

She hurried across to her seat, her heartbeat thundering in her ears.

He opened his door and slid the gun to the back seat before climbing in, bringing rain and the smell of the grassy fields with him.

She didn't know what to say. Wasn't sure if she could talk.

He pressed a dial on his phone, and a sleepy voice answered.

"Who is this and why are you calling me so early?" The voice was female and young. Tired-sounding.

Trent sighed. "Hi, Dr. Mills. It's Trent, and I just shot a mountain lion that tried to attack me."

Blankets rustled. "Did you try to scare it first?"

"Of course," Trent said, his face a hard mask of stone. "Darn thing came at me anyway."

The woman sighed across the line. "I'll need to check it for rabies, then. Were you scratched or bitten at all?"

"No. Nothing on me, but he took down a couple cows. Probably more. I'll scout the fields later today and let you know." Trent gave the location of the downed cat and promised the gates would be unlocked. "Call me when you have results." He ended the call.

Even though Hallie was sitting, her legs shook. Her whole body trembled.

Trent turned toward her. "Baby? What's wrong?" His thick hair was wet and rain still slid down his face. He wiped it off, focusing on her.

She couldn't breathe. If she was honest with herself, she had been caught in a silly little daydream involving life with Trent. He'd claimed her, whatever that meant. So yes, she'd been picturing herself in that sweet ranch house living the dream, if she survived the killers after her as well as the possible incriminating evidence against her. "I had no idea ranching was so dangerous," she whispered.

He set the phone down gently. "That was nothing. Horses get spooked, cattle rampage, and Mother Nature likes to take a bite or two once in a while." Then he caught her expression, and he sobered. "It's okay. A little mountain lion can't hurt me."

Her stomach lurched. "Little? He was at least a hundred pounds." Her voice rose as her fantasy faded away. "You had to shoot him."

"Only because he probably has rabies. Otherwise, he would've run when I shot into the air. It happens."

Rabies? Well, that wasn't dangerous or anything. She sucked in air. "And you have a wolf who hangs around you. A real, wild, sharp-toothed wolf." By the last word, she was almost screeching.

The wolf snorted in the back seat.

Trent just studied her, his eyes a soft green while the storm beat around the truck. He reached out and gripped her chin, looking deep. "I'm not sure what's happening right now, but we have to get to the clubhouse and the meeting. Tell me what's wrong so I can fix it."

She swallowed and pulled her face free. Never again would she tie herself to a man with a dangerous job. She'd already faced losing the one person in the world she loved, and she wouldn't do it again. "There's nothing to fix," she said quietly.

After he paid her that night, she'd go.

Trent kicked back in the conference room of the club with a mug of coffee in hand, his mind still turning over his odd interaction with Hallie in the truck. She'd been so pale, and her eyes had seemed to fill her whole face. Did she have some phobia about mountain lions? Or rabies?

Austin continued the meeting with the eight present members of the lodge. "Wyatt, Levi, Doc, and Boone have checked in, and they've secured the woman and already taken her to a military hospital in Germany. One of ours."

Trent focused. "How badly was she hurt?" The woman was a journalist kidnapped for ransom.

"Not as bad as she could've been," Austin said. "They wanted money, not her."

Well, that was something. "Is the team wheels up?" Trent asked.

Austin looked at his watch. "In about ten minutes." Then he looked around the table. "Any other business before we get to the shit show Trent has brought to us?"

"You're welcome," Trent drawled.

Zachary snorted and took another deep gulp of his coffee.

Trent nodded and told them about the mountain lion. "I called the vet and she's headed out to see if it has rabies." Which was more than a possibility since the animal hadn't reacted as it should have when he'd shot into the air.

Zeke straightened. "Mills is going out there by herself?"

"Yeah. She's the vet." Trent turned toward his brother. "I killed the animal. There's no more threat."

Zeke didn't answer.

Austin's gray eyes flicked over them, and then he nodded to Jesse. "You're up. What did you find?"

Jesse leaned over his keyboard and typed rapidly, his thick black hair wavy behind his ears and his light brown eyes reading code faster than most people could think. The screen at the far wall lit up. "Meet Silas, Charles, and Brad Montgomery."

Photographs of three men appeared on the screen. They looked like accountants. All three wore golf shirts, khaki pants, and earnest expressions. Trent hated them on sight. The elder had thick gray hair and his sons light brown hair. All had blue eyes and fairly fit physiques.

Another picture came up. "Marc Lewis," Jesse confirmed.

Lewis was younger than Trent would've guessed— maybe early forties. He had thinning blond hair, squirrely brown eyes, and a gut.

Then another picture of a man about the same age with darker blue eyes. "John Bixby," Jesse said. "According to a police report, he's been missing for three months and there's been no sign of foul play. According to his partner, good old Marc Lewis, Bixby had a gambling problem, and there's a notation in the file that he owed money to some very bad people."

Trent tapped his fingers on the table. "Did Bixby really have a gambling problem?"

"No," Jesse said, reading his screen. "I went through all of his financials for the last twenty years, and there's no indication of gambling. He spent too much money on self help books, but he didn't gamble." He typed some more, and banking records scrolled across the screen. "It was fairly easy to track down the embezzlement records, to be honest. These guys are good but not great."

"Can you clear Hallie from the records?" Trent asked.

"Already did," Jesse affirmed. "At least from the computer records. We'll have to go in for hard copies of everything, which I figured we'd want to do anyway. Her last name is Rose, by the way."

Trent's eyebrows lifted. "Rose? Like the flower?"

"Yep," Jesse said.

Mac grinned. "That's freaking adorable."

Yeah, it kind of was.

Austin snorted. "I liked Smith better. I still can't believe she said that."

Yeah, his woman wasn't made for subterfuge, that was for sure. Trent took a sip of the strong brew. "Did you track the men?"

Jesse nodded. "Brad and Charles are hunting her, and based on phone records I hacked, Marc Lewis is looking to hire hitmen. Like right now."

Everything inside Trent went cold. "Well, then. I guess we should make ourselves available."

Jesse leaned forward, his gaze intense. "I've learned everything I can about this girl, and she's pure, man. Not even a speeding ticket. She ain't gonna like it if you go around killing people. Even if they're trying to kill her."

Trent straightened his shoulders. "We take out the threat. That's what we do." But Jesse's words made sense, and he wasn't sure what to do with them. Losing Hallie because he wanted to protect her wasn't an option.

Austin pursed his lips. "We could set them up. Let the law handle them this time."

Zeke twirled his mug in his hands. "The dead don't come after you for vengeance." He shrugged. "Usually."

Trent nodded, in full agreement. "Did you find any connection between the Montgomerys and the law in Boise?"

"No," Jesse said. "Which means there isn't any. They were lying to her to scare her. Good ole Silas doesn't have the law in his pocket."

Well, at least that was something.

Austin looked over at Trent, his gray eyes darker than the sky outside. "This is your call."

Trent scrubbed both hands down his face. "I agree with Jesse, even though I don't want to leave loose ends out there. Let's get the evidence to the authorities, but first, I want to pay a visit. If we're doing this the right way, they're gonna know we could've done it another way and might always change our minds."

Zeke grinned. "Now you're talkin'."

Jesse looked over at Ford, who hadn't spoken yet. "I sent the schematics of their offices and homes if you want to come up with infiltration plans. We're gonna want to spend some time with Marc Lewis to discover the location of Bixby's body, so I'm thinking their homes are our best bet. It's up to you, though."

Ford scratched one of the many scars on his strong face. His eyes were black, his hair even darker, and his temper blackest of all. "I'll get the location from him."

"I will," Trent interjected. "This is my op and my woman. They need to see my eyes on this, just to understand."

Zachary leaned back in his chair, and it squeaked in protest. "How much are you going to tell her?"

Trent swallowed. "I'm not sure. It's not like we've been in this position before. Any ideas?" His brothers all looked back at him, just as clueless as he when it came to reordering their lives and trying to include women in them. "I'll think of something?"

"Good luck with that," Austin said grimly.

CHAPTER TEN

Hallie wiped the bar in the clubhouse party room until it sparkled, still keeping an eye on the wolf. He lay across the sofa, watching her with those golden eyes. Sometimes it looked as if he was really thinking something. "What?" she whispered.

His nose twitched.

Man, she was really losing her mind. Now she was talking to wild animals, although this one seemed rather domesticated. They'd spent the entire morning together, and she was getting hungry. The pretzels she'd found in a bag beneath the bar hadn't lasted long.

Two men loped from the back hallway and halted.

"Hi." The first one stepped forward and held out a hand. "I'm Ford." He had black eyes with dark hair and was taller than the others. Maybe six-six? Scars lined the right side of his face, many of them, making him look dangerous. Although his grip was gentle when they shook.

Ford? Seriously? She held her breath until he released her.

"I'm Jesse." The second guy had intelligent eyes and dark hair that curled around his ears. His right arm was scarred around his wrist as if it had gotten caught in barbed wire. "It's nice to meet you." He, too, was a big guy. Not as tall as Ford but definitely as wide.

She shook his hand and stepped back. "Ford and Jesse? Did your parents find a book on cowboy names, or what?"

Jesse flashed a grin, showing two surprising dimples. "Something like that."

The two men headed for the door, their cowboy boots clipping on the now clean floor.

Hallie cleared her throat. "Do any women belong to your club?" There had to be cowgirls around, right?

Ford kept right on going through the door, while Jesse paused, settling a laptop bag over his shoulder. "No. Twelve of us created the co-op, and we put this clubhouse in the middle of what will eventually become our ranches. Women are welcome, though. Well, not to be members, but they're always welcome here."

She stiffened. "Why can't women be members?"

He pushed his cowboy hat farther back on his head. "Because we formed the club for the twelve of us when we created the co-op." His tone indicated he wasn't sure why he had to repeat that fact.

"Why aren't there women in the co-op?" she asked.

His gaze cleared. "That's a story you should probably get from your man."

Butterflies winged through her abdomen and she shoved the girly happiness away. "I don't have a man."

Jesse grinned. "You might want to tell Trent that." Whistling softly, he strode out into the wild rainstorm.

Yeah, she definitely would. Maybe she could get one more kiss out of the cowboy first. Oh, she was leaving, but that man could kiss, and she needed something to keep her warm in the nights to come.

She finished with the bar and looked around. She'd already cleaned the small kitchen and the bathrooms. The conference room was still in use, so that only left the personal suites to work on. Trent hadn't asked her to clean them, but she could at least tidy his, since she'd stayed there. Maybe as a thank-you to him before she left.

Making her way down the hall, she double-checked her vacuum marks on the carpet. Perfect. The vacuum and cleaning supplies she'd found in the small laundry room had been surprisingly good. She entered his room, removed the sheets from the bed and jogged down to the laundry room to start another load. Then she returned and dusted before vacuuming. There wasn't much else to do; it didn't look like he stayed there often.

She sat on the bed and took a deep breath, inhaling his scent. She'd never smell wild grass or leather again and not think of him.

A figure passed by, and Zachary poked his head in. "Whatcha doing?"

"Laundry," she said, pushing hair out of her face. "I didn't know if I should clean all of the suites or just Trent's."

"Just Trent's," Zachary confirmed. "Who knows what you'd find in some of those other quarters. We have a lot of parties out here."

That's what she'd figured. "I've heard of co-ops, but I didn't think they were a good idea tax-wise. How does yours work?"

Zachary's eyebrows rose to his hairline. "Who told you about the co-op?"

She just shrugged. If it was a secret, why get Jesse in trouble over it? "Does that matter?"

"Not really." Zachary leaned against the doorframe,

reminding her of a lazy panther that wasn't so lazy. While he appeared to be good-natured compared to his brother, his gaze lacked the lightness his body exhibited. "The co-op purchased all the land, and we each work equal portions of it, sharing in the profits and losses. Since ranching is such a risky business, that grants us more stability overall."

Their approach made sense. "Oh. So that first day, when Trent said that the Newberys had a bad calving season and the donation was one calf each, that was a co-op adjustment?"

Zachary shook his head. "No. The Newberys aren't in the co-op. But they're neighbors, they had a rough season, and we're going to help them out. It's what we do."

That was kind of sweet. She angled her neck. "Where's your brother? You two seem to be together all the time."

Zachary grinned, and the smile finally reached his eyes. "Zeke discovered that the pretty veterinarian was headed out to Trent's field all by herself, and he went to make sure she didn't trip over a rock or something."

She matched his smile. "I take it Zeke has a crush?"

Zachary pushed away from the doorjamb. "Heck if I know, but he has something. Makes him ornery, too."

Sounded like Zeke was a lion with a thorn. Maybe the vet would take it out and even the odds around the lodge. There was way too much testosterone around. The washing machine dinged.

She stood. "Zachary? Ranching is dangerous, isn't it?"

"Definitely. Danger comes from every direction, it seems." He tugged the brim of his hat. "I'll see you later."

No, he probably would not. She had to get out of there.

* * *

Trent drove carefully through the storm, keeping an eye on the quiet woman in the passenger seat.

She crossed her arms. "I wasn't finished with your sheets yet. They're in the dryer, but now they'll be all wrinkled by the time somebody takes them out and puts them on the bed."

That somebody would be her, but apparently she thought she was going ahead with her crazy plan. He took her hand. "We need to grab lunch, sweetheart. You worked hard, and you have to be hungry."

She tilted her head in acknowledgment, just like a queen.

He grinned as he pulled to the curb in front of the one diner in town. "I'm treating you to lunch, and we're going to have a talk." He'd been working through how to explain the plan to her without scaring her. There was no need for her to know everything about him or what he could do, although he did want her to feel safe. It was a tightrope he was walking, but he could handle it. "Wait here."

She waited patiently as he exited the truck and ran around to open her door, hustling her across the wide sidewalk and into the entryway of Sandra's. They shook rain off on the rubber mat right inside the door.

The familiar smell of cheeseburgers, chicken, and pie assailed him, and he breathed deep. "I more or less live here when I can." Putting his hand to the small of her back, he propelled her inside and down to a blue booth, nodding at folks as he went.

She scooted in her side and reached for a menu. "I love the colors in here. Pretty blue, light peach, white. It's refreshing and inviting. Peaceful, even."

All right. He knew where the exits were, what could be used as a weapon, and the best place to dodge a bullet, but he'd never noticed the colors. "I like that you notice stuff like that." She blushed, and he liked that even more. Who blushed these days?

She read through the menu. "Everything looks so good."

"Hi, Trent." Sandra gracefully set two glasses of water on the table, and she smiled at Hallie. "You must be Hallie. I'm Sandra, and the lunch special is a Cobb salad, but the shrimp is fresh in, and that salad looks amazing, too." Sandra had to be in her midtwenties with deep green eyes and curly blondish hair with red in it that looked natural.

"Hi," Hallie said, smiling. "I'll have the shrimp salad."

Sandra nodded. "Drinks?"

Trent took a sip of his water. "Sandra has an excellent wine selection. I'll have a Wallace Red. It's a good beer, if you like beer."

Hallie looked from him to Sandra. "I'll have the same. Thanks."

Sandra nodded and turned for the kitchen.

Hallie frowned. "She didn't take your food order."

He shrugged. "She knows what I want." Sandra was magic like that. Had been since she'd purchased the diner recently.

"Really?" There was something odd in Hallie's voice.

It took him a minute, and when he recognized the tone, he had to cough away a chuckle. "Yes. You sound jealous." Would she be honest about it?

She looked him right in the eye. "That is one beautiful woman, and she knows your tastes well enough that she didn't take your order. You've been kissing me lately, like a lot. I'm not jealous. I'm irritated."

That was fair. He flattened her hand beneath his, enjoying her little struggle to reclaim it. Fire lanced her eyes when she glared at him, her hand staying right where he wanted it. She huffed out a breath, and he leaned toward her. "Sandra is a friend and a very good cook. I have never, and I will never, kiss her. The only mouth I've taken lately has been yours, and after one taste, nobody else will ever do." He let her see the truth in his eyes.

Her eyes widened. "You can't say things like that."

He didn't see why not. It was time to explain things to her. "Did you meet Jesse?"

"Yeah. So far, I've met you, Jesse, Zachary, Zeke, Austin, Mac, and Ford. Who does that leave in your little He-Man Women Hater's Club?" She gripped her water glass with her free hand.

"Doc, Boone, Nash, Levi, and Wyatt," Trent said easily.

She chuckled, watching him over the rim of her glass. "You hear those names, right? I mean, it's cowboy central. Did all of you grow up here in the wilds of Wyoming?"

If he explained the names to her, he'd have to explain everything, and that wouldn't do. "Anyway, Jesse is a computer genius, and he managed to hack into all of the Montgomery records. He's expunged any sign of you, as well as prepared a case file for the local police, who do not have a connection to Silas or his idiot kids."

She stiffened. "Hacked? One of your friends, another cowboy, is a hacker?"

Sandra set the glasses of beer in front of them and hustled down to the booth at the far end.

Trent took a deep drink. "Yeah. Hackers are everywhere. Anyway, the key is that the law will soon be involved, and you're out of it." He set his beer down and released her hand. "I'll deliver the information and make sure to get all physical records from the office before I do so."

Her hand halted in reaching for her beer. "How do you plan to do that?"

His palm felt empty since he'd let her go. "I learned a certain skill set in the military, and I was well trained. I'll break in, get any information that might implicate you, and be out before they know it."

She shook her head. "The office has an alarm system and cameras."

He barely kept from rolling his eyes. "Good. Then I won't be totally bored."

"Absolutely not." Her small nostrils flared. "We are not breaking the law to fix things."

They already had, considering the hacking. "I told you that this was out of your hands, and it is. Today is Tuesday, and I can't go until Friday, so that's our plan." He couldn't go until Friday because stupid Silas was out of town until then, and Trent needed to meet face-to-face with him to get his point across. "Until then, I'd really appreciate it if you'd continue working at the ranch. Once you're clear of this, you can go wherever you want." Of course, he was going to try to keep her close, but that had to be her choice.

"I don't think so," she murmured.

He sighed. "I didn't want to tell you this, but we found information that Charles and Brad are after you right now, and Marc Lewis is trying to put a hit out on you. We're taking care of it, but you're not safe anywhere but here right now."

She turned so pale, a fine blue line showed on her temple. "A hit?"

He reached for her hand again. "I've got you, baby. You're safe. Trust me."

CHAPTER ELEVEN

Hallie super-cleaned Trent's house the next two days, settling into a routine of cooking and then hanging out by the fire with him. Both nights different members of the lodge showed up to drink wine or beer and watch the fire, almost as if they wanted her to get used to them. The feeling of camaraderie was comforting, until she remembered there might be a hit on her head.

Trent worked the ranch both days, returning dirty, tired, and starving. He hadn't kissed her again, and she told herself that made her happy.

It did not.

She tried to reason with him about going to Boise, but he refused to listen. On the other hand, if his plan worked, she'd be free of the Montgomerys as well as Lewis. If his plan didn't work, she'd have to visit him in prison for breaking and entering. It was enough to make her a nervous wreck.

Thursday night found her curled into her chair with a glass of Chianti in her hand. Trent sat next to her, his legs outstretched toward the fire. She wasn't surprised when Austin, Mac, and Ford loped around the side of the house and took chairs, having brought their own beer this time. Rumor had it the twins were out on dates and that Zachary had roped Zeke into hanging out with his date's sister.

Apparently Zeke hadn't been amused.

Mac looked at her across the fire. "I should have your car ready by Monday or Tuesday."

She perked up. "That's good news. Any idea on the cost?"

He shrugged. "Don't worry about it."

"No. I will pay." She tried to make her voice as firm as his.

He glanced at Trent.

She wanted to get irritated, but it had been a long day, and the wine tasted delicious. Plus, it was mellowing her out a little, and she didn't want to lose that sense of peace. She cleared her throat. "We need to talk about tomorrow night."

"No." Trent rolled his neck. "Did you guys fix those fences along the western ridge?"

"Yes." Hallie sat straight up. "I've let you ignore the subject for almost three nights, but we're going to discuss it now." Her gaze swept the men on the other side of the fire. "None of you can think this is a good idea."

Not surprisingly, they remained silent.

So she focused on the sheriff. "Austin? Speak."

Surprise, amusement, and then wariness flashed across the sheriff's face. "I'm sure any plan Trent told you about is a good one."

She jerked to face Trent. "Any plan you told me about? What don't I know?"

He took another drink of the wine. "I told you the plan. We've already scrubbed you electronically from the data. Tomorrow night I'll go in and destroy physical copies.

Then we're turning everything over to the police in Boise to handle. Once the Montgomerys and Marc Lewis are in custody, you're safe. It's pretty simple."

Darn if three heads didn't nod across the fire. She took a big drink of the Chianti and barely kept herself from coughing. The stuff was strong. "I don't think you should risk everything you've built here by breaking the law in Idaho. It's just silly."

"He'll be fine," Ford said, lounging in the chair in a way that looked casual but felt anything but. The firelight danced across the white scars on the right side of his face, putting the other side into darkness.

She shivered.

Trent's phone buzzed, and he tugged it from his pocket, reading the face before lifting it to his ear. "Hey, Jesse. What's up?"

He listened and then sat up, pulling his legs in. "Got it. We'll be right there." He stood just as the other three men did the same, all with that same alert readiness. "We have a mudslide on the north ridge, cattle in trouble. The rain has been horrible."

"We can get there faster on horseback," Austin said, setting his bottle near the fireplace. He turned toward the nearest barn with Ford and Mac flanking him.

Thunder pounded and lightning zagged in the distance. The smell of ozone filled the air. Hallie stood. "It's going to rain again, and it's dark out there. No moonlight. It's not safe."

Trent snagged her around the waist and dragged her against him, kissing her hard. Then soft. Then deep.

She moaned, leaning into him. Fire flushed through her, setting every nerve pounding.

That soon, he released her. "We'll be fine, sweetheart. I'll be late, so don't wait up."

Then he was gone.

Hallie startled awake on the sofa and listened. Rain beat against the windows and the wind gnawed on the house with sharp fangs. She blinked and pushed her hair off her face.

Another sound caught her attention. Footsteps.

She sat up and looked toward the kitchen. "Trent?"

"I told you not to wait up." His voice was strained.

She stood and hurried into the kitchen, flipping on the light as she did so. Then she stopped. He stood at the back sliding glass door and gingerly removed a long black slicker. Blood flowed from a wound in his right cheek and one along his left wrist. "What happened to you?" She moved toward him.

He shoved his boot into a wooden thing on the ground and tugged it off before doing the same with the other one.

She blinked. "What is that thing?"

"A bootjack." He plunked his hat onto a hook on the wall. Mud and blood coated his throat, and he reached toward the countertop and the paper towels while remaining on the small rug by the door.

She hustled toward him, trying to see how badly he was cut. "Come in and sit down."

"I'm a mess. Don't want to ruin your clean floor." He grinned, and blood slid down to cover his upper lip.

She took the towel from him and wiped off his neck, her hands shaking. "You need stitches in your cheek." Probably. She wasn't sure. "I'll drive you to the hospital."

"Honey, I don't need a hospital." He ripped his T-shirt

up and over his head, and the shift of muscle was something to see.

She reached for his damaged wrist, gently patting it with another paper towel. "This looks deep, too. What happened?"

"Spooked cattle and barbed wire," he muttered, looking long and lean in his muddy jeans.

Her knees bunched, and she had to fight the urge to run. Right now he needed help, so she'd help. "At least tell me where the first aid kit is." Maybe she could somehow bandage the wound so his skin would knit together. "Though we really should go to the—" A huge, quickly purpling bruise on his left shoulder, right above a healed bullet wound, caught her eye. "What the heck?"

He looked down. "Oh. Got kicked. Darn cow."

Kicked? He'd been kicked in the chest by one of those huge beasts? "Is anything broken?" she whispered as the room started to tilt.

"No. Honey, sit down. You're turning white." He grasped her arm and tugged her into a chair by the nook. "You afraid of blood?"

"No. Just your blood." She shook her head and stood. "I can help you."

He pushed her back down. "Just sit."

The sliding glass door opened, and Ford stomped inside, dropping his slicker onto the floor and slamming his hat onto a hook next to Trent's. "How bad you hurt?" He opened a cupboard by the door and removed a large first aid kit.

"Not bad. You?" Trent pulled out the chair next to Hallie and dropped into it.

"Just bruises." Ford's hair was slicked back, and a new bruise showed along his jawline beneath his existing scars.

He leaned in to study Trent's face, his dark eyes serious. "Not bad. I can get you closed up fast." He set the kit on the counter and rummaged through it.

Hallie forced herself to stand. "What can I do?" Her voice wavered but not very much.

Ford didn't look her way. "Two shots of whiskey from the bar in the living room. Bring the bottle."

She hustled into the living room and the bar on the far side, scrambling for whiskey. There were several bottles of different kinds. Shrugging, she went with Bulleit Bourbon because the bottle looked cool. She snatched two shot glasses and ran back, pouring liquid into them quickly and setting them on the table.

Trent instantly grabbed one and downed the whiskey, holding the glass out for another shot.

She filled it up, and he did the same thing, pained lines fanning out from his mouth.

Ford finished threading a needle and reached for his glass, upending it quickly. He nudged the glass her way.

She frowned, holding tightly to the bottle. "How about I give you more *after* you stitch up his face and wrist?" She couldn't have their pseudo-doctor drunk.

Ford grinned and leaned in to pierce the skin on Trent's face. "Your woman is bossy."

Her stomach dropped and her knees buckled.

"Whoa." Trent caught her with his good arm and prodded her into her vacated chair. "I told you to sit. So sit and look the other way."

She'd argue, but she was trying really hard not to vomit. "Sorry. I've never seen, well, that." The image of that needle sliding so easily through the skin on his face would haunt her forever. "Ranching is too dangerous."

Trent set his hand on her thigh and squeezed. "It's no big deal, baby."

"Stop talking," Ford growled. "I almost stabbed you in the eye."

Bile bubbled up from Hallie's stomach. She swallowed, refilled Trent's glass, and tipped back the entire contents. Heat exploded in her midsection, spreading out.

"Wrist," Ford muttered, his voice low and hoarse.

Hallie turned to see a bandage already in place on Trent's handsome face. She needed to toughen up a little bit so she could cope. "Would you guys like coffee or anything to eat?" She stood. "We have leftover chicken Parmesan in the fridge."

"I'm good," Trent said quietly.

She turned to look at Ford as he bent over Trent's arm and then gently put a bandage over the stitches. "Ford? Are you hungry?"

He looked up and grinned. "No thanks, Hallie. Can I have another shot now?"

She rolled her eyes and poured him another shot.

He drank it quickly. "All right. Austin and Mac should be done bedding the horses down, and we'll head out. See you tomorrow, Trent." He patted Trent's shoulder, leaned over and placed a quick kiss on Hallie's head, grabbed his coat and hat, and was out the door into the storm.

She swallowed, tears threatening the back of her eyes.

Trent pulled her down onto his lap and snuggled his nose into her neck. "He likes you. They all do. This is what family feels like, Hallie."

Her heart swelled with so much longing, she could barely breathe. This ranching life was too dangerous. The men got hurt so much they knew how to stitch each other up. She wanted Trent, and she wanted to be with him, but having his love and losing it would be too much. However, right now she had this moment, and she had him. She swung her leg to his other side and straddled him, careful of his injured wrist. Then she kissed him.

CHAPTER TWELVE

Trent was on fire for the little minx. She straddled him, her mouth soft and sweet with a taste of his good whiskey. There was a certain desperation in her kiss, in her touch, but she was careful of the bandage on his face.

He let her play, his hand resting at her hip. The whiskey in his blood warmed him but the woman on his lap shot fire right through him. The flames licked and teased, torturing him until it hurt not to take over.

Even so, he contented himself with kissing her back.

Until she bit his bottom lip.

Electric sparks zipped through his mouth, straight south, catching him by surprise. His blue-eyed woman had a vixen in her, and he leaned back to stare. "You bit me."

Her smile was catlike. "Don't tell me one little bite from me hurt you. Want me to call Ford back and see if he can stitch you up?"

Amusement warred with the arousal rushing through him. Cute and sassy—now if she got sweet again, he'd lose his mind. Those were only three of the many facets of this woman, and an entire lifetime of being with her wouldn't show him all of them. He just knew it. "Brats who bite should prepare for the consequences," he murmured.

Interest swept across her face. "You're wounded, cowboy. You shouldn't make threats."

He stood in one smooth motion, his hands at her butt, her legs wrapped around his hips. "A couple of stitches won't slow me down, city girl. You might want to keep that in mind." To his surprise, his Kentucky twang emerged faintly. He had to watch himself with her.

She leaned in and pressed a sweet kiss against his lips. "I'm sorry if I hurt you."

He leaned back, easily carrying her weight. Yep. That was humor in those eyes. It wasn't as if she'd broken the skin, and he liked a little nip once in a while. "You might want to remember that I have teeth as well, and I'd bet mine are sharper than yours." He leaned in, satisfied when her breath caught. "And I won't bite your lip."

With her thighs against his hips, she still looked rather daring. "Really? Where exactly do you want to bite me?"

He let one of his dark eyebrows rise. "You're feeling rather brave tonight, aren't you?"

She shrugged, a small smile playing over her bow-shaped mouth. "I guess. You're leaving tomorrow, and when you get back, things will be different. My car will be fixed, and hopefully I'll be out of trouble. If you're not in jail, that is."

It sounded as if she planned to leave him. Interesting. "Since you don't have anywhere to go, why don't you stay in town? Then I can date you properly." He had no clue how to take things slow with her. She was the one. The only one who'd dug right into his chest and planted herself there. But if she needed slow, he'd give it to her. What he wouldn't do was give her up.

She shook her head. "You don't understand. I like you, too. Usually." She said the last quietly.

He couldn't help but smile. "*Usually* works just fine for me." He wasn't the world's most likable guy, and he did get bossy, which she probably didn't like. He also probably wasn't going to change. His hands clenched into her rear end on their own, and her soft gasp almost had him doing it again. "What's on your mind?"

She held still, her eyes deepening to the darkest of sapphires. "I don't want to talk. Let's go back to kissing."

Tempting. Definitely tempting. "Oh, we'll go back to the kissing, but first, you're going to tell me what's going on in that head of yours."

She frowned, looking adorable. "Maybe you should put me down."

"Nope." He could hold her all night, even though the bruise on his chest was making itself known. "I've learned you like to run instead of talk, so we're staying right here until you talk to me." He was fairly comfortable, truth be told. Her ass was a handful, and he finally had his palms right where he wanted them. Although there was a lot more of her to explore. But first things first.

Her eyelashes swept down.

"Eyes on me, baby." He put command into his voice.

Her gaze shot up. "You are so bossy."

"Yeah. Now talk." It was after midnight, and he had an early morning the next day, when he'd be heading to Boise to take care of the killers after her. "I'm losing patience, and you don't want that." It was only fair to be honest with her.

She swallowed. "Fine. Here it is. You'll think I'm weak, but you want the truth."

There was nothing weak about this woman. "All right. Truth?"

She sighed. "I can't do it again. Be with a man who does a dangerous job. Losing Paul was enough for me. I know you love your life, but it's dangerous. You got kicked by a cow tonight."

Understanding wafted through him. The sweetheart. He leaned in and placed a gentle kiss on her nose. "If you were any sweeter, I'd get a toothache," he muttered. "I get it. Yes, you've lost people, and so have I. But Hallie, life is dangerous. Just living is a risk." He knew that better than most. "You're an accountant, which should be one of the safest occupations possible, yet you're on the run for your life. There might even be a hit out on you." He kept his voice gentle.

She blinked. Once and again. "That's a good point."

Yeah. He had them once in a while. "People get sick and die every day. The point is, you have to live. We all have to live." He'd learned that the hard way. He and his brothers still learned it, every day. "I'm good at my job, and I don't take unnecessary risks. Either you trust me to do my best, or you don't."

Panic and then a softer light entered her eyes. "I do trust you."

Well then, it was about time. He needed her to catch up with his understanding of their situation. The attraction between them had been instant, and pursuing it might involve risk, but as he'd told her, living was what mattered. "We good now?"

She swallowed, her gaze dropping to his lips. "Yeah. We're good now." Her voice had gone low. Husky. Sexy.

"Good." He finally gave in and took her mouth the way he wanted. Hard and fast.

* * *

The kiss was beyond anything Hallie had ever experienced. He possessed her, took her over, securing everything she'd ever been and leaving the most intense longing in his path. The storm outside faded to nothing along with her worries and fears. There was only Trent Logan and his hands on her, his body easily holding her aloft.

His mouth was hot and insistent, demanding her surrender in a way that should've scared her but thrilled her instead. He had stopped asking and now commanded.

The taste of whiskey on his breath tantalized her tongue, while that kiss became electricity that zipped down her throat and flew throughout her body, wilder than she could've dreamed. His hold tightened on her, his fingers gripping her butt and the proof of his arousal hard against her core.

She moaned against his mouth, her fingers curling over his hard shoulders, feeling muscle and power.

He tore his mouth free and kissed her jawline, nipping and licking, snapping her earlobe between his lips. His movements were controlled and just rough enough to have her gasping for more. Needing more. Wanting all that was Trent Logan—the fire and the danger.

She could taste both on his skin as she licked her way up his neck to his chin, where his whiskers scratched her. Everything about him was masculine, and she reveled in the sensations, feeling safe in his arms.

Then he was moving. Easily carrying her through the house, his mouth once again on hers, demanding and fast. Each movement of his legs jolted her against him, and her nipples sharpened, rubbing against his hard chest in a way that spiraled need through her so fast her head swam.

The world tilted, and she found herself on her back on Trent's big bed. He loomed over her, a wild cowboy in his element. "You sure about this?"

She nodded, unable to speak. Instead, she reached for him.

He caressed up her sides, his thumbs beneath her shirt, the calloused pads sliding over her soft skin. "Nodding isn't good enough, baby. You need to tell me you're okay with this. If not, no worries. We have plenty of time to get to know each other better." His voice was a low, gruff rumble.

She needed to start living again, not just existing. He'd been right about that. "I don't know what's going to happen next, but I want this moment with you." Maybe a lot more moments with him. Okay. Definitely a lot more moments with him.

He leaned over her, one knee on the bed beside her, his mouth starting to wander along her cheekbone as if they had all the time in the world. "Just this moment?"

It was as if he could read her mind.

She slid her hands up all of that smooth muscle, feeling scars and power. A warrior's body. "It's too fast and it's too crazy, but you make me believe it's possible." She ached more than she would've imagined. For him. Only him.

He kissed her, his mouth working hers like he owned it. Then he leaned back just enough to speak, his lips still brushing hers. "I'm not sure why, but it seems like people who've been through pain, who've survived it, know what they need when they see it. Know what they want. You're in here." He put her hand on his chest. "Whether we understand it or not, you're right there, and I'm not letting you go."

"Maybe I'm not letting *you* go," she whispered, caught by the gleam of his green eyes through the darkness.

He licked along the shell of her ear, his hands finally pushing her top all the way off. "I ain't gentle, baby. I'll try for you, but it's not me."

She arched against him, her mind reeling. "If I wanted gentle, I wouldn't be here with you. Give me all of you."

His grin was a flash of white in the darkness before his hands settled on her breasts. "That I can do."

CHAPTER THIRTEEN

Silas Montgomery lived in a fancy gated community in Boise. His house was imposing, with thick columns, wide wooden doors, and a crap alarm system. The man had been divorced for nearly a decade, and based on the phone records Jesse had hacked, currently enjoyed the company of several widows in the area once in a while.

Tonight, he went to bed alone.

Trent had followed him all day, noting he kept to a normal routine. If his sons were hunting Hallie, he was cool and collected about it, not showing any stress to anybody who might be watching. Now Trent waited on the roof, observing the quiet street below and making sure no nosy neighbor was out walking a poodle or some other animal.

"The light just went off in the master bedroom and the shades are drawn," Austin said through the earpiece.

Trent looked up to see Austin on a mansion rooftop across the street, sniper rifle in place. Mac was on another rooftop, one with a vantage point of the entire neighborhood.

"Go now," Austin said.

Trent rappelled down to the back door as Ford did the same from the top of the garage. They landed silently and coiled up their ropes, then remained still for several minutes.

"The alarm system is disengaged," Jesse said, sounding downhearted.

Mac snorted. "Sorry it wasn't a challenge for you, brother."

Jesse sighed loudly.

Ford shook his head and turned, ducking and expertly picking both locks on the door without leaving a trace. He pushed it open and they waited, just in case.

No sound.

Yep. The system hadn't been a challenge for Jesse. They needed to find him a better job soon, or he was going to get cranky again. Jesse cranky was never a good thing.

Trent went first, taking in the kitchen area with its dirty dishes still on the counter. He'd already memorized the layout of the house from the blueprints Jesse had acquired, but he still stepped carefully around the table and moved silently through the darkened house. If he hadn't felt the heat of Ford's body behind him, he wouldn't have known his brother was there.

They entered the bedroom, and Trent flicked on the light.

Silas Montgomery bolted upright in his bed, his gray hair mussed, his eyes already pissed. "Who the hell are you?"

Aggression. Nice. Trent moved forward while Ford did the same. "I'm Trent. I'm also the guy who decides if you live or die tonight."

Ford shut the bedroom door. "I vote die, just so you know."

Silas was dressed in fancy blue pajamas that looked pressed. Like people on television wore. He looked at them both, swallowing rapidly.

Yeah, Trent knew what he saw. Two men, dressed in all black, scars on their faces and blades in their glove-covered hands. He let the killer in him show in his eyes.

"What do you want?" Silas apparently went with brave, because his chin rose and he settled back against the bed.

Trent stripped the covers from the bed in one smooth motion, leaving Silas revealed and vulnerable. The pajama bottoms matched the pressed top. He paused. "He wears socks to bed." He looked at his brother over his shoulder. "You ever heard of that?"

Ford shrugged. "Maybe he has feet problems. We can cure him of that." He twirled his knife in his hands.

Silas drew his legs up. "I have money in the safe."

"Don't need money," Trent said casually, studying the man's eyes. "I need answers."

"So ask," Silas said.

Trent watched him carefully. "I broke into your office after closing and took any documents proving Hallie Rose worked on the Bixby and Lewis file. Are there any other documents that weren't in your office?"

Silas's eyes widened. "You're working for that woman?"

"Sure," Trent said easily.

"She did it all," Silas spat. "We're covering for her."

Trent moved fast, slicing down Silas's buttoned top, making sure to scrape skin as he did so. Blood welled but not too much.

Silas cried out, his hands going up.

Trent flashed his teeth. "You're talking about the woman I'm going to marry, so you might want to watch yourself. Before we get back to that question, do you know where Bixby's body is buried? You'll save your friend Marc Lewis a lot of pain if you do."

Ford coughed. "Marry? Really? I thought you'd keep your head buried about her and we'd have to slap you silly to wake you up. Good for you, brother."

Trent grinned. "I know, right? I'm evolving. Definitely marrying that girl." He tilted his head. "Well, I'm not evolving too fast. I still like causing agony. Talk, Silas."

Silas swallowed rapidly, his eyes finally showing understanding of the moment. "What do you know about Lewis or Bixby?"

"Everything," Trent stated. "Well, almost everything. My brothers are with Lewis right now, and they're not as patient as I am. Not even close. I'd bet anything he's already bleeding . . . a lot worse than you are. *So far.*"

Ford nodded. "Truth there."

Wyatt and Boone had arrived earlier that morning to help, since their previous mission had been concluded. Wyatt had no patience, actually. He preferred to get to the torture first and think about answers later. He felt things went quicker that way. But Trent didn't want to tick Hallie off too much if she ever found out about this. So he was taking it easy. For now.

Silas looked around frantically for help. "How did you get inside my house?"

"Your alarm system sucks," Trent said, tapping the blade against Silas's arm. The man jumped.

"Get a dog," Ford suggested. "Dogs are better than any alarm system." He rolled his neck. "Can I cut him now? This is boring."

Drool slid from Silas's mouth.

Trent snarled. "You're afraid of the wrong brother here, friend. Right now, your moronic sons are after my woman, which means they'll probably die. I'm fighting really hard not to start cutting pieces off you, just for fun. Just for causing her fear. You're gonna want to start talking. We can start with where your sons are right now, move to the location of Bixby's body, and then discuss any additional documents that may implicate Hallie. I'll probably have to stab you a few times and maybe cut a few things off. It happens."

Silas gulped and his shoulders slumped.

Now they were getting somewhere.

Hallie couldn't manage to eat dinner, so she sat on the sofa and petted the wolf. His head lay in her lap, and he snored gently, seemingly content. Where was Trent? Was he all right?

The front door opened, and both Zeke and Zachary walked inside.

She'd become accustomed to all of the gang appearing at the house whenever, so she just looked up. "Have you guys heard anything from Trent?" she asked, her heart rate kicking in.

"Nope," Zachary said.

Harley lifted his head and sneezed, while remaining close to Hallie.

Zeke studied her. "Stop worrying. Trent knows what he's doing. We're having an impromptu party out at the lodge, so grab your stuff."

She blinked. "I'm not going to a party."

"Honey, you're going to a party," Zeke corrected, his

tone almost gentle. "We promised Trent to keep an eye on you, which was easy since we worked his ranch today, but now we're having a party and you're going with us. Plus, it'll take your mind off Trent."

She sighed. It wasn't as if she was doing anything else, and now she could put the sheets on his bed at the club. "Fine." Stretching her back, she stood. "Have you noticed that you all are too bossy? Way too bossy?"

"Zeke is bossy," Zachary said, smiling. "I use charm."

She rolled her eyes and looked down at her jeans and cream-colored sweater. Her hair was up and her makeup done, just in case Trent returned, so she was ready to go. "All right, but I'm not staying out all night. And if things get too wild, I'm bringing a book to read in Trent's room."

"You party animal," Zeke teased.

She grinned and then followed them outside into a light rain. At least the weather was giving them somewhat of a break. "When does it stop raining around here, anyway?"

Zachary snorted. "Right when we don't want it to stop raining."

Figured. The drive to the clubhouse was quick, and it looked like the party was in full swing when they arrived. She sighed and jumped from the truck, preceding the twins inside. They flanked her so easily it seemed natural, and she noted nobody could get to her without going through one of them.

The sense of safety warmed her.

Then she walked inside, and a blast of heat smashed her. Music beat from the speakers, couples danced on a makeshift floor by the sofa, and the beer was already flowing freely. She recognized a couple of the women from the other party, and she nodded and then smiled at some of the brothers.

Zeke herded her to the bar. "You thirsty?"

"Not yet." She patted Harley's head to calm him. While he seemed to want to stay close to her, he was still a some-what wild animal and surely couldn't deal with the noise or the strangers. She had to help him. "I'm going to go finish Trent's sheets, and then I'll be back." The music was already giving her a headache.

Zachary was putting his arm around a full-bodied blonde who was falling out of her shirt. "All right, but check in every once in a while. You're safe in the club-house."

Men were morons sometimes. She shook her head and strode through the party and down the hallway, not sur-prised when the wolf followed her. He didn't seem to like the music any more than she did. "You're a good boy," she murmured, patting his head and letting him into Trent's room before continuing down to the laundry room to fetch the clean sheets.

She buried her nose in them, almost sorry they smelled like a fresh breeze instead of Trent. Laughing at herself, she entered the room and quickly made the bed. Within seconds, Harley jumped on top and settled himself at the foot of the bed.

"Harley," she objected without any heat.

He snuggled down, and it looked as if he smiled. Crazy animal. Trent had been wrong to say that Harley was wild and rarely came close to any of them. The wolf wouldn't leave her alone.

Maybe she should cuddle with him and just relax. She looked around the room; it was still clean and dusted. Then she lay on the bed, closing her eyes. Within minutes, with the wolf guarding her, she was asleep.

Something awoke her hours later, and she sat up groggily,

looking for the clock. It was well after midnight, and the music was still pounding in the other room. For goodness' sake. She yawned and then stretched. The wall across from the bed caught her eye. What in the world? Part of the paneling looked askew. It appeared misaligned with the panel next to it.

Curiosity caught her, and she moved forward, settling her fingers against the uneven edge. Then she pulled. A door opened to reveal a narrow closet. She gasped. Guns of all kinds were mounted on the wall along with knives of every size. More weapons than she could count. A shelf to the left held all sorts of bullets and more knives. She gulped. It was a munitions cornucopia. Why did Trent have so many weapons?

Feeling guilty, she glanced over her shoulder, but only the wolf watched her.

She looked back at the closet, her gaze catching on a silver box on the shelf. Her hands shook but she took it out and flipped the lid open. She'd expected more bullets or something. What she found were passports. She filtered through them. Each one held Trent's picture with a different name. A couple of USA passports, Russian, Belgian, Scottish . . . there were at least a dozen of them from as many different countries, and his look varied in each one.

But it was Trent.

Her hands shook so hard, she had to close the lid and slide the box back onto the shelf. Leaning to the side, she saw a bigger box beneath the bottom shelf. Biting her lip, holding her breath, she pulled it out, grunting with the effort. Swallowing down panic, she opened the lid.

Money. Tons of cash, all in different currencies.

Who was this man? She hurriedly closed the lid and shoved the box beneath the shelf, closing the secret door.

She leaned against it, her breath panting wildly. He had weapons and passports and currency. Was his name even Trent? Who were these ranchers? What were they really involved in?

None of it seemed good. How could it be?

He had told her he was a killer. He'd said the words, looking right in her eyes. Were they some sort of hitmen? She realized Austin was one of them, as well as being the sheriff right now.

She had to run.

Taking a deep breath, she grabbed her purse and opened the door to the quiet hallway. Then she hurried toward the exit at the end, pushing the door open and rushing into the rain. Avoiding the trucks of the cattlemen, she looked at the other cars parked there. One of them had to have keys.

She scored with an older blue Honda and left the lights off as she drove away until she was out of sight.

None of this seemed real. No matter how she looked at it, Trent had lied to her. He'd promised her forever, and he hadn't even told her who he was or what he did. At best, he was hiding from something. At worst, he was some sort of assassin or something crazy like that.

Either way, she did not know him. At all.

CHAPTER FOURTEEN

Hallie's hands shook on the steering wheel, and she had to squint to see through the rain. Something on the car dinged, and she caught sight of the fuel gauge. Wonderful. Almost empty.

The thunder billowed in the distance and the rain pelted down during yet another impressive storm.

She bit her lip and drove to the end of town, swinging into the lone gas station. Grimacing, she pulled out her last ten dollars. Trent hadn't had a chance to pay her yet. Why the heck hadn't she stolen some of the money from his closet? The idea hadn't even occurred to her until right now.

She was the worst fugitive ever. She wished she'd brought the wolf, already missing him.

Gulping, she ducked through the rain and paid the cashier, a teenager who barely looked up from her book. It was nice the place was open twenty-four hours. Then Hallie dashed to the pump and carefully used the ten dollars, choosing the least expensive fuel. "Sorry about this," she murmured, hoping she could ditch the car somewhere so the owner would find it easily.

Trent had turned her into a car thief.

Her anger was at a slightly higher level than her hurt, and at least that was something. He owed her an explanation, but she needed some time and distance first. Plus, what would he do? She couldn't imagine in a million years that he'd hurt her, but it wasn't as if she really knew him. Maybe the charm and promises had been as fake as his many passports. This was all so confusing.

Yeah. Time and distance were her friends. Oh, she was going to confront him and make him explain everything, once she'd gotten to safety. For now, she just needed some time and space to *think*. Then she'd figure out how to confront him.

"Hello, Hallie." Something hard pressed into her back.

The world ground to a harsh halt. Her head hung. This was impossible. She partially turned to see Brad Montgomery, his handsome face twisted, a three-day scruff covering his face. Even his eyes were bloodshot. It was too much. Everything was too much. "You can't be here right now," she snapped, losing her mind.

He reared back. "Excuse me?"

The gun pressed harder into her rib cage.

She threw out her hands as her sense of reality completely deserted her. "You can't be here. Seriously. I have enough to deal with, and there's no way you could find me. Get that gun out of my side."

His brows drew down as if he wasn't sure how to respond. "Listen, you psycho. We've been sitting here for three days waiting for you to make an appearance, and I've had it. Get in my car before I just shoot you."

She glared. "Waiting here?"

"Yes." He pushed even harder, and she winced at the pain. "We knew you were here and there's only one major way in or out of this stupid little town. We knew you'd show at some point, and it's about time."

She looked around, panic finally sinking through the fog she'd been in. The area was quiet, and the teenager inside was faced away from the pumps, reading her book. "How did you find me?" She had to get away from him.

He grabbed her hair and pulled, yanking her away from the car and the lights. She fought him, but he shoved the gun to the side of her head, and she grew still, her mind grasping for a way to escape. "We traced the phone call. You'd be shocked the people we know who can help us."

"You'd be shocked the people I know," she countered, unable to move far with the weapon at her temple. "I used a burner phone."

"We didn't trace *you*." He opened the back door of a nondescript brown car and shoved her inside, keeping the gun on her as she followed.

She perched on the worn leather seat, frantically looking for a way out. "You traced my neighbor's phone." She should've thought of that, but she'd had to check on Mrs. P.

"Yeah." Brad slammed the door. "I knew you'd check on that old bag, and you did."

Charles turned around in the driver's seat, his face an angry red. "It's about time. I am done with this job." He started the car and drove away from the gas station and Hallie's last sense of safety.

Fear climbed through her as the shock receded, helping her focus. "This day just keeps getting worse." She cautiously reached for the door handle.

"It's childproof locked," Brad said, facing her with the gun pointed somewhere in her stomach area.

She froze. If she could get the gun from him, she could at least shoot Charles and stop the car. "What do you want from me?"

"Oh. A lot, and we'll get to that," Charles said grimly.

She studied Brad in the darkness. "You seemed like a good guy to me."

"I am a good guy." He waved the gun, spittle flying from his mouth. "If you'd just listened to me, we wouldn't have had to chase you for a solid freaking month. You don't seem to understand that you put all of us in danger. Marc Lewis isn't messing around, and he's going to hire hitmen on all of us if you don't promise to keep quiet about everything."

"I promise," she said instantly. "Is that all? I haven't told anybody, and as you can see, it's not like I went to any authorities." Which was the absolute truth. Sure, she was planning to turn them in, but so far, they couldn't know that. Hope spun through her.

Brad set the gun on his thigh, his hand securely over it. "That's true."

She nodded and patted his knee, so close to the gun. "I know. You scared me, and I ran. But I haven't turned you guys in. That has to count for something."

Brad looked toward his brother, and her heart sank.

Charles met her eyes in the rearview mirror. "My brother might think you're sweet and truthful, but I think you're full of it. Whichever is true, we're going to find out the hard way."

Brad's shoulders slumped and he barely looked at her. "We'll figure something out, Hallie."

That didn't sound good. Fear made it hard to think, but she watched the ranch land speed by outside, trying to figure out a way to escape. Soon Charles pulled onto a dirt road and followed it, stopping in front of a small, quiet log cabin.

Her mouth went dry. "Where are we?"

Brad reached for her arm. "Rental in the middle of nowhere."

Charles turned and smiled. "I hope you're a screamer."

The helicopter landed smack dab in the field behind the clubhouse as lightning struck too close, and Trent was the first off, ducking and running full bore for the building. He'd gone stone cold the second he'd heard that Hallie had been taken. Emotion threatened to knock him to his knees, so he returned to being the killer they'd made of him. It was the only way he could handle the situation.

He entered the clubhouse first, nearly bowling Zeke over. "Talk to me." His team was on his heels, ignoring the rain pounding them. Remains of a party littered the floor around them, but the place had been cleared out the second Hallie had gone missing and Zeke had called Trent.

Zachary looked up from a laptop while still typing furiously. "She took off about an hour ago, and here's footage from the gas station." The video feed came up, showing Hallie being taken by Brad Montgomery. He held a gun in her side and then to her temple.

Trent breathed out, his body going hot and then back to cold. Freezing, killing, desperate ice.

Zeke scrubbed both hands down his face. "She was sleeping in your room, and I didn't think she'd ever run. I would've planted myself right outside if I'd even had a hint."

Levi looked up. "She found your stash. Didn't you tell her about you? About us?"

"No," Trent muttered, fury catching in his throat and forcing his Southern accent out in full force. Fury at himself, at Hallie, at the Montgomery brothers, who were going to bleed. "Where. Is. She?"

"I'm working on it," Zachary said. "Last CCTV is the gas station, and the car doesn't make it to Smalltown. They have a new camera system to catch speeders right before town. So she's somewhere in that strip of land between the two towns."

That strip of land was comprised of a hundred miles. How was Trent going to find her in that stretch of land before they hurt her or worse? He'd finally found her—the one woman in the entire world made just for him. He'd known it the second he'd touched her, and now he might lose her.

Wyatt dropped his pack on the floor. "If they've been staying around here, there's only one area to rent cabins between here and there. The rest is private ranch land."

Austin reached for his phone and pressed a button, holding the phone to his ear. "Hey, Murphy. Sorry to wake you, but it's the sheriff. Are any of your cabins rented to a couple of men going by the name of Montgomery?" He waited and shook his head. "Any rented to just a man?" He listened and held up a hand. "Which cabin? No, don't go down there. It's official police business, and I'll handle it. Go back to bed and tell Loretta that I'm sorry I woke you both." He hung up. "One guy, renting the cabin on the far east side. Said he was a novelist who needed space and quiet."

Trent fetched his Glock from his bag and shoved it into

his waist. "Six of us can fit in the helicopter." It'd take an hour by car and probably a half hour by horse.

The storm outside would mask their arrival.

Austin grabbed his arm. "We dropped all of the evidence off with the police department in Boise instead of taking out Silas Montgomery and Marc Lewis. If we kill the Montgomery sons, there will be questions and a spotlight on us. I'm fine with it, but this is your call."

Ford shoved his knife in the sheath attached to his thigh. "We can make them disappear. Maybe nobody will connect them to Wyoming. It depends how much of a trail they left traveling here. They obviously tried to stay under the radar, but we found them in five minutes. If they're the ones in the Murphy cabin, anybody else looking might get lucky, too."

Trent sucked down anger and tried to breathe. Was she being hurt right now? Would they kill her? He couldn't bring the attention of the authorities to his brothers, but he was torn. What should he do?

Zeke shook his head. "This is why we don't leave witnesses. Should've taken out both Silas and Lewis."

"I'm not disagreeing," Trent said grimly. He had tried to tamp down the reality of who he was, for Hallie, and it had put her in danger.

Austin dropped his pack as well as the case for his rifle. He took out a pistol. "Either way, we need to get the girl. Are we shooting to kill, or do we need a plan B?"

Trent moved for the door. The harsh journey he and his brothers had endured to find this place and become who they were spun through his head. The image of Hallie with her sweet smile and her belief in him landed hard in his chest. Somehow, he was her hero. Or he had been. He was so far from a hero it wasn't funny, but she'd looked at him like that. His brothers, his woman, his family.

"Trent?" Austin asked.

Trent straightened his shoulders and gripped his weapon. There was only one solution. "I am plan B. Let's go."

CHAPTER FIFTEEN

Hallie sat with her wrists tied to the chair arms with rough rope that cut into her skin. A fire crackled in the small woodstove, so different from the cheery fire she'd sat in front of every night with Trent. The Montgomery boys sat in chairs across from her, arguing quietly about what to do with her.

Charles took a knife out of a backpack on the table. "There's only one way to know if she's telling the truth."

Her eyes widened, and she couldn't look away from the firelight glinting off the sharp blade. "Um, I'm telling the truth. Is the law after you? No. Is there any hint of the police being involved? No. Brad?" She tore her gaze away to look at the man she'd once considered charming. "You know I haven't turned you in. I thought you liked me."

"I did. I do," Brad said, his voice almost a whine. Even for a kidnapping, he wore a blue button-down shirt with pressed jeans and brown loafers.

So different from Trent's torn jeans and tough cowboy boots. She missed Trent. She wanted him right then. She might not know what he was involved in, but he'd protect her. She just knew it. For now, she had to figure her own way out of this disaster, so she stared at Brad.

"If you like me, how can you let your brother threaten me with a knife?" She silently implored him to act like a man and protect her from his sociopathic brother, who was staring at her with way too much interest while he caressed the handle of the dangerous-looking knife.

Brad looked at his brother and sighed.

It was obvious who was in charge. She shifted her focus to Charles while gingerly testing the ropes around her wrists. They were tight and painful. Her feet were loose, so she could kick whoever came at her. But there were two of them and one of her, and they had knives and a gun. Why hadn't she taken one of Trent's many weapons? She shivered.

Charles smiled. He had the same jawline and eye color as Brad, but his face was wider and the shape of his eyes meaner. "You know we can't let her live. Even if she hasn't turned us in, she knows too much, and she'll always be a threat."

Her stomach revolted and she coughed. "Have you ever killed anybody, Charles?" Maybe she could talk him out of it.

"No," Charles said. "I've hit a few people in my time, but I've never had reason to kill anybody. Until now." He looked as if he could do it—as if he wanted to kill her.

Brad made a small sound of distress.

She closed her eyes and took several deep breaths before reopening them to find the brothers staring at her. "I thought Brad said that the evidence incriminated me, too. So I can't talk to anybody about it." They didn't know about Trent and his friends, and who knew, maybe Trent hadn't gone to take care of her problem. He could be anywhere in the world right now.

"Actually," Brad whispered, "we've arranged it so it's all your fault."

"Which means she has to die so she can't raise any doubt." Charles stood and walked toward her, the knife in his hand.

She opened her mouth to scream just as the front door burst open.

Men poured in, and she recognized Trent right before he threw a knife across the room, embedding it in Charles's shoulder. Charles screamed and dropped his knife, grabbing at the handle protruding from his flesh. Blood welled around his fingers.

Zeke had Brad in a headlock within a second, and his brother shoved Charles into his vacated chair.

Trent came at her, his face a hard mask. He looked her over, his gaze intense, his body one long line of pure fury.

She cringed, unable to help herself.

He dropped to his haunches, whipped another knife out of his boot, and cut through the ropes. "How badly are you hurt?" His voice didn't even sound like him. Harsh, guttural, deadly.

She swallowed and shook her head.

His head jerked up, and he cupped her jawline, his touch gentle. "Hallie. Answer me."

"I-I'm not hurt," she whispered, her voice trembling.

His knuckles smoothed over the raw rope burns on her arms. "Tie them up. Use ropes on their arms and make them too tight." His gaze didn't leave her abused skin. "Anywhere else?"

"N-no," she said.

He lifted her shirt to her bra and angled his head. "There's a bruise on your ribs. From the gun?"

She gulped and nodded.

He looked over his shoulder to where Zeke and Zachary were tying Brad and Charles to chairs. Brad was babbling and Charles was coughing, still trying to dislodge the knife from his shoulder. "Their ribs are where I'll start," Trent said, slowly standing.

Hallie stood, reaching for his shirt. "Trent—"

"No." He whirled on her, lifting her into his arms and striding for Austin at the door. "I'll deal with you when I'm finished with them." He deposited her in Austin's arms. "Take her to my place." He leaned in, his eyes so dark the green was almost gone. "You'd better be there, baby. I'm mad enough as it is. Do you understand me?" His voice dropped several octaves, which was much more menacing than if he'd yelled.

She gulped and nodded.

"Say it," he ordered.

"I understand. I'll be there," she whispered, her entire body shaking.

He turned away as Austin carried her out into the raging rain and a waiting helicopter. Apparently the team felt safe enough to fly in the storm, although she had her doubts. The first scream came from the cabin just as the craft lifted away from the field.

Hallie paced by the fireplace while the wolf snored on the sofa. It had been hours. At least two. Austin had dropped her at the house, and she knew, *she just knew*, he was watching from somewhere outside. Maybe not only him. They were out there to make sure she didn't try another run for it. What they didn't know was that she'd meant her promise to Trent. She had no plans to leave until after he explained everything to her. *Everything.*

Lightning struck outside followed by more thunder.

He walked through the front door and hung up his jacket and coat before turning to stare at her. No expression lived in those green eyes. "Sit down, Hallie."

Normally, she'd take exception to the order, but right now, she just didn't have the energy. She pushed the wolf farther up the sofa and sat, crossing her hands in her lap. "Where are Brad and Charles?"

"They're not your concern. I am." He crossed in front of her. With the fire lighting him from behind, his face was shadowed and his expression impossible to read. He tucked his thumbs in his jeans pockets and studied her, the feel of his gaze physical. "I love you. Don't know how it happened so fast, but it's the truth. Thought I'd start there."

It wasn't what she'd expected. Her heart started to pound, and her body burst wide awake, reacting to him as it would to no other. She swallowed. "You have passports."

"Yeah. I have a lot of passports." He didn't move. "I was with a specialized team in the navy and was taken prisoner and presumed dead."

Harley stood, turned around, and set his face on her knee. She absently started petting him, already hurting for Trent.

He continued. "The group that took me didn't have a country or even a name. They tortured us and trained us, forcing us to carry out missions. They were smart. First they forged bonds between us that couldn't be broken. Or maybe we did that." He ran a rough hand through his hair.

She shook her head. "I don't understand."

"That's because it's something that shouldn't be understood," he said. "I was with them for seven years. Zeke and Zach for five years, Austin for ten. They hired us out to the highest bidder, and if we failed on a mission, one of our brothers was murdered. They were tortured until we returned. There were fifty of us."

She couldn't breathe.

"Now there are twelve. We killed our captors and we got free. Only twelve of us survived, and we came here. Started over." He rubbed the back of his neck, his fingers digging in so hard she could see the force in them. "There was a kid, younger than the rest of us. His name was Harley, and he came from Wyoming. Used to talk about the wide-open spaces and the freedom. That's what we wanted. Needed."

She petted the wolf, already knowing the answer but having to ask anyway. "Harley didn't make it?"

"No. We all chose cowboy-style names when we reinvented ourselves. When we got here, the wolf kind of adopted the group from afar. Seemed like maybe Harley was still looking out for us."

She perked up. "What was your given name?"

He was quiet for a moment. "I was called Kevin Track, but he died years ago. I don't even know that guy anymore."

She nodded. He did seem much more of a Trent. "Okay."

Trent sighed. "Even so, reinventing ourselves has been difficult. We're still trying to figure it out."

All of the different passports ran through her mind. "How many languages do you speak?"

"Dozens. We were from all different countries, and we taught each other during the darkest times. It was a way to survive and keep our minds busy. Only two of us in the club are actually from this country." He shook his head. "It's not up to me to tell you who. Their secrets are their own."

Fascinating. Today, they all sounded like they came from Wyoming. She remembered his accent. "You were from the South?"

"Kentucky. Born and raised. But this is my family. I want to make them yours, too." He moved toward her then, dropping to his knees in front of her. "I know it's not normal, and I know it probably seems frightening. But we'll protect you until the end of days, and we'll love you. I'll love you as mine. They'll love you as family. But once you're in, Hallie, you're in. Take your time and think about it, because this is your one chance to leave. I'll let you." He placed his hands so gently on her knees. "It'll rip out my guts, but I'll let you go if that's what you want. This once."

She'd known he was a good man, even though there were so many mysteries surrounding him. Now she understood some of him, and she wanted more time to know all of him. He was hers. When she spoke, it was from the heart. "I choose you, Trent. I don't understand your world, but I want you. Need you." It felt good to finally go with her heart and not her fears. Tied to a chair in a scary cabin, she'd realized what she wanted for her future. Who she wanted in her future. "I love you. No matter what."

He sucked in air. When his hand cupped her face, it trembled. "Make sure you're certain, baby."

She leaned into his touch. "I'm sure. And stop calling me baby."

He grinned, leaning in to kiss her. "I'll call you anything you want."

The kiss flowed through her, promising everything. "I guess baby is okay." Then he kissed her again, and she forgot all about nicknames.

CHAPTER SIXTEEN

A month later

"Would you relax?" Austin once again tried to tug Trent's tie back into place. "We have the whole town here, and we need to look like normal people. So freaking relax before I have to knock you out, and don't think I won't do it. You'd only be out long enough to compose yourself."

Zeke looked up from the chair near Trent's fireplace, his feet on the coffee table. "I think the groom is supposed to be terrified or nervous. That is normal."

Austin gave him a look. "How do you know how a groom is supposed to feel? You can't even keep a girlfriend around."

"Sorry, Mom," Zeke said, apparently forgetting that Austin had taught them all how to kill more efficiently with bare hands. "Maybe I just haven't found the right woman." His gaze caught on somebody outside near the quickly built gazebo, and his boots hit the floor.

Trent looked outside to see the pretty veterinarian winding her way through the crowd. "Why don't you just ask her out?"

Zeke flashed him a grin. "I'm not the ask-them-out

type. Zachary is. I like them to show up at the club, take off their clothes, and say thank you afterward."

Trent snorted. "You can be such a jerk."

"Sometimes they say that, too," Zeke admitted. "Even so, there's something about a woman with shadows in her eyes that calls to me. That woman calls to me, although she has way too much attitude."

Ford loped into the room and eyed the sunny day outside. "I don't understand why we have to wear suits, too. Trent is the one getting married." He lapsed into a combination of languages that included one he'd invented just for them.

"It's a summer wedding," Austin snapped. "It said in that bride magazine that everyone wears suits."

Trent shook his head before Ford could give Austin a hard time about the bride magazine. His older brother had been pushed enough for the day. "Hey, I heard the sheriff is back."

"Yeah, but he wants to retire and thinks I should take the job." Austin reached for a flask and downed a healthy swallow, handing it over to Trent. "I'm kind of interested, since it'd keep us involved in the town. I'm thinking about it."

Ford read the face of his phone. "Just heard from our contact in Boise. Silas, his sons, and Marc Lewis all pled guilty to homicide and embezzlement after reaching deals for long prison sentences. There was no mention of Wyoming or Hallie Rose."

Austin nodded. "You did a good job with them."

Trent shrugged. "I just made it clear what would happen to them if they talked, and they believed me."

Zeke stood. "Enough focus on the past. Let's go work on the future."

Trent took another deep breath and followed Zeke outside and down the path to the gazebo, smiling and nodding at the townspeople as he did so. It had been so long since he or any of his brothers had tried to live with normal people. No doubt Hallie would help them all with that. It was a good town, and he wanted to stay here.

He tugged on his tie again as he stood next to the preacher and Austin, with his brothers in the audience giving their full support.

The music started, and Hallie walked out of the other side of the house.

A hush came over the crowd.

He couldn't breathe. She was the most beautiful woman in the entire world. Her dress was white and flowy, and little flowers were dotted through her hair. Her eyes were the bluest of blue, and they were laser focused on him, with love shining in them.

Austin tried to grab his arm, but it was too late. Trent hustled toward her down the aisle, ignoring the twitters of laughter until he reached her. "You're beautiful."

She faltered, and her smile chased away any clouds that would ever exist. "What are you doing?"

"Making sure you don't change your mind." He was being an idiot, but he didn't care. He lifted her and swung around.

"You go, Trent," Zeke called out.

Yeah. Zeke got him. Trent carried her all the way to the altar and then stood there in front of the preacher. "I do, she does, so say we're married." His mouth moved toward hers.

Austin smacked him on the nose, halting his progress.

Trent snarled, for the first time wanting to hit his older brother.

Then Hallie laughed, the sound sweet and free.

He paused and let himself bask in the sound. She was his. All of that joy and kindness, and he'd protect it and her with everything he'd ever be.

She settled against his chest and put an arm over his shoulder, tossing the bouquet. Trent watched to see where it landed.

Ford caught the flowers and his eyes widened in what looked like horror.

Then Hallie turned to the preacher. "I think we should get right to the vows before this cowboy tries to get right to the honeymoon."

The preacher, an older gentleman with a kind smile, nodded. "That's a good idea." He rattled off the vows and Trent answered quickly, holding his breath until Hallie said *I do.*

The second she did, he took her mouth in a kiss, even as the preacher dubbed them husband and wife. She filled parts of him he hadn't realized were empty. He kissed her again and then leaned back, still holding her securely in his arms. "I love you, Hallie Logan."

She nipped his bottom lip in that way he adored. "I love you, too. Always."

Yeah. He had an *always* now. He kissed her again, giving her the same thing.

Always.

Please turn the page for an exciting peek at:

THE SNOW MAN

by
Diana Palmer

Available at bookstores and e-retailers

Meadow Dawson just stared at the slim, older cowboy who was standing on her front porch with his hat held against his chest. His name was Ted. He was her father's ranch foreman. And he was speaking Greek, she decided, or perhaps some form of archaic language that she couldn't understand.

"The culls," he persisted. "Mr. Jake wanted us to go ahead and ship them out to that rancher we bought the replacement heifers from."

She blinked. She knew three stances that she could use to shoot a .40 caliber Glock from. She was experienced in interrogation techniques. She'd once participated in a drug raid with other agents from the St. Louis, Missouri, office where she'd been stationed during her brief tenure with the FBI as a special agent.

Sadly, none of those experiences had taught her what a cull was, or what to do with it. She pushed back her long, golden blond hair, and her pale green eyes narrowed on his elderly face.

She blinked. "Are culls some form of wildlife?" she asked blankly.

The cowboy doubled up laughing.

She grimaced. Her father and mother had divorced when she was six. She'd gone to live with her mother in Greenwood, Mississippi, while her father stayed here on this enormous Colorado ranch, just outside Raven Springs. Later, she'd spent some holidays with her dad, but only after she was in her senior year of high school and she could out-argue her bitter mother, who hated her ex-husband. What she remembered about cattle was that they were loud and dusty. She really hadn't paid much attention to the cattle on the ranch or her father's infrequent references to ranching problems. She hadn't been there often enough to learn the ropes.

"I worked for the FBI," she said with faint belligerence. "I don't know anything about cattle."

He straightened up. "Sorry, ma'am," he said, still fighting laughter. "Culls are cows that didn't drop calves this spring. Nonproductive cattle are removed from the herd, or culled. We sell them either as beef or surrogate mothers for purebred cattle."

She nodded and tried to look intelligent. "I see." She hesitated. "So we're punishing poor female cattle for not being able to have calves repeatedly over a period of years."

The cowboy's face hardened. "Ma'am, can I give you some friendly advice about ranch management?"

She shrugged. "Okay."

"I think you'd be doing yourself a favor if you sold this ranch," he said bluntly. "It's hard to make a living at ranching, even if you've done it for years. It would be a sin and a shame to let all your father's hard work go to pot. Begging your pardon, ma'am," he added respectfully. "Dal Blake was friends with your father, and he owns the biggest ranch around Raven Springs. Might be worthwhile to talk to him."

Meadow managed a smile through homicidal rage. "Dariell Blake and I don't speak," she informed him.

"Ma'am?" The cowboy sounded surprised.

"He told my father that I'd turned into a manly woman who probably didn't even have . . ." She bit down hard on the word she couldn't bring herself to voice. "Anyway," she added tersely, "he can keep his outdated opinions to himself."

The cowboy grimaced. "Sorry."

"Not your fault," she said, and managed a smile. "Thanks for the advice, though. I think I'll go online and watch a few YouTube videos on cattle management. I might call one of those men, or women, for advice."

The cowboy opened his mouth to speak, thought about how scarce jobs were, and closed it again. "Whatever you say, ma'am." He put his hat back on. "I'll just get back to work. It's, uh, okay to ship out the culls?"

"Of course it's all right," she said, frowning. "Why wouldn't it be?"

"You said it oppressed the cows . . ."

She rolled her eyes. "I was kidding!"

"Oh." Ted brightened a little. He tilted his hat respectfully and went away.

Meadow went back into the house and felt empty. She and her father had been close. He loved his ranch and his daughter. Getting to know her as an adult had been great fun for both of them. Her mother had kept the tension going as long as she lived. She never would believe that Meadow could love her and her ex-husband equally. But Meadow did. They were both wonderful people. They just couldn't live together without arguing.

She ran her fingers over the back of the cane-bottomed rocking chair where her father always sat, near the big stone fireplace. It was November, and Colorado was cold. Heavy snow was already falling. Meadow remembered Colorado winters from her childhood, before her parents divorced. It was going to be difficult to manage payroll, much less all the little added extras she'd need, like food and electricity . . .

She shook herself mentally. She'd manage, somehow. And she'd do it without Dariell Blake's help. She could only imagine the smug, self-righteous expression that would come into those chiseled features if she asked him to teach her cattle ranching. She'd rather starve. Well, not really.

She considered her options, and there weren't many. Her father owned this ranch outright. He owed for farm equipment, like combines to harvest grain crops and tractors to help with planting. He owed for feed and branding supplies and things like that. But the land was hers now, free and clear. There was a lot of land. It was worth millions.

She could have sold it and started over. But he'd made her promise not to. He'd known her very well by then. She never made a promise she didn't keep. Her own sense of ethics locked her into a position she hated. She didn't know anything about ranching!

Her father mentioned Dariell, whom everyone locally called Dal, all the time. Fine young man, he commented. Full of pepper, good disposition, loves animals.

The loving animals part was becoming a problem. She had a beautiful white Siberian husky, a rescue, with just a hint of red-tipped fur in her ears and tail. She was named Snow, and Meadow had fought the authorities to keep her in her small apartment. She was immaculate, and Meadow brushed her and bathed her faithfully. Finally the apartment manager had given in, reluctantly, after Meadow offered a sizable deposit for the apartment, which was close to her work. She made friends with a lab tech in the next-door apartment, who kept Snow when Meadow had to travel for work. It was a nice arrangement, except that the lab tech really liked Meadow, who didn't return the admiration. While kind and sweet, the tech did absolutely nothing for Meadow physically or emotionally.

She wondered sometimes if she was really cold. Men were nice. She dated. She'd even indulged in light petting with one of them. But she didn't feel the sense of need that made women marry and settle and have kids with a man. Most of the ones she'd dated were career oriented and didn't want marriage in the first place. Meadow's mother had been devout. Meadow grew up with deep religious beliefs that were in constant conflict with society's norms.

She kept to herself mostly. She'd loved her job when she started as an investigator for the Bureau. But there had been a minor slipup.

Meadow was clumsy. There was no other way to put it. She had two left feet, and she was always falling down or doing things the wrong way. It was a curse. Her mother had named her Meadow because she was reading a novel at the time and the heroine had that name. The heroine had been gentle and sweet and a credit to the community where she lived, in 1900s Fort Worth, Texas. Meadow, sadly, was nothing like her namesake.

There had been a stakeout. Meadow had been assigned, with another special agent, to keep tabs on a criminal who'd shot a police officer. The officer lived, but the man responsible was facing felony charges, and he ran.

A CI, or Confidential Informant, had told them where the man was likely to be on a Friday night. It was a local club, frequented by people who were out of the mainstream of society.

Meadow had been assigned to watch the back door while the other special agent went through the front of the club and tried to spot him.

Sure enough, the man was there. The other agent was recognized by a patron, who warned the perpetrator. The criminal took off out the back door.

While Meadow was trying to get her gun out of the holster, the fugitive ran into her and they both tumbled onto the ground.

"Clumsy cow!" he exclaimed. He turned her over and pushed her face hard into the asphalt of the parking lot, and then jumped up and ran.

Bruised and bleeding, Meadow managed to get to her feet and pull her service revolver. "FBI! Stop or I'll shoot!"

"You couldn't hit a barn from the inside!" came the sarcastic reply from the running man.

"I'll show . . . you!" As she spoke, she stepped back onto a big rock, her feet went out from under her, and the gun discharged right into the windshield of the SUV she and the special agent arrived in.

The criminal was long gone by the time Meadow was recovering from the fall.

"Did you get him?" the other agent panted as he joined her. He frowned. "What the hell happened to you?"

"He fell over me and pushed my face into the asphalt," she muttered, feeling the blood on her nose. "I ordered him to halt and tried to fire when I tripped over a rock . . ."

The other agent's face told a story that he was too kind to voice.

She swallowed, hard. "Sorry about the windshield," she added.

He glanced at the Bureau SUV and shook his head. "Maybe we could tell them it was a vulture. You know, they sometimes fly into car windshields."

"No," she replied grimly. "It's always better to tell them the truth. Even when it's painful."

"Guess you're right." He grimaced. "Sorry."

"Hey. We all have talents. I think mine is to trip over my own feet at any given dangerous moment."

"The SAC is going to be upset," he remarked.

"I don't doubt it," she replied.

In fact, the Special Agent in Charge was eloquent about her failure to secure the fugitive. He also wondered aloud, rhetorically, how any firearms instructor ever got drunk enough to pass her in the academy. She kept quiet, figuring that anything she said would only make matters worse.

He didn't take her badge. He did, however, assign her as an aide to another agent who was redoing files in the basement of the building. It was clerical work, for which she wasn't even trained. And from that point, her career as an FBI agent started going drastically downhill.

She'd always had problems with balance. She thought that her training would help her compensate for it, but she'd been wrong. She seemed to be a complete failure as an FBI agent. Her superior obviously thought so.

He did give her a second chance, months later. He sent her to interrogate a man who'd confessed to kidnapping an underage girl for immoral purposes. Meadow's questions, which she'd formulated beforehand, irritated him to the point of physical violence. He'd attacked Meadow, who was totally unprepared for what amounted to a beating. She'd fought, and screamed, to no avail. It had taken a jailer to extricate the man's hands from her throat. Of course, that added another charge to the bevy he was already facing: assault on a federal officer.

But Meadow reacted very badly to the incident. It had never occurred to her that a perpetrator might attack her physically. She'd learned to shoot a gun, she'd learned self-defense, hand-to-hand, all the ways in the world to protect herself. But when she'd come up against an unarmed but violent criminal, she'd almost been killed. Her training wasn't enough. She'd felt such fear that she couldn't function. That had been the beginning of the end. Both she and the Bureau had decided that she was in the wrong profession. They'd been very nice about it, but she'd lost her job.

And Dal Blake thought she was a manly woman, a real hell-raiser. It was funny. She was the exact opposite. Half the time she couldn't even remember to do up the buttons on her coat right.

She sighed as she thought about Dal. She'd had a crush on him in high school. He was almost ten years older than she was and considered her a child. Her one attempt to catch his eye had ended in disaster . . .

She'd come to visit her father during Christmas holidays—much against her mother's wishes. It was her senior year of high school. She'd graduate in the spring. She knew that she was too young to appeal to a man Dal's age, but she was infatuated with him, fascinated by him.

He came by to see her father often because they were both active members in the local cattlemen's association. So one night when she knew he was coming over, Meadow dressed to the hilt in her Sunday best. It was a low-cut red sheath dress, very Christmassy and festive. It had long sleeves and side slits. It was much too old for Meadow, but her father loved her, so he let her pick it out and he paid for it.

Meadow walked into the room while Dal and her father were talking and sat down in a chair nearby, with a book in her hands. She tried to look sexy and appealing. She had on too much makeup, but she hadn't noticed that. The magazines all said that makeup emphasized your best features. Meadow didn't have many best features. Her straight nose and bow mouth were sort of appealing, and she had pretty light green eyes. She used masses of eyeliner and mascara and way too much rouge. Her best feature was her long, thick, beautiful blond hair. She wore it down that night.

Her father gave her a pleading look, which she ignored. She smiled at Dal with what she hoped was sophistication.

He gave her a dark-eyed glare.

The expression on his face washed away all her self-confidence. She flushed and pretended to read her book, but she was shaky inside. He didn't look interested. In fact, he looked very repulsed.

When her father went out of the room to get some paperwork he wanted to show to Dal, Meadow forced herself to look at him and smile.

"It's almost Christmas," she began, trying to find a subject for conversation.

He didn't reply. He did get to his feet and come toward her. That flustered her even more. She fumbled with the book and dropped it on the floor.

Dal pulled her up out of the chair and took her by the shoulders firmly. "I'm ten years older than you," he said bluntly. "You're a high school kid. I don't rob cradles and I don't appreciate attempts to seduce me in your father's living room. Got that?"

Her breath caught. "I never . . . !" she stammered.

His chiseled mouth curled expressively as he looked down into her shocked face. "You're painted up like a carnival fortune-teller. Too much makeup entirely. Does your mother know you wear clothes like that and come on to men?" he added icily. "I thought she was religious."

"She . . . is," Meadow stammered, and felt her age. Too young. She was too young. Her eyes fell away from his. "So am I. I'm sorry."

"You should be," he returned. His strong fingers contracted on her shoulders. "When do you leave for home?"

"Next Friday," she managed to say. She was dying inside. She'd never been so embarrassed in her life.

"Good. You get on the plane and don't come back. Your father has enough problems without trying to keep you out of trouble. And next time I come over here, I don't want to find you setting up shop in the living room, like a spider hunting flies."

"You're a very big fly," she blurted out, and flushed some more.

His lip curled. "You're out of your league, kid." He let go of her shoulders and moved her away from him, as if she had something contagious. His eyes went to the low-cut neckline. "If you went out on the street like that, in Raven Springs, you'd get offers."

She frowned. "Offers?"

"Prostitutes mostly do get offers," he said with distaste.

Tears threatened, but she pulled herself up to her maximum height, far short of his, and glared up at him. "I am not a prostitute!"

"Sorry. Prostitute in training?" he added thoughtfully.

She wanted to hit him. She'd never wanted anything so much. In fact, she raised her hand to slap that arrogant look off his face.

He caught her arm and pushed her hand away.

Even then, at that young age, her balance hadn't been what it should be. Her father had a big, elegant stove in the living room to heat the house. It used coal instead of wood, and it was very efficient behind its tight glass casing. There was a coal bin right next to it.

Meadow lost her balance and went down right into the coal bin. Coal spilled out onto the wood floor and all over her. Now there were black splotches all over her pretty red dress, not to mention her face and hair and hands.

She sat up in the middle of the mess, and angry tears ran down her soot-covered cheeks as she glared at Dal.

He was laughing so hard that he was almost doubled over.

"That's right, laugh," she muttered. "Santa's going to stop by here on his way to your house to get enough coal to fill up your stocking, Dariell Blake!"

He laughed even harder.

Her father came back into the room with a file folder in one hand, stopped, did a double take, and stared at his daughter, sitting on the floor in a pile of coal.

"What the hell happened to you?" he burst out.

"He happened to me!" she cried, pointing at Dal Blake. "He said I looked like a streetwalker!"

"You're the one in the tight red dress, honey." Dal chuckled. "I just made an observation."

"Your mother would have a fit if she saw you in that dress," her father said heavily. "I should never have let you talk me into buying it."

"Well, it doesn't matter anymore, it's ruined!" She got to her feet, swiping at tears in her eyes. "I'm going to bed!"

"Might as well," Dal remarked, shoving his hands into his jeans pockets and looking at her with an arrogant smile. "Go flirt with men your own age, kid."

She looked to her father for aid, but he just stared at her and sighed.

She scrambled to her feet, displacing more coal. "I'll get this swept up before I go to bed," she said.

"I'll do that. Get yourself cleaned up, Meda," her father said gently, using his pet name for her. "Go on."

She left the room muttering. She didn't even look at Dal Blake.

That had been several years ago, before she worked in law enforcement in Missouri and finally hooked up with the FBI. Now she was without a job, running a ranch about which she knew absolutely nothing, and whole families who depended on the ranch for a living were depending on her. The responsibility was tremendous.

She honestly didn't know what she was going to do. She did watch a couple of YouTube videos, but they were less than helpful. Most of them were self-portraits of small ranchers and their methods of dealing with livestock. It was interesting, but they assumed that their audience knew something about ranching. Meadow didn't.

She started to call the local cattlemen's association for help, until someone told her who the president of the chapter was. Dal Blake. Why hadn't she guessed?

While she was drowning in self-doubt, there was a knock on the front door. She opened it to find a handsome man, dark-eyed, with thick blond hair, standing on her porch. He was wearing a sheriff's uniform, complete with badge.

"Miss Dawson?" he said politely.

She smiled. "Yes?"

"I'm Sheriff Jeff Ralston."

"Nice to meet you," she said. She shook hands with him. She liked his handshake. It was firm without being aggressive.

"Nice to meet you, too," he replied. He shifted his weight.

She realized that it was snowing again and he must be freezing. "Won't you come in?" she said as an afterthought, moving back.

"Thanks," he replied. He smiled. "Getting colder out here."

She laughed. "I don't mind snow."

"You will when you're losing cattle to it," he said with a sigh as he followed her into the small kitchen, where she motioned him into a chair.

"I don't know much about cattle," she confessed. "Coffee?"

"I'd love a cup," he said heavily. "I had to get out of bed before daylight and check out a robbery at a local home. Someone came in through the window and took off with a valuable antique lamp."

She frowned. "Just the lamp?"

He nodded. "Odd robbery, that. Usually the perps carry off anything they can get their hands on."

"I know." She smiled sheepishly. "I was with the FBI for two years."

"I heard about that. In fact," he added while she started coffee brewing, "that's why I'm here."

"You need help with the robbery investigation?" she asked, pulling two mugs out of the cabinet.

"I need help, period," he replied. "My investigator just quit to go live in California with his new wife. She's from there. Left me shorthanded. We're on a tight budget, like most small law enforcement agencies. I only have the one investigator. Had, that is." He eyed her. "I thought you might be interested in the job," he added with a warm smile.

She almost dropped the mugs. "Me?"

"Yes. Your father said you had experience in law enforcement before you went with the Bureau and that you were noted for your investigative abilities."

"Noted wasn't quite the word they used," she said, remembering the rage her boss had unleashed when she blew the interrogation of a witness. That also brought back memories of the brutality the man had used against her in the physical attack. To be fair to her boss, he didn't know the prisoner had attacked her until after he'd read her the riot act. He'd apologized handsomely, but the damage was already done.

"Well, the FBI has its own way of doing things. So do I." He accepted the hot mug of coffee with a smile. "Thanks. I live on black coffee."

She laughed, sitting down at the table with him to put cream and sugar in her own. She noticed that he took his straight up. He had nice hands. Very masculine and strong-looking. No wedding band. No telltale tan line where one had been, either. She guessed that he'd never been married, but it was too personal a question to ask a relative stranger.

"I need an investigator and you're out of work. What do you say?"

She thought about the possibilities. She smiled. Here it was, like fate, a chance to prove to the world that she could be a good investigator. It was like the answer to a prayer.

She grinned. "I'll take it, and thank you."

He let out the breath he'd been holding. "No. Thank you. I can't handle the load alone. When can you start?"

"It's Friday. How about first thing Monday morning?" she asked.

"That would be fine. I'll put you on the day shift to begin. You'll need to report to my office by seven a.m. Too early?"

"Oh, no. I'm usually in bed by eight and up by five in the morning."

His eyebrows raised.

"It's my dog," she sighed. "She sleeps on the bed with me, and she wakes up at five. She wants to eat and play. So I can't go back to sleep or she'll eat the carpet."

He laughed. "What breed is she?"

"She's a white Siberian husky with red highlights. Beautiful."

"Where is she?"

She caught her breath as she realized that she'd let Snow out to go to the bathroom an hour earlier, and she hadn't scratched at the door. "Oh, dear," she muttered as she realized where the dog was likely to be.

Along with that thought came a very angry knock at the back door, near where she was sitting with the sheriff.

Apprehensively, she got up and opened the door. And there he was. Dal Blake, with Snow on a makeshift lead. He wasn't smiling.

"Your dog invited herself to breakfast. Again. She came right into my damned house through the dog door!"

She knew that Dal didn't have a dog anymore. His old Labrador had died a few weeks ago, her foreman had told her, and the man had mourned the old dog. He'd had it for almost fourteen years, he'd added.

"I'm sorry," Meadow said with a grimace. "Snow. Bad girl!" she muttered.

The husky with her laughing blue eyes came bounding over to her mistress and started licking her.

"Stop that." Meadow laughed, fending her off. "How about a treat, Snow?"

She went to get one from the cupboard.

"Hey, Jeff," Dal greeted the other man, shaking hands as Jeff got to his feet.

"How's it going?" Jeff asked Dal.

"Slow," came the reply. "We're renovating the calving sheds. It's slow work in this weather."

"Tell me about it," Jeff said. "We had two fences go down. Cows broke through and started down the highway."

"Maybe there was a dress sale," Dal said, tongue-in-cheek as he watched a flustered Meadow give a chewy treat to her dog.

"I'd love to see a cow wearing a dress," she muttered.

"Would you?" Dal replied. "One of your men thinks that's your ultimate aim, to put cows in school and teach them to read."

"Which man?" she asked, her eyes flashing fire at him.

"Oh, no, I'm not telling," Dal returned. "You get on some boots and jeans and go find out for yourself. If you can ride a horse, that is."

That brought back another sad memory. She'd gone riding on one of her father's feistier horses, confident that she could control it. She was in her second year of college, bristling with confidence as she breezed through her core curriculum.

She thought she could handle the horse. But it sensed her fear of heights and speed and took her on a racing tour up the side of a small mountain and down again so quickly that Meadow lost her balance and ended up face-first in a snowbank.

To add to her humiliation—because the stupid horse went running back to the barn, probably laughing all the way—Dal Blake was helping move cattle on his own ranch, and he saw the whole thing.

He came trotting up just as she was wiping the last of the snow from her face and parka. "You know, Spirit isn't a great choice of horses for an inexperienced rider."

"My father told me that," she muttered.

"Pity you didn't listen. And lucky that you ended up in a snowbank instead of down a ravine," he said solemnly. "If you can't control a horse, don't ride him."

"Thanks for the helpful advice," she returned icily.

"City tenderfoot," he mused. "I'm amazed that you haven't killed yourself already. I hear your father had to put a rail on the back steps after you fell down them."

She flushed. "I tripped over his cat."

"You could benefit from some martial arts training."

"I've already had that," she said. "I work for my local police department."

"As what?" he asked politely.

"As a patrol officer!" she shot back.

"Well," he remarked, turning his horse, "if you drive a car like you ride a horse, you're going to end badly one day."

"I can drive!" she shot after him. "I drive all the time!"

"God help other motorists."

"You . . . you . . . you . . . !" She gathered steam with each repetition of the word until she was almost screaming, and still she couldn't think of an insult bad enough to throw at him. It wouldn't have done any good. He kept riding. He didn't even look back.

* * *

She snapped back to the present. "Yes, I can ride a horse!" she shot at Dal Blake. "Just because I fell off once . . ."

"You fell off several times. This is mountainous country. If you go riding, carry a cell phone and make sure it's charged," he said seriously.

"I'd salaam, but I haven't had my second cup of coffee yet," she drawled, alluding to an old custom of subjects salaaming royalty.

"You heard me."

"You don't give orders to me in my own house," she returned hotly.

Jeff cleared his throat.

They both looked at him.

"I have to get back to work," he said as he pushed his chair back in. "Thanks for the coffee, Meadow. I'll expect you early Monday morning."

"Expect her?" Dal asked.

"She's coming to work for me as my new investigator," Jeff said with a bland smile.

Dal's dark eyes narrowed. He saw through the man, whom he'd known since grammar school. Jeff was a good sheriff, but he wanted to add to his ranch. He owned property that adjoined Meadow's. So did Dal. That acreage had abundant water, and right now water was the most important asset any rancher had. Meadow was obviously out of her depth trying to run a ranch. Her best bet was to sell it, so Jeff was getting in on the ground floor by offering her a job that would keep her close to him.

He saw all that, but he just smiled. "Good luck," he told Jeff, with a dry glance at a fuming Meadow. "You'll need it."

"She'll do fine," Jeff said confidently.

Dal just smiled.

Meadow remembered that smile from years past. She'd had so many accidents when she was visiting her father. Dal was always somewhere nearby when they happened.

He didn't like Meadow. He'd made his distaste for her apparent on every possible occasion. There had been a Christmas party thrown by the local cattlemen's association when Meadow first started college. She'd come to spend Christmas with her father, and when he asked her to go to the party with him, she agreed.

She knew Dal would be there. So she wore an outrageous dress, even more revealing than the one he'd been so disparaging about when she was a senior in high school.

Sadly, the dress caught the wrong pair of eyes. A local cattleman who'd had five drinks too many had propositioned Meadow by the punch bowl. His reaction to her dress had flustered her and she tripped over her high-heeled shoes and knocked the punch bowl over.

The linen tablecloth was soaked. So was poor Meadow, in her outrageous dress. Dal Blake had laughed until his face turned red. So had most other people. Meadow had asked her father to drive her home. It was the last Christmas party she ever attended in Raven Springs.

But just before the punch bowl incident, there had been another. Dal had been caught with her under the mistletoe . . .

She shook herself mentally and glared at Dal.

Connect with Us

Visit us online at
KensingtonBooks.com
to read more from your favorite authors, see books
by series, view reading group guides, and more.

Join us on social media

for sneak peeks, chances to win books and prize packs,
and to share your thoughts with other readers.

facebook.com/kensingtonpublishing
twitter.com/kensingtonbooks

Tell us what you think!

To share your thoughts, submit a review,
or sign up for our eNewsletters, please visit:
KensingtonBooks.com/TellUs.